THE GIRL WHO DARED TO LEAD

THE GIRL WHO DARED TO THINK 5

BELLA FORREST

Before the Tower, humanity was free in the only way that truly mattered—humans had an implicit understanding that they could express their emotions however they pleased. Some people were quiet and even stoic, yet shared their love through patience and action. Others were scared, terrorized by past horrors over which they couldn't quite seem to gain control. Even more were driven by greed, lust, jealousy, hope, pride, pleasure, love, compassion, justice... The list was endless, yet filled with a myriad of emotional states that could twist a person's heart and affect their life. But all of these feelings were understood, and could be met with compassion.

Now, however, humanity couldn't be bothered to waste time dealing with such trifles. Things like happiness were a luxury, and grief an anathema. Dwelling on any emotions only distracted from the mission of keeping us all alive. It served no purpose other than to satisfy a selfish and petty urge to feel connected. Want to feel connected?

Work harder and dedicate yourself to the Tower and to Scipio, our benevolent—and broken—AI overlord. Want to feel emotions? Don't. The Medica will make sure that you don't have to anymore.

Before the Tower, humanity was free to laugh, sing, play, and cry. Now, we weren't expected to do any of that anymore. Instead, we were expected to bury our emotions like we buried our dead, and forget everything.

Except I couldn't seem to stop feeling. I felt everything like it was a raw, festering wound buried deep inside, right next to the names of those I had lost: Cali Kerrin, former Lieutenant to Devon Alexander, both of whom I had killed in one way or another. Roark, the man who had saved me from a fate worse than death, and Ambrose Klein, a man whom I'd failed to protect.

And now my mother. My mother. Holly Castell. Gone.

I was pretty sure no one had been as surprised as I was at the depth of my grief. It didn't make sense—we hadn't been close for the past twenty years of my life—but I couldn't seem to control the aching pain in my chest that only got worse as time dragged on.

My eyelids slid open, and for a moment I just stared, waiting to see if the tears would come or not. They hadn't during the last two nights, but I couldn't always predict when they would. Nor could I predict what sort of tears they would be. Would it be the kind of crying where I curled up into a ball and wheezed out my tears in the grip of panic, or would it be the one where tears slid down my face in silence?

Yet another thing I couldn't control. Sometimes I hated the tears when they came, but they often came nonetheless when my thoughts drifted toward her.

No tears. None ever seemed to come in the cover of darkness.

Maybe it was because there was no one awake to witness them, or maybe it was because on this night, just like the past two, I had a sort of grim purpose that seemed to supersede everything else, including my own grief. Either way, I found myself only with dry eyes that ached in the minimal lighting of the room.

For several long seconds I lay there, listening to the sounds of soft breathing filling the small compartment that was my room. I didn't remember going to bed—when I hadn't been a crying mess, I'd been left with a strangely disconnected sensation that made it difficult to remember parts of the day—but I was unsurprised by the company. My friends had been holding a weird sort of vigil by my side. And that included slumber parties, apparently.

I was grateful to them. I knew they were doing everything in their power to be here for me. I just wished I could give them what they wanted: for me to talk.

But how could I talk when I couldn't make sense of the feelings inside of me? Why was I so torn up about a woman who had treated me like crap? Yes, we had been on a path to working out our problems. My mother had begun to look past the veil the Tower had placed over her eyes. She'd chosen to believe me.

She'd told me she'd loved me.

Then she was gone.

And I couldn't seem to stop hurting.

And I couldn't understand why.

It was why I kept getting up when I should be sleeping and slipping past my friends like some sort of thief in the night. But it was the only way I could be alone, and I desperately needed it.

I'd made the journey twice before, on the two previous nights, but my thoughts were still jumbled and chaotic. And I had to clear them. Today was too important for me to be anything but clearheaded.

As rational as that reason was, there was another, darker purpose behind my midnight escapades, which was currently in the living area of my apartment.

Getting to it, however, was slightly tricky.

I stared at the back of my best friend Zoe's head, studying her body. Her shoulder and side moved up and down with slow, even breaths, telling me she was asleep. And why wouldn't she be, at three in the morning? She wasn't plagued by the memories of falling, or the nightmares peopled with what-ifs. She wasn't dreaming of getting my mother to the Medics in time and saving her... only to wake up and find that she was still gone and nothing had changed.

Scipio help me, I hated how much that realization hurt, almost as much as I hated my mind for playing tricks on me in the first place.

I sat up slowly, careful not to make any noise or pull too much on the blanket Zoe and I were sharing, for fear it would wake her. At the foot of the bed, I heard a soft snort and froze, lifting my head slightly to peer along the edge of the blanket to where a small girl was sleeping, her legs propped up against the wall. Her eyes remained closed, her breathing soft and even, and I quickly seized the opportunity to wriggle my feet out from under her and carefully ease my way out of bed. Tian, the youngest member of our group, didn't move as I did so, and I felt confident I hadn't woken her.

My feet hit the cold floor, and I curled my toes in tight as I stared at my final obstacle: the tall, muscular girl spread out like a starfish on the floor. Maddox. Her blanket was twisted up around her, and her pillow was being used to cushion her knee, creating an obstacle course that I would have to navigate quickly and carefully, lest I wake her up.

I reached out, grabbed my robe from where I had hung it next to the bed last night, and slipped it on, sliding my hair out from under the edge of it. I held my breath for a second, and then stood up, crossing the floor with a light step. I didn't stop until I hit the button next to the door, causing it to slide open with a pneumonic hiss that seemed unnaturally loud in my mind. I stepped through quickly, and then took a look back over my shoulder.

Nobody had moved. Three sets of lungs inhaled and exhaled softly, Maddox's breath ending in a slight snore. They were still asleep.

I pressed the button on the outside and closed the door, feeling a hollow pang of regret as I did so. I knew what I was doing wasn't what they wanted. They were all waiting for me to speak to them, to let them in. And I desperately wanted to, but how could I even begin to describe it, when I didn't understand it? It was frustrating because I just wanted this to stop, to go away, but I couldn't seem to make it. It was like there were two Lianas inside me, fighting for control. Or maybe not control, but just the right to... feel... something?

I didn't know. Nothing made any sense.

I supposed I could just try to talk to my friends again. I knew exactly where I'd start. *My mother died three days ago. She was murdered three days ago. I feel...*

There were so many words to choose from. So many different flavors of grief. Too many, if you really thought about it. Regret, shame, rage, loss, absence, melancholy, depression... And not a single one quite nuanced enough to encapsulate the myriad of emotions that I couldn't seem to control. They made me afraid of what I would say and to whom I would say it if I opened my mouth. Afraid of what would happen when I did speak. Afraid to even admit she was gone, for fear that I would start crying again. So I stayed quiet instead. It was better that way, anyway; the last three days had passed in a haze of grief, and it had helped me cope when all the questions and investigations started.

Not that those resulted in much, either. Nothing had changed since the end of the Tourney. I had been named Champion—the leader of the Department of Knights, meant to protect the Citadel—but it was being held up, pending the investigation by the council and Scipio into what had caused the situation with the sentinel that had killed my mother and her friend, Min-Ha Kim, during the final challenge. Oh, and a further investigation into why I had just happened to have a sentinel-defeating (and completely illegal) weapon on me during an official challenge.

The official story was that the sentinel had been authorized as an additional obstacle for the last challenge, but that something had, of course, gone terribly wrong. The designers had no clue what; hence the three-day-long investigation that had stalled everything.

But it was just that—a story—whereas the truth was a touch darker: someone had put a rogue AI fragment named Jang-Mi into that sentinel and ordered her to kill off the competition so that one specific candidate would win.

Speaking of which...

I padded down the hall, cinching my robe tighter around myself as I entered the shared living area. The three males in our group were sharing Maddox's room across the hall from my own, but made sure someone was always in the front room in case our enemies tried to attack us. They'd broken the night into shifts and hadn't bothered to change the order since.

What they hadn't thought about was that Eric, Zoe's boyfriend and one of my oldest friends, couldn't stay awake past midnight—a byproduct of being raised as a Hand in the farming department. His internal clock was set to rise early, hours before the rest of the Tower, and fall asleep not too long after sundown. The others hadn't caught on yet because he woke up an hour before everyone else did. I wasn't sure why he hadn't mentioned it to the others. Maybe he thought he'd only dozed off for a few minutes or something. Either way, it was a flaw, and a big one that needed to be addressed—but it didn't stop me from taking advantage of it now.

Sure enough, it was Eric's turn in the front room, and there he was, splayed out on the couch, using the arm as a pillow. His own arm was resting across his head, keeping the light from reaching his closed eyelids, and he had thrown one leg over the back of the couch. His breathing was deep and even, the large expanse of his chest rising and falling rhythmically.

I stood in the center of the room watching him for a second, and then lowered my gaze to the table in front of the couch, where a clear plastic box with glowing purple and green lights sat, the lights pulsating with life. An intense stab of hatred hit me as I gazed at it, but I stoically pushed it away and scooped the box up, carrying it over to the entryway.

I pulled out the spare set of clothes I had stashed in the closet next to the front door—black, and with no insignia to show what department I was from—and quickly got dressed, not bothering to mask my sounds. Doing so would only create irregular noises, something we were trained to identify when we were sleeping, as a matter of survival and self-preservation. Trying to hide what I was doing would only give Eric's sleeping mind a greater chance of noticing and waking up to investigate, and I didn't want that. It would defeat the purpose.

Once dressed, I slid the box of light into a bag that I had also stored in the closet and draped the bag over my shoulder, resting it against my hip. One last thing—a hat—completed the ensemble, and I quickly hit the button for the door and stepped out into the wide hall. I waited for the door to close, and then left, not even bothering to make sure my escape was clean.

My walk was robotic, my eyes fixed on the ground. It was stupid to be out alone, but I didn't care; I had been taking this walk for the last three nights, and no one had tried anything. In truth, I kind of hoped that they would—it would give me an outlet for some of the deep-seated rage that boiled just under my skin. If they would just strike, I could finally have a target, something I could wrap my hands around and punish for everything they'd done to me, to my mother, to Ambrose, to the Tower. Maybe I'd even keep one of them alive, and make him talk, tell me who my enemy was. A name was all I wanted. The name of who was in charge.

But no one bothered me. The hat did its job in disguising my most noticeable attribute—my amber eyes—and it was early, which meant that only the grave shift was on duty. But the hat was only to prevent me from being recognized in the halls, keeping me hidden from people who might try to make me do the one thing I didn't want to do: talk. It would do nothing to stop my enemies from tracking me. All they needed to do was have access to the sensors and the Citadel, and they could find me easily enough.

But I wasn't exactly trying to hide from *them*. Just everyone else.

And though the halls were more heavily patrolled, if you knew the way around the patrols, you could find clear paths easily enough. Plus the stairs were always free. As they had been for the past three nights.

I made my way down them until I reached the floor I was looking for, and slipped back into the halls. I was stopped only once—at the

exit leading to the bridge that connected to the outer shell of
the Tower.

"Down here again, girl?" Lewis asked gruffly, sliding into place
next to me as I walked toward the dark archway that served as the
exit. "Why aren't you asleep?"

I gave him a look from the corner of my eye, noting the dark bags
under his own blue eyes, and the white scruff that was now forming
on his cheeks and chin. Only his mustache seemed in order, if
heavily tugged upon. I arched an eyebrow and tilted my chin up
enough to meet his gaze for a second.

"You're one to talk," I said softly.

Talking was hard—my vocal cords seemed resistant to use—but I
forced the words out anyway, barely managing a volume above a
throaty rasp. Still, Lewis heard me, which wasn't particularly hard in
the relative emptiness of the reception area, and sighed heavily.

"Scipio help you, Liana, where are you going each night? Why
are you even going out? You know Astrid wouldn't like the idea of
you leaving the safety of the Citadel and exposing yourself like this!
You can't keep doing this. You need to talk to someone."

Even though his observation was perfectly reasonable, and a part
of me wanted to do just that, I got frustrated instead, my mouth
drawing into a thin, flat line. Frustrated and downright angry. I was
still in the process of trying to figure it out, and everyone just wanted
me to be able to explain every little thing. I wasn't ready—if I were,
then I could figure out why the heck this kept eating at me as
intensely as it did, deal with it, and move on.

But no, I had to be ready to go on their timetable, to just open my
mouth and talk about her, about the complicated mess of our relationship, and about how I felt now that she was gone.

Tears bit into my eyes as the hollow ache of simply *missing* her hit me like a sledgehammer, coupled with the knowledge that I would never see her again. Wetness spread to my lashes, and I could tell that if I left it, it would turn into tears that would slowly roll down my cheeks. It was so strange to have cried so much for a person I had spent most of my life resenting, but I couldn't seem to gain any control over it.

And that only made me feel even worse.

My vision grew blurred, signaling that my tears were about to spill over, and I dragged my thoughts back from the edge. I didn't want Lewis to see me cry—didn't want to be vulnerable like that in front of him—and quickly lowered my head and wiped my eyes, doing my best to disguise my actions while pushing the pain back.

I managed to keep my breathing even, trying for some semblance of calm (although who knew what that felt like anymore), and repeated the argument that had gotten him to leave me alone for the past three nights. "Lewis, you and I both know that you voted for me to be the Champion. And you yourself told me that in your mind, that *made* me the Champion. So as your Champion, I'm asking you to get out of my way."

We had come to a stop just under the archway, and I turned to face him directly, letting him look fully into my eyes and inviting him to see the bleak darkness within them. I knew what they looked like: hollow and dead, devoid of any emotion save a deep, vacant emptiness that made me feel like I was nothing but muscle and skin, carved out and gutted like a pumpkin.

He sucked in a deep breath, his pupils dilating slightly. "Liana..." He trailed off, his brows drawing close as pity flooded his eyes. I looked away, not needing to see it. I didn't want his pity; I just wanted to be alone so I could think.

Lewis reached out and touched my shoulder. My eye twitched,

but I didn't jerk away from him, even though I wanted to. My mother had touched me there, too, once. My mother had squeezed me there, just as Lewis was doing now. My mother had told me she loved me, that she was proud of me.

God, what was wrong with me? She'd told me she loved me—once—and she'd *never* told me she was proud of me. Why was my brain inventing crap like that? Why was it trying to revise our history into one that justified all of this pain?

Why was it making me hold my breath, imagining that her voice would be the next one I heard? Imagining what it would be like to be pulled into her arms one more time, to hear her telling me that it was all a mistake, that she was safe and sound.

And why did it make me want to cry when all Lewis did was give me a gentle and gruff "Be careful" before letting me go?

Like she had let me go.

More tears came, but I angrily fought them back, moving forward instead, stalking onto the bridge, guided only by what I could make out through my blurred vision, and the grim determination that I had to fix myself.

Because I couldn't keep going on like this.

2

My tears eventually dried as my feet unerringly followed the route I had taken every night for the past three nights, led by memory alone. I took an elevator buried inside the narrow halls that riddled the inner walls of the Tower and rode it all the way up to the hundred and thirtieth floor. Once there, I followed the uniform passages, navigating them like I had done since I was fifteen years old.

I reached a door and pressed a button, bracing myself. The door slid to the side with a hiss, revealing nothing but open space and a view that was breathtaking. From here, I could see into the heart of the Tower, from the white, gleaming walls of the Medica to the geometric precision of the Core, illuminated in blue, to the dark, twisting architecture of the Citadel, all of it laid out before me, one structure right next to the other.

I stepped through the opening onto a ledge that was eight inches wide, and then slid along, using handholds cut into the wall to help guide me. The door closed behind me with a hiss, but I ignored it, focusing on making my way down the narrow walkway and around the corner. As soon as I was past that, the ledge I was walking on widened, leading to a platform roughly five feet wide and eight feet deep, framed on three sides by the sloped edge of the interior part of the shell.

Zoe, Eric, and I had discovered this area years ago, and it had become our official meetup spot when our classes and duties took us farther and farther away from one another. Now, it had become my refuge—the only place I could go where I didn't have the prying eyes of the Tower on me at all times. Sure, Zoe and Eric would probably think of it if they woke up and found me gone, but they hadn't the past two nights, so the odds were in my favor that they wouldn't tonight.

I stepped onto the platform and walked along the edge until I was roughly at the middle. Then I sat down and dangled my legs over the side. I pulled my hat off and set it down behind me, so I wouldn't accidentally knock it over the ledge, and then lifted the bag over my shoulder and set it next to me.

I took a moment to stare out at what had once been one of my favorite views in the Tower, trying to find some semblance of beauty in it. I failed. Instead, I was left with an emptiness, a lack of... anything. Nothingness. Oblivion.

And rage. It seethed and twisted deep inside me—yet another unchecked thing that had formed since my mother's death. It was the other half of what had dragged me up here, a vicious compunction that I couldn't seem to shake. Even though I'd never given in to it before, still it came, and for a moment, I was powerless to stand against it.

I closed my eyes and exhaled. Then I turned. I opened the bag. Stared at the glowing, clear box inside. Pulled it out, gripping the edges of it tightly between my hands. Ignored their trembling as I extended my hand, and the box, away from the bag and toward the ledge. Held it over empty space.

My breathing had intensified, and I stared at the box. My eyes burned. My lips trembled.

"Just drop it," I told myself bitterly. "It's what you want, isn't it? Vengeance, right? Plain and simple, short and sweet? Or would it be justice? She made your mother fall. She killed her. You could just let her fall. Never mind she didn't want to do it. Never mind that she was forced to. Never mind that it won't help you find the bastards who really did it. Just do it. Just let her go."

My grip tightened around the box in my hands, so much so that the entire thing creaked slightly. Or maybe it was my knuckles—I couldn't tell. They were bone-white from the pressure with which I was pressing my fingertips into the box. Even though the anger in my heart screamed at me to do it, just do it, my words helped keep me anchored, prevented me from letting go.

But, Scipio help me, I really wanted to do it. I wanted it so bad that I could taste it. If I just relaxed my fingers, it would happen. *She* would die. The thing they put into the sentinel to make it kill. Jang-Mi.

And all I had to do was let go.

Yet my fingers stubbornly refused to do so, and after several agonizing heartbeats, I pulled my hands back and thrust the hard drive containing Jang-Mi back into the bag. A moment later, I pushed the bag backward, away from me, and then wiped my hands against my pants, trying to scrub them free of the taint of holding her. Repulsed by her, myself, what I had been thinking about doing...

This was the worst part of everything I was going through. The anger, as misdirected as it was, burned in my gut, telling me that the thing in the hard drive should die. Even though I knew it was wrong, it kept finding ways to creep up on me when I least expected, forcing dozens of images of me destroying the hard drive into my head.

It took everything in my power to keep from dropping her. She was important, not only for tracking down the monsters who had directed her toward my mother, but to help Leo fix Scipio.

Because someone—likely the same people who put Jang-Mi in a four-hundred-and-fifty-pound death machine and sent her on a murder spree—had done something to the great AI. Something that everyone in the Tower thought was impossible. They had tampered with his programming, carving out massive chunks of codes and then hiding it from the members of the IT Department, which was responsible for and dedicated to protecting him from harm. All in order to control him and make him do what they wanted.

For what reason, you might ask, and to that I would tell you, "I have absolutely no friggin' clue."

I only knew certain things. The innovator and creator of the Tower, Lionel Scipio, had created Scipio using five AI programs based on sophisticated scans of his neural pathways, and those of the other founding members. Those AI programs were then run through a battery of simulations that would emulate problems in the Tower, forcing them to find solutions and deal with their ramifications, over and over again, until only one remained—Lionel's, in point of fact. Those who failed were not discarded. Instead, Lionel had heightened the strengths they demonstrated during their simulations and then incorporated them into Lionel's AI clone, forming the completed version of Scipio, who was now housed in the Core.

Later, the council would decide to destroy the original prototypes, but Lionel saved one of them—his own—against the council's wishes. That one was Leo, and he was currently housed inside a net inside the body of my braindead boyfriend, Grey, trying valiantly to repair the damage to *his* brain and restore him to the man he once was.

And I was pretty sure he had a crush on me.

Which, in my current emotional state, was just another litany of problems I couldn't deal with. And wouldn't until I figured out why I was spiraling out so badly. It was why I was up here, for crying out loud! Yet every time I sat down, out came Jang-Mi and the anger, and I kept hovering on the edge of something dark and sinister, barely able to hold it back. It scared me—not only because of how intense it was, but because I couldn't seem to control it.

I never would've imagined my mother's death would affect me this badly, and I needed to stop this vicious cycle. Every second of each minute that had passed since my mother's death, I had been failing to focus on the multitude of problems we were facing, the biggest one being the secret group that was in all likelihood trying to kill me. Legacies, these secret groups were called, and each of them seemed to be undetectable to the scans of the Tower. In fact, they were *hiding* themselves within the Tower, with an ease and access that was as incredible as it was terrifying.

Then, there was Jasper, another AI fragment I had befriended in the Medica. He'd saved my life twice, only to be ripped away before I even knew what he was. I'd been aching to go after him since I'd learned what happened, but everything had gotten derailed by the

Tourney. Not to mention, he had been downloaded directly into the head of IT's computer terminal.

Having met CEO Sadie Monroe, I had no doubt that Jasper was there against his will. I had so many questions about him, *for* him. Yet the answers were elusive, and largely irrelevant. I needed to focus on how to rescue him, not only because he could help us figure out what we needed to do to save Scipio, but also because he was my friend, and I owed him. To make matters even more complicated, he was the only one who knew the formula for the drug called Paragon—the drug that could mask an individual's rank (often confused with someone's *worth*), and which we desperately needed in order to recruit people and make our escape.

Which was why rescuing Jasper, and getting the formula for Paragon, was so important. But I was at a loss for how to even go about it, considering every five minutes my mind would drift back to my mother and my heart would begin to ache from loss.

It seemed like my entire life was like that now. Just when I thought I should contact Lacey to find out what was going on inside the council regarding the Tourney, I'd start to cry, thinking of the final challenge, of the line being cut, of my mother falling to her death, and felt certain that I couldn't ever bear to go through anything like that again.

Rationally, I knew it would help me prepare for the off chance that they decided to re-do the last challenge. But I also knew that she held me responsible for the death of her cousin, Ambrose.

Should I even do the challenge again, if the council decided to repeat it? It might be a moot point, though; if I was found guilty of cheating, they wouldn't let me compete, anyway. But if they let me do it... would I?

The very idea was downright exhausting, and pointless, unless I could get myself under control. If they set me loose on the Tourney now, I'd likely fall to pieces at the drop of a hat.

"Why do you feel like this?" I asked out loud. "Why do you miss her so badly?"

Was it guilt? I did feel guilty; that much was certain. I replayed the moments leading up to her death a thousand times in my head, imagining different ways that I could've saved her and then stopped the sentinel. All of them burned a hole in my stomach, making me feel a thousand times smaller, but that didn't explain why I kept imagining us as if we had been better than we were.

Tears burned hot tracks down my cheeks, rolling over my chin and dropping onto my hands, which I noticed were grasped tightly into fists, shaking. I felt the press of my nails into my palms, and squeezed tighter, numb to all pain save the one raging inside the tattered place where my heart had once sat. A place that was now an empty, cavernous space that seemed to hold only the echo of a heartbeat.

I sat frozen, but inside I struggled to resist the torrent of pain, trying to understand the source of all of it. It wasn't guilt. Could it just be loss? The very thought that I was never going to see her again?

It was frustrating not being able to peek through the veil and find the root of the problem. It was in my nature to fix things when they were broken, even myself, and the only one preventing me from doing so was me.

Time passed—I wasn't sure how much—and I just stared out at the Core, searching for answers and finding none. Then a soft scraping sound just around the corner of the ledge pulled me back into the present. I had enough energy to shift my eyes over, and watched as a crimson-clad leg swung into view, followed by an arm, and then a familiar head with dark blond hair that was slightly mussed and a strong, square-cut jaw speckled with a few days' growth.

It was hard to look at Leo without seeing Grey. It was his body, after all.

Leo stepped onto the platform and then slid his hand through his hair, pushing the tangled mass back. He met my gaze and opened his mouth.

"Are you alone?" I asked, cutting him off as I turned back to my view. "Or are the others right behind you?"

"I am alone," he announced softly. "May I sit?"

I considered his question, but I still wasn't ready to talk. So I shrugged by way of an answer, and a second later his legs appeared over the edge at my side, swinging into place about a foot away from my own.

We sat there for a long time, the silence between us spinning out slowly.

"Liana, tell me what I can do to help you," he finally said, clearly unable to stop himself.

I blew out a breath. He'd been saying something like that constantly for the past few days, and it was one of the most frustrating statements anyone had made to me. It filled me with a resentment and irritation that was hard to push aside because he was basically asking me to advise him on how to advise myself. And clearly, given my late-night obsession with coming up here every night to hold Jang-Mi's hard drive over the edge and really contemplate the justice of dropping her... I needed the help. But help with *what*?

Was it failure? That had definitely been the source of my guilt with Ambrose, but here it didn't ring true. I didn't feel like I had failed her. We had been working as a team. She had gone after my father—that was a mistake—but I had let her. Had I failed her by letting her go after him?

"How did you find me?" I asked, deliberately changing the subject, still trying to figure it out.

Leo sighed softly. "I woke up and found Eric sleeping and Jang-Mi's hard drive gone. I woke Zoe and asked her where you might be, and she suggested here. She said it was your favorite place, which makes sense, considering you like a good view. It really is beautiful."

As he said that, the lights on the walls of the Tower changed and began to grow brighter, indicating that the sun outside was rising. The dim settings for night—a white that was almost blue— began to shift in tone, the blue shade lightening and then disappearing altogether. The white dimmed slightly, and then suddenly changed to a warm, dusty orange, brightening until streams of light were hitting the three structures inside. I'd watched the simulated sunrise dozens of times, and each one had felt more spectacular than the last.

But this time, the sight did nothing for me, except remind me that it was a new day. A new and terrible day. A day that I had been dreading since I got the announcement.

"Not from where I'm sitting," I replied, suddenly feeling drained. I was exceptionally tired. Scipio help me, I wasn't ready for today. I hadn't fixed a damn thing. I glanced over at him, eyeing him warily. "You sure Zoe isn't with you?"

"No. I convinced her that you were probably craving some alone time, and it would be better if I came by myself. I just wish you had told someone. You shouldn't be out here alone." His voice held a note of reproach, and I shifted as a dull throb of guilt hit me. My friends cared about me—were concerned for me—and I was willfully ignoring them. It wasn't very thoughtful or considerate of me, and it certainly didn't make me a good friend.

At the same time, his implication that coming up here was unsafe struck me as unusually funny, given that I had gone out the past two nights unescorted and nothing had happened to me, and I laughed bitterly, in spite of myself.

Leo cocked his head at me, his facial expression reminding me of a baffled dog who didn't understand what was happening. I decided to let him in on the joke. "Nothing's happened the last two nights I've come up here, Leo. If anyone was going to try anything, they would've already."

I looked back out at the Citadel, suddenly growing morose. Maybe I had been wishing they would try—or even succeed. Maybe that was why I had been drawn here night after night, like some sort of ghostly echo of a girl who used to be. Maybe it wasn't guilt, or failure, or loss. Maybe I was trying to punish myself.

"I made it easy enough for them."

The words escaped me without me choosing to let them, giving Leo a glimpse into the dark inner workings of my brain. I cursed it bitterly for betraying me. That was why I didn't want to talk to people. You had to give up a part of yourself to do it, and I wasn't prepared to share my pain. Especially today.

"You've come up here the last two nights alone?" he asked, raising an eyebrow. "With Jang-Mi?"

I looked at him from the corner of my eye. I wasn't surprised that he had noticed her absence, but the slight question in his voice made me burn with shame and resentment. I hadn't hurt her—I'd managed not to the last three nights—but I was embarrassed that he knew I had taken her. I hadn't wanted anyone to know.

"She's in the bag," I said. "I didn't do anything to her."

"Yes, but—"

"Leo, I—" I faltered. What was I even going to say? What excuse did I have for my bad behavior? Irritated by the fact that I still hadn't seemed to figure out the source of everything, I mumbled a quick, "Never mind," and looked away, feeling helpless and inexorably broken.

"Okay," he replied, clearly trying to placate me.

I needed to get out of here. I couldn't stand his guilt over my inability to fix myself. I couldn't handle this. "I should go."

I slid back from the ledge and stood up. Leo twisted around so he could watch me, his brown eyes heavy with sorrow. "Liana," he pleaded. "You have to talk to someone. You can't keep all of this bottled up inside."

A part of me wanted to shout at him. Tell him that I knew that, and that I was trying, dammit. I was trying to figure it out, process my grief, move on... but I felt stuck. And today was coming at me with the force and weight of terminal velocity.

But that anger was misguided and wrong. "I wish I could give you what you want," I told him simply.

Leo's eyes grew softer. "You can," he said carefully. "You just have to try." He gave me a hopeful look, but I couldn't meet his gaze, and he sighed. "Is Jang-Mi... okay?"

I stared at him for a long second, and then snatched up the bag and thrust it at him, the anger coming hot and fast and impossible to stop. "Yes, your precious, murderous friend is still here," I said. Maybe some of the anger was directed at him, for even thinking I could do it. But most of it was directed at myself for not dropping her —and for wanting to in the first place. For not being able to stop the hatred I felt for her. I just couldn't see straight where Jang-Mi was concerned, and I seemed to hate that Leo would still want to protect her after what she had done.

Get yourself together, Liana, I ordered myself.

Leo grabbed the bag, looking both confused and hurt. "I've made you angry. I'm sorry, I didn't mean—"

"I know you didn't," I said, remorse blossoming in the wake of my emotional outburst. "I'm sorry. I just..." God, what was the magical combination of words that would let me unlock the mystery of all of this torment! I sought them, but try as hard as I could, they continued to elude me. "Forget it," I finally said. I had to get away and figure this out. There wasn't any time, only these scant few hours before I had to face her, and I needed every second. "I gotta go."

"Wait. Please."

I stopped partway to the wall and my escape, and turned to see him standing up. I watched him over my shoulder for a second, and then turned when he came toward me, facing him fully. I wasn't sure why I stayed, but there was something in his voice that I couldn't seem to resist, a hopeful yearning that I wasn't able to bring myself to ignore.

He studied my face, his eyes sad. "I would do anything I could to remove all that darkness from your eyes," he breathed softly, one hand coming up to cup my cheek. "Liana, I care about you. We all do. All you have to do is talk to us, and we will help you. I know we can, if you just let us in."

I stared back at him. His hand on my cheek was like fire, daring to try to spread life back through me, and for a second, I was sorely tempted to just give in and submit to his care.

But that would be selfish of me. It wouldn't make me feel better. It wouldn't change anything at all. It would just be a distraction. One that I would use to try to forget—if only momentarily—about what today was going to bring.

"I know you can," I said, taking a step away from him to get a little distance between us. I stared at him for a long moment before being as honest as possible, and adding, "I just need more time."

I didn't stick around for his reaction. I simply left, stepping out onto the ledge and swinging around the corner, chased away by the pain in my heart and spurred on by a grim sense of purpose.

Today was my mother's funeral, after all.

3

The last three days had felt like watching several different vid files in sequence, but with nothing in between them to connect them. Every time I blinked, I found myself in a new place with different faces around me. Blink—sitting on the living room couch, barely listening to Maddox as she tried to reach me. Blink—standing in the bathroom, my hair wet, staring at a girl in the mirror whose face should be familiar, but was that of a stranger's. Blink—walking down the corridor with my friends and family, each step closer to our destination filling me with dread.

Blink—staring at two dark gray metal boxes on the dais constructed in the back of the cafeteria, long crimson banners laid across them, the tails touching the floor.

The room was a den of noise, filled with the thousands of incidental sounds that were produced when a large number of people gathered. The squeaking of chairs being dragged against the floor, the sharp barks of coughing, the creak of uniforms, skin sliding on skin, the constant murmur of voices, each one like a strike against my cold and clammy skin.

Someone said something just next to me, their voice sounding as if it was coming from underwater, but I couldn't hear the words over the whoosh of the blood rushing around in my head. My mouth was dry, and when I swallowed, it felt like my esophagus had been filled with small rocks, tight and choking. My knees trembled, my breath came out in a wheeze, and then a hand, warm and solid, slid into mine and squeezed slightly.

I looked over to see the strong lines of my brother's face peering down at me from behind his thin wire spectacles, and felt like I was seeing him for the first time, even though I vaguely remembered seeing him and my father earlier in the hall. I blinked at the thick, dark beard that had sprouted on his normally cleanshaven face. His thick, wavy hair was also a touch too long, like he'd forgotten to get it cut, and was tied at the top of his head in a small, neat bun.

He looked concerned and sad, and there was something in his eyes that told me his heart was broken, and he really didn't know what to do about it. I knew exactly how he felt. My efforts to sort through my own emotional turmoil still hadn't yielded any results, and now that we were here, I was woefully unprepared.

I turned away and looked back up at the boxes we were drawing near, my breath catching in my chest. Alex guided me the entire way, moving forward at a resolute march, his back and spine stiff, and I allowed him to lead me. Up the stairs we went, the steps creaking loudly in my ears. Then between the two boxes, up, up, up, until he stopped just short of the top.

I stared at the floor for a second and struggled to find the courage to look, while Alex's hand tightened in mine. I heard his sharp intake of air, followed by a slight, choked sound, and squeezed my eyes shut, knowing who he was looking at.

Knowing who *I* had to look at.

I lifted my chin, pointing it in the direction of the top of the box, and then slowly slid my eyes open, confident that this would be the only way I could do it, and hating myself for being such a coward.

My mother was lying there, nestled inside like a pearl in an oyster. Her skin was pale, almost translucent, her eyes closed. As if she could be sleeping. Sternly.

I would've laughed at my own observation, but my heart went ahead and decided to break instead, horrified that I could even think of cracking jokes at a time like this. These were the final moments I was going to get with her, and I still didn't know what to say.

Scipio help me... she looked so lifelike. I half expected her eyes to open. For them to focus on me, and for her to smile at me—something she had almost never done when she saw me, until the end. She began to blur around the edges, and I realized that the tears were coming again. My eyes seemed to have a never-ending body of water contained within them these days.

Ugh, I was doing it again! If she woke up right at this moment, she wouldn't smile. She'd probably be like, "Liana, crying is a selfish use of your time. You should be doing something productive like catching my killers."

The thought only made me want to cry harder as her imagined words reignited the feelings of failure that haunted me.

Alex shifted beside me and slid his hand from mine to move a piece of her hair out of the way so that he could rest his fingertips against the high arch of her cheekbone. "She's so cold," he said, his voice empty and devoid of any emotion.

I swallowed back my tears, trying to put on a brave face. I realized it was Alex's first time seeing her since the vid of the challenge had been broadcast live to the entire Tower.

"When was the last time you saw her?" I asked, my voice barely a whisper.

Tears escaped my brother's eyes as he blinked, looking at me. "When was the last time I was home?" he asked in way of answer.

That had been... almost a year ago. When he'd come home to celebrate our birthday. I looked up at my brother, my heart aching for him, understanding almost perfectly the agony he was experiencing at this moment. He was angry at himself for not going to see her more, and feeling selfish for not making time for her.

It was funny how we forgot things in moments of grief. My mom hadn't exactly been the kindest or most comforting individual while we were growing up, and she and my brother had butted heads constantly about his decision to join IT. Not that Mom hadn't supported him serving the Tower in any way he could; she just didn't understand why he couldn't use his skills inside the Citadel as a Knight. Her words, not mine, and the very ones that had led to a massive fight between the two of them. It was why he hadn't been home in a year.

I licked my lips and looked away from him, envious that he, at least, could understand the source of his pain. I had regrets as well, but they were just part of the equation. I wanted the whole picture. The real one, not the one my imagination seemed to procure.

Like how life would've been had she survived the Tourney. I always seemed to picture the three of us sitting together and having dinner, just talking and laughing, but finally getting along. My mother helping me figure out what was really going on in the Tower, working side by side.

If you had asked me three months ago if I had ever thought that picture was possible, I would've laughed in your face. And to be honest, if my mother had survived the Tourney, that image of us would still be unrealistic. There had been miles and miles between us that would've taken a long time to cross.

But maybe it hurt so much *because* it hadn't been that far outside the realm of possibility.

There was something there, some hidden truth that I hadn't accepted, and I started to dig deeper, wondering if that was it—the source of all of my pain.

Someone cleared their throat behind me, breaking my thoughts into a thousand pieces, and I slowly turned to see my father standing there, a hostile look on his face. "People are waiting," he rumbled, and I felt a sharp spike of anger. My hands curled into fists.

The urge to hit him was so strong that it was blinding. How *dare* he try to rush me through this. This was the last moment we were ever going to have with our mother, and he wanted us to just move it along?! I was finally getting somewhere with my own issues!

My brother grabbed my wrist before I could even lift my arm to swing, knowing my body language well enough to understand what I was about to do. He pushed me back behind him, and then stood nose-to-nose with my father, glaring at him.

A sudden hush told me that people were noticing the standoff. I honestly didn't give a damn what they thought, and would've allowed Alex to knock the ever-living crap out of my father, but I couldn't let him. Much like he'd stopped me seconds ago, I had to return the favor. Because we couldn't do this in front of her. Not at her funeral. She'd be so angry with us for ruining the last day we were ever going to be together, and I'd never forgive myself if I let her down like that.

God, even dead, she was making me feel like a ten-year-old child who'd been caught doing something wrong.

"Stop it," I said sharply, tugging on my brother's arm. "Not here. Not in front of her."

Alex looked back at me over his shoulder, his dark eyes glistening, and then nodded once, not even bothering to give one further glance to our father. He stepped around me, clearly needing some space, and I gave him a moment alone with Mom so he could say his goodbyes.

I used the time to stare at my father. He glared back at me, but I ignored it, suddenly too tired to care. Instead, I just looked at him. He'd lost weight in the face, and now his beard seemed to wilt instead of bristle. The lines in his face had deepened, becoming almost crag-like, and the bags under his eyes gave them a droopy look, like they were almost too heavy to look at anything but the floor.

Even with him looking like crap, though, I couldn't find a shred of sympathy for the man. I resented every inch of space he was taking up. I blamed him for my mother's death. Blamed him for being too weak to rescue *himself* from the sentinel. Blamed him for poisoning her own team against her. And most of all, I blamed him for not believing me—and for turning against my mother when *she had.*

Neither of us spoke for a long, tense moment, and after enough time had passed, I realized that neither of us would. So I simply turned my back to him. Alex was pressing his lips to Mom's forehead and whispering something in her ear, and suddenly the pain was back in full force. He glanced at me, offered me a tremulous smile, and then moved away, heading for where Astrid and a few other individuals were standing behind a podium and talking quietly.

I watched him go, and then turned to my mother and took a step closer to her coffin. For a long moment, I wasn't sure what I should do. All I could do was stare down at her.

And then, for the first time since she'd died, I talked about it. Softly, gently, and in a voice only she could hear.

"I'm going to be honest with you... I'm not sure what I'm supposed to do here," I said hoarsely. "I've been... This has been hitting me really hard, Mom." So far, so good, but this was harder than I'd thought it would be. *Just be honest,* I told myself. *It's not like she can yell at you anymore.*

I gave a weird chuckle at my own dark joke, and then immediately felt bad again. She was dead. She could probably hear my thoughts. I looked around, chagrined, and then sighed again.

"I guess there are no more secrets between us, huh? Which is good, I suppose. It makes things a lot easier. Although, it feels a little bit one-sided." I paused, the realization that she was gone hitting me all over again and trapping me in a moment of pain. I pushed it aside, and tried. "Mom, I think... I think what I'm the angriest about is that... is that time was stolen from us." I sighed and wiped my tears away. "Stupid, right? I mean, you were a hard woman, Mom, and I've been used to doing stuff on my own for so long now. We probably would've torn each other apart long before we ever figured out what was going on and –"

That was unfair, and I stopped. Once again, I was talking about unknowns. And that was the problem—there were too many of them. I had no way of knowing whether our relationship would've gotten better or fallen apart, and I needed to stop pretending I did and just admit that my grief was a byproduct of the knowledge that I was never going to find out.

And that hurt. I'd lost any chance of ever getting to find out, and it was tearing me apart. I was torn between a young girl who desperately craved her mother, and a young woman who knew that our relationship hadn't been perfect, but had wanted to work on it anyway. And there was no way of ever finding out now what that would've looked like.

"I really wanted us to get better," I told her, my voice coming out thick from the tears that were now spilling over. "I really wanted us to be a family. I know it's stupid and sentimental, but that's really what I wanted. I thought I'd never have it—I gave up hope—and then you... you decided to try. You... You gave me hope, and now it's just gone, and I'm so hurt... and mad. I can't seem to get my head on straight about it. I just... I just wanted you to be my mother. That's all I ever wanted." I paused, and then in an even smaller voice, added, "And I was starting to think it's what you wanted, too."

And I now had to accept it wasn't going to happen. That it had never been mine to have in the first place.

"I'm sorry, Mom," I finished lamely. "I'm going to get through this, and then I'm going to find the people behind this and make them pay. They stole something from us that we can't ever get back, and even though I can't predict what would've happened between us if you had lived, I can go after them for what they stole from us. I hope it's enough." It didn't feel like enough, but it was the best I had.

I leaned forward and kissed her on the forehead, like Alex had. Her skin was like a slab of marble, cold and hard. Another tear slipped down my cheek and splashed onto her forehead, and I quickly wiped it off, knowing that she wasn't able to do it for herself anymore.

I took one last look at her, trying to memorize every detail I could, and then moved away, heading for where Alex was talking to Astrid. Astrid looked up and greeted me, but the numbness had settled back in, like a heavy mantle around my shoulders. Reality seemed to fall away, and even though I was looking right at it, I remained unmoved by it.

Blink—Astrid walking to the podium. Saying a few words. Stepping off.

Blink—Min-Ha Kim's son, Yeong-Jay, saying something, standing tall and stoic under the bright lights of the stadium.

Blink—another speaker. Lieutenant Zale. I stared at him, a seething anger burning in me. He abandoned his team—my father, Min-Ha, and my mother—to try to win the challenge, and now two of them were dead. He had no right to stand there and speak for them. None at all!

Suddenly my brother reached out and grabbed my hand, and I realized I had balled it into a fist and was shaking all over. I withdrew back into my numb state, not wanting to start a fight.

Blink—speaker after speaker comes and goes. Friends of my mother, friends of Min-Ha, all of them talking, sharing stories, and saying goodbye.

I was glad that I had decided not to give a speech, though I knew people out there would condemn me for it. I didn't care. I hadn't talked about my mother with my friends, so there was no way in hell I was sharing anything with the public. Besides, my feelings weren't for public discussion. I'd only just discovered the source of my pain, but that didn't mean it faded away immediately, and the moments between us were extremely personal. Especially after I'd spent my entire life sharing her with others—not just my family, but the Knights who had worked with her, who knew her better than I did in so many ways.

What I had was private because the good moments with her had been few and far between, and I couldn't bear to part with them, especially now that I understood the source of my pain came from the uncertain future between us. They were part of our history, and the truest memories of her, for good or bad. I mourned over the fact that I'd never hear her say "I love you" again, or get annoyed at her meddling, but I didn't share. The thoughts were mine, and I wasn't going to share them with anyone.

And it seemed my family agreed, because my brother and father also stayed silent. I found myself hoping that Mom would understand our reticence. That our thoughts were now open to her, our motivations clear, and completely un-malicious. We just... didn't want to share.

So we stood there for hours while other people spoke, one right after another, a parade of faces and voices that all seemed to blur together until suddenly I looked up and realized that Astrid was back at the podium, speaking.

This was it—the end was in sight. I straightened my spine some and pushed through the haze, forcing myself back to reality to hear the final remarks before making my escape. I had no intention of staying behind for the wake, but there was only a narrow window of time when I could get out before anyone spotted me and tried to draw me into conversation, or offered their condolences. I couldn't handle it, and I wouldn't, so I needed to know the moment Astrid was done speaking.

"—know that this loss will linger in the days to come, and I realize that the tragic circumstances regarding the final challenge have left us all hurting and filled with confusion." She sighed and glanced at me, her mouth pinched slightly, her eyes remorseful. "I have been authorized to help assuage some of that confusion. As you are all aware, a sentinel—a robot created by the Knights to help establish order in the aftermath of Requiem Day, all of which were retired shortly thereafter—was used as another obstacle during the Tourney.

Scipio lost connection with the sentinel shortly before the start of the challenge, and attempted to shut it down remotely, but failed, and as a result, two fine Knights lost their lives. An intensive investigation by the council has determined that faulty firmware in the sentinel kept a critical software update from occurring, one that was necessary for Scipio to maintain the connection. This was a well-documented problem with the sentinels in the past, and although both the IT Department and the test designers thought they had compensated for it, it seems they had not."

I frowned, trying to understand what she was saying. It didn't make any sense to me—and it definitely wasn't the truth. If there had been a real investigation, it would've been looking into where the sentinel, an obsolete and defunct piece of tech created a hundred years ago, had even come from. Because I knew from our past brushes with it that it hadn't been a part of the Tourney. In fact, it had been working for someone else entirely.

But Astrid hadn't mentioned that, which meant this was a cover-up. This must be the story made up by the council so that they could conduct further investigations in secret without alarming the public. The council didn't want anyone knowing that someone had stolen one of their sentinels—it would make them look weak and ineffective.

They didn't want to take responsibility for the actions, or lack of action, as it were. They didn't want to see that Scipio and the Tower were corrupted. They didn't want to admit their little system was broken.

I narrowed my gaze at Astrid and clenched my teeth, wondering if she had anything to do with it.

"Those responsible for the failure have given themselves up freely, and have been penalized with a lowering of their rank, for their failure to perform their duties correctly. They have also been demoted within their department, and are expected to write personalized apology letters to the families of those who were lost. I understand that many of you feel this isn't enough, but this was an accident."

She turned and looked at me again, and I met her gaze, letting my anger bleed through. Astrid had been my mother's mentor. Her friend. If she was participating in a cover-up, then I wanted to know *why*. Her eyes widened, and then narrowed derisively, and she turned away to face the crowd. Her reaction confused me a little, because while she looked angry, it didn't seem to be directed at me.

"I know it's hard to accept in the light of all the tragedy, and we're all looking for someone to blame, but this incident was not malicious. If anything, we were fortunate that more lives were not lost to this situation. To the families of Min-Ha Kim and Holly Castell, there are no words I can offer that will comfort you in this time of darkness, and for that, you have the sincerest condolences of both myself, and the council.

"Now, I know many of you must be asking what happens next, and wondering about the future of the Knights. With the investigation now concluded, I have been authorized to make one more announcement regarding the council's determination concerning the results of the Tourney. While the tragedy surrounding the final challenge may be close to our hearts, it still pleases me greatly to be able to make this announcement, here in the presence of all of you. And most importantly, in the presence of our future Champion and her family. After much consideration and due diligence, the council has determined that the results of the Tourney will be upheld. Liana 'Honorbound' Castell is the confirmed Champion, and rightful leader of the Knights!"

The crowd burst into applause and cheers, but all I felt was horrified and enraged. They'd made their determination and decided to announce it *here*? Right after feeding us that pack of lies about the sentinel "malfunctioning"? I couldn't believe this—couldn't believe that Astrid would even play a part in this. They'd covered up my mother's and Min-Ha's murders, and now they were distracting from that with "good news", and Astrid was acting as the mouthpiece. How could she do that to me, to my mother? Didn't she or the council have *any* sense of decency?

I glared at her as she stepped down from the podium and made a line straight for me, coming to a stop a respectful distance away.

"If you'll accompany me," she said to me, dismissing my brother and father with a respectful bow of her head. "I'll show you to your new quarters." I stared at her, and then nodded. I clearly had a few things that I needed to ask her about, and this gave me an excuse to get out of here before I was swarmed by people.

She studied me for a second and then turned to head toward one of the side doors that was guarded against the general public's use. I started after her, but stopped when Alex continued to hold my hand. Glancing back, I saw him looking at me with a speculative light in his eyes, and he took a step closer.

"I want to say congratulations," he said, his voice soft. "But first, something tells me that what Astrid said up there was a pack of lies. And you haven't told me anything about what happened. I know that sentinel was the same one we saw at Dinah's, and I know someone was controlling it. You and Dinah said as much. Liana, what is going on?"

I opened my mouth to tell him, and then hesitated. Alex was in a precarious place already, given that he was a member of IT and under heavy scrutiny from the head of the department just because he was my brother. He already knew too much, and even though he was protected by Dinah Velasquez, a powerful and mysterious woman who had been helping us from early on, that protection would only go so far. If he tried to get involved, he could get caught— and I wasn't about to lose somebody else I cared about.

And yet he stared at me, determination and anger glittering in his dark eyes, and I found I couldn't lie to him, either. So I stalled instead.

"Not right now, Alex," I replied, carefully pulling my hand from his. "I'll net you later, once things calm down."

Then I left, pointedly ignoring my father's scathing look and following Astrid out into the hall and away from my mother.

4

I followed Astrid down the hall, walking a few steps behind her and trying to wrap my head around what had just happened. I felt as if I had just surfaced for the first time in a long time, and could focus again. Maybe coming to terms with my mother had helped, I wasn't certain, but now that I could think more clearly again, some of my anger toward Astrid was fading fast as I considered the cover-up and what it really meant.

I supposed it was naïve of me to hope that they would reveal any aspect of the truth regarding my mother's murder. If they had discovered that the sentinel was stolen, which was more than likely, they wouldn't want to broadcast that to the Tower. What's more, if they found out there was a group behind the theft, they wouldn't want to cause a panic inside with the knowledge of a potential terrorist cell.

I was still angry that she and the council had used my mother's funeral as a stage to broadcast the news that I was the Champion, but

I found the questions I had for Astrid were far more pressing than that, and decided to use the walk to the Champion's quarters to let my temper cool off some.

The Champion's quarters, like every department lead's apartment, were a well-guarded secret, to the point that most of the department didn't know where their lead lived. Not only were their locations hidden, but each housed some of the most sophisticated defense systems in the Tower, in case anyone tried to attack the leader of a department directly. It hadn't happened, but councilors continued to keep their quarters hidden over the years for this reason alone.

A lead's quarters also served as a sort of fallout shelter, should a catastrophe large enough to destroy the Tower occur. They were supplied for any event imaginable, with hundreds of thousands of liters of water that were refreshed daily to prevent stagnation, and food stores that could last months or years, depending on how many people a councilor stuffed into their apartment. Each had direct access to the outside in some way, and could be ejected from the Tower if needed. Supposedly, anyway. No one really knew, so much of what I had gleaned was based on rumors—and many of them were ludicrous, so I had taken in only the ones that made the most sense.

I had always daydreamed about what the Champion's apartment would actually look like.

Astrid led me into the elevator, which scanned our nets to ensure that we were authorized for use. I winced as the net in my skull began to vibrate, sending waves of discomfort through my brain and skull and setting my teeth on edge. It ended moments later, and a digitized feminine voice said, *"Champion Liana Castel, 25K-05, and retired Knight Commander Astrid Felix, 165K-58, you are cleared for elevator use."*

A thin, flat disc slid from the wall into the open shaft and hovered in place, and Astrid and I stepped onto it. I started to turn around as it began to lift us into the tube, to face the entry portal, but paused when I saw Astrid still facing the wall behind us.

"What are you doing?"

She looked over at me and offered a small smile, the lines around her eyes crinkling. "Liana, what's on the other side of this wall?"

I frowned and looked at the wall, trying to think. This elevator was one of the six that ran through the centermost part of the Citadel. There wasn't anything on the other side, except for the internal support structure that allowed the structure to hang from the ceiling.

"Nothing but a massive steel rod and brace beams," I replied, letting some of my confusion show.

Her smile deepened, and she looked up. "Stop the elevator between the thirty-first and thirty-second floors on my authority, Astrid Felix 165K-58." The elevator slowed to a stop, and I tensed, taking a step away from her that was purely reactionary. All I could think was that I was alone with a woman I wasn't sure I could trust, and that she had just shut the elevator off in a way that left me completely alone with her for some unknown reason.

I was certain I had just walked into a trap.

She noticed it, cocked her head in confusion, and then blinked rapidly in alarm. "Oh Scipio, Liana, no! I'm not going to attack you! I'm sorry for the theatrics. I just thought I'd surprise you. Your quarters are on the other side of the wall."

Her voice carried a slightly flustered tinge, and I could tell she was mentally kicking herself for not thinking about how her actions would affect a recently traumatized and paranoid young woman. And I could've smiled, if the sight hadn't made me sad. She knew now that I didn't trust her, and while that wasn't entirely true, it wasn't exactly wrong, either. It made me feel guilty for even reacting like that toward her. And it made me hate the people who had put that seed of paranoia in my heart.

"It's all right," I replied, relaxing slightly and trying to shake it off. "Show me to my quarters."

As if on cue, a door in the wall separating us from the heart of the Citadel slid open. Astrid gave me a pleased smile, and then stepped through the door and into the darkness. I hesitated for a second... then followed. The door slid shut behind me with a slight grating sound, and then lights came on overhead—terrible bright white things that stung my eyes.

"It's a bit bright in here," I said, raising my hand to shield my eyes so I could peer around the room. Before I could even get my hand up, though, the lights dimmed to a tolerable level.

"My apologies," a dry masculine voice announced. "Your predecessor preferred the light settings to be much higher. If you wish to make these your new settings, please say so. If not, you can order them higher or lower, based on your preference."

I blinked and looked around, searching for the speaker. Only, the floor was empty. Just a flat, circular dome with lights gleaming from the ceiling. "Who said that?"

"That's Cornelius," Astrid said from beside me. "He's your personal assistant, and can answer almost any question you have regarding protocol and procedure."

I blinked again, still confused. We had computers that spoke, after a fashion—the elevator scanners were a prime example of that—but they were automated, programmed with only a small variety of things to say and commands to respond to. They couldn't sustain a dialogue with anyone, and even if they could, I doubted they would be as ingratiating as this voice had sounded.

"Cornelius?" I repeated.

"Yes, Milady Champion," he replied. "How may I be of service?"

I looked over at Astrid. "I'm really confused."

She smiled. "Cornelius is an advanced program, much more advanced than others in the Tower. He's not sentient—only Scipio is, of course—but he can feel rather lifelike due to his broad vocabulary. He can take commands, as long as they are worded generally and are within his purview, and he can find almost any record within the Citadel or the council's private server, should you need it."

Huh. That was new and exciting. And also a little terrifying. The group of people I thought were behind the sentinel, and the attack on Scipio, had definitely proven they had a way with computers, and Cornelius could have been one of their targets. For all I knew, he had been hacked long ago. Especially considering that his former user, Devon Alexander, had been part of a legacy group that had been working to steal parts of Scipio's code. Even if he hadn't, the legacies we were up against had proven incredibly adept at manipulating the security systems around the Tower—which made Cornelius a potential threat. I'd have to be careful about what I told him and how I used him, or he could become a huge vulnerability that our enemies could exploit.

"I see." I took another look around the room while I considered the problem and how to solve it, and was momentarily taken aback by how underwhelming the room was.

Because that was all it was: a room. A large, empty space with nothing save a column in the middle and a dome-like roof overhead.

"This isn't what I expected."

Astrid smiled warmly and then nodded to the column. "Wait until you see what it can do," she replied mysteriously. "Come here."

I followed her to the column and watched as she pressed her fingers against a dimly glowing spot halfway up. Instantly, a five-foot section of the column dropped open, revealing a three-dimensional holographic image of the room in red. There was also some sort of interactive screen over it, with several drop-down menus that read *Layout, Furniture, Level, Appliances, Accessories.* I jabbed my finger at the last one, feeling a tingle of electricity in my fingertip as I poked the word *Accessories,* and a moment later the screen changed, showing me an array of blankets, pillows, dishware, cookware, vases...

I looked over at Astrid and raised an eyebrow. "I can design the room?"

She nodded and reached over me to hit the back button. "You can," she replied excitedly, swiping her finger through the entry marked *Layout.* The image of the room immediately got closer, and I watched as she drew a wall just to the left of us. A second later there was a soft grating sound, and a wall slid from the floor up to the ceiling. There was a flurry of movement overhead as a table was placed against the wall and topped with a vase, both delivered from above through the use of a robotic crane.

I gaped, astonished at what I was looking at, and gave her a wide-eyed look. "How is this possible?"

"You and the other councilors have access to a storehouse of furniture and different supplies in the top levels of the Citadel. Whenever you order something, it's delivered. The room is adjustable according to your needs and wants, so you can lay things out in a way that makes you most comfortable. I would suggest that you create a large seating area, though, as you'll be expected to meet with the Knight Commanders once a month to listen to their reports."

I nodded, but inside I was feeling slightly anxious. This was a lot to take in. A room that I could change to my own desires, complete with a computer program assistant who could possibly be spying on me? Not to mention the idea that I was going to be hosting meetings with the Knight Commanders once a month...

Scipio help me, only five minutes as Champion and I was overwhelmed—and certain that this wasn't even the tip of the spear.

"Is there anything else I need to know about the room?" I asked.

Astrid nodded, and hit the *No* button under a line that read, *Accept changes to the room?* Seconds later the wall, table, and vase had been whisked away, leaving the floor empty and vacant again. I watched as she selected the *Level* button and keyed in the number 65, suddenly wondering why she was doing it manually.

"Hey, can't Cornelius handle this?"

She chuckled. "He's programmed to do a lot, but someone decided that giving him too much control wasn't necessarily a good thing, as even computer programs can break down or get glitches. You'll need him to help sift through the massive amounts of historical data we've collected, should it come up, but you don't need him to work the room when this terminal can do it just as well. This also gives you peace of mind that Cornelius won't bug out and decide a wall was needed right in the middle of your bed."

I shuddered at the image and took a quick glance at her, trying to decide whether she was joking or not. I couldn't tell, and something told me I didn't want to know, so I didn't ask. I wouldn't sleep for a month if I learned a councilor had been killed by their virtual assistant.

She hit the enter key, and the floor immediately started to shake as the entire room began to lift up. My new home, it seemed, was also a giant elevator. "It runs all the way through the top of the Citadel to the very top of the Tower. You can exit through any of the marked doors—" she pointed at the six rectangles with designations over them as they slid by "—and be in one of the six main elevators. It just has to be lined up in between two floors, as that was where the doors were built leading to the normal elevators. You can give whomever you want permission to come and go, if you desire, but be aware that the defense system is designed to use lethal force, so you should never send anyone in here if you haven't authorized them to enter. The defenses will be configured to your new home as best as possible, but you will have some say in that configuration. That section is found under a subheading in the *Appliances* option. Cornelius can walk you through it. Now, do you have any questions for me?"

I stared at her, and then crossed my arms over my chest. I had been momentarily distracted by the intriguing possibilities of my new home, but now I remembered my questions from earlier.

I wanted to know what the council had really uncovered, and what they were doing about it.

"I want to know what the council really found in their investigation into my mother's death," I said roughly.

Astrid's smile wilted, leaving a sour look on her face. "Liana..." she said, trailing off. "Look, I know you think that your mother and Min-Ha's deaths are connected to Ambrose's murder, but I led this investigation personally. I questioned the designers and the techs thoroughly, with Scipio watching their emotional states through their nets to see if they were lying. I had multiple experts from the Mechanics Department and IT running tests and comparing their findings, independent of each other. The sentinel was torn apart and meticulously studied. Their deaths were tragic and horrifying, but I am convinced that they *were* accidents."

My brows drew together in confusion at her words. She had *personally* run the investigation? And hadn't found any evidence that the sentinel had been stolen, or that it was being controlled by anyone else? I fought back a groan as I realized that there were only two things that made sense: Astrid had forced the investigation to a conclusion that she wanted because she was working with the legacies, *or*... she had discovered exactly what she was meant to, so that the legacies could continue to move around freely. Of the two of them, the last was far, far more likely.

Even if I didn't want to believe it.

"So you're saying that there was no one actually controlling the sentinel, but that it was supposed to be an obstacle in the Tourney... and just went haywire?" I asked, needing the confirmation. If Astrid wasn't lying, then was it possible someone above her was? The only people who had been above her in this had been the council... A chill hit me as I realized that it was entirely possible that someone on the council was a legacy, or controlled by one.

"Unless you count Scipio, then no," Astrid said, folding her arms over her chest. "But if you don't believe me, feel free to ask Cornelius for access to the council file and take a look at the reports yourself. It'll be filed by date, but you can use general search words, like your mother's name, or even the sentinel—although that would pull up other information as well." She speared me with a sharp look and added, in a dry tone, "Do let me know if you find anything that I might have missed."

"I'll do that," I replied, refusing to be cowed by the steeliness of her gaze. I knew I had upset her by insinuating that she had missed something, but I didn't care. I wanted to find out what had happened. I didn't want to believe there was another enemy legacy on the council—that made everything even more dangerous. I supposed it was possible that the legacy group just had a lot of well-placed connections and had been able to set all of this up, cover-up and all? Could the entire council have been duped? It was also a possibility, but I couldn't see how. I needed those files.

I looked up to see Astrid staring at me expectantly, waiting to see what I would ask next, and thought for a second. If she was truly satisfied with the investigation, continuing to question her would just make her angry. So I moved on to my next question, one that wasn't as pressing, but was burning in the back of my mind all the same.

"Whose idea was it to make the announcement during my mother's funeral?"

She rolled her eyes, but again, I got the distinct impression that it wasn't directed at me. "Look, kid, I didn't agree with that decision, and fought against it, but the council was adamant that all of this be put to bed... if you'll excuse my awful choice of words there. So was Scipio. He felt it would be good for the Citadel's morale, and the Tower itself, to get the Knights represented so that the department could get back on track. And since they planned to announce the conclusion of the investigation at that point anyway, they figured why not let them down and then try to lift them back up?"

I looked away. Her answer made a certain amount of sense from the council's point of view—they didn't want morale to fall—but I didn't like the greasy sensation of it, which made my stomach twist. "It wasn't right," I replied, and to my surprise, Astrid nodded.

"I agree. I'm sorry that I sprang that on you, Liana, but I was under orders from the council and from Scipio himself. You understand?"

I met her earnest look, and then sighed. I did understand. It wasn't her fault that she was following orders; it was the way we were all brought up. You did what Scipio told you to because if you didn't, then you were clearly an enemy of the Tower.

But what Astrid didn't know was that Scipio's will wasn't exactly his own these days. I'd seen him manipulated once already—at my trial for the murder of Devon Alexander—and knew from Lacey that there was another group controlling him even more directly, influencing his decisions. I just wasn't certain they'd go as far as to influence when and where information was distributed. If they were going to affect anything, they would've made Scipio tell the council to reject me and re-do the Tourney, so their chosen candidate could win instead.

Speaking of which...

"I understand," I said carefully, wondering just how to ask her what I wanted to know. "How did this even happen?" was what I finally decided on.

"You mean, how did you become the Champion?" I nodded, and Astrid sighed. "I'll admit that you entering the arena armed with an illegal weapon didn't earn you a lot of favor, especially with the Medica. Chief Surgeon Sage was very upset to learn that the voltage on those little shocker things could've easily killed a human being, and argued that for all anyone knew, you'd brought them to use against the candidates, and just happened to save lives instead. IT was also dead-set against accepting the results. I don't know what you did to that woman, but Sadie Monroe hates you, kid."

That was unsurprising; she had hated me since the day she met me. It was surprising, though, to hear that Marcus Sage had sided with her. The Chief Surgeon of the Medica was over a hundred years old, and had seemed mostly disinterested with my trial. Now, it was very possible that his concerns were what Astrid said—merely based on safety—but still, I marked it and filed it away. No one was above suspicion, and if Sage was somehow involved with the legacy group, then I wanted to know.

"Anyway," Astrid continued, shifting her weight to her other leg and crossing her arms, "your saving grace was that you admitted to everything."

"I did?" I asked, unable to hide my confusion. The interview after the Tourney was one giant blur, and I honestly couldn't recall exactly what I had told her by way of explanation.

"Yes, you did, remember? You told me that you overheard a group of designers talking about how they were planning to use a sentinel for the final challenge and created the shockers to stop it, to give yourself an advantage. My favorite part was when you said, 'Yes, I cheated. But if I hadn't, then more people would be dead. You're welcome.'"

"I said that?" I looked away, surprised at hearing my own words for what seemed like the first time and shocked that I had been able to fabricate something that believable and had delivered it in such a way. Scipio help me, it seemed so callous now. Hours after my mother's death and I had been acting like *that*? "Wow."

"I agree," Astrid said. There was a long pause, and then she added, "You're a good kid, Liana, with a kind and strong heart. It's something the Citadel needs, more than you might think. But I also know that you've been pushed to a breaking point, and I want to tell you that you're not alone. You can come to me if you need help, or advice... or even just a shoulder to cry on."

I rubbed my hands together and nodded absently. I'd heard those words a thousand times by now, and a certain amount of bleak hopelessness rose up to greet them before they could ever settle in, reminding me that she was wrong. I *was* alone. Completely and abjectly alone. Maybe not in the physical sense, but certainly in my soul, where I was trapped by memories of what had been and dreams of what could've been.

And there wasn't anything anyone could do about that.

But still, I gave her the empty platitude I had given everyone else. "Thank you. I'll be sure to do so, if I feel the need."

Her mouth flattened into a thin, displeased line, and I could tell that she didn't believe me, but she didn't press. "Good. Now, before we finish here, there is one little matter of who will be serving as your Lieutenant. Traditionally, the Champion picks someone from their team. I understand that Grey Farmless is quite popular. Will he be taking on that role?"

I considered the question for a second. Leo would be a good Lieutenant, but I knew he wouldn't want the job. He'd helped us during the Tourney because we were being forced to do it, but his heart and soul were dedicated to the mission of helping Scipio, and being Lieutenant would only distract him from his cause.

Besides, Maddox was my first instinct. Not just because of Leo's situation, although that was a part of it, but because she was the best fit for the job. She'd dreamed of being a Knight since she was little, and though she hadn't been educated inside the system, she knew it inside and out, thanks to her mother's education and her own determination. Beyond that, she had tested out of being a Squire within two days—an impressive feat, considering she didn't have a photographic memory or enhanced reflexes like Leo did.

"No, he will not," I said, feeling confident about my decision. "Maddox Kerrin will."

"The undoc?" Astrid asked, her eyes widening in alarm. "I'm not sure the other Knight Commanders will like that, considering she's the daughter of two people they consider to be traitors."

"Camilla Kerrin was not a traitor," I snapped, wanting to defend not only Maddox, but the memory of her mother as well. Cali might have run away from the Citadel, but she'd had little choice in the matter; she had done what she did to save her child and stay alive. "She tried to alert the council to Devon's treachery, but he found out and ran her off. She fled, pregnant with their child, and hid, knowing that Devon would kill her long before she could get to the council. So you will talk about her with respect, and tell the Knight Commanders to treat Maddox as if they were talking to me."

Astrid's eyebrows shot straight up in surprise, but behind it I could see a glimmer of respect that was steadily growing, and mentally patted myself on the back. "I will do that, but keep in mind, kid, I go back to teaching in the Academy now. My investigation is over, and I'm retired. Maddox is going to have to earn the Commanders' respect in her own way, but I've seen the vid files from the Tourney, and I'm sure she'll be fine."

I wasn't certain how to respond to that, so I just smiled and nodded.

"Do you need anything else?"

"Yes," I said. There was one more thing I needed, and that was a step toward finding the legacy group. Which meant looking into *every* investigation—not just my mother's. "I need everything you have on the investigation into Ambrose's murder, including copies of your personal notes. I'll be taking over and handling it personally."

She frowned, a line forming between her gray eyebrows. "Liana, are you sure? You were on his team, and while you've been eliminated as a suspect, you aren't exactly impartial."

"I'm sure," I told her, ignoring her complaints. I needed everything she had and more if I was going to find the people who'd killed my mother and Ambrose. I knew that the same people were behind it

—it was the only thing that made sense—and I needed to find them. Not only because I wanted to know what they had done to Scipio, but also to punish them for what they did to my mother and Ambrose.

I couldn't decide whether it helped or hurt that I was being blackmailed into doing it by Lacey Green, the head of the Mechanics Department, who was holding evidence that made it appear as if I had tampered with Scipio. Originally, the deal had just been for me to keep her cousin, Ambrose, safe, but when I had failed at that, I had promised that once I won the Tourney, I would do everything in my power to bring his killers to her for justice. And I still intended to do so.

I just wasn't sure if anyone I found would make it back to her in one piece. I supposed I would have to make an effort to get her a few of the people who were responsible, just so she wouldn't have me and my friends brought up on charges of terrorism. I really didn't want to become public enemy number one again.

"Very well," Astrid said after a long moment. "I'll send them to you in a few minutes."

"Thank you," I replied. "Now, if you don't mind... I'd like a little time alone in my new room."

"Of course," she replied with a nod. "Champion Castell, it has been my privilege to serve you." She bent her head forward, offering a small bow, and then straightened. "Cornelius, the door?"

A door slid open to the right, and Astrid departed, leaving me blissfully and completely alone.

5

"I am ready to serve you," Cornelius announced as soon as Astrid had left. "Shall we go over the tutorial?"

I sighed and closed my eyes, rolling them back into my skull with my annoyance. I had forgotten that I wasn't *actually* alone. In fact, I had been left to deal with a new flavor of problem: was Cornelius actually safe, or was he spying on me?

Or... was he secretly an AI fragment, like Jasper and Jang-Mi, but being forced to impersonate an unassuming assistant program?

If so, that would be super convenient, if a little weird. Because if Devon Alexander had been hiding an AI fragment, wouldn't his followers have come into the room and removed it before the next person moved in?

I wasn't sure, but I was beginning to grow tired of all the supposition and guesswork. I wanted data, evidence... a clear way forward that I could use to track down the people responsible for everything.

Which didn't mean coming up with more things to guess at. It meant going over each piece of evidence and fact that we had, filling in the pieces of the puzzle step by step, and treating no detail as insignificant or unrelated.

But first, I needed to understand the ins and outs of my new home, and that meant dealing with the program installed inside it first. "Oh, Cornelius," I sighed, folding my arms across my chest. "What am I going to do with you?"

"I do not show any matches for that query. Please refine and specify."

His reply was given in that same ingratiating voice that was just a hair too chipper in my opinion, and I sighed again, rubbing my forehead with one hand. The tone made me fairly confident that he wasn't an AI fragment, but that didn't alter my belief that he could be a risk if someone managed to hack into his system.

"Who has access to you?" I asked, curious about what he would tell me. "Is it possible that someone has hacked your program?"

"Only the Champion has access to me," Cornelius replied. "I have been successfully hacked only twice during my lifetime, in tests performed by our internal security teams to check my systems and firewalls. The tests were designed to find any faults and fix them, and none have been found in the subsequent seventy-five years. Would you like to see the reports?"

I considered his question, then realized that it didn't matter. I wouldn't be convinced that he was all right until Quess and Leo checked him out. Which meant I should probably get them up here sooner rather than later. My period of solitude was going to be shorter than I would've liked, but I needed to get over it.

As much as I wanted to withdraw and go it alone, I knew they'd never let me. Even worse, they would probably get themselves killed trying to help me.

"No, thank you," I informed Cornelius, trying to stay on track. "Tell me, what are your duties?"

"I monitor your quarters at all times to ensure your safety, as well as assisting you in finding procedural solutions to any and all problems that arise in our department. I liaise between you and central command, so your orders are delivered correctly and effectively. I also inform you of your daily schedules and pending messages that require your attention, and help you prepare for your weekly council sessions."

I blinked, realizing that I was about to lose my excuse for ever being late again. Because Cornelius was going to play lord of my schedule and force me to deal with every issue as it came in.

"Fun. So... is everything I do in here recorded?"

"Yes. There are multiple cameras recording at all times."

I definitely did not like that. If he was hacked, my enemies could be watching me right now. "Who has access to those cameras?" I asked.

Because the next step was obvious. Devon Alexander had been working with the legacy group—and he might have given *them* access to Cornelius's system.

"Only you and whomever you authorize, Champion Castell," Cornelius replied simply.

I considered his answer, and knew I couldn't be certain about that, either—not until Leo and Quess got here. But the idea that I was being recorded got me thinking even more about the former Champion, and the fact that if what Cornelius was saying was true, he had been recorded as well. Were those vid files still there, inside of Cornelius? A surge of excitement shot through me as I considered it, and I found myself already imagining that they were, and that I could access them and discover who Devon was working with by finding clues in the recordings Cornelius had made.

"What happens to the security files after a Champion dies?" I asked carefully. I wasn't sure if there was a special way to access those files, but if I asked directly about them, anyone who might be watching could figure out what I was getting at and preemptively delete the backups.

"They are deleted."

That didn't make any sense. The council would want a record of everything, wouldn't they? "What happens if a Champion is accused of a crime, and the council requires the vid files to prove it?"

"Only with a warrant unanimously agreed upon by the other members of the council can I release that data."

"So there *is* a way to access the vid files after a Champion is dead?" I asked, excited that I might have caught him in a mistake.

"Clarification. In your earlier question, I presumed the Champion accused of a crime was still living, which would mean the data would be available. However, to answer your question more specifically, it would be possible for a technician to come in and recover the deleted file from the buffer, but those would be fragmented, at best."

"Was a warrant ever issued for Devon Alexander?" I asked, my skin tingling. If so, that meant that those files, even fragmented, would be a part of the council's records. Definitely in the file with my trial—undoubtedly sealed—but there, nonetheless. And now that I was a counselor, I could gain access to them and watch.

"No. The council has never had a unanimous decision to issue a warrant like that. Not once in the entire history of the Tower."

I blinked, disappointment flaring through me. "I see."

"Would you like to see the records of the attempts to gain

warrants in the past?" he inquired by way of response. "Perhaps this can help you with your investigation."

"No, it's fine," I muttered. I was grasping at straws, anyway. I should've known it wouldn't be that easy. Still, it was mildly reassuring to know that, should Cornelius check out, this room was completely private and safe from prying eyes. My friends and I would finally have a safe place to plan things out without the risk of being discovered.

I looked up at the column, taking in the dimensions of the room using the interactive hologram, and studied it. The elevator pad was massive, with a diameter of a hundred and fifty feet, creating an area that measured a little under seventeen thousand square feet. I had never had so much space available to me in my entire life, and suddenly I was curious to see what I could do with all that room.

I pressed the back button and examined the drop-down menu for a moment or two before pressing *Layouts*. There were a few mockups of potential floorplans in the archives, but after a short perusal of them, I decided that none were to my liking, and moved on, flipping through the options until I discovered a way to draw directly onto the image using a stylus that slid out of the wall, to show exactly where I wanted the walls to go.

The program was very intuitive, and within minutes I was tinkering with ideas, checking spaces and dimensions, and trying to come up with the most defensible design. I settled for something that looked like a snail's shell and widened into oval-shaped rooms before narrowing into a hall again. The first room was a sitting area, complete with a tactical table, several monitors, and comfortable seating. I planned for this room to be where I had my monthly meetings with the Knight Commanders, as well as being a general reception room, should I ever feel inclined to invite anyone over. From there, the layout became a more intimate dining area and kitchen. I learned that I could also alter the depths of the floor somewhat—three feet, either up or down—and could add stairs if I wanted to. So I made the kitchen slightly higher than the dining room.

Another long hall came around, and here I created two bathrooms. I was delighted to learn that not only could I have a bathtub, but I would also no longer be restricted by water rations (although Cornelius still warned me about overuse). I could take a bath for the first time in my life, and it would just be like... swimming in one of the bodies of water in Water Treatment. Only hot, private, and luxurious.

So I gave both bathrooms a tub, and moved on. I created four bedrooms, all on the same side of the hall, with connecting doors between them as a security measure. One was for Zoe and Eric, one was for Quess and Leo, one was for Maddox and Tian, and then the last one was for me. I put in basic furniture where I thought it would look best, and was delighted when the mechanical cranes suddenly got to work, dropping everything exactly where I had placed it in the model.

In fact, the transformation of the room was conducted so seamlessly while I worked that I lost notice of the whir and scrape and the flurry of activity as I adjusted, tweaked, modified, and refined my design, only moving when the program notified me that I was in the way of something, until the final wall slid into place, followed by the final bit of furniture.

I turned in what was now the center of my snail shell, looking over the final piece of my design, which I was planning to call the war room. It had two levels, the lower of which held a long table that was another tactical table (only far superior to the one I had dropped in the front room). Curved steps climbed up six feet to where I was standing, creating a small dais with a desk in the middle of it that overlooked the table. Screens circled the dais and desk, giving whoever sat at the desk a three-hundred-and-sixty-degree view of whatever was being projected there. Cornelius helped me set each one of them up, adjusting until I had live images from the Citadel piping through each one.

I stared at it for several moments, and then decided to take a quick tour to admire my work and search for any problems. I walked through the spiraling hall, up stairs and down them, and found myself smiling at the space I had created. A space that was now all my own.

I can't wait to show my friends this place, I thought, and then stopped dead in my tracks as it suddenly hit me. I had been so distracted by fiddling around with the versatility of the room that I had forgotten to net them and tell them where I was.

I sighed and ran a hand through my hair, trying to release the sudden tension that had formed. I was making progress in over-coming the problems from the last three days, but even though I had come to terms with things, I still wasn't sure if I was ready to talk about them. It was a little embarrassing to admit that I had broken down all because I had been robbed of a potential future with my mother.

And then it hit me all over again. She was gone, and nothing was ever going to be fixed between us. I'd forever carry the memories of the good and the bad (more bad), and it made everything inside ache and rage. In spite of me recognizing it for what it was.

My strength deserted me, and I leaned against the wall for support, wondering where she was right now. They would've closed her casket at this point, to transport her through the Tower with respect, which meant there were no more chances to say goodbye—

unless I wanted to walk through the fields of Twilight, a greenery where the dead were left to create new soil that helped maintain the fields we needed for farming. It was a process that took decades, so if I truly wanted to, I could go up there and visit her.

But that would require being comfortable with the idea of seeing her decomposing corpse. The respect was finished as soon as the casket bearers reached the greenery and her body was upended from the box onto soil that needed replenishment. It was a brutal and callous thing to do to the dead—something that had never sat well with me—and yet was a practical solution for keeping the soil we had rich with the minerals necessary for growing things.

And that was where Sybil was buried, and Ambrose. Devon was probably there as well. And now my mother and Min-Ha. All of them sharing what would become one final task before they were completely obliterated, unified by the only equalizer my world seemed to know or understand: death.

I knew in my heart that I would join them up there too, one day. I could only hope to accomplish something good before it happened —something that would *help* people rather than hurt them. I believed that, more than anything, was the legacy my mother wanted me to have. She had believed I had a destiny once, after all. And if destiny meant helping people instead of hurting them, then I was okay with it.

Once again, my heart began to wish and pray for her to be here with me, guiding me and telling me what to do, and I wanted to beat my head against the wall, frustrated that I still couldn't push the torrent back. Maybe it was unrealistic, given the hour or so that had passed since the funeral, but I just... I wanted to be better.

I *needed* to be better. There was no time for this—I had too much to do. Finding my mother's killers, rescuing Jasper, saving Scipio, keeping my friends safe, learning how to be Champion... The list was endless.

I sucked in a deep breath, trying to calm myself. It took me a moment, but I realized that I was on my knees in the hall, just before the sitting area. Pathetic.

I scrubbed my cheeks clean, wiping away the wet residue, and sniffled to clear my nose so I wouldn't sound nasal or stuffed up. I was shaking slightly, and exhausted by how much energy all that emotion had eaten up.

Of all the things mourning had put me through, these moments of weakness were the worst, and I couldn't keep going on like this. I had to find a way to compartmentalize everything so I could function. Every time I broke down, I was giving our enemies free time to plan their next move. Not to mention, my friends were depending on me to figure out what we would do next. They were probably already climbing the walls, wondering where I was and what I wanted them to do.

Yesterday, I wouldn't have been able to tell them, but now...

Now I had answers, even if I wasn't sure I was ready to share them yet. I could keep going, if I just reminded myself what it was I was really upset about, and remained in the moment. It was going to take time, but at least I had a path forward. I just had to focus on it, and try to keep calm whenever the pain hit. It would pass. I hoped.

I picked myself up off the ground, climbing back to my feet on shaky knees. My friends were waiting for me. People were depending on me. I could do this.

"Cornelius?" I croaked, my voice hoarse.

"Yes, ma'am?" he replied. "How can I serve you?"

"I need you to contact Zoe Elphesian for me," I said, leaning heavily on the wall as I slowly maneuvered myself into a standing position. "Tell her to get everyone, and then direct her here. She and her guests have permission to enter."

"Yes, ma'am. Doing so now. While I do, I would like to inform you that the Medica has sent you a notification that your neural transmitter is ready for implantation at your convenience. They want to know if you wish to do it in the Citadel or go to the Medica."

I blinked, confused by what he was talking about. It took me a minute, but I realized that a neural transmitter was the special implant that only the council members got—one that allowed them to communicate nonverbally. The technology used to be fairly prolific, but as the materials for these types of nets became harder and harder to produce, they became limited, until their use was restricted to council use only.

But I was about to get one, and could have voiceless conversations with whomever I wanted. If I was ever being attacked or needed backup, I would be able to communicate orders without giving our enemies any clue what I was up to. Couple that with the legacy net that Quess was hopefully going to get back to me soon, and Cornelius, and I'd have access to more information than I would know what to do with—and be able to talk about it without actually having to *talk* about it.

It was exciting.

"Right, tell them I will come down in two hours, and remind me fifteen minutes before then. I'll notify them if I need more time."

"Order logged. I have received confirmation from Zoe Elphesian that she is on her way. You are also receiving a vid chat request from Engineer Lacey Green. Should I connect it to your desk station terminal?"

Vid chat request, huh? That was fancy; no citizen in the Tower had that ability. I considered his question for a second, and where I was in my new home, and then said, "No, connect it to the video screen in the parlor. I'll take it in there."

My breath caught for a second as a stab of anxiety rocketed through me, and then I took a moment to compose myself. I had been expecting this, and while I had been certain it would come sooner, I still wished it had happened later. I was not ready to deal with Lacey Green right now—but if I put her off, she'd make sure that my stint as Champion was the shortest one in Tower history.

And I'd no doubt be joining my mom in Twilight sooner than I'd hoped to.

6

I faced the screen on the wall and waited. A second later, Lacey's face filled it.

She... did not look great, but that was understandable given that Ambrose had died a little over a week ago. It felt like a lifetime since it had happened, but it was still fresh on Lacey's face. Her dark skin had an unnatural paleness to it, but the bags under her eyes were black, making them looked bruised. Her eyes were tinged with red, and even the brown and blond curls of her afro seemed to droop.

Still, the look on her face was anything but sad. Because her expression was lined with a hostility that almost matched the one my father had demonstrated earlier, during the funeral. As soon as I registered it, I immediately felt guilty—and then angry in my own right. Lacey might have blamed me for Ambrose's death, but in my mind, *she* was to blame for my mother's death! She'd forced me into the Tourney, made me participate just to help her plans along! It had made me a target, and my mother had gotten caught in the crossfire.

Lacey glared at me for a second or two, resentment simmering delicately in the browns of her eyes. "I'm sorry about your mother," she said suddenly, a slight snap to her words.

More rage poured over me, until my skin felt like it was sizzling. *Don't start a fight,* I told myself sternly, trying to rein it in. *Remember to be patient, and that she owns you for as long as she has that so-called "evidence" against you.* I managed to pull myself back—but just barely.

"Thank you," I replied tersely.

She nodded, just once. "Congratulations on becoming the new Champion, as well."

I stared at her, thinking about Astrid's speech and the knowledge that the council had put her up to it. Lacey was a council member. Had she agreed to that little stunt, or had she had the decency to at least vote no?

"Did you have anything to do with the strategy for delivering the news at my mother's funeral?" I demanded, unable to help myself. If she had, I'd be livid that she'd stoop that low.

Her eyes widened, and then narrowed slightly. "No, I did not!" she hissed. "I've barely weighed in this past week. The only thing I did was keep appraised and pass my votes on through Strum as proxy. Scipio was the one who made the decision on your fate, and for some reason, the enemy chose not to alter it. Or maybe they couldn't; it seems like sometimes Scipio fights them on things, though I'm not sure."

I blinked. She had told me more about Scipio's current state than anyone else had been able to. Scipio's program was an amalgamation of several different AI fragments, but at his core, he was Leo—whose determination to keep the Tower moving had made him the central program on which Scipio was based.

I wondered if that part of him was rebelling against his controllers—if that was what Lacey had just told me. Still, I was a little suspicious. How could she determine that Scipio sometimes fought them? Did she have a way of monitoring him?

"How do you know he fights them?"

She frowned, instantly displeased. "Me and my big fat mouth," she muttered, running a hand over her face. "Look... we have a way of monitoring Scipio's emotional state. Basically, whenever he's being manipulated, his emotional state shifts to extremes, almost like someone with bipolar disorder. However, there have been times when we start to see it happen, and then the entire thing breaks down before it finishes. It's hard to explain, but that's what happened with the decision."

"I see." That was a lie. I wasn't entirely sure what she was talking about, but I made a mental note to ask Leo about it. Maybe it would help him figure out what was wrong with Scipio, which could help him find a way to fix the problem. I also decided to change the topic, as I was certain that if I continued to press Lacey about this, she would shut down and refuse to reveal anything more. I needed her relaxed so she would be more willing to let things slip.

Once she stopped glaring at me like she wanted to see my throat torn out. Or when I managed to stop doing the same.

I sighed and rubbed a hand over my head. "Look, I know why you're calling, and I'm waiting on the files from the investigation to be sent over to me. But I also need the files from the investigation into the sentinel. The people who stepped forward to assume responsibility are lying, and I want their names so I can hunt them down and ask them questions."

Ever since Astrid told me about the results, I had been itching to get my hands on them and tear into them to get to the truth of the matter. The people who had taken responsibility were clearly lying about what happened. And I wanted to know why.

"Liana..." Lacey studied me for a second, and then looked to one side. "You can't do that."

"The hell I can't," I snapped back, incensed that she would try to block any line of inquiry from me. "Those people were told to lie! I will find out who told them to, then track them down to find out who told *them* to do it, and go up the chain until I am standing face-to-face with the person who is responsible for my mother's death."

"And Ambrose," Lacey hissed sharply. "Don't you dare forget about him, Liana."

"Believe me, I haven't. Now, are you going to send me those files?"

"No, I'm not. You can access them if you want, but let me lay this out for you: those people weren't lying. Or at least, they didn't think they were. They checked out a sentinel between the challenges to prepare it for the last one. It disappeared shortly after the final checks were completed, about an hour before the final challenge. Around that time, our monitoring of Scipio showed an extreme mood shift that normally accompanies someone making him do something, and we assumed the other group made him move it. Then a sentinel appeared in the arena and started attacking people with a Class B weapon. Astrid and everyone else on the council assumed it was the same sentinel that those engineers had lost, and by the time the sentinel you disabled in the arena showed up in the investigation rooms, it *was* the original sentinel—serial numbers and all."

"Wait, are you telling me there were *two* sentinels in play, and they switched them?" A second later, I realized that if that was true, that meant one of them was still unaccounted for—and in their hands. They might not have Jang-Mi to pilot it for them anymore, but that didn't mean they couldn't work around the problem.

She nodded. "It's not the first time something like this has happened, but believe me when I say they are good at this. They've been setting people up like this for years."

A chill ran down my spine. I knew my enemies had a significant number of people, but the fact that they had managed to steal not one, but two of the sentinels the Tower had kept because of the Technological Preservation Act, in order to cover their tracks, was impressive. And terrifying.

No wonder I rarely felt safe anymore.

"Fine," I said, giving it up and focusing on a new question. "Then here's a question: how secure is my little personal assistant thing? Is it possible Devon had it hacked? Could someone be monitoring us right now?"

Lacey's eyebrows rose, and a surprised smile flashed across her face... and was gone again in the blink of an eye. "Okay, dial back the paranoia and relax. The program is fine. They are systematically wiped and reinstalled between department heads, so even if he was hacked, that hack is now gone. You're fine."

That was a relief, but only a mild one, and quickly it gave way to a different line of questions. "What about recovering Devon Alexander's vid files from this room? If we could do that, maybe we could figure out who he was working with on the council."

Lacey rolled her eyes and leaned back in the chair she was sitting in, leaning onto one of the armrests. "It's not possible. Those files are gone, destroyed in the system wipe. Even if we tried to recover them, they'd be severely degraded and next to useless. Let this go and move on to more productive things."

"I seriously don't buy it," I insisted. "Every system has a redundancy, just in case. There's got to be a ghost server somewhere, and if we find it, we can just—"

"You are going to waste time on this," Lacey cut in flatly, her face growing hard. "I want Ambrose's murderers yesterday, and trying to dig out the old vid files on Devon is only going to slow you down in finding them. Let it go and move on."

I pressed my lips together and fought the urge to push harder. I was right about this—I knew I was—but Lacey was apparently finished with the subject. Still, something about the exchange was weird, and after a moment's consideration, I filed it away for later pursuit. "Fine. What now?"

"Now that you're on the council, you'll obviously need to know how to vote on certain issues. I'll get you a cipher key through Zoe. Use it to decrypt messages from us on how we want you to vote, and on points we might want you to bring up during a council meeting."

I narrowed my eyes. "You'll give me my own discussion points? Am I at least allowed to add or detract from them so I can best represent my department, or am I just going to be your little vote-generating machine?"

"The last one, definitely," Lacey deadpanned. It took me a second, but I realized she was serious and rolled my eyes, amazed by the presumption that I would just blindly follow her lead. "Let me make this perfectly clear, Liana. I know you're only in this for as long as it takes you to get out from under my thumb. I'm a reasonable woman, and I don't want you for an enemy, so I'll keep my word as soon as you deliver Ambrose's killers to me. But I won't be surprised

when you run after that. And why wouldn't you? You never wanted
to do the Tourney in the first place."

She spoke with a sneer so intense I was certain that if it were
weaponized, it would instantly vaporize anything with which it came
into contact. Luckily for me, they were just words. But as one of my
instructors used to say, "them's fightin' words", and a wash of anger
erupted at the tail end of them.

I raised my eyebrows at her. "I stepped in after Ambrose died,
knowing what was at stake and in the balance if I didn't."

"You stepped in to cut a deal for yourself to keep me from
turning you in," she replied. "Don't pretend it was for some noble
cause."

"Screw you, Lacey," I shot back, my temper exploding. "You
have no idea how hard this was to do, knowing that losing the
Tourney meant losing thousands of people when that other group
finally does what it plans to do! I lost my *mother* getting involved in
your little legacy war, so you could accomplish your goals!"

No, what I lost was a chance to have a good relationship with her,
I reminded myself firmly. I needed to remember what was behind
this fiery response, and pull it back.

"For which I am truly sorry," she said, sighing. "I knew they were
capable of some depraved things, but this one went above and
beyond."

Her apology and admission helped curb some of the anger I
hadn't managed to push back, but only a bit. It was still there, tightly
capped but ready to explode. "Yeah, well, once I find the bastard
behind all of this, I plan to rip him limb from limb."

"You'll get him *if* there's anything left to have after I'm through
with him," Lacey replied haughtily. "You promised me Ambrose's
killers, and that means all of them."

And with that, the anger was back in full force. How dare she try to hog all of them for herself? I had just as much right as she did to exact revenge, and if she tried to take it from me, there'd be hell to pay.

Once again, I considered arguing with her, but put it aside, knowing that if I did, it would only invite her to mistrust me. "Fine," I spat from between clenched teeth. "Is there anything else?"

"Yes," she replied primly, looking away for a second. "There's a council meeting tomorrow. Cornelius has the agenda for you to peruse, but I wanted to tell you that the expulsion chamber law is up for a vote. It—"

"It is?" I asked, suddenly very interested. The expulsion chambers were disgusting, and the fact that we used them to murder ones —legally—was even worse. It spoke to a dark part of our humanity that we should turn our backs on. Except nobody had. I couldn't wait to change that law.

"Scipio initiated the process to repeal it right after your trial, but without a full council, it has been waiting on the docket for review and voting," she replied, and I realized she was trying to answer my vague question.

I hadn't realized that, but it made sense; you couldn't make important decisions like that without having each department represented. "Have they at least suspended the expulsions until after the vote is completed?" I asked, knowing that the answer wouldn't be the one I wanted.

"Of course not," Lacey said with a shake of her head.

"Then it's a good thing we're voting on it tomorrow," I replied. "'Cause that law has got to go."

"Yes, well, Strum and I are still coming up with suggestions for what to do with the ones after they are caught, so—"

"Oh, interesting," I said, interrupting again as I grew even more excited. "I bet I could whip up quite a few ideas between now and then."

"Yes, but it's not that simple. You should know the process will take some time once it starts."

"So what? I'll give orders to stop using the expulsion chambers in the meantime. We'll convert the chambers into cells and get some beds and food down there for those people while we wait."

Lacey shook her head and sighed. "Look, I'm late for an appointment, and I am not in the mood to fight with you. I'll explain to you why that's a bad idea later, but for now, just hold off on doing anything rash, okay?"

Oh man, I could tell this was going to get old real fast. Lacey was already treating me like I was a child about to mess everything up, and if that went on for much longer, we'd fight, and it wouldn't be pretty. I was barely keeping it together as it was.

"All right," I said guardedly. "I'll see you tomorrow, then?"

"Tomorrow?"

"For the council meeting?" Had she forgotten already? If so, I could understand; grief had a funny way of making you absentminded.

She stared at me for a second and then smiled. "Right. That. Have a good afternoon, Liana."

"You too," I mumbled, caught off guard by the weird shifts and ambiguous nature of her response. There was something going on there—something she wasn't telling me—but I imagined I would find out soon enough, during the meeting.

The screen went dark seconds later, and I rocked back on my heels. All in all, I wouldn't say the conversation went spectacularly well, but at least I knew what she expected of me. I didn't like it, but

I could play along for a while until I got a handle on things. And in the meantime, I could sit down and talk with my friends to establish some sort of game plan.

Just as soon as I figured out what we were going to do next.

7

I was busy scribbling things down on my pad when Cornelius suddenly said, "Zoe Elphesian and her guests are in the elevator requesting access. Should I let them in?"

I paused mid-stroke and looked up. "Yes. Show them back here. And give them a tour while you're at it."

"It is my honor to serve."

I leaned back in my chair and looked at my indicator, swiping across the glowing ten of my rank and going to the time. It'd been just a few minutes since Lacey and I had finished talking, and I had attempted to figure out what we should do next, but it was hard when there were three different goals: getting out of the Tower, restoring Scipio, and finding the people responsible for what had happened.

Escaping the Tower had always been the original plan, but without a steadily flowing supply of Paragon, we were powerless to recruit any more people toward accomplishing it. We were barely able to keep up with the people Roark had already recruited, and that was after we made the doses weaker. What we had wouldn't last, and without the people we had recruited, we would be unable to build an escape vehicle large and safe enough to pass through the radioactive wasteland that surrounded the Tower. They were people I had never even met, and yet they were an integral part of this mission. What was more, we needed further recruits. Which meant making more Paragon. Which meant we needed to go after Jasper, so he could give us the formula.

Jasper could also help with fixing Scipio, another one of our goals, so going after him was really doubly important. Getting him, however, wasn't going to be easy. Sadie Monroe, who currently had him, lived in an apartment similar to my own, and entering it wouldn't be a simple task. We'd have to figure out a way to get around *her* computer assistant so our passage wouldn't be recorded— and we wouldn't be killed before getting through the door. We'd also have to coordinate some sort of distraction to make sure she was out of there at the time, so we didn't risk running into her.

Finding Ambrose and my mother's killers was important, too, though, because of Lacey, and because that was what I wanted to do the most. However, I was self-aware enough to realize that it was also dangerous for me on a personal level. I was too emotionally compromised—and too hungry for vengeance—to trust myself. If I found even *one* of the bastards who'd had anything to do with the sentinel...

I exhaled and straightened as I heard Cornelius's voice drawing closer through the speakers he had set up after I finished designing the rooms, alerting me that the tour was nearing completion. Standing up, I took a look around my new war room, and then decided that I shouldn't be on the raised dais when they came in. It'd make me look imperious and arrogant.

I went down the stairs I had created, feeling slightly anxious. I hadn't exactly been at my best over the last few days, and I knew my friends were worried about me. They were the closest thing I had to family now, next to my brother of course, but I hadn't been able to let them in. I hadn't wanted to talk about my mom because I didn't know what to say.

Now that I did, I still wasn't ready, it seemed.

But luckily, I didn't have to yet, either—I had something we all could focus on. Which meant, I hoped, that we could get back on even footing again.

Cornelius's voice was still droning on about the bedrooms, so I just about leapt out of my skin when he abruptly announced, "You have an incoming net transmission from one Alexander Castell. Shall I connect him?"

I took a moment to calm my beating heart and then frowned. I had forgotten to net Alex after Astrid left, but then again, I really hadn't wanted to. He didn't need to be involved in this, not with his position in IT being so precarious. Still, I couldn't exactly ignore him. He was my brother.

"Yes, please," I said to him. "Directly to my net."

"Of course."

A second later, a fine-tuned buzz began to erupt from the filament strands draped over my cerebral cortex, setting my teeth on edge.

Liana, I am still in the Citadel. Where are you? My brother's voice was hot and angry in my ear canal, causing me to wince slightly.

"Alex, I'm in my new quarters getting things set up." Okay, not a total lie, but not the complete truth, either. As good as I was at lying, I really didn't like doing it to the people I cared about, but the less Alex knew, the better. I didn't want his temper getting the best of him—and besides, it wasn't like I had much to tell him. "It turns out my first council meeting is tomorrow, and I need to prepare. I'm going after the expulsion chambers. I'll be able to put them out of commission."

To hell with that, Liana. What about Mom? The investigation, tracking down her killers!

I bit my lip and sighed. I knew my brother well enough to know that when his family was threatened, he became the most protective. But his questions were dangerous and liable to draw even more attention to him. Hell, the legacies could be watching him right now and listening in, trying to see how much he knew. I needed to be careful about how I handled him and what I revealed.

"Alex, I don't have access to those files right now," I told him. "I know you expect me to jump in feet first, but I have a really big job now, and I need a little time to get a handle on it."

That's bull. I saw Zoe and the others leave the wake together, and I know they're going to meet you right now. I know it's going to come up. I want to be in on this meeting. I can help you.

I pursed my lips. Alex *could* help us to a certain extent, given that he was in the IT Department and could figure out where Sadie's quarters were, if he didn't know already. But Sadie was also watching him, and the slightest misstep on his part could get him caught up in charges of terrorism and treason—charges that came with a death sentence. I couldn't risk him getting caught doing anything, and I couldn't risk telling him anything that might lead to rash action on his part.

Still, I did need to get him to ease off a little, and for that to happen, I had to approach this reasonably.

"Yes, the others and I are going to have a meeting. And yes, we will be talking about Mom's death, but only so that I can tell them to let it go for the time being. The council is watching everything closely right now, and if anyone starts digging, they'll be all over it, wondering why. I promise you that as soon as it's safe, we will look into it together, but for now, I just need you to keep your head down and watch your back, *comprende?*"

"Comprende" was our word, the last connection with our heritage from before the End. I was hoping that using it would make Alex see the wisdom in my words—lies that they were—and back off.

I don't believe you. Let me come to the meeting. She was my mother, too!

I almost caved. Almost. The hurt in his voice was so raw it touched me, and I felt myself start to soften.

But I couldn't do it. My brother was already too close, and now in danger due to how much scrutiny he was under. Better to keep him away and let those who might be watching think we'd had a falling out, so they wouldn't go after him to get to me.

I had to keep him safe.

"I'm sorry, Alex. I know you think I'm going after this, but I'm not... I promise you I'm not." I looked up as Zoe entered, a bag thrown over one shoulder. She'd recently re-shaved the sides of her head, as the hair there had been getting too long, but the center mass was still long and held back in its customary braid. Her face was curious as she put the bag on the ground, but she didn't interrupt me. "Look, I really have to go. I love you."

There was a long pause on my brother's end, followed by a soft, *Coward,* said in a bitter and angry tone.

The single word was like a slap to the face that also cut right down to the bone, flaying me open. I knew he wanted to be involved, but that was a bit harsh, even for him. Not to mention uncalled for—I was doing the best I could. And he should have understood that.

"Alex, I—"

"He has terminated the call," Cornelius said, just as the buzzing in my skull suddenly cut off, confirming what he was saying. I sighed, pinching the bridge of my nose between two fingers.

"That jerk," I muttered, frustrated by my brother's response to things.

"Your brother is many things," Zoe said carefully, straightening up from where she had deposited the bag onto the floor. "But a jerk isn't one of them. What's up?"

"Nothing," I said, shaking my head. "He just wants to be part of the investigation into what happened with..." I trailed off, my throat tightening around her moniker. It felt wrong saying it now that she wasn't here.

"Of course he does," she said, running her hand over her braid and fidgeting with the end of it. "And we're doing one, right?"

I blinked, surprised at her. "You want to? I would've thought..."

"Hey, going after Jasper is also very high on my list, because of the Paragon, but knowing who these people are will help us understand what their goals are. And that will help us figure out what we can do to stop them."

I was opening my mouth to reply when Quess and Maddox entered, both of them carrying multiple bags. They came to a stop on the top of the stairs I had created at the end of the hall, and Tian pushed between them, darting down the stairs right toward me.

"Liana!" she said, leaping into the air, her arms spread wide.

I opened my arms and braced myself, and seconds later the body of a fourteen-year-old girl slammed into mine, knobby arms and legs going everywhere. I hugged her tightly to me for as long as I could hold her weight, taking solace in the feel of her warmth and vibrancy, and then gently eased her down onto the floor.

"Hey, Tian," I said quietly. "What do you think of our new home?"

She placed a finger on her chin and looked up and around, drawing her lips and eyes tight in a severe and speculative expression. After a second, she smiled broadly and went up to her tiptoes, raising a hand to the side of her mouth. "I love it," she whispered loudly.

I smiled, pleasure radiating from her praise, and then looked up to where Maddox and Quess were coming down the steps, Leo and Eric right behind them.

"Yeah, I have to agree with Tian," Quess said. "This place is pretty killer. Not sure about Cornelius, though. Do you want me to check him out?"

"You and Leo both," I said, relieved to know that Quess and I were on the same page, security-wise. "Lacey assured me that the entire terminal was wiped after Devon died, but I want you to make sure. I also want you to see if you can find any ghost servers that might store the previous Champion's vid files. Apparently, this apartment is always monitored, but it's supposedly as private as private can be. Find out if that's true."

Quess raised his eyebrows as he slung his bag onto the floor, next to where Zoe had set the one she was carrying. "Well, hello there, stranger," he said roughly. "That's more than you've said in the past three days. Are you..." He paused and fidgeted before meeting my gaze, a mixture of hope and hesitancy in his eyes. "Better?" he finished.

I looked up for a moment, and then exhaled slowly, the answer too complicated. "Let's just not worry about how I am," I said. "There's too much going on to dwell on that. Can you get started on Cornelius, please?"

He frowned, and then nodded slowly. "Yeah," he said, his voice filled with caution. "Whatever you need, Liana."

"Thank you," I replied. I looked at the pile of bags that was rapidly growing at the foot of the stairs. "You guys packed up the apartments?"

"Oh yeah," Eric said with a grunt, tossing his three bags into the pile. "We figured it would be more efficient this way." He looked around for a second, his hands on his hips. "This is some living space."

"Came with the job," I said dryly, and his lips twisted into a shadow of a smile, some of the concern in his eyes lightening. "Well, I've got a room set aside for Zoe and you, because I figured you guys would want to share, and then Quess and Leo are sharing, as are Maddox and Tian, so you can pick out rooms and move your stuff into them while Quess and Leo take a look at Cornelius."

Silence met my statement, and my brows drew together. Clearly I had missed a beat and they had already made decisions about their sleeping arrangements without me. I waited, looking around expectantly, and it was Zoe who explained.

"Eric and I are going to stay in Cogstown," she said, lowering her eyes. "I think it's better if we stay as close to Lacey as possible."

I narrowed my eyes at her as I considered what she was saying. I knew there was more to it than that, but wasn't entirely sure why she was being so cagey about telling me. "Okay," I said, drawing out the syllable to add an implied "and?" to the tone.

"And..." She trailed off again, looking oddly guilty. Her blue eyes

lifted so she could look at Eric, and suddenly it clicked: Zoe wanted
to be alone with her boyfriend, and I could understand that. She
probably just didn't want to hurt my feelings, which explained her
behavior.

"You know what, it's okay," I said softly as she grew more and
more flustered. "I get it. You and Eric are just starting up, and this
stuff is definitely a source of stress. If you think you're safe there,
then I'll trust your judgment."

I expected her to smile, but the look she gave me made me feel as
if I were being peered at through a microscope, getting pressed flat
by two pieces of glass so everyone could see right through me. I
suddenly felt awkward under that gaze, and added, "Don't look at
me in that tone of voice."

This time she did smile, and relief poured through her eyes.
"You're back," she said, stepping close and wrapping her arms
around me. I stood stiffly for a second, and then returned the gesture.

"In a manner of speaking," I said gently. I let her hold me for a
second or two longer, and then pulled away. "Anyway, I can leave
the room open for you, or I can change the rooms to make them a
little bit bigger if you all want."

"Actually," Maddox said carefully, dropping into a chair at the
tactical table, "Quess and I are going to be sharing a room for a little
while."

She brushed her fingers lightly across the tabletop, but a dull
blush formed in her cheeks. I swiveled around to look up at where
Quess was standing on the dais to see him staring down at us, both
his thumbs raised high and a broad smile revealing all of his teeth.
My jaw dropped, and I looked back and forth between the two of
them several times.

I wasn't sure why I was so surprised. Up until the last challenge, he and Maddox had been sharing a room. That had changed after my mother had died and I shut down, but now it seemed they wanted to go back to that arrangement.

"And that means I can have my own room!" Tian chirped excitedly. "And so can Leo! And we're single, so we don't have to share!"

I looked over to where Leo was kneeling behind the desk, a screwdriver in hand, and saw him already watching me, his eyes a warm brown. Something passed through me—a jolt of electricity—and I quickly moved my gaze away, afraid he would see it. I was lonely, and he was curious.

Or at least, I hoped that was all it was on his end. I couldn't even consider how I would feel if it was something more than that.

I took a moment to clear my throat, and with it my thoughts, and then looked around. "Okay. Well, I think we should just jump right in, if that's all right with everyone. We've got a lot to talk about and some decisions to make, and as always, there's not a lot of time. So let's start with what we've got."

I held up my pad and hit the *Project* button, and a second later, the table began to glow.

8

Moments later, a three-dimensional representation of a timeline that I had been working on earlier was projected into the air, marking what I thought were the most mission-critical events.

"Whoa," Zoe said, taking a step closer to the table and leaning her hands against it. She studied the lines and my handwritten notes, and then her eyes narrowed. "Why'd you start the timeline twenty-five years ago?" she asked, her head swiveling around to look at me.

"Two reasons," I said. "First of all, because of something Alex told me before we first met Cali and everyone: that the number of accidental deaths in the Tower showed a five percent increase around that time period, and that it's been steadily increasing since then. I know it seems strange, but I think it has something to do with the alien girl Roark's wife met."

"In what way?" Maddox asked, leaning forward. "I mean, someone popping by the Tower for a visit doesn't immediately equal a higher death rate."

"Except I think it does," I said hurriedly. I had given this a lot of thought, and I was convinced that the visitor to the Tower had, for some reason, kicked things into overdrive for our mysterious legacy group. The timing was just too perfect for it to be unconnected. There was every possibility that I was wrong, but something about the way Roark talked about what had happened afterward—his wife disappearing, council members dying—made me suspect that a cover-up had been implemented. "Cornelius, can you add Head Farmer Raevyn Hart's death to this timeline?" I asked.

"Searching," he replied a moment later. I looked over my shoulder to where Quess and Leo were still hunched over my terminal, presumably going over Cornelius's code with a fine-toothed comb, and was pleased that they hadn't taken him offline to do it. I didn't want to delay this conversation while we waited for him to come back online.

"What does the death of my department's previous leader have to do with anything?" asked Eric, his dark eyes meeting my own.

"She was one of two councilors who reportedly met with the alien girl that day, along with two Knights," I explained. "The other was Devon Alexander. They wound up taking the girl to a Medic station where Roark's wife, Selka, was working. Selka was taken from their home some time later, when they were trying to plan their escape, and was never heard from again. Roark assumed she was dead, and I think he was right."

It seemed so obvious to me now—they must have killed her to keep the alien girl's existence a secret. They couldn't risk the citizens of the Tower learning that there was life beyond the Wastes. They might want to leave.

"Head Farmer Raevyn Hart's death, ma'am," Cornelius interrupted while I was taking a breath. "Will there be anything else?"

I paused when I saw Raevyn's name added to the timeline, the date marked right at the start of it, just past where I had written "visitor". I looked at it, and then took a shot in the dark. "Yes, I'm also looking for the recorded death of a Medic by the name of Selka, married to another Medic named Roark—last names unknown to me, but it would have been within weeks or months of Raevyn's."

"Searching."

"That seems like a bit of a leap, Liana," Maddox said doubtfully. "I still don't see the connection. Are you sure you're not just... trying to manufacture something?"

I stared at her for a long moment and then sighed. I knew it seemed half baked, but I was following my gut on this and trying to piece together an explanation for what was going on. She had a point, but in my mind, Raevyn's death had happened too early—too close to when this all started—for it to be coincidence. I wasn't sure what had made her a target, but whatever it was, I was going to figure it out.

"You may be right, but just hear me out. I think that all these things are actually related, once you consider who is behind them."

Her black eyebrows drew together, forming a tight line over the bridge of her nose, and she wore a pensive expression for a moment or two. "Okay," she said, drawing it out. "I'm gonna need more than that."

"Then give me a second to explain," I said, trying not to let my exasperation show. "Cornelius, any luck?"

"There's no death record for anyone matching the first name Selka," Cornelius replied. "Perhaps the individual is still alive?"

"Or Liana's right and they didn't want a death record for her," Leo said casually from behind me. "Maybe you could use her personnel records? Are you sure you don't remember her surname?"

I considered his question for a second, and realized that I did have the date of Roark's death. I quickly asked Cornelius to run another search, hoping it would lead to his surname, but was unsurprised when Cornelius replied with a, "No searches match your query."

Even though I wasn't surprised by his response as it had been a long shot to assume that Devon had even reported him dead, I was still aggravated that I had never asked Roark's surname—not once in the entire time I had spent with him and Grey. I crossed my arms and rocked back on my heels. Grey would know it, but he wasn't in a position to remember much at the moment.

"No," I said with a weary sigh. "Roark never told me. Only Grey knows."

I swiveled around to look at Leo, and saw him wearing a small, pensive frown. "I've only just started repairing Grey's memories, but what I'm working on is mostly his childhood. Those neural pathways are the most important to restoring his personality as you knew it. If you want to know the name of the piglet he grew attached to when he was young, I can help you. But anything from his older years is beyond his or my abilities at this time."

"Grey was attached to a piglet?" Tian asked, leaning forward. "That's so cute!"

Leo gave her a sad smile, but when he met my gaze, I saw darkness there, and I knew that at some point or another, Grey's parents

had likely forced him to kill the poor creature. The idea was to indoc-
trinate children to the harsh realities of the Tower, but my heart
broke for him a little bit right there.

For him and for Leo both.

"The piglet was indeed very cute," Leo informed Tian softly.
"The fact remains that I cannot rush this process. I don't know
Roark's last name."

That sucked, but it was okay. I had other things that would add
to the timeline. I was resolved to find out what had happened to
Selka and Raevyn, somehow—but now wasn't the time.

"Don't worry about it right now," I said. "There are other things
that factor in. Like the date when Scipio passed the law that
condemned anyone who fell to a rank of one to the expulsion chambers. Cornelius, can you show the date when that law passed?"

It came up, and I felt a grim sense of satisfaction. It had
happened almost exactly a week *after* Raevyn's death, when Head
Farmer Plancett had been elected. "That's not a coincidence," I said,
already wondering if that election had been tampered with like the
Tourney had been. If that were the case, there was every chance that
Plancett had been working with the enemy and was still doing so
now—he was still the current leader of the Hands. I opened my
mouth to add that speculation, but decided to hold it back, worried
that it might be too much for them to swallow.

It was already a lot.

"But that's not evidence, either," Zoe replied carefully. I looked
over at her, surprised by the fact that she couldn't see the connections like I could. The people we were up against had more than
proven that they were capable of a cover-up, given that they'd never
even been caught. The connections existed purely in the events

themselves, the things they had changed, the ways events had happened. "It is suspicious," she added as soon as my eyes hit hers. "But there's no evidence, and her death is attributed to... Cornelius, help me out?"

"A heart attack," he replied a moment later, and she gave me a look with a raised eyebrow that said "beat that".

I stared at her and then shrugged. "Look, you and I both know that a heart attack can be medically induced and easily covered up, and the legacy group we're after is good at that! They certainly proved it with the Tourney. But I'm certain about this—I think they escalated their plans for the Tower after the visitor came."

And I thought they did it because they wanted to get as much control as possible to make sure that no one else left. *Why*, I didn't know—but I was going to find out.

"Escalated?" Zoe asked, looking up at me. "You mean they didn't just start getting control a few years ago—that they've been working on it for centuries? I thought Lionel said that it would take centuries for them to even get into the Core in that vid we watched!"

She was talking about the vid where Ezekial Pine had murdered Lionel, and they'd been talking about a terrorist cell called Prometheus—the progenitors of the legacies—who didn't believe an AI should control humanity's destiny. During the conversation leading up to the attack, Lionel had admitted that it would take centuries for Prometheus to hack into Scipio, but I figured he'd been wrong. It hadn't taken the legacies all that time to break in—it had taken them that long to break apart what he had created so they could slowly tighten up the reins of control. They didn't have it completely yet, but I felt certain that they would, soon, if we didn't do anything.

"I think they were slowly gaining control in the background long before that point," I replied. "Remember what Leo said about the ranking systems never being meant to last? That they were only supposed to monitor the people who survived the End, and a few generations afterward, for depression or suicide?"

"Yeah, Lionel didn't want people hurting themselves because they couldn't cope with what they had lost," Zoe shot back, a slight irritation in her voice. "But what does that have to do with this?"

I realized that I was frustrating her with all of this supposition. I could only imagine what I looked like: a girl in the depths of sorrow trying to make connections between things without any evidence.

And the problem was that there probably *wouldn't* be any evidence. The lack of Selka's death record proved that. The people who were behind this knew how to cover their tracks. They'd been doing so for who knew how many decades, if not centuries. So there wouldn't be evidence, not like Zoe wanted.

But half of what I was extrapolating was based on what I believed their goal to be: absolute mastery over Scipio and the citizens of the Tower so that they could run things as they saw fit, and not based on Scipio's advice. If that were the case, they would need ways to exert their control, and the ranking system fit into that perfectly. They'd done it intelligently as well, first by making the rankings visible through the indicators around our wrists, and then by spreading fear by villainizing those who dropped too low on the spectrum, accusing them of shirking their duties to Scipio.

Every step was a slow tightening of the noose that had become an ingrained part of our society. We'd become accustomed to it. Started to accept it. Even play into it. And it had made us their puppets, giving them absolute control of our lives.

"There's an easy way to check to see if Liana's right," Leo said, and I turned to see him coming down the stairs toward us, Quess right behind him.

I arched an eyebrow at Quess, and he gave me a nod and a thumbs up, indicating that Cornelius was clean. Relieved that I could cross at least one thing off my worry list, I turned back to Leo, who was moving to stand next to me. "How do you propose we do that?"

"We check the council records for the incident in question. If you're right, Liana, then the two Knights who were there would also have died, probably in some sort of accident."

I closed my eyes, feeling like an idiot for not having figured that out sooner. I was a councilor now, which meant I had access to those records. "Cornelius, run a search on any instance of a person coming to the Tower involving Raevyn Hart, Devon Alexander, and a Medic named Selka twenty-five years ago."

"Searching."

I waited, my breath caught in my throat, hopeful. I knew this was a leap, but anything I could find out about that day could go a long way toward explaining why things had suddenly seemed to escalate. If I could figure that out, then it would be a piece—something that I could maybe use to find out who was behind it.

"There are no records that match your inquiry," he said a moment later, and I frowned.

Was it possible that Roark had been wrong this entire time? Could it have all been a story? If that was the case, then my entire assumption that the visitor changed something for the legacy group fell apart, and I had just wasted everyone's time.

"Cornelius, is it possible that there are sealed records that Liana cannot access?" Leo asked, and I looked back up, hope rekindled. It was a good question, one that I hadn't thought of but which made total sense. Of *course* the record of a visitor would be sealed. The council would never want that information getting out, no matter what side of the legacy war they were on.

"Yes. There have been times when the council records have been sealed to prevent later councilors from accessing them, classified as need to know."

"How would I go about getting them?" I asked, excited all over again. There had to be a way, a precedent that would allow access to them after the fact.

"You would have to petition the council and give adequate reason regarding what you hope to achieve or prove with such information. Scipio will make his recommendation, and they will vote accordingly based on that."

Well, that was not going to work. Whoever our enemy was had direct access to the council, whether it was because they were on it, or were working with someone who was on it, I did not know. But if I began poking around that incident, it would draw attention—something I was trying to avoid.

"I'll look into it," Leo said, offering me a little smile that softened the serious lines of his face.

"Thank you," I said sincerely. I looked back at the timeline and sighed. On to the next matter at hand. "Astrid is sending over her notes—"

"*Has* sent, ma'am," Cornelius interjected, and I took a second to absorb that before continuing. She had gotten those to me fast, which I really appreciated, and I made a mental note to thank her for that.

"And findings about Ambrose's investigation," I concluded. "But I think it might be a good idea to go even farther back than that to try to find these individuals. Quess, do you remember when we broke into the Medica to get Maddox out?"

"You mean the day we killed Devon Alexander?" Quess asked, stepping closer to the table. "Yeah. Literally one of the most terrifying moments of my life. Who can forget it. Why?"

"Remember that he was meeting with those Inquisition agents?" I asked. I hoped he did, because I was fairly certain those two were the ones we needed to focus on. Given the conversation they had been having with Devon at the time, they were legacies, and clearly had intimate knowledge of who was in charge. They—Baldy and Plain-Face, as I had named them—had been in the room and fought with us, meaning that they probably went into hiding shortly after to keep from being questioned too closely, but enough time had passed without anyone coming for them that they had to think the coast was clear. We had a better chance of finding them than the people who murdered Ambrose, because odds were *they* were still in hiding, and would be for a while.

But if we could find Baldy or Plain-Face, well, then that would be a step toward something. The only problem was how to do it. The legacy group had proven to be adept at creating fake nets that allowed them to avoid detection by the scanners. They had to have nets, or the thermal sensors would pick their body heat up and send out an undoc alert, but if the nets had been fabricated...

The only method we had left for tracking them was through facial recognition software. They had to be somewhere, and we knew for a fact they were working for the legacy group with which Devon was allied, which might be the same group that had infiltrated the Tourney.

If we could locate them, and they could tell us where the infiltrators were hiding, we could turn *them* over to Lacey—and then I could get the name of the person in charge, and finally put an end to all of this.

"Yeah, sure," Quess said. "Why?"

"I think we should run a facial recognition search on them," I said. "They would've been lying low since the Medica, but with everything that's happened with the Tourney, they might assume that people have forgotten about what happened there. Maybe they'll be moving around freely. We've got to try. We should also pass their pictures on to Dinah, to see if she can find out who they are."

"We'd need the video of the attack, Liana," Maddox said, folding her arms across her chest. "Do you have that?"

"We should," I replied. "It would've been part of the investigation for my trial. Cornelius, pull up the vid file from the Medica that shows the death of Devon Alexander."

"Searching." Another long pause, followed by, "There are no records that match your inquiry."

"What?" I said, frowning. "How is that possible?"

"No formal request was ever made to the Medica to turn over the vid files, and they did not voluntarily submit them," Cornelius replied. "If you wish, I can submit a request on your behalf to Chief Surgeon Sage."

I considered the question. We needed that vid file if we were going to track down Baldy and Plain-Face, but asking for it might have the same repercussions as trying to get the council to unseal the record of the alien girl in the Tower. Going to Sage was risky, especially now that I knew he was upset about me having the shockers in the final challenge of the Tourney. But then again, I might not have any choice.

"Ma'am, I would also like to remind you that your appointment in the Medica is in fifteen minutes. Would you like me to reschedule?"

"Yes," I said reluctantly. I really wanted to get the neural transmitter installed, but we had more left to talk about here. "Let's just set it up for tomorrow after the council meeting."

"I will send them an update."

"You're going to the Medica?" Zoe asked curiously. "What for?"

"To get the special mouth-free talking device," I said tiredly.

"Oh," she said, looking vaguely disappointed. "That's too bad... I was kind of hoping you were going to maybe talk to someone about what happened."

My forehead wrinkled in surprise, and suddenly I felt very defensive. But I pushed it aside, recognizing it as a knee-jerk response to my childish behavior. "I'm not ready yet," I told her. "But I'm coping."

Zoe gave me a doubtful look. "I'm not sure I believe that, Liana. You haven't exactly been 'coping' the last few days. We were barely able to get a word out of you, or food into you. You were positively lifeless. So yeah... was kinda hoping that if you weren't talking to us, you were at least talking to someone else."

I shifted my shoulders and looked away. She had a point, and I could understand why she didn't believe me. I hadn't exactly kept it together over the last few days, and she just wanted to make sure I was taking care of myself. Still, her implication that I would go to the Medica for this was a bit comical. The doctors there would barely care about someone who came in grieving, would prescribe a fistful of drugs, and call it a day. Talking things out was only reserved for special cases, where they'd almost died. I hadn't, so I was expected to just be all right.

I was suddenly reminded of Dr. Bordeaux, the man my parents had sent me to after my rank had dropped to three. He had given me pills to help my rank improve, but they'd sucked everything about my individuality right out, leaving some sort of mindless automaton blindly devoted to the Tower. I had hated it. Just like I had hated the appointment with Dr. Bordeaux.

The only good thing to come out of that was meeting Jasper, and that had been...

I stopped myself mid-thought and played it back in my head, making sure I had gotten it right. As soon as I confirmed it, I felt the urge to smile coming across my lips. If I could just get an appointment with Dr. Bordeaux, then maybe I could ask him a few questions about Jasper and see what he knew. Maybe he'd let something slip about why the council had put Jasper in the Medica in the first place, and who the driving force had been. I had dozens of questions, and this could be a way of getting them answered.

"All right," I said. "Cornelius, contact the Medica and make a special request for Dr. Bordeaux to be my physician."

Zoe wrinkled her nose. "Isn't that the guy who gave you the drugs that turned you into a rank-obsessed idiot?"

"He is," I said. "Now, not to rush things, but we have other things we need to hash out."

"I agree," said Maddox. "Because what I really want to know is what we're doing about getting the heck out of here. That is still the plan, right?"

"Of course it is," Zoe said before I could formulate a response. "But you know Lacey wants us to find Ambrose's murderers, and if we aren't working toward that, she's going to find out and have Liana and Leo arrested!"

Sullen silence met her remark, telling us that it had hit home, but I ignored it, pressing onward. "The way I see it is we have two ultimate goals," I said carefully. "Both of them equally important. One is getting Jasper out of Sadie's hands. I have no idea where

Sadie stands, but if she is with the legacies, then we have to get him out, or else risk him winding up like Jang-Mi. He's a priority." I paused and let that sink in for a second, and then continued. "We also need to track down the people who killed Ambrose and my mother. To that end, I suggest we divide and conquer. Maddox, I'm putting you in charge of hunting down the legacies. Work on finding the legacies we know, like Baldy and Plain-Face. Quess, you're going to be helping both of us out where we need you."

"Does that mean I'm getting a special promotion?" Quess asked, his eyebrows waggling. "Because I would just like to point out that as a lowly Squire, I have no authority whatsoever."

I rolled my eyes. "You've got to finish the tests, but yes, you'll be promoted. We'll talk official titles later."

"We'll do it now because it's simple," Quess said with a cocky smile. "I'm your new head of the Citadel's internal server police."

I thought about it for a second, and then nodded. It was the perfect position for him, even if it was one he had just made up, because it was something the department desperately needed, given how easily our security systems had been overcome by the infiltrators. With him in charge of the few tech-savvy Knights we had, we'd be able to beef up our cyber-security. He could also help us in other ways, like developing algorithms that would help the Knights locate people faster, while secretly searching for our own mysterious enemies. It was a double win.

"What about me?" Maddox asked. "How exactly am I supposed to hunt the legacies down without any resources?"

I smiled for what felt like the first time, pleased to share this particular decision with her. "I already informed Astrid that you're my new Lieutenant," I told her.

Her green eyes widened and her jaw dropped. "You want *me?*" she asked, incredulous. "After everything from before?"

"Absolutely," I told her in all seriousness. "You're perfect for the position. It's kind of in your blood."

She flushed with pleasure as I compared her with her mother, Camilla Kerrin, who had been Devon Alexander's Lieutenant before Zale.

"I don't know what to say," she managed thickly. "Thank you."

"Don't thank me," I said. "You earned it."

She continued to smile, clearly happy at my decision, and I felt a shadow of warmth slide through my ever-present grief. Fleeting though it was, it was a victory that proved that the tattered remains of my heart wouldn't always be broken. I'd heal.

It would just take time.

Leo cleared his throat softly, and I looked at him. "Does that mean I'm going to be looking into recovering Jasper?" he asked.

"Yes," I said, remembering that I hadn't finished handing out orders. I took a moment or two to ground myself, and then continued. "You and Zoe both. I want you looking for a way to hack into Sadie's terminal remotely. I'd like to avoid entering if possible, but if we can't avoid it, then Zoe will need to get hold of some blueprints of the Core to see if we can figure out where her quarters are. I don't expect them to be obvious, but hopefully Zoe can figure out where they are in spite of that."

"Zoe hopes she can, too," she said. "But yeah, I'll get on the Cog server and see what I can find."

"Actually, you might not have to do that," Leo said lightly. "I'm already quite confident I can breach their defenses."

"Really? How?" I asked, unable to stop myself.

"By sending an AI to do it," he said excitedly. "The terminal in which Cornelius is housed is the same size as the one in Lionel's office, which means it has plenty of room for an AI to fit inside comfortably."

"You want to download yourself into my terminal?" I asked, unable to help myself. The idea seemed shocking for multiple reasons, but mostly because he was talking about leaving Grey before he was finished healing. Would that hurt him?

"Not exactly," he replied carefully. "If you'll permit me to, I'll download Jang-Mi from the hard drive onto the—"

"No," I said, a hot flash of blinding anger followed by a cold chill of fear pouring over me like a waterfall. I didn't want Jang-Mi anywhere but in her own hard drive. She was crazy, and... oh yeah... *she killed my mother.* She may not have wanted to, but she had, and I hated her for it. I didn't want her presence in my new home. I didn't even want her *alive.*

I tried to swallow it back, fumbling to remind myself that it wasn't her fault. There were people who had turned her into what she was and then pointed her toward us.

But it didn't matter. The fact that she had personally robbed us of any chance for further reconciliation boiled inside of me, and I couldn't seem to stop hating her for it.

Leo looked at me expectantly, and I realized he was waiting for some sort of explanation as to why, and quickly found one. "There are automated defenses and weapons in here that she could hypo-thetically access if you put her in that terminal."

I was surprised at how reasonable that all sounded considering my heart was pounding so hard in my chest that I was certain I could taste blood in my mouth... but then looked at Leo to see what his reaction would be.

"I can create a firewall that will prevent that from happening," he said simply. "But getting her into the terminal is necessary. If I can get her to help me, then she can just go in and get Jasper for us."

I pressed my lips together. I recognized he was making a good point, and one that was far safer than the idea of actually going to Sadie Monroe's office to get the other AI, but I couldn't seem to make myself say that. All I knew was that Jang-Mi had to stay in that hard drive. She was too unstable, and I wasn't about to risk my friends against the defenses in my new home if Jang-Mi up and decided to murder everyone.

I convinced myself that was the one and only reason that I was refusing, even though I knew it was a lie. Knew that a small, twisted part of me was supremely gleeful at the prospect of keeping her trapped on the hard drive forever as a punishment for what she had taken from me. And that I was letting that feeling win.

"I'm not risking it," I said. "It's too dangerous. I'm not losing anyone else to that thing."

"Liana!" Tian gasped, sitting forward. "Jang-Mi's not a thing!"

I almost said something snarky, but caught myself just in time. Tian was attached to Jang-Mi, thanks to her time as a prisoner of the deranged AI fragment, and way more forgiving than I could be at this moment. "You're right, Tian," I said, the words leaving an acrid taste on my tongue. "I'm sorry, but the fact remains that you'll have to find somewhere else to put Jang-Mi. She's not going in the terminal." The last part I directed at Leo, and hated myself for doing it. But I also couldn't seem to stop or change my feelings about this, at all.

His brown eyes grew hard, and his jaw tightened, but he didn't say anything. He just nodded. I looked around the room and sighed. It seemed I still had a long way to go before I was all right, but I could work on this Jang-Mi thing. I just needed more time to get comfortable with the idea that she wasn't to blame.

"All right, gang, let's go ahead and get settled in. Feel free to use anything you want in here—I'm giving you full permissions—and I'll see you guys in the morning."

"The morning?" Zoe asked, looking up. "Where will you be?"

"Well, before she goes anywhere," Quess interjected before I could formulate my response, "she's going to sit down and let me change out her net with Lacey's legacy net." At my surprised look, he smiled sadly. "I had some time to work on it, and with Leo's help, we figured out how she was preventing you from retaining certain memories. It should be fixed now, but the only way to know is to put it back in and see how it works. I can do it now."

I realized he was talking about the time after my mother had died, and had a moment of sadness of my own, but pushed it aside, focusing on what he was saying. Of course I wanted him to, but I worried about someone discovering it when I went in tomorrow. "I have to go to the Medica for the transmitter," I said. "Won't they notice?"

He frowned. "Hey, Cornelius. Where does a neural transmitter get placed?"

"In the temple," the computer replied a heartbeat later.

Quess grinned. "Then you should be fine. They'd have to cut it out to notice that it was different. So... do you want it now, or would you rather wait?"

I smiled—I definitely wanted him to do it now. There was important information about this legacy war on it, and I needed every bit of information I could get. Lacey was hiding something, and I was betting something on here revealed what that was. "Absolutely," I told him, turning around and moving my hair away from my neck. "I'm ready."

Quess chuckled, and I heard him rustle around behind me, while Zoe came around to face me. "Okay... but what about after that?" she asked, wrinkling her nose. "What are you going to do all day?"

"I'll be in my room," I replied, my elation quickly transforming into exhaustion at the fact that I still wasn't done, yet I felt good that I could at least distract myself with something germane. "I have to get ready for my council meeting tomorrow."

9

I woke up early the next morning and got ready quickly, eager to do at least one good thing today. I'd been up late going over the other issues for the council meeting and writing messages to Lacey with questions about them, and I wanted to see if she'd gotten back to me yet.

I made a quick cup of tea in the kitchen, and then carried it and the savory breakfast tart that Cornelius ordered from a nearby cafeteria—which had been delivered by one of the robotic arms before my tea had finished steeping—into the war room. I climbed the steps tiredly, and then sat down at the table, setting my tea and tart to one side and dusting off my fingers.

"Cornelius, pull up the schedule and my messages, please," I requested, picking up my cup and taking a sip.

The screen on the desk immediately split into two different sections, the left side filling with messages, and the right one with my schedule. The council meeting was marked in gold, with my appointment in the Medica marked right after it. The rest of the time was denoted as *Champion Transition Period*, which I had learned from Cornelius was the month I was given as a break from normal duties so that I could familiarize myself with what those would be. I was expected to spend time with the Knight Commanders under me in order to start forming professional relationships with them, and consult with the other councilors about what to expect on the council.

I leaned forward, taking another sip of tea before setting the mug down, and then studied my messages. There were actually quite a few, some of them from people I had known at the Academy, offering their condolences, congratulating me for winning, or condemning me for cheating. I quickly asked Cornelius to separate messages like that into three separate folders, with the negative messages being marked as priority. Anyone who sent hate mail was a potential enemy that I needed to keep an eye on. The congratulatory ones I deleted, with no small amount of bitterness. I didn't like the idea of being congratulated for something that had cost my mother her life. The other ones I ignored, unable to look at their words without falling to pieces. Maybe later, but now? No way.

Three in particular caught my eye, though, thanks to the authors. One was from Lacey, one was from my brother, and the last one was as surprising as it was pleasing to see. The corners of my lips twitched slightly as I reread the name there, and I automatically opened it, curious as to what he had to say.

Hey Liana,

I just wanted to say I'm really sorry for what happened to your mother. I can't imagine what you're going through right now, but I'm here if you ever need to talk.

I know you probably don't want to hear this. I mean... you're going through all this stuff right now, and how you make me feel doesn't help you in the slightest, but I still want to tell you that you've given me hope again. Before I watched your incredible climb, I was convinced that an eight was all I would ever be. It filled me with such shame, Liana, because I wanted to be good, but I was clearly being betrayed by my own treasonous thoughts. I now know that if you can overcome your low rank and become the Champion, then one day I will be able to do so as well.

I thank you for that gift, and look forward to proudly serving under you one day as a Knight Commander, once I've proven my worth to you.

Sincerely,

Theo

I smiled sadly. Theo was the first boy I had ever liked, the first one I had kissed, even. We'd bonded over our poor ranks, and then lost touch right after he graduated from the Academy. I ran into him again a while later, and his rank had improved dramatically, thanks to the Medica's intervention services and the big, fat, red pills marked MSM-7.

Theo was exactly the reason why the ranking system was so reprehensible to me: he felt like he was a failure because he hadn't been able to move past an eight. So he had let the Medica give him pills that wiped away his emotions—which he had because he wasn't content with the stifling life in the Tower.

But so what if he couldn't be happy all the time? That didn't mean he was a bad person. He was entitled to his feelings for as long as he had them, and to tell him he was bad for being who he was inside was cruel and counterproductive. That was how I felt about the matter, anyhow, and the fact that he was actually thanking me for demonstrating that even those with a low score could actually change was just... very sad.

I considered his message for a long time, then asked Cornelius to mark it as unread and create a folder between Theo and me for personal correspondence, and instructed him to remind me to respond later. When I had some sort of wisdom or hope to offer him.

Poor Theo. He just wanted to succeed here, but the very system he ascribed to was keeping him from being happy.

I turned to the next two messages, and then decided to leave my brother's for last. I knew he was upset with me, and I understood why. I had cut him out. I needed to find a way to make it up to him, to include him somehow, but I was struggling to think of something. He'd want to focus on our mother's death, with good reason, but I couldn't trust that he wouldn't fly off the handle. We had to be very careful with our next moves, or else all of us would be exposed.

I just wasn't sure how to sum all that up in a message, and I wasn't sure I was ready to deal with his recriminations about how I was failing him as a sister.

So I turned to the other. I had sent several messages to Lacey last night, and was disappointed to see only one waiting for me this morning in reply. I clicked on it, thinking that maybe she had just condensed her answers into one message, and then paused when I saw the words written there.

Liana,

Direct your messages to Praetor Strum in the future. I have neither the time nor the patience to sort through all of this, and given the number of messages you sent me through the night, I am beginning to think you're already reneging on your promise to find Ambrose's killers—since I received messages about everything but

that. Messages that clearly took time to research and compose. Time
that could've been used to do what I've told you to do.

Let me make this perfectly clear. I am not your mentor. You're in
the position of Champion to help us (Strum and me) vote in certain
ways, to keep our enemies from destroying the Tower further. All you
need to do is vote the same way we do on issues, and focus on finding
Ambrose's killers. That's it. If you can't get on board with that, we'll
take our chances with the next Champion.

Lacey

I let out an irritated sigh and leaned back in my chair. Lacey's
concern that I was going back on my promise to find Ambrose was
understandable, since I had spent a lot of time researching issues and
writing her messages last night that had nothing to do with him or
that investigation. But the rest of it was not. Didn't she want me to be
an effective leader for my department? Did she think I would just
capitulate to her and Strum's orders without saying anything? If so,
she had a rude surprise in store for her, because I was not going to let
her dictate every vote to me.

I considered writing a reply with something to that effect in it,
but held off on doing anything until I got through Alex's message.

I took a deep breath, and then clicked on it.

Lily,

I'm coming by the Citadel later today to visit Dad. I know you
won't come see him, but I am expecting you to sit down with me and
tell me exactly what is going on with the investigation. I gave you a
day, but I want in on whatever it is you're doing. I'll be there from one
to two, and don't give me any crap about being busy. You're the head
of a department now, which means you control your own schedule.
Message me back with the location of your new quarters.

Alex

P.S. Still miffed at you, but looking forward to seeing your new home. I hear those things are friggin' cool—at least Dinah says Sadie's is, anyway—and I'm dying to know. Don't let me down.

I smiled at his postscript, glad that he wasn't furious with me, at least. If he had been, he'd never have included the last bit. The rest of it, however, filled me with anxiety, and I scraped my hands over my face, trying to clear it away. It occurred to me that the last time I had included a family member in a fight, they had died, and suddenly I was beyond terrified for Alex.

A thousand things could go wrong if I let him in on this. He could jump the gun or lose his patience while we investigated. He could run off full tilt after someone without any backup. He could get caught by the Inquisition snooping around in the mainframe. He could accidentally expose Dinah's relationship with me.

Not to mention, working with us would make Sadie suspicious. Hell, just having him in the Citadel to visit my father would make her question his loyalty. I knew Dinah said she could get Sadie to back off by feeding her false intelligence reports on my brother's movements, but it was naïve to think that Sadie wasn't having Alex followed or monitored in some way.

Especially now that I was the Champion. Even if she wasn't with a legacy group, she wouldn't like the idea of my brother acting as a potential spy for another department. She would be looking for any excuse to cut him from *her* department.

I knew I shouldn't let any of that bother me. My brother had the ability to reason, and he had the right to be there. I could always let him back in the Knights—as long as he wasn't found guilty of sedition and terrorism.

But if I had been this torn up over my mother's death, how awful would it feel if I lost Alex? He was my twin, my best friend, my brother... I wasn't sure I could survive his death. I didn't even want to entertain that possibility.

So I let fear rule my decision and decided to reply to his message later, with an apology that I was still getting the hang of my new role and had missed his message. He'd be angry, yes, but it'd be a believable excuse. Maybe I could come up with an excuse for a delay on my part, and then, when we finally had something solid, I could bring him in?

Suddenly something dark moved into my field of vision, and I tensed, my hand going to my baton before I even turned my head to see what it was. Seconds later I let the baton go and exhaled in relief as Leo entered the room, looking alert and neatly dressed in his uniform.

"Good morning," he said. "I'm your escort to the meeting this morning, as Maddox has several meetings to take with the Knight Commanders, and Quess has to go take his tests."

"How's Tian occupying herself?" I asked quickly, trying to disguise my earlier alarm by standing up to gather my things. It was a little early, but not so much that I minded leaving now. It would give me time to think about the responses I was going to deliver to Alex, Lacey, and Theo.

"She's going to resume her quest for a new Sanctum, just in case we need it sooner rather than later," he said with a small smile.

I considered that for a moment, remembering what had happened the last time she went out by herself, but decided not to make an issue of it. Tian had a penchant for getting in and out of any place she wanted to, and I had no doubt that if we forbade her from going, it would only make her want to do it more. It was better not to argue, and hope that she could take care of herself.

"Right," I said, putting my brother problem aside. "Shall we?"

Leo nodded and turned to lead the way, leaving me to follow.

The luxury and richness of the Grounds that made up the bottom floor of the massive atrium where the three core structures hung bothered me, even if the sight managed to take my breath away. Tall, non-fruit-producing trees ran rampant across the floor, rooted deep in soft, rich dirt that had to be at least fifteen feet thick. Artificial waterways and manmade paths cut through them, weaving meandering walkways through the thick vegetation and giving the entire floor a serene and peaceful feeling.

Peaceful and empty—and devoid of any sign of human movement save our own. Which made sense, considering access to the Grounds was restricted to anyone who had an appointment with the council, or who was there by official invitation, like Leo was as my bodyguard.

It wasn't our first time down here. We'd been once before, on the day of our trial. It hadn't been that long ago—only two weeks, now—but I had never once in that entire time imagined myself returning, and especially not like this. Not with a position that could actually allow me to make positive changes in the Tower.

"Nervous?" Leo asked as the domed shape of the Council Room drew into view over the tops of the trees. We headed toward it, crossing a wooden bridge that spanned a fish-filled stream, and I considered his question.

"Not so much nervous as... apprehensive. I must've asked Cornelius a dozen questions about what to expect, and he was less than helpful."

Leo frowned. "He didn't offer enough information?"

I gave him a wry look. "No, quite the opposite. Way too *much* information on procedures and rules and points of order. It really did nothing to reassure me. Neither did Lacey, for that matter."

Leo came to a stop, turning around to face me. "You're going to do brilliantly at this. First step is getting rid of those gas chambers. The second is getting rid of the ranking system. Baby steps, right?"

I gave him an incredulous look as I listened to his words. "Was that a joke?" I asked. If so, it was one of his funnier ones—which wasn't saying much, as his jokes tended to be a little odd.

"Yes," he said, immediately pleased that I had recognized it. His features took on a boyish light, and I couldn't help but smile at the simple validation I had given him just by recognizing it. "I finally got one right."

"I'm really proud of you," I told him, wanting to praise him further. Other people might've found his reaction odd, but Leo struggled with the concept of humor and joke delivery, and had for a while, according to his own admission. It showed a marked change in him—and one for the better.

He met my gaze, and suddenly that spark of electricity was back, that need and desire to move closer to him and let him wrap his arms around me and hug away my nerves. I stared at him, imagining what it would feel like to be held tightly by him, and lost myself in that image, driven there by acute loneliness and a need to feel connected, if only for a moment.

Leo lifted his hand and stroked the backs of his fingers over my cheek in a gentle swipe that made my heart miss a beat and my breath catch in my throat. "You just got sad," he murmured, clearly concerned. "What did I do?"

I almost laughed at his question, and then shook my head.

"Nothing," I said, carefully moving his hand away from my cheek. "I was just thinking about something."

"Your mother?"

I closed my eyes, pain washing over me, and then nodded. It was a lie, but not that far from true; thoughts of my mother were always there, in the back of my mind. Besides, it was easier than being honest.

"I'm still not ready to talk about it," I admitted before he could offer. "I'm just trying to keep it together for this meeting."

"All right," he said carefully, taking a step back. "After you."

I moved before he even finished speaking, eager to get a little space between us so I could have a break from the confusing feelings Leo always seemed to generate in me.

Of all the concerns on my laundry list of concerns, my AI friend's attraction to me was literally the last one I wanted to deal with.

We walked over another bridge in silence, and I was starting to turn my thoughts back toward the meeting, when Leo interrupted them, scattering them into oblivion with one simple question: "Can we talk about Jang-Mi, then?"

Anger gripped my spine immediately, and I grated my teeth together. "No," I said flatly. "I made my decision about this last night."

No, I thought angrily. *You made a purely emotional decision based on anger and hatred, and dismissed a valid argument against it. Stop. Being. Angry.*

I really, desperately wanted to. But I couldn't disassociate Jang-Mi from the people who had controlled her. I felt trapped in a cycle, powerless to stop the unmitigated hatred I had for her.

And the blinding resentment that came whenever anyone advocated for her.

Please, let it go, Leo, I prayed. I was so close to boiling over at the sheer mention of her name, and if he pushed, I wasn't sure what I was going to do or say, and the uncertainty terrified me.

"Liana, I know you're worried, but I can take precautions to keep—"

"No," I said, cutting him off, my rage so blinding that all semblance of reason deserted me. "I'm not letting that *thing* anywhere near a computer system. For all I care, she can stay in that hard drive from now until eternity."

Leo's eyes widened in horror. "Thing?" he said, his voice filled with hurt. "You think she's a thing?"

My fists balled, immediately defensive. "You know what I meant. I'm not backing down on this."

"No, I don't know what you meant," he said indignantly. "Liana, she may be an AI, but she has feelings and is clearly unstable. Who knows what she is doing to herself inside the hard drive? It isn't exactly the most stimulating place for an AI to be. It's awful, as a matter of fact, and by keeping her there, we're torturing her!"

"Good!" I snapped back, spite burning through me. I wanted her to suffer, and if the hard drive was like a prison for her, then all the better. "She *killed* my mother."

"It wasn't her fault!" he sputtered. "How can you say that?"

"It *was* her fault," I shouted back, temper snapping like a brittle twig. How could he stand there defending her after what she had done? When he knew the opportunity she had robbed me of? "She clearly had enough control to save Tian, but couldn't resist killing Min-Ha or my mother. She's weak, insane, and just as responsible as the men who used her to do it! That thing is lucky to even be alive, even if she *is* trapped in a damned hard drive!"

As soon as I fully heard the words I was saying, it was like a switch had been flipped, and all of my anger drained away, replaced instead by an icy feeling of dread. I was shocked by my own behavior, embarrassed that I had lost control, and mortified that I had even said any of that. I knew that Jang-Mi was our best option for getting Jasper—or at least the safest one.

But my feelings didn't agree with my logic, and it seemed they were intent on winning, no matter how much I fought against them.

The blood drained from Leo's face, and his features hardened an instant later, his entire body going rigid. "Well, if you'll excuse this *thing*, I think I've heard enough," he said stiffly. "Pardon me."

He turned and stalked away. I stared at him for a second, knowing that I should go after him and apologize... but afraid of him mentioning Jang-Mi again and my anger taking control. I needed to get it together if I was ever going to get past this and give Leo the answer he deserved to hear.

But that wasn't going to happen in the next fifteen seconds. Even now my anger was threatening to return and swallow me up. I'd go to the council meeting, distract myself with council business, and then sit down and figure out how I could get over this Jang-Mi issue so I could apologize to Leo and we could move forward.

Hopefully.

With that in mind, I turned and headed toward the Council Room. Everything else would have to wait.

10

To my surprise, the Council Room was empty when I entered. I quickly checked my indicator for the time, and realized I was about fifteen minutes early. The other councilors were undoubtedly on their way, and would be here any minute.

I rolled my lips between my teeth, exceedingly nervous about how it might appear to them if they found me here waiting for them. Half of me wanted to slip right back out of the circular room and go after Leo, but I resisted the urge. If I had time to further prepare for the meeting today, then I wasn't about to waste it. Especially when I knew that running after Leo might only make things worse between us—which would do nothing to help my nerves.

I took a deep breath and stepped farther into the circular room, refamiliarizing myself with it. Wood stretched up the walls from the floor to a midway point, where I knew from experience that councilors' desks sat, some fifteen feet up and overlooking the floor below.

I had stood on the small dais in the center of the room and felt the weight of their eyes upon me in silent judgment—and I'd hated it. Now, I was a part of it. Weird, right?

I walked around the perimeter of the circle, taking in the carved relief in front of each desk. Carvings depicted the insignia for each department—the rudimentary outline of Cogstown set against a mechanical gear for the Mechanics Department, where Lacey would sit; the five parallel pipes bound together by a single one inside a water droplet for Water Treatment at Praetor Strum's spot; the Farming Department next to his, marked by a chaff of wheat; and then Scipio's place, a spot marked by a Tower wreathed in lightning. Marcus Sage's position was marked with the Medica's cross, and Sadie's by the insignia of IT, an eye circled by lightning, echoing Scipio's own sigil to signify their devotion to his wellbeing.

My spot was between Sadie's and Scipio's, delineated with the Knight's symbol: a fist thrust straight up. I stared at it, trying to find some meaning in its lines and design, some inspiration that would help boost my confidence, but all I could see was my mother and that sigil burning over her breast. The insignia was a point of pride for her. She'd loved the Knight's Department more than any other, and had truly believed in what they stood for.

Even if it had caused her to do some grim things, like murdering ones.

But I put that aside, back into the little box I had created just for her and those feelings. As guilty as it made me feel, I did not want the council members coming in and seeing that I had been crying. I couldn't afford to look weak in front of any one of them—even Lacey and Strum.

I cleared my throat and approached the spot marked by the Knights' sigil. As soon as I was within five feet of the area just below it, a panel slid open, revealing a recessed area. I stepped in and found a narrow set of stairs to my right. They doubled back halfway up, and I had to duck my head to avoid hitting an overhanging ceiling, but that was easily surmounted.

At the top, I found a small office space behind a desk that overlooked the area below.

The desk was simple, with a larger screen waiting to be synced up to my pad. I quickly pulled it out and did just that, projecting my correspondence onto the screen. Several new messages had appeared since I left my quarters, and I realized they were all welcoming letters from the other councilors.

I clicked through them, but it didn't take me long to pick up on the rather generic nature of the greetings. *Welcome to the council; we are here if you have any questions; the fate of every citizen of the Tower rests on us...* Blah blah blah.

I focused instead on the agenda items. The repeal of the expulsion act was right at the top, but there were other issues that needed to be addressed as well. When I had gone to bed last night, my docket had been filled with ten items, five of them jurisdictional disputes between Water Treatment, Farming, and the Cogs.

Three of those were now marked as having been resolved at some point during the night, and a quick look at the notes showed that agreements had been reached privately between the departments in question, with no further need for council action. The other two were still marked active, but there was nothing I needed to do about them, as they didn't involve my department. My department and the Medica were the only ones without jurisdictional disputes, as the entire Tower was our jurisdiction.

The others, however, were always fighting about who got to repair what when it broke down. Water Treatment would insist that all water-related repairs be done by them, but if the issue was a mechanical one, the Cogs always wanted to get involved. The Farmers just never wanted anyone to tamper with their carefully cultivated crops, and fretted over everything from water temperature to pH balance changes that could affect them—something no farmer worth his salt would willingly allow.

The last two items were conflicts between Water Treatment and the Cogs, but I had a feeling they would be resolved soon enough, as the two were actually quite close. I was betting Lacey and Strum manufactured these reports to keep people from realizing they were working together, and wondered how they would act toward each other once the session began. For a second, I imagined them arguing with each other fiercely in mock anger, waving their fists and arms, and then dismissed it as pure fantasy. There was no way they'd get that theatrical about it. They were both too practical for that.

The other pending items were requests from departments to run drills or tests on equipment, which required the council's approval so that announcements could be made to prepare any people affected during the tests. Two were from the Farming Department, the first to run the biannual cleaning of their condensation rooms during the harvest season on Greeneries 4, 6, 11, and 13. I checked the records, saw that it was right on time, and made a mental note to look into my own department's requests later, to make sure I knew which ones I needed to submit requests for, and when. The second one was also routine, announcing the repair and maintenance on the harvesting machines and loading systems.

The last one was from Water Treatment, regarding the draining and cleaning of several of the treatment pools in the water purification section. It was also pretty standard, so I moved along, planning to let it pass without challenge.

The only other item beyond all those was an action request from Farming to the council, asking if an investigation was necessary to account for missing animals. Apparently a cow, two goats, a pig, and seven chickens were unaccounted for inside the Menagerie, the greenery where we raised our animals. I narrowed my eyes, considering the request. This seemed suspicious, though it was possible that one of the Hands on duty had simply been negligent, and that the animals had gotten out of their pens and then out of the greenery. It wouldn't be the first time that had happened... but still.

I minimized it as the chandelier hanging from the domed ceiling high above flickered in warning. Checking my watch, I realized time had slid by much faster than I anticipated, and looked up, expecting to see Strum or Lacey in position.

But their desks were empty, devoid of any signs of life—as was the rest of the Council Room. Confusion rippled through me, and I glanced down at my wrist, confirming the time. Then I looked over at my schedule to see that yes, the meeting was indeed at eight o'clock, like my indicator said. Where was everyone?

There was a sharp click and a hum from above, and I stood up to see beams of light starting to stream from the dome above, thousands of them, streaking from what appeared to be holes in the ceiling. I recognized the effect immediately, and was relatively unsurprised when they drew together and combined to give shape and form to Scipio through holographic technology.

It was breathtaking to watch as they lined his strong jaw, luminous blue eyes, and inky black hair. Seconds later he was there, the beams of light suddenly gone, while he remained.

"Greetings, Champion Castell," he said formally, inclining his head.

"Hey, Scipio," I said, not bothering with the formalities. "How are you doing?"

It was a loaded question—and one I wasn't even sure why I asked —but there it was, out there. I watched him closely, trying to gauge his reaction. His face didn't change, but I got the distinct impression from his eyes that he was surprised by my interest.

"I am well," he replied, managing a polite smile. "Are you ready to begin?"

I blinked and looked around. "Aren't we going to wait for the other council members?"

"They are logged in remotely," he replied. He nodded toward my terminal, and a moment later a chat log appeared, already filled with messages from the heads of the other departments. The messages were routine, showing what time they logged in, that they were ready for the minutes to begin, and my brief conversation with Scipio, but seeing them there—realizing that I was going to be alone in the Council Room—shocked me, and I could only stare.

"Allow me to begin." As Scipio spoke, the words were generated in the log, and I realized that he was recording everything in text form. "There are seven issues before the council today. We will start with the repair orders, then move to jurisdictional disputes, then investigation requests, and finally attend to pending protocol changes. Are all parties agreed?"

The screen lit up green with yeses, and Scipio looked at me. "You may agree verbally or on record, or lodge a complaint in the same manner."

I stared at him, still taken aback by the fact that no one was in the room. He raised an expectant eyebrow, and I realized that everyone was waiting for me to answer. I couldn't find a reason to launch a complaint—not that I would, over the order of issues—and said, "Yes, the agenda is fine."

"Then I will proceed," Scipio said with a nod. "The first item on the agenda is the maintenance request from the Farming Department, to clean the condensation rooms and service harvesting machines. No services to other citizens will be hampered, and this is a biannual event. Does the council agree to the dates submitted by the Farming Department?"

A slurry of yeses hit the screen faster than I could blink, and once again, I found Scipio looking at me expectantly.

"Yes," I said, still a bit overwhelmed by how quickly everything was moving, given the fact that there was literally no one here.

"The next issue is Water Treatment's request to drain and clean the water purification ponds. No services will be hampered, save that water purification on that day will be cut approximately in half, but all reservoir tanks are full. This is an annual event. Does the council agree to the dates submitted by Water Treatment?"

Again, a bunch of yeses, and this time I just tapped the *Yes* button on the screen, not bothering to articulate it. This was nothing like I had imagined, and I felt isolated and insignificant.

"Next, we move on to Water Treatment's claim on cleaning and servicing the cooling pipes around the air processing units in Cogstown. This is a jurisdictional issue that was resolved in Year 59 of the Tower, resulting in jurisdiction being given to the Divers. Engineer Lacey Green is asking that the issue be reopened. Both department heads will be allowed to make statements for their case."

On the screen, Praetor Strum sent the first message. *Lord Scipio, Engineer Green and I have come to an agreement, but it involves council approval on not only this issue, but on the other jurisdictional request pending in today's docket as well.*

"Go on," Scipio both said and wrote, and I resisted the urge to roll my eyes at them both. This was so stupid. Whatever they were trying to accomplish was rather irrelevant, given that they were allies. If Lacey wanted her Cogs to fix something, she and Strum could just work it out on their own. They were clearly manufacturing issues between the two departments to keep up the appearance of being at odds.

The other jurisdictional dispute is about the Cogs' claim to the repairs on our pumps for Greenery 2—a decision that was also reached around the same time as the last one. Because of the inter-departmental training programs, we have cross-trained enough of our people so that there is no need for either department to further service the other's machines. Engineer Green's people can clean the cooling pipes, and we will maintain the pumps.

There was a pause, and I looked over at Scipio to see a pensive look on his face. "I will need time to ponder the matter," he said finally. "It is rare for jurisdictions to change, and I will need to do some research into the issue to ensure that doing so will not cause undue harm to the Tower. I move to table these two discussions until next week's meeting. All those in agreement?"

Again, a flurry of affirmatives, to which I added my own. I didn't really understand why Scipio needed to do research—the solution seemed reasonable enough to me—but I held off on asking about it, unsure what the other councilors would think, and waited.

"Next, we have a request from Head Farmer Plancett regarding a matter of disappearing animals. I understand you are requesting an investigation into a potential poaching ring?"

Yes, Plancett replied on the screen. *But I wanted to consult with you first, to hear your recommendation.*

"Animals going missing in the Tower is not an uncommon

phenomenon," Scipio said. "As long as it remains under ten percent during the period of a month, it is well within the margins of error. It is more likely that the animals escaped and we will find them stuck in the vicinity of Greenery 1. If the council wishes to overrule my recommendation and launch an investigation anyway, please hit *No*. Otherwise, please select *Yes*."

This one gave me pause. Ten percent a month was the indicator for criminal poaching? That seemed a bit high, but without knowing the number of animals we actually had, it was difficult to tell. Not to mention, a cow and a pig were pretty large animals. They'd be impossible to miss, even down at the bottom of the Tower.

To me, it seemed likely the animals were getting poached, and that an investigation needed to be done, in spite of Scipio's recommendation. However, I had no idea what it would mean if I hit *No*. One look at the screen told me it was a moot point anyway, because everyone else had already agreed, even Plancett. Recording a negative at this point would only serve to separate myself from the consensus, which wasn't a great idea.

Reluctantly, I hit *Yes*—but I couldn't help but think of it as a mistake.

"The request is marked resolved, with no action needed," Scipio announced. "Archiving it now."

I leaned forward, suddenly excited. This was it—the moment I had been waiting for. I pulled up the notes I had made last night, decided to speak them rather than type them out, and waited.

"Now on to the final item for the day," Scipio announced. "The expulsion law that authorizes humane executions of all rank ones in the Tower is under review due to illegal tampering by Devon Alexander, deceased. There is no precedent on this matter, so I will open the floor to the councilors on discussion and debate."

I opened my mouth to speak, but then stopped when a new line of text appeared on my computer screen, from Sadie Monroe.

Requesting the debate be tabled until the IT Department can finish its investigation of Scipio, to ensure that there are no remnants of the virus that was used still embedded in his code.

I stared at the screen, blinking. She wanted to wait to perform an investigation into *that*? Hadn't Scipio already cleared himself at my trial? I knew he was being manipulated, but why wouldn't Sadie take his word for it? Everyone else would—because they were supposed to. The fact that she looked like she wasn't was... odd. What the hell was this?

"Request received. Does anyone second the motion?" Scipio asked, and I looked up, alarmed. This wasn't right; if they postponed the discussion, then the law would still be in place, and the ones already being held in the bottom of the Citadel would continue to die! I couldn't let that happen.

"Uh..." I said, trying to figure out how to stop this. The screen shifted again, and I saw that Plancett had seconded the motion. My heart sank lower in my chest. When was *I* going to get the chance to say something?

"All those in agreement?" Scipio asked, and I blinked in surprise as everyone hit *Yes*, including Lacey and Strum. What the hell? Why hadn't they voted it down? Lacey had told me herself that she hated those chambers, and had even manipulated Scipio into pointing to the vote to implement the rooms as evidence of Devon's interference! So why were they suddenly letting Sadie slow everything down? We had the votes to stop it—at least tie it and challenge the motion.

"Opposed?" he asked, looking at me.

I stared at him, and then looked back at the screen. "Am I allowed to make a different request?" I asked.

"If this one fails, then yes," he replied. "If it passes, you will have to wait one week for the next vote."

A week? My stomach twisted and my eyes bulged. "I see," I lied, because no, I did not! How could they let what was happening down there continue for even a day longer? It was anything but humane, as Scipio had called it. Those rooms were deplorable and monstrous!

I hit the *No* button, this time unable to resist, and uncaring about Lacey's order that I should vote with her and Strum. There was no way I was going to agree to anything that left those rooms in use a moment longer, and even though it was pointless, it was a matter of pride.

"Four agreed and one negative. The motion passes. This discussion will be continued in one week's time."

I fumed in my seat, angry at what I had just seen and been a part of. No one in the council had even bothered to show up, and then they had just done practically nothing, certainly nothing of any importance. And what was worse, they were fine with it!

I couldn't speak, couldn't think straight, so I missed Scipio's final remarks regarding the next meeting.

It wasn't until the councilors left the chatroom, creating little bonk sounds as they exited, that I came back to myself. I looked up to see Scipio giving me a sad smile before evaporating into thin air, leaving me alone.

For a long time, I just sat there, feeling helpless and impotent thanks to what had just happened. This had been a moment when we could've saved lives and changed things for the better, but it had slipped away.

No, it had been *thrown* away. And for what? Some investigation into Scipio that clearly wouldn't reveal anything, considering that no one in IT, save my brother, had even seemed to figure out that he was dying. If they couldn't see that, then how the heck were they going to find any speck of a virus that was used twenty years ago? And the request came from Sadie Monroe, the head of IT, a woman who should definitely have known what was going on with her charge. Scipio was literally her job, and yet she had never reported any problems.

Which meant that she was in on it, somehow. She *had* to be. The alternative was that she was incompetent, and while I was familiar with many of her negative qualities, that wasn't one of them.

And if she *was* in on it, then delaying the repeal of the expulsion chambers had a purpose—likely tied in with the legacy group's need to exert control and create a state of fear. As long as rumors that the Knights were authorized to kill those who fell from Scipio's grace remained, people would work harder, keep their heads down, and, most importantly, obey Scipio. Who was being controlled by someone else. I wasn't about to let that pass... but I wasn't sure what exactly I could do about it.

So I tabled this subject for now and stood up to collect my things.

My appointment with the Medica awaited.

11

"Hello again, Liana," a masculine voice announced.

Blink. There it was again—that untethered sensation that had haunted my days and nights lately. I looked around the room, searching for the owner of the voice, but only saw the obnoxiously pure white glow of the Medica's walls. The last time I had been here was when we had tried to rescue Maddox... and Leo had killed Devon Alexander. That room had been heavily damaged in the process, but this one was clean and tidy.

My eyes finally landed on a man who had just emerged from a hole in the wall, the portal behind him already closing up. Dr. Bordeaux hadn't changed a bit since the last time I saw him. He was a rotund man, with skinny legs that made it look like he was waddling slightly as he walked in, his gaze on the pad in his hands. He still wore a pair of thick, horn-rimmed glasses over his dark brown eyes, and the bottom half of his face was obscured by a heavy brown beard. His hair was a mixture of thick curls that reminded me vaguely of Lacey's afro.

"I see you're here for a neural transmitter?" he said, his voice questioning. "I'm not entirely sure why you would request me for this. Any Medic can do this procedure easily."

I narrowed my eyes as I picked up the slight recrimination dusting his words, and realized that I had wounded his pride by requesting him as my doctor. Evidently, he thought he had better things to do than "grunt" work, and by asking that he do the procedure, I had insinuated that I didn't think him capable in his current position within the Medica.

Tough cookies, I thought as I raised my chin up to meet his gaze head on. "You know that my mother died recently," I said—although it was harder than I'd thought it would be. The words were like rocks that I had to force out of my throat one by one. I swallowed when I was done, and then doggedly pushed forward. "I'm having a hard time processing that. But you know the Tower. If they hear that the Champion is suffering from depression..." I said as I rolled my eyes. On that point, I wasn't lying. The Tower thrived on gossip and drama, and any hint of a depressed council member would be talked about for weeks. I did not want that to happen, which was why it made for a believable excuse.

"Ah, yes," Dr. Bordeaux said, coming closer to take a seat across from me. "I apologize for my tone before. I should've realized that you had not made the request arbitrarily."

I smiled, but it was a bitter one. Dr. Bordeaux may have looked the same, but now that I had soothed his wounded ego and reminded him of my rank and position, his manner had shifted from condescending to obsequious in a matter of moments.

He leaned back in the chair and looked at his pad. "Even though we try to endure it, loss can weigh heavily on certain more... sensitive individuals. How have you been sleeping?" he asked.

I narrowed my eyes at the backhanded insult. "Sensitive individuals?" I said, my tone icy. Okay, to be fair, I was sensitive about my mother's death. Clearly and maddeningly so. But I didn't like the insinuation that my pain was a weakness. It was something I was processing, yes, but it didn't make me weak.

Just... y'know... irrational when it came to certain topics. It was a work in progress.

He blinked owlishly at me, and I had the distinct pleasure of watching his expression morph into one of alarm as he realized his mistake. I didn't have direct power over him, but I was a member of the council, and I was certain he knew I could find fun and interesting ways to make his life a living hell if I wanted to.

I wouldn't, but I could see the thoughts drifting behind his eyes, the fear of it growing as he carefully struggled to backtrack.

"My apologies," he managed slowly. "I did not mean that how it sounded. Your case comes with a certain amount of trauma associated with it. Your mother did not simply pass due to old age. The accident in the arena was tragic and sudden, and that can also have an effect on the grieving process. Now, back to your sleeping habits the past few days... How have they been? I want to make sure I prescribe the right medication."

Medication? That was so not happening, even if I *was* having problems sleeping at night. I wasn't just going to swallow a pill that would steal my grief away. It was mine, and I wanted it. And it bugged me that it was his instant go-to. He didn't ask how I was feeling; he only cared about the physical side effects that could prevent me from doing my job.

Not that I was surprised. It was the Medica's way to prescribe drugs rather than provide therapy. You had to insist on the latter if you wanted it, and then the doctor would send you to a "specialist." In other words, a first-year medical student who spent more time asking you about your aversion to pills than your actual problems.

It didn't matter anyway, because I did not want to actually talk about it. I was here for two reasons, and neither of them revolved around talking about my mother. Luckily, I had a good cause to delay, in the form of my first objective.

"Before we do this, can we get the transmitter implanted? I might get called away unexpectedly on Citadel business, and I need to make sure that's done first."

He looked up from his pad, his mouth forming a surprised O, but then quickly nodded. "Of course," he replied earnestly, hefting himself up. I started to join him, but he raised his hand, indicating that I should remain seated.

He walked over to the treatment bed that lay along the wall and pressed a button. A section of the wall dropped away, revealing a terminal. "Neural transmitter for Liana Castell, 25K-05," he said out loud.

The screen flickered to life, and my credentials immediately filled it, the crimson background a harsh contrast to the white glow of the Medica walls. A little window appeared over my profile, containing the word *APPROVED*. There was a hum, and then another section of the wall dropped.

I couldn't see what happened next, as Dr. Bordeaux reached for it, his body blocking my view, but when he turned around, he was holding a white, cylindrical object with a black tip. A pneumatic injector.

He approached me confidently, but my eyes drifted back to the terminal as I realized that this was my in for switching over to the *other* reason I was here: Jasper.

"What happened to Jasper?" I asked casually, looking back at the doctor as he closed the distance between us.

He frowned for a second in confusion and came to a stop in front of me. "The computer program?" I nodded, and his frown deepened. "The project was terminated right after you killed..." He trailed off, his eyes widening as he realized what he was about to say. "That's... Well... I mean..." He sucked in a deep breath, his cheeks darkening some. "What I meant to say was that it was terminated on the day Devon Alexander died," he finally managed without stammering.

It was an odd feeling to realize that you were making someone nervous, and an even odder one to recognize that at the heart of that anxiousness was fear. He was now *afraid* of offending me, afraid of saying the wrong thing—and afraid of how I would react now that he had botched it. For a second time.

"I know what I did," I said, in an attempt to make him more comfortable. "So do you. It's not going to hurt my feelings to talk about it."

He slowly looked up at me, relief evident in his dark brown eyes. "Here, let me do this," he said, holding up the injector. "Can you tilt your head up toward me, please?"

I lifted my chin, and he reached out and touched me on the side of my head, forcing me to tilt slightly away from him. Then he pressed the tip of the injector to my temple. I felt a sharp pain as he clicked the button, but it faded quickly, leaving only a dull sense of pressure. Then the injector was removed, and Dr. Bordeaux carried it back over to the wall for disposal.

"Is that it?" I asked, massaging the spot with my fingertips, searching for any sign of the implant—a hard nub or something—but finding nothing.

"Not yet. We're going to test it right now," he replied, turning around and lifting his hand. "Contact Liana Castell, 25K-05."

A moment later, the net in my head began to buzz and my indicator lit up, showing Dr. Bordeaux's name and identification number. I accepted the call, and then looked up at him. "What do I do?"

"Just think hard about what you want to say. You'll know when it is sent."

That sounded easy. Too easy. And also... what should I even think at him?

I thought about it for a moment, and then focused intently. Pressure formed at the injection site on my temple—tiny and not exactly painful—and was followed by a soft pop. And I knew in that moment that I had just transmitted *I feel stupid doing this* to Dr. Bordeaux.

To my surprise, he smiled. "It worked," he said, and I had the added bonus of hearing it twice—once in real life, and then a second later in my ear, transmitted through our open net connection.

Cool, I thought at him, smiling as the pressure/pop sensation went by faster. *Ending the transmission.* I touched the indicator on my wrist to end the call a second later, and exhaled. It wasn't exactly what I had been expecting, but having it was like gaining a measure of privacy that I had never had before. Now I didn't have to worry about my side of a net transmission being overheard; I could just let it all play out in my head, and no one would know.

Well, they might in the beginning. The sensation was a little distracting, and I was certain that I would have an odd look on my face the first few times I used it. Still, I was happy to have it.

Dr. Bordeaux had moved back over to the chair while I was

dwelling on the new freedom I had with the neural transmitter, and now pulled his pad back around. I realized I had gotten distracted from my original line of inquiry, and that he was about to resume dissecting my emotional state. But I needed to get back on track about Jasper—before Dr. Bordeaux could bring up my mother.

"So what happened with him?" I asked, taking a moment to reposition myself casually in the chair and cross my legs. The movement was calculated on my part. It, coupled with the idle curiosity in my voice, would hopefully signal to him that this was just small talk and nothing more.

He blinked as he settled back into his chair. "I suppose there is no harm in telling you," he said, crossing his own narrow legs. "You *are* a member of the council now. The program apparently had too many bugs in it, and IT recalled it to fix them."

"I see." I scooted my hip over a little bit more, fidgeting slightly. "Still, he was a bit odd for a computer program, wasn't he?"

"How do you mean?"

His question sounded genuine. He was intrigued, but I couldn't tell whether that was good or bad. He might never have thought much about Jasper before, but if I spent too much time asking questions about the AI, he might get questions of his own and start asking around, and who knew what sort of trouble that would create. I had to be smart about this.

"Well, I just mean he was so incredibly lifelike. Honestly, it felt like I was having a conversation with him, not just ordering him around, y'know? It freaked me out a little, because I thought Scipio was the only one like that."

He chuckled. "You'd be surprised how many people don't like the realistic voices the computer programs have around the Tower. In certain cases, it creates feelings of anxiety and paranoia, but it's important to remember that it's just a program. I also found it to be incredibly realistic—perhaps one of the most interactive programs ever invented, really. But it was only a program. And a buggy one as well. I was glad when they pulled it."

"They?" I asked, perking up slightly. He narrowed his eyes at me, just for a second, and I realized I had gotten a little too eager, which had aroused his suspicions. I gave him my most winning smile and hoped it would be enough to keep him talking.

"IT and Chief Surgeon Sage," he said. "It was Sage's idea to have a sort of... mentorship program for the less experienced Medics. A support structure that could offer advice and confirm diagnoses. It was an intriguing idea, just one that didn't pan out, I'm afraid."

He didn't sound too disappointed by it, though, and the casual disregard for Jasper made me slightly upset. But Dr. Bordeaux was a typical example of how a true citizen ought to be: completely trusting of the system. If those in charge told him the program was broken, he bought it. Hook, line, and sinker.

So I ignored my irritation at his callousness and focused instead on his answer to my question. It made sense that the heads of both the Medica and the IT Department would be the pioneers of a mentorship program for the Medica—IT had helped several different departments develop programs over the years. There was nothing wrong with Sage making a request for an interactive teaching program for his workers, and, unless he was working with the legacies, I doubted he would know an AI fragment from a regular program.

But Sage being involved was an intriguing thought. He had voted against me becoming Champion. That could make him a part of this in some way, if it meant he was working with my enemies to try to keep me out. But that didn't feel right to me, for a number of reasons.

First, he had cited my shockers as the explanation for his vote, and from his perspective, I could respect the concern about me potentially having them with the intention of attacking another candidate —even if it wasn't true. Not to mention, the man was over a hundred years old, and while he still looked surprisingly young for his advanced age, there had been whispers that his mind was not what it once was. While I wasn't certain about that last part, I found it hard to imagine that he was the man I had been running around the Tower trying to fight in a legacy war. It was a little laughable, if I thought about it. Honestly, it just didn't seem very likely that he was involved in a criminal conspiracy to take down the Tower, but I couldn't eliminate him until after I talked to him—something I was going to have to do sooner rather than later, it appeared.

Sadie Monroe, however, was a completely different story. Jasper had been transferred to her terminal. She had to know what he was at this point. But had she known *before*? Maybe she had discovered the truth after he was at the Medica and transferred him back to figure out what he was, but I didn't think so. If that was what had happened, she would've shared it with the council. Discovering another AI would have been a big deal.

But she hadn't, which made me think she knew more than she was letting on. She'd taken Jasper—whom she must have known was an AI—without telling anyone. I wondered if messing with one AI fragment could mean messing with another. Because if so... then she had to be involved in what was happening to Scipio.

It would certainly explain why IT had never reported any problems with Scipio to the council. And made it imperative that we find a way to get Jasper away from her. I feared what had become of him already.

"Liana?"

I blinked, and saw the doctor staring at me, his thick brows pulled high and tight on his wrinkled forehead. "Yes?"

"You spaced out there for a second. Are you all right?"

I nodded, and then shook my head, immediately changing my mind. I wanted to leave now, and this was an open way out, calling my name. It just needed to be handled delicately.

"No," I said. "I'm really not. Look... I want to talk about this, I do, but I'm just not comfortable with it yet. I'll see about making another appointment next week."

Dr. Bordeaux frowned at my abrupt about-face. "Are you sure? If you're not feeling well, then maybe you should stay."

I shook my head again, emphatically. "I'm sorry, it's just... the council meeting this morning was very frustrating, and I suddenly feel so drained. I think I'd rather take a nap and see if I can get my head on straight."

"Take a nap?" he asked, arching an eyebrow. "That is another signal of depression, and one that is a waste of Tower resources. Are you sure I can't prescribe you something? A stimulant for now, followed by a sedative later, so you can sleep?"

"No," I replied, irritated by the fact that he didn't actually seem to be listening to me or hearing my emotional distress. *Some doctor you are,* I thought, before adding, "I'm not a big fan of medicating people's emotions away."

His jaw dropped as I stood up, but I ignored it and sauntered out of the room. I hadn't learned much. But the fact that Sage had been involved in Jasper's presence was interesting, and I made a mental note to ask the councilor about it when I saw him.

After all, in his welcome letter he'd offered to give me advice if I needed it. All I had to do was schedule an appointment, which I could do as soon as I got back to my quarters.

eo was waiting for me in the reception hall when I exited the Medica proper. I came to a stop when I saw him standing just to one side, his back to a wall, and he pushed off the wall and came over, his face a careful mask.

"Hey," I said carefully, raking him with a look. I was surprised to see him after our little tiff this morning—plus I still hadn't had time to come to terms with everything. I wasn't sure I was ready for this. "How'd you know where to find me?"

"Cornelius told me where you were," he said simply, and I realized that he could. I'd given everyone unfettered access to my quarters.

I narrowed my eyes at him, wary of why he was here. "Are you here to change my mind about Jang-Mi?" I asked. I didn't care that I had wanted to apologize just hours earlier. Thinking of Jang-Mi only caused my anger and resentment to return in full force, even though I was actively trying not to have that reaction.

"Look, Jang-Mi can *help* us," he snapped, and my anger intensified, my rationality slipping some.

Please don't do this, I prayed, and I couldn't tell whether it was directed at myself or Leo. I knew I needed to listen—Jasper's rescue was critical, and if Leo had a safe way to rescue him, I should hear him out!

"She's a threat!" I retorted, heedless of my inner wisdom. "She's crazy, and she'll kill us all."

The skin on his face seemed to tighten, but he took a deep breath and exhaled slowly, relaxing the muscles strand by strand. "Peace, Liana," he said. "I don't want to fight with you about this."

I stared at him for a second, struggling to gain some semblance of control before this spiraled again, and then noticed that people around us were beginning to stare. My words to Dr. Bordeaux rang in my ears, and I realized that snapping at one of my inferior officers in public was something that would get around.

Besides, this irrational anger toward Jang-Mi had to stop. I knew it did. I kept telling myself it did. Putting her in the mainframe wasn't the end of the world. Leo was completely capable of taking care of the security measures—he had more than proven himself, time and time again.

Yet every time I opened my mouth to tell him that it was fine, everything would come to a grinding halt, and a surge of rage would rush up and start to fill me. I just couldn't stand the thought of Jang-Mi having a voice... when my mother now had none.

I backed off a few steps and looked at him. "Okay," I said slowly. "Then why are you here?"

His expression became downcast, one of deep sorrow and regret.

"I came to apologize. I left you alone and undefended after vowing to keep you safe. Liana, I am so sorry. I should never have lost my temper."

I softened instantly, and for a moment or two, I wasn't sure what to say. It touched me that he cared enough to apologize for leaving me, even though it was my fault he'd gotten angry in the first place. I knew I was being unreasonable about Jang-Mi and insensitive toward Leo. And I needed to tell him that. I needed to tell him what was going on with me.

But... maybe not while standing in the middle of the reception hall of the Medica. "Take a walk with me?" I said, raising an eyebrow toward him in question.

He gave me a surprised look, and then nodded hesitantly. "Of course. I'm your bodyguard, after all."

A surprised chuckle escaped me, and I found myself smiling at the self-deprecating tone in his voice. "Leo, you had every right to be angry with me," I said softly, starting to walk. I sucked in a deep breath and prepared to eat a little crow. "I know I'm being unreasonable where she's concerned. It's just... every time I think of Jang-Mi, I get this... uncontrollable rage toward her. I know it's not her fault, but she... she shot that beam at my mother! She didn't fight it, didn't resist! She just followed orders!"

I finished my rant with more force than I intended, and immediately looked over at Leo to see him watching me, sorrow lining his face. "I am so very sorry for what you lost, Liana," he said hoarsely. "I know what it's like to have someone taken away from you, and not be able to stop it."

I thought of Lionel, and how Ezekial Pine, the founder of the Knights—and the founder of one of the first legacy groups to try to take Scipio down—had suffocated the old man with a plastic bag, and for the first time since Leo had told me that story, I was able to reach out and touch him, resting my hand on his forearm. "Oh God, Leo. I never realized, but you must've felt awful. How did you cope?"

He gave a bitter chuckle and looked out over the bridge we were now crossing. "Not well," he admitted hoarsely. "I was all alone, remember? For almost three hundred years."

My heart swelled, and I found myself stepping closer to him, wrapped up in the hurt in his face. I hated seeing it there. "Maybe you should talk about it," I suggested lightly.

The look he gave me was bone dry and full of irony. "Those words sound oh so familiar," he said teasingly. "Do you still have the expression about a pot calling a kettle black, or will I need to explain that idiom to you?"

Another surprised laugh escaped me. "That was surprisingly rude, coming from you. What's gotten into you?"

Leo smiled and then shook his head, his pace slowing down and forcing me to slow as well. "I'm not really sure. I just found it pretty ironic that you want me to share when you yourself have not been doing so." He came to a stop, and I mirrored his movements so that we were face-to-face. "Although I guess I can't use that any longer, considering you did just kind of open up about her, in talking about Jang-Mi."

There was an idleness in his tone that I didn't like—that made me want to get defensive. "Talking about Jang-Mi isn't the same as talking about my mother." At least, I hoped it wasn't. Because I still wasn't ready to open up about her death. I was afraid of what might happen if I did.

Leo gave me a doubtful look. "If you say so," he said after a moment. "All I know is that when Lionel died, I felt scared and alone. I was mad at him for being so trusting, and had a deep-seated rage toward Ezekial. I used to imagine what it would be like to kill him, over and over again. Long after he died, I'm sure, but I couldn't stop dreaming about it."

I smiled, remembering Leo cutting through the statue of Ezekial Pine on the mock Champion's Bridge the designers had constructed for the Tourney. "Guess that's why you looked so happy cutting that statue down."

"He didn't deserve to be there," Leo spat, his eyes blazing. "Not there, not across from Lionel like that! He didn't deserve to breathe the same air as him, let alone stand there for all eternity, like they were equals!"

"Calm down," I said soothingly. He shut his mouth for a heart-beat, clearly upset by the line of thought, and I felt another burst of empathy for him resonate deep inside. "Honestly, it looked a little cathartic," I told him. I fidgeted. "I'd be lying if I said I didn't want that sort of catharsis of my own. But Jang-Mi's all I have, and, as irra-tional as it is, I just can't seem to get past it."

I looked down, slightly embarrassed, but he reached out and caught my chin, refusing to let me. "I'm going to do everything I can to help you find the bastard who did that to your mother," he vowed solemnly. "You're going to get the vengeance you deserve. I promise you that."

The air in my lungs turned gelatinous, and I found it difficult to breathe with him staring down at me like that. I couldn't believe that he was unbothered by my new thirst for blood. If anything, he seemed ready to embrace it, feed it, whereas I was still trying to determine whether unmitigated and blind revenge was a path I was even ready to walk.

But it was unimportant next to the way he was making me feel— like I was the center of everything for him, like he would tear the world apart to make me happy, or to spare me pain. An impulse seized me, and this time I couldn't resist. I stepped close to him and slid my arms around his waist, hugging him.

"That is probably one of the weirdest, yet sweetest things anyone has ever said to me," I murmured. "Thank you."

Leo was stiff for a second, and then carefully extracted me from the embrace without returning it. "You don't have to do that," he said as he did so, not quite meeting my eyes.

I took a step back, confused. "What did I do?"

He glanced at me for a second and then sighed. "Nothing. I just..." He hesitated and shook his head. "It's nothing."

"No," I said, blocking his path when he made to move away. "It's not nothing. I'm sorry if hugging you made you uncomfortable."

"Liana, it's not that. If anything, I want you to hug me. If I'm perfectly honest, I want you to do a lot more than that." He paused, a blush forming on his cheeks. "But I understand that you can't look at me without seeing Grey. It's not fair that I even put any of this on you, it's just..." He met my gaze again, and this time his eyes were sparkling with something that both scared and excited me. "I look at you, and I get this... strange, twisty sensation in my stomach, and I feel like at any moment I'm either going to fall down face first in front of you and make myself look like an absolute idiot, or I'm going to do something that makes you smile—and that smile is going to make me soar. I have no experience with any of this, and it's very frustrating and terrifying, and I just... I get so confused around you."

I stared at him for a long second, but found no reproach in his voice. He wasn't upset at *me*; he was upset at himself for feeling attracted to me, and confused by the sensations themselves.

And why wouldn't he be? Leo had never had a physical form before. He didn't understand fear as I knew it, as more of a sensation than a quantifiable data stream, or whatever made up his programming. Being introduced to a body was teaching him how humans experienced emotions—which was not easy to process, even for a human.

I would know, after all. I wasn't exactly doing my fair share of healthy processing these days.

But the way he talked about how I made him feel... I had to admit it made *me* feel very flattered. Leo was an amazing individual. He was kind, caring, and smart. Even after being alone for three hundred years, he had remained open to the world. He was doing everything he could to embrace and fight for it. He was amazing, in more ways than one.

Suddenly I realized how close we were standing. How there were just inches separating us. I looked up at him, and saw him studying my face with that same hooded hunger that he had just been complaining about. His eyes dropped to my mouth, and I could practically feel the heat from the kiss we had shared after Ambrose died. He didn't remember it, but I did, and it had been incredible.

Before I had realized that it was him and not Grey I was kissing.

But then again... it hadn't exactly been Leo, either. I bit my lip, recalling the earnest look in his eyes and the words he had said when we talked about it later.

Is it wrong that I'm sorrier that I don't remember it?

Leo cleared his throat and ducked his head, breaking my train of thought, and I was disappointed when he took a half step back, self-consciously rubbing his hand up the back of his neck. "Look, I know it's awkward to talk about these feelings like this, but I can't really talk to anyone else about it. It feels... wrong."

"Why?" I asked, genuinely curious. But I had a suspicion—and blurted it out a second later. "Is it because of Grey?"

"In a way, yes. I suppose it's just because they're my feelings for *you*. You are the only one who should know about them, for that reason alone. But also..." His eyes turned darker, a hint of fear in them. "What if these feelings aren't really mine?" he asked, and I suddenly understood the darkness inside of him.

"You think they might be remnants of Grey's feelings for me?" I asked.

He held his breath, his eyes growing distant, and then shook his head. "No, I don't. I think they're mine. But I can't help but wonder, sometimes, especially after what happened that night."

I exhaled. On the one hand, it would be much easier if it was Grey at the root of Leo's feelings toward me. Not only for him, but for me as well, as selfish as that sounded.

But I couldn't deny that there were moments between Leo and me... Moments when I didn't see Grey, just Leo. And as much as I would have loved to write it off as my attraction to Grey in spite of Leo being in his body, I knew it wasn't that simple.

Feelings never were.

I looked around and realized that we were standing in the middle of the bridge, talking about something that required way more privacy than we currently had.

"C'mon," I said lightly, catching his eye. "Let's go take that walk, and we'll... we'll talk about it, okay? See if we can't figure out what's going on with you."

He stared at me, as if he didn't know what to make of my offer. Then he smiled. "I'd like that," he said with a nod.

"So would I," I replied. And it wasn't a lie.

13

"So how did the implantation session go?" Leo asked idly as we stepped onto an elevator. I wasn't sure where we were heading, as Leo had picked the floor and I hadn't been paying attention, but I guessed it didn't matter as long as it was private. "Can you now communicate nonverbally, as I can?"

I cocked my head at him. "Yes. How do you do that, by the way?" It was a safe enough question, I supposed. We'd both agreed to the conversation about Leo's emotional state regarding me, but it wasn't exactly something we could dive right into, either. He needed to set the pace and tone. I was just here to listen.

And to remain impartial, I reminded myself firmly. I couldn't allow myself to see things that weren't there, no matter how much I wanted to. A part of me sort of hoped Grey was at the heart of Leo's feelings toward me, but that didn't mean I could overanalyze every little thing Leo said, looking for Grey. I had to sit back and listen, and not judge unless he did something utterly Grey-like.

"The net in which I am stored has a transmitter inside of it," he replied.

"Huh," I said, slightly confused. I had been under the impression that the neural transmitters were a separate implant, as evidenced earlier, but maybe they hadn't always been separate? Maybe they'd been packaged together at some point?

It made a certain amount of sense. After all, the original nets had been created to keep and store the memories of the users who came before. But they had also been recyclable, meaning that after they were removed from one citizen's head, their data could be erased and new credentials uploaded. This led to criminals inside the Tower resorting to stealing them from other citizens, often even killing for them. Supposedly, the new nets were designed to prevent it from happening, but now I wondered if that entire story had been a fabrication, created by a legacy group early on, and used as an excuse for tightening the reins of control over the population by restricting their access to the knowledge the nets had provided. It didn't matter, either way. To outside eyes, it was just another innovation that had been backward-engineered into a cruder version of itself, a bastardized copy with limited capabilities, but infinitely more controllable than before.

Suddenly the net in my skull began to vibrate slightly, and a second later, I was caught in the grips of a memory that was not my own.

"I don't care what the reports say," I said, *waving my hand emphatically through the air. "These nets are the only connection our people have to the past, now that Pre-End history has been abolished."*

"Not this again," came a snide voice, and I turned to look at Lead

Farmer Vladimir Strutz, a middle-aged man with broad shoulders and a thick, dark beard. "The vote to remove that course from our education was based on Scipio's analysis that it was a root of discontent for the citizens. This vote is about allowing IT to manufacture new versions of the net that can't just be stolen from the backs of our citizens' necks! People are being murdered because the current nets are transferrable!"

"But getting rid of them at the cost of denying people the memories of their ancestors?" I argued. "The people won't stand for it!"

"They will," replied a feminine voice, and I pivoted in my seat so I could regard Praetor Ressa. She was young—twenty-five—but smart and insightful. I was a little surprised to find her agreeing with Strutz, since the two hated each other, but I leaned back and let her have her say. "Lead Engineer Summers, you know that Farming, Cogs, and Water Treatment all bear the brunt of these net thefts in the form of human lives. We have to do something to preserve our population and the peace, and this is the course that Scipio and IT have come up with, backed by the resources they have available. We weren't prepared to redesign these nets because we never anticipated that people would steal them in order to escape the sensors. Because of that, we don't have the resources to recreate the nets with advanced security features, and mineral production in the Core wasn't designed for some of the elements necessary for recreating the functionality of our pre-End-designed nets. Maybe if we could go outside to hunt for some, but we can't. So we're forced to adapt, and this is the best way. I don't like it either, but the survival of humanity is more important than the memories of the past."

She had a point, though it was easily defeated with a simple question: how did we know that we didn't have the resources? I didn't know how to make a net. No one but IT did. We were taking their *word that they couldn't fix the flaw in the existing nets, and their word that they couldn't recreate the technology that allowed people to imprint their memories into them. I hated the idea of another law coming into existence that would further restrict people from knowing about their past, and I couldn't help but feel that there was something dark and sinister behind this.*

But there was nothing I could do. The rest of the council had made their decision based on Scipio's recommendation, and we were supposed to trust in him. He knew what he was doing—he'd been programmed for this. Maybe I was being too sentimental. After all, people were getting murdered for their nets. Something had to be done.

But I would be damned if they were taking my net from me. It was the only connection I had to my father.

I jerked out of the memory with a soft gasp, feeling slightly dizzy and disoriented. A strong hand wrapped around my forearm, keeping me on my feet as I blinked rapidly, expecting to see the Council Room, but only finding the shell.

"Are you okay?" Leo asked, concern in his voice. "Was it a memory?"

I nodded, unable to speak. I needed a moment to process what I had just seen. I didn't recognize the name "Summers", but that wasn't surprising. There had been many people on the council over the years, and not all of them were particularly memorable. Strutz and Ressa should have been clues as well, but I was the first to admit that I wasn't familiar with many of the other departments' past leaders. They weren't particularly relevant to me, but I'd do a little research to figure out when all this had gone down.

But the decision... the actual decision that changed the nets was there, embedded in the legacy net that Lacey had given me? And this

Summers had decided to keep his net because he didn't want to lose his connection to his father? It was fascinating—and made me think my guess about the neural transmitters had been spot on. The transmitter had to have been another one of the accessories built into the original net, likely eliminated to make it easier to monitor citizens' net conversations.

I sucked in air, using it to calm myself, and then focused on Leo. He was still watching me, a concerned expression on his face. "Sorry," I said, straightening. "It just caught me off guard."

"It wasn't bad?"

I shook my head and blew out. "No. Just... informative. About the law that got the original nets changed out."

"Ah." He let go of my arm. "Anything of note?"

"More of a distraction, actually," I said. "I'm going to have to learn to control my reaction to them. They're pretty disorienting."

Leo nodded sagely. "Lionel said as much. I'm sorry that it's so disorienting."

"It's okay," I said. "At least it helps to answer some of my questions. I wish I knew how to control it. It seems to happen randomly."

The elevator slowed to a stop, and Leo stepped out first, his expression pensive. I followed him, and moments later realized we were at one of the bottommost levels. It was a curious choice, but one that would ensure some privacy, so I didn't question it. Instead, I followed him as he led me through the narrow halls, heading for some unknown destination.

"I wish I could help you with that," he said. "Lionel told me a lot about the science behind them. He also tried to explain what it felt like, but I have to admit it was difficult to comprehend. I'm sure you'll get the hang of it."

I smiled at that. As odd as it was to hear him talking about the founder of the Tower, I also loved it. My entire life, I had grown up hating the man because of the system I'd thought he created, but Leo had taught me that he was much more than that. Now I saw him for what he really was: a human. Flawed, but with honorable intentions.

"I really like it when you tell me about him," I admitted.

"Really?" Leo smiled, his eyes growing light. "I feel like I could talk about him forever. He really was my best friend."

"Don't you find that to be a little bit weird?" I asked before I could stop myself. It wasn't the most appropriate question, but I couldn't help but ask it. "You *are* technically him, right? You were created from his neural scan?"

To my surprise, he chuckled. "I guess in a way that's true. But it's a little more complicated than that. The memories that made us the same were taken away from me, so that only the underlying aspects of Lionel's personality remained—the things that drove him or helped him to survive. The rest of this is me, and believe me, we were very different."

"In what ways?" I asked, too curious not to. I knew we were supposed to be talking about him and me, but this was too fascinating to pass up.

"I'm a lot more patient," he replied automatically, and I could tell he'd thought about this a lot in the past. There was no hesitation, no arrogance—just blunt honesty. "And I tend to be more self-aware with my feelings than he was. He was better at jokes, though."

"You are getting better with joking," I told him, and he glanced at me long enough to give me a smile before turning his attention back to the halls we were in and continuing to lead us at a languid pace.

Silence lapsed between us, and while I felt a need to fill the air with conversation, I remained silent, wanting to give him some space to focus on the real reason we were taking a walk together.

"Is Grey funny?" he finally asked a minute later.

I thought about it, and hated myself for having to do so. I should have been able to remember something like that so easily, but it felt like I had known Grey a lifetime ago. "He is," I replied to his question.

My answer didn't please Leo, who frowned. "I see."

I studied him, and sighed when I realized that he was now questioning whether his newly developed sense of humor was his... or a result of being implanted in Grey. "Leo, just because you have been making jokes more successfully does not mean that it's Grey influencing you. You just didn't have anyone to practice on for a while, is all."

He seemed to consider this as we came to a slow stop in front of a sealed door. I glanced at it, and then back to him, watching as he reached out toward the door controls. "Where are we?"

"A place I wanted to show you," he replied cryptically, and pressed the button.

There was a roar of sound and a burst of air as the door slid open, carrying with it a slightly damp feeling. I looked through the door to see a metal catwalk, and then realized I knew exactly where we were: right in the heart of Water Treatment, where the hydro-turbines were.

I stepped out into the roar, my heart pounding. We were forty feet from the bottom floor, which held several collection pools and the massive, rotating turbine. Water spilled over and around it, creating a fine mist that seemed to sparkle in the artificial lighting. Catwalks laced the horizon and the walls, cutting multiple pathways through the open space, but they were largely deserted, as it was the middle of a shift.

Leo stepped out past me, his hands gripping the rails on the catwalk. "Isn't it beautiful?" he said with a smile, leaning his weight forward so he could stretch out over the edge a little. "When I found it, I immediately wanted to bring you here. But there's never really been a good time to show you."

I looked up at him, and then back out at the sight, uncertain of how to reply. No, scratch that. I wasn't sure *if* I should even say it. It was clear by the enthusiastic sparkle in his eyes that he was beyond ecstatic about getting to share this place with me, and it only made me want to swallow back the words and simply smile at him, pretending nothing was wrong.

But I couldn't do that to him. He deserved to know the truth.

"Leo..." I said, searching for the right words. When he'd asked me to talk about his feelings toward me, to try to determine whether they were Grey's or his own, I had hoped for an easy way out. Now that I was staring one right in the face... I looked around the room again. Nothing I was coming up with was nearly good enough, and I wondered if I should even utter anything—and risk hurting him.

"He brought you here?" he asked, and my heart broke at how small the words made him sound.

"Not exactly," I said, looking back toward him, but not able to meet his gaze head on. "And not to this exact spot. I followed him—I thought he was a criminal, and..." I trailed off as Leo turned away from me. I wanted to reach out and touch him—comfort him—but I worried it would confuse the issue in his mind.

He needed a moment to come to terms with the fact that I'd been in Water Treatment with Grey long ago, and that his desire to bring me back here was probably a result of that. Which meant his feelings for me were now even more in question.

Time stretched on like a thin rubber band, and I felt anxious that I had somehow broken his heart with the revelation. I wanted to say something, but there was nothing I could say. I could only wait, watch, and be ready to listen when he spoke next.

"It doesn't mean anything," he finally said.

I had been completely unprepared for that reaction.

"Excuse me?" I asked, needing to make sure I had heard him correctly. "It doesn't mean—"

"Anything," he declared, whirling back around to face me. There was a ferocity in his eyes that made my breath catch in my throat, and the hair on the back of my neck rose up as I saw the underlying hunger, which was blatant with longing. "It means nothing. I know how I feel. I know what I want."

As he spoke, he stalked nearer, pressing close until we were inches apart. I sucked in a breath at his proximity, overwhelmed by the sheer confidence he was exuding and the impression that he was causing all of the air between us to disappear. My body responded, a throb of excitement strumming through me, and I had to look away, my cheeks heating with embarrassment at my body's reaction to him.

I told myself that it was because I was so lonely. I told myself that my body's reaction to him was because it was Grey's body. I told myself that I was just looking for something—anything—to distract me from my own problems.

I told myself all those things, but when Leo reached down, gently pressed his fingers under my chin, and slowly lifted it, those excuses evaporated under the scorching heat of his eyes as they traced over the lines of my mouth, as if he were already imagining what it would be like to have his own mouth fitted to them.

I licked my lips without meaning to, and watched as his eyes tracked the passage of my tongue, his hunger mounting. "You don't know how badly I want this," he admitted hoarsely, and my heart thundered, galloping madly across my ribcage. "I've thought of little else since I met you. You constantly amaze me, Liana, with every-thing you do."

I knew I had to stop this. We were standing on a precipice, and if I let it go on, we were both going to tumble over the edge. "Leo, I—"

"No," he said, his eyes blazing. "I have something to say, and dammit, I'm going to say it." He took a step closer, his hands grabbing my shoulders. I wished I could say it was aggressive, but it wasn't. If anything, it was tentative, almost as if I were part of a dream that was about to fall to pieces at any moment. And that only served to confuse my body and mind even more.

"You asked me how I survived my grief after being alone for so long when Lionel died, and the truth is, I'm not sure all of me did. I was beyond distraught. I was downright melancholic." His eyes grew distant for a second, trapped behind a distant memory. "I even considered suicide. Especially when there was no one around to talk to about it. I thought I'd go mad from the lack of interaction, and who knows... maybe I did.

"I was so isolated and alone. I had no way of knowing what was going on with the Tower, and no way of gaining revenge for Lionel's death. I don't even know how I survived those first few years. I was so lonely.

"I found ways to pass the time that helped distract me from my loneliness. I'd use my imagination to create holographic stories, revis-ited old conversations with Lionel, invented games for just one player, and most importantly, I didn't give up. I kept hope alive that someday someone would find me and rescue me. And you did."

The air in my lungs disappeared completely, and I struggled against the impulse to close the gap between us.

"I know you feel something for me, too."

I opened my mouth to protest, but it died on my lips. He wasn't wrong; I was clearly feeling something for him right now. But there was a massive problem with all of this, and he knew that.

"But Grey..." Leo's grip tightened slightly—not painfully, but I could tell he didn't like this train of thought, so I stopped, trying to find some other way to phrase the argument.

"I know this is confusing for you," he said moments later, while I was still struggling. "I know that looking at me and seeing his face is confusing. But I also know that you can see beyond this exterior and see *me* inside. You're one of the only ones who does, really. I know you want this to be a result of Grey's feelings toward you, but I promise you that it's not."

"But how can you know that?" I whispered, wondering how he could possibly be so certain.

"Because he knows what it's like to taste your lips, whereas I can only come to places like this, and imagine."

I gaped at him, and his hand came up to grip my chin, pressing my mouth closed. I expected his hand to leave me, but it didn't. Instead, he ran his thumb over my chin, right under my bottom lip. Shivers erupted from the places where his calloused finger gently grazed my lip, and a gasp escaped me before I could snatch it back.

"And, God help me, I have spent so much time imagining what kissing you would be like. How you would react when I skimmed my lips over yours, pressing my tongue against the seam of them and begging for entrance. And you opening your mouth to me. Just me. I have always been endlessly fascinated by what it must feel like, and now..."

I grew lightheaded at his words, arousal crashing into me as if someone had flipped a switch. I bit my lip, and Leo zeroed in on the action, his own lips parting on a small groan. Pleasure blossomed in me at the raw look on his face, knowing that I had put it there.

I really, *really* needed to stop this.

"Leo, I—"

"Screw it," he muttered, and then he dragged me to his chest and smashed his mouth to mine.

Shock shot through me at the brazenness of his actions, making me freeze—which was all the invitation my body needed to take over. It responded where I could not, melting into his touch like butter in a pan.

His velvet lips massaged mine roughly, his tongue running along the seam of it, begging entrance, and my jaw relaxed, parting my own lips. He seized the opportunity immediately, his tongue sweeping in to establish dominance and control. His hands left my shoulders, only to slide into my hair and cup the back of my head.

He was relentless, using his tongue and teeth and lips in ways that sent shivers down my spine. Lightheaded, I reached for him, needing something to hold me up before I fell, and he made a low noise of pleasure in the back of his throat and then dragged me closer, one hand going to my hip and holding me there.

He ripped his mouth away moments later and looked down at me, his eyes wild with passion. "I never knew it could be so... soft," he murmured, before dipping his head back down to reclaim my mouth.

A disappointed moan slipped from me as his lips only pressed against mine, my body clearly hungry for more, and then his mouth was drawing a soft line up to my ear. I gasped when he captured my earlobe with his teeth and gave a gentle tug, before running his tongue over the shell and sending even more delicate shivers down my spine... and right to the special place between my legs.

"You know that it's me," he whispered in my ear. "Yet you're still responding to my touch."

"It's just physiological," I managed weakly, unable to come up with a better excuse. "It's not—"

His tongue swept over my ear again and I gasped, all the words I had somehow managed to screw together into a passable argument against this falling apart.

"It is," he growled insistently. "Shall I prove it? Shall I tell you exactly how I pictured kissing you here? Backing you up against the railing and pressing myself into your softness. Drinking in your moans and your cries, teasing you relentlessly. I want to savor every moment of touching you I have, because I know it can't last. Grey will be restored, and I will have to leave him eventually. But this isn't for him. It's for me."

He moved to kiss me again, but this time I turned my head away, unable to let him do it. I wanted to—Scipio help me, I really wanted to—but as soon as he'd mentioned Grey, the moment was gone, leaving me physically frustrated and guilty. We couldn't do this. Shouldn't, even.

"Leo, I—"

A sharp *crack* cut me off, and I watched in confusion and then horror as Leo's eyes rolled into the back of his skull, his grip on me slackening before slipping away as he tumbled to the ground, boneless.

Behind him, a man wearing nondescript black clothing was staring at me with a smug grin, twirling a pipe around in his hand.

"Well, well, well," he said with a smirk to the people standing just behind him—five of them, unless I miscounted. "Lookie here, gang. The newly elected Champion, far away from the safety of her own department, and with a poor excuse for a bodyguard. Should we help her out, or just congratulate her on her victory?"

14

This was bad.

Really, *really* bad.

I eyed the handful of people, searching for weapons as they spread out around me and split into two groups of three to block any escape. Nothing was in their hands, save the pipe that the first one had used to knock Leo out, which he was twirling lazily in the air. A small smile played on his lips, like he was a cat who was about to swallow a mouse whole.

And I was that mouse.

That look told me everything I needed to know. These people weren't here to talk. They were here to fight. And they were confident, which meant they had weapons, even though I couldn't see any. They outnumbered me, and I was all alone.

And running wasn't an option. Even with them surrounding me

on either side of the catwalk, I wasn't about to leave Leo unconscious like that. I couldn't risk him falling into anyone's hands while he was inside of Grey's head—nor would I risk Grey's life.

But then again, I really didn't *want* to run. These people wanted to attack me? Fine. Then we would dance. I was spoiling for a good fight, and these guys had given me a reason. I wanted to know why they had decided to attack Leo too, and that meant sticking around was the right answer. I just had to make sure I kept Leo safe while I did it.

I immediately began checking out my surroundings, gauging what I had to work with. We were next to the hydro-turbines, which meant that there was humidity everywhere, making my lashes ineffective. They relied on static technology to connect, and the moisture would make that impossible to generate. Quess had developed lash-ends that *could* work in the high humidity, but I hadn't put them on when I got my new lash harness. Honestly, I hadn't even thought to do it.

But that didn't mean I couldn't use my lashes anyway. I just needed to think. And maybe buy some time before the fighting broke out.

"Greetings, citizens," I said with a bright smile. "Care to explain to me why you felt the need to attack one of my Knights?"

There was silence for a second, and then someone coughed. "Is she stupid, or..."

I looked in the direction of the hushed voice, and whoever was speaking stopped. I continued to smile at them, my mind whirling. Could I get Leo under the catwalk somehow? It would make it harder for them to get to him, while leaving me free to fight.

It was possible. I just needed to figure out how to do it.

"I don't think I'm stupid, but you never know with us Knights, right? All brawn and no brain?"

"I don't know about that," the first man—I was marking him as their leader—drawled, and I looked at him again. I'd never seen him before, but there was something familiar about his voice that gave me pause, and I studied him closely. "From where I was standing, it looked like you and your little boyfriend were all hormones. You sure he's not trying to sleep his way to the top?"

"Do we know each other?" I asked, ignoring his comment. Inside, I was a little embarrassed—and scared. But more than anything, I was angry. And I couldn't overreact; I needed more time to plan. If I could lasso the railing using Leo's lashes, I thought, I could throw him over and let him dangle while I took out the others.

But I dismissed the idea a second later. They'd be on me before I was even halfway done. *C'mon, think, Liana,* I told myself, trying not to panic.

"You could say that," he said wryly, dragging a finger around the side of his face as his mouth twisted into a grimace that bared his teeth.

I cocked my head as his voice once again sent warning signals through my mind, the familiarity of it screaming at me. I'd heard that voice before somewhere... but I still couldn't place it.

"You really shouldn't have wandered so far from home, where no one can help you."

"Yes, but then I wouldn't have been able to sneak away with my boyfriend," I pointed out. If I couldn't get Leo away from them, I'd have to find a way to keep them away from him. But how?

Somebody laughed, but it stopped with a short "oof". The laugh gave me some hope, but only a small bit. I wasn't going to be able to stall forever.

The man rolled his eyes and opened his mouth, but I quickly cut in with a question, wondering whether I could draw him out. "So... what's up with the attack on my Knight?"

The man smirked again. "Inter-departmental dispute. Now, are we done wasting time? Nobody's gonna accidently stumble in here and save you, Champion. You're decidedly alone."

I stared at him for a second as his words hit me, and a thought occurred to me that almost made me smile before I could catch it. Because I *wasn't* alone. Not entirely.

Cornelius? I thought, focusing my thoughts. A moment later, my net began to buzz gently.

Yes? his voice transmitted. *My scans of your indicator show that your adrenaline is high. Is there a problem?*

You could say that, I thought at him, trying to focus on the idea so the message got across. But it was difficult keeping my thoughts clear enough to transmit. I needed to hurry if this was going to work. *Contact all the Knights near the hydro-turbines and get them here now. Tell them to make it quick, or they'll be holding another Tourney.*

"What are you doing?" the leader demanded, and I glared at him as my carefully ordered thoughts nearly fell apart with the distraction.

"I'm thinking," I snapped, and then thought, *Tell them to hurry up.*

ETA two minutes, he replied. I grated my teeth together in annoyance. Two minutes was a long time when death was only about ten feet away, especially given how long I'd already stalled. I wasn't going to get much more conversation out of them, but I still hadn't figured out how I was going to fight off six people alone.

Think, I ordered myself. I had lashes and a baton. Going for the baton would be too obvious, and would kick things off before I could get to it, but I could maybe do something with my lashes. Something that would help me keep them back—control their attack, somehow. If I was fast...

"What is there to think about? You're surrounded and about to die."

Well, that confirmed that—they weren't here to play nice. But now I was curious as to who they were and why they were here. What was their issue with me, really? Were they legacies? Were they finally making a play to take me out?

"My final words?" I snapped back on impulse, placing a hand on my waist to let my anger show. "Clearly you jerks are about to kill me, so can I just have a moment to make sure that whatever I say is really good? I don't want to get stuck with 'Why'd you hit my boyfriend,' as the last thing I'm ever remembered for, all right?"

Silence met my remark, and then someone behind me sniggered under their breath. "Knock that off," the leader snapped, his eyes narrowing thoughtfully at me. "What are you up to?"

Once again, I was hit by the familiarity of his voice, which made the hair on my neck stand up. I stared at his face even harder, trying to recognize him. His eyes were blue, his brows black, downward slashes over them. His nose was perfectly straight and narrow, his jaw soft and slightly rounded. His head was balding at the top, and he kept his hair cut short in a buzz. I recognized nothing about him.

And yet I couldn't get over the feeling that I knew him from somewhere. Somewhere bad.

"What do you want?" I asked, continuing to stall.

"Stop talking to her," a feminine voice said from behind me, and

I turned to the group and raised an eyebrow toward the three people there.

"Why?" I asked, keeping my voice light and innocent. My heart pounded against my chest, and my adrenaline spiked. I already knew why—I was dangerously close to being out of time, and they knew I was stalling. I needed to move. Now.

"She's right," the leader said, hefting up his pipe. As soon as I saw it, a plan fell into place, and I seized it. "Let's finish thi—"

Whatever he was about to say was cut off as I snapped my arm at him, my weighted lash-end whipping toward him. And I wasn't aiming at him, exactly, but the pipe. I flicked my wrist the way Dylan Chase—my competitor and teammate during the Tourney—had taught me, which caused the line to wrap around the piece of metal. Then I yanked.

The pipe swung free, and I immediately lifted my hand over my head and went to my knee, twisting my wrist and swinging the lash-end and pipe over my head in a circle. I felt and heard the sharp crack as it hit someone's head, followed by their cry of pain, and sent the line in another circle over my head, and then another, keeping them at bay with the added weight the pipe created at the end.

"Grab her!" the leader shouted, and a flurry of movement erupted at his order. I looked around, watching as my attackers began to pull out weapons, and zeroed in on the two who had produced pulse shields. They were weapons that IT's security teams used, and they emitted a burst of... something that felt like a brick wall if it hit you. Having them meant that some of these guys were in IT, or connected to them somehow. It was exceptionally difficult to find a pulse shield outside the Core—the Inquisitors rarely stepped outside the Core with them on—and yet they seemed to be the legacies' weapon of choice.

It only added fuel to my suspicions about Sadie. She had to be working with them.

I growled and yanked my hand down, then flicked my wrist so that the lash-end snapped back up, hitting the first of them in the hand. There was a *crack* as the pipe broke his arm, followed by a scream, but I was already twisting the line and flinging it back, aiming for the second man.

This one I caught around the wrist, and I immediately pulled the line, yanking him off his feet. A hand grabbed my shoulder, and I twisted with it, thrusting the heel of my hand up toward the area where my attacker's face should be. I felt the cartilage in their nose break as my blow hit home, and immediately grabbed the hand on my shoulder and rolled them off my back and onto the floor, then slammed my boot into their face.

Another set of arms wrapped around my waist and arms, then, and dragged me into a massive chest, where they held me captive. But I didn't panic. Instead, I brought my knees to my chest, surrendering my weight completely to him. He was prepared for me to fight, but not for that, and he grunted in surprise and staggered, his balance offset.

A person—a woman with blond hair—charged at me with a knife gleaming wickedly and pointed right at me. I bared my teeth, angry that she would dare try that kind of crap right now, and lashed out with both my legs when she got close enough, kicking her square in the chest and pushing the guy behind me even further off balance.

He fell back, his arms slackening, and I swung my legs up over his head into a flip and landed on one knee behind him. I snapped three sharp punches to his head the moment he turned around, right against his nose, until he went limp.

Then I looked up to see the leader grabbing Leo, a knife in his hands, and yanked on the line with the pipe, trying to retract it. If I could get it swinging again, I could hit him and stop him from using that blade on Leo. But it only pulled in a few inches before it came to a grinding stop, the gears whirring, and a quick glance showed me that it was tangled around the second man's wrist, and that he and several others were gripping the line. I wasn't sure if I had caught them trying to trip me or they were helping their friend get free; all I knew was that they were surprised, and keeping me from using my lash to help Leo.

So I hit the disconnect button on the entire cable, letting them fall victim to gravity as they lost the resistance I was providing, and turned back to Leo to see the leader drawing back the knife, clearly about to drive it into his chest.

I screamed, an enraged, wild thing as the man started to slam the knife down, and he stopped, looking at me in surprise.

I charged him, uncaring that he was turning the knife toward me, lifting it up to fight. He was not going to kill Leo.

I stepped under his first swipe and threw a punch, but he deflected it neatly. Still, it forced him to take a step back from Leo, and that was all that mattered. He reversed the knife and punched it toward my side, and I leapt away so that it missed me by inches, and then surged forward, swinging my fist at his unprotected jaw.

I caught a glimpse of his foot from the corner of my eye, and then suddenly my head snapped back and my vision went dark for a second. I landed hard on my side and rolled, stopping when my back hit the railing. The pain was exquisite, but it was met with a wash of adrenaline and fear, forcing me to pry my eyes open rather than give in to oblivion. My jaw ached violently from where he had caught me with the roundhouse kick, but I ignored it and tried to locate him.

White and black flashes blurred my vision, though, and I blinked my eyes rapidly, struggling to figure out what I was looking at.

I caught a flash of a shadow through the blobs of light, and instinctively brought my hands up to shield my face. I felt his forearms strike against my own with a heavy, pushing weight, and knew in my bones that he was trying to stab me. In my face. He grunted as he bore down, and I fought back, keeping my eyes wide open. They began to focus.

The point of the knife was millimeters from my left eye, a great gray blob that filled me with icy fear. I grunted and pushed back with my arms, trying to force more distance between us, but he pressed harder, his teeth bared.

I gasped and tried to wiggle my hips, make some room to pivot, but found nothing.

"Just die, like your mother did, bitch," he spat, his spittle landing on my cheeks.

And at that, anger clouded everything. I snapped my head to one side just as I released his arms, letting him drive the knife home. There was a tug on my earlobe, followed by a burning sensation as the edge of the blade bit into the soft flesh there, but I ignored it, ripping my arms out from between us and twisting around. I brought my elbow back with a sharp snap into his face, and his weight shifted off of me.

I didn't bother getting to my feet. Instead, I twisted around and grabbed the knife off the floor. The tip had snapped off in the corrugated walkway, but it was still plenty sharp.

Climbing to my feet, I gripped the handle and faced off with the leader, who was already standing. So were some of his people, though almost all of them were nursing wounds that made me feel a savage rush of pride. I shook my hair out of my face and straightened, trying to catch my breath.

"Had enough yet?" I taunted, fingering my other lash-end and looking for something else to lasso. It had worked well the first time, and I could make it work again.

The leader straightened slowly and wiped away the blood that was trickling down his nose. "You—"

"CHAMPION!" a voice shouted, thundering loudly in the cavernous space and cutting him off. He looked past me, and his eyes grew wide. I smiled then, realizing that it was my backup.

"Leave her and run!" he shouted, and immediately his people sprang into action, stopping only to grab their unconscious friend.

I moved to intercept one of them, unwilling to let them all get away, but the leader was already there, his arms and feet flying. I parried his first blow and ducked the second, but was forced to retreat slightly before I launched a counterattack with a roundhouse kick. He was surprisingly ready for the move, and caught my leg, wrapping his arms around it. He did something with his hands, and then the next thing I knew, my knee had exploded into agony unlike anything I had ever felt before.

I screamed as the leg holding me up crumpled, and attempted to pull the injured limb to my chest, but as soon as I tried to flex my knee, the pain intensified so much that tears formed in my eyes, purely on reflex. I expected the final blow to come any second, but to my surprise, opening my eyes revealed only the ceiling above me, slightly obscured by the mist.

Shapes darted over me moments later, leaping across my prone form, and I followed them, realizing it was a pair of Knights chasing after the man. I struggled to push myself up, but my knee was not having it, and I bit back a cry of frustration.

"DO NOT LET THEM ESCAPE!" I shouted after them, pissed off that I couldn't pursue. I struggled to a sitting position, and then hands were there, helping me.

"Liana?" a feminine voice said, and I twisted around to see Dylan Chase staring at me, her eyes wide. "Are you okay?"

Alarm immediately coursed through me. What was she doing down here? Was she with them? I'd had my suspicions about Dylan since she had technically won the Tourney, having actually completed the challenge, and had wondered if she was the candidate the legacies had been supporting.

It was possible she wasn't, and had simply been better than their candidate, but I couldn't know for certain.

Well, I guessed I could, depending on how she handled this exchange. But then again, that wasn't an indication of anything; she could still be pissy over the results of the Tourney. She may have won, but the Knights had voted for me anyway, and the last I had seen her, she had not been happy about it. Now I was down, my leg broken or worse—it felt like it had been ripped off below the knee—and vulnerable. Was she going to finish me off? Was she working with my enemies?

Her eyes raked over me and settled on where I was gripping my thigh just over my knee. She immediately pressed her hands there, right into the joint, and I hissed, fighting the urge to slap her hand away.

"It's dislocated," she said with a scowl, removing her fingers a second later. "I can pop it back in for you now, or we can call the Medics."

I stared at her for a second, suspicious. "Why are you down here?" I asked. Was it planned, or just coincidental?

Dylan wrinkled her nose in confusion and then raised a wry

eyebrow. "I'm on patrol duty in Water Treatment with my squad. We were doing our rounds when your call came in. What happened?"

I considered her for a second and then nodded toward my knee, giving her permission. I wasn't sure what I had been expecting. If she was with the legacies, her answer would be the same. Still, I wanted to believe her. It would be so nice to take someone off my potential enemy list for once.

"This is gonna suck for a second," she said, her eyes flicking to mine and filling with sympathy. "Grab on to something."

I looked around, reached out, and grabbed the handrail, pulling myself back and ignoring the feeling that my shin and foot were only along for the ride because they were held there by my skin. I pressed my back against the lowest rung and rested my arms on it, fisting my hands around the cold metal.

I took a moment to collect myself, and then nodded at her. "Do it."

With a steady move, she grabbed my shin, twisted it slightly, and then pushed. My knee popped back into place with an excruciating burst of pain, and then it instantly lifted, making me feel I could breathe again.

I sagged back, sweaty, and looked at her. "Thanks," I offered tentatively.

"No problem," she said, standing up from her squat and offering me a hand. I took it, allowing her to help me up. It was awkward—I was favoring my newly reconnected joint and limped a lot, too afraid to put any weight on it—but she didn't complain. "So what happened?"

"Grey and I were jumped," I told her. "They hit him from behind and surrounded me."

"What department were they from?" she asked sharply.

"I don't know," I replied honestly. "They weren't wearing depart-ment uniforms. Get after them. I'll get Grey out of here."

"Medics are on the way, ma'am," a male voice said from my left, and I looked over to see another Knight kneeling over Leo, checking him over. "Farmless is still unconscious. He isn't going anywhere."

That wasn't good. If the Medics got here and started scanning him, they might notice the special net he was using. I couldn't let that happen, as it would raise too many questions and draw way too much attention. I wasn't going to risk Leo like that.

"Do you have salts?" I asked him sharply.

"*I* do," Dylan said, reaching into one of her pockets and pulling out a long plastic tube. I took it from her, hobbled over to Leo, and handed the salts to the Knight. He quickly snapped them open and waved them under Leo's nose, releasing the ammonia smell.

Leo came awake with a start, looking around. "What happened?" he demanded. His eyes settled on me, and his brows drew together. "Liana, you're bleeding."

Confusion hit me, until I remembered my ear and the sharp pain I had felt there. My hand went up, searching for the wound. The entire edge of my ear was wet with blood, but I found the spot easily enough, as it was the only part that hurt. I felt the edges and realized he had sliced right through a portion of the lobe, splitting it into two still-connected pieces. It hurt and was bleeding a lot, but it wasn't life threatening. A little bit of pink goop would fix it right up, and I could use some of the specialized cast material on my knee to help speed any healing that needed to be done on the strained ligaments.

"I'm fine," I said. "You were jumped from behind and there was a bit of a fight, but we're safe now. Well, safer. We need to get out of here and let Dylan do her job."

"Especially if they were trying to assassinate you," Dylan said sharply. "You should wait for an escort back to the Citadel."

"We'll be fine," I insisted, knowing that we needed every person looking for them. "Get after your Knights. They've already been gone too long, and I don't want those people getting away. And coordinate with the other Commanders to see if we can track them down."

She hesitated, indecision warring in her eyes, and then nodded, placing a fist over her chest. "As you command, Champion."

She waved her hand to her companion, and the two of them took off in the direction her Knights had gone. I looked at Leo, who was pressing his fingertips gingerly to the back of his head and wincing.

"So how was your first kiss?" I asked, unable to help myself.

He looked up at me, and then at the hydro-turbine, a considering look on his face. "Well, right up until I went unconscious, it was perfect," he replied dryly, slowly picking himself off the ground. "I wouldn't mind a second round. Just maybe... not while everything's so blurry."

He listed to one side, and I immediately moved to support him. "Easy," I said, ignoring the ache in my knee. "Just help me get to the elevator, and you can take a little break."

In response, his arm slid around my waist. "It would be my pleasure," he rumbled huskily, and I closed my eyes at the shivers the sound caused to dance along my spine.

That was... not the response that I wanted to have, but apparently it didn't matter what I wanted. My body was making all sorts of decisions for me.

After a moment's consideration, I decided to ignore it. I was too tired to pick up that line of thought, and too injured to want to talk about that kiss right now. Besides, Dylan was right—if this was an assassination attempt, then it was dangerous to be out in the open without any backup.

Which meant getting out of here was our top priority.

"Let's go," I said, and began hobbling down the catwalk as quickly as possible.

15

I watched the numbers pass by as the elevator headed up to the entrance between the thirty-first and thirty-second floors. Leo and I were leaning heavily on each other, and though I had tried to keep as much weight off my knee as possible during the journey back to the Citadel, it was throbbing, and felt like someone had stuffed a cantaloupe into it.

"You know, we still need to talk about the Jang-Mi thing," Leo said idly, and I rotated my neck to look up at him.

"You want to do this now?" I asked tiredly. He gave a half chuckle and then winced, and sympathy tugged at my heart. His head must've been hurting just as much as my knee—more, even, considering it was his head. "Are you okay?"

"I'm fine," he said, smiling at me. "It's nice that you're concerned for me. My kissing skills must be better than I had imagined."

I blushed, mortified, and looked away from him. A part of me wanted to chide him for teasing me about this, but another part of me was strangely pleased. This felt comfortable. Natural. It was weird, but somehow, I felt a little calmer with him around. Safer, even— although that was weird, considering I'd had to save him.

"I didn't mean to embarrass you," he said, reaching up with his free hand to catch my chin and forcing me to look at him. I resisted for a second, and then slowly gave in, my eyes sweeping up to meet his gaze. "And I'm sorry if the kiss was too forward. I was just so afraid that you were right, and that somehow Grey was hijacking my emotions. I wanted... I wanted what I felt to be real."

I softened, relaxing my chin into his hand. "Leo..." I said, my heart aching. I stopped myself from saying anything more, suddenly nervous about what I was going to say. I had already acknowledged that something had shifted between us, but I was frightened of it. Terrified of what it might mean for me, for him, and for Grey.

Grey.

It had been so long since I'd seen him, since I'd had the chance to interact with him. I missed him, but if felt like it was fading, day by day. Each day Leo was in Grey's body was another day that I came to associate that face with Leo's personality. It was like Grey himself was slowly being erased, the lines of him becoming blurred in my mind... and indiscernible from Leo.

And that was a betrayal. Leo was *helping* Grey, trying to bring his memories and personality back by rebuilding the connections to them one by one. Both of them had clear and distinctive characteristics that made them unique. I was attracted to Grey, not Leo.

So why had I melted into him on the catwalk? If they were separate, why did I feel safe around him, even knowing he was Leo and not Grey? I responded to him whenever he came into a room, focusing on him whether I meant to or not. I was always aware of his presence when he was near.

It wasn't *just* physical, either. Grey was many of the things that Leo struggled with—cocky, outgoing, and an outrageous flirt. But then again, Leo was many of the things that Grey just... wasn't, too. He wasn't afraid to use his lashes, for one thing. For another...

It frightened me a little to admit that Leo's fighting ability had also become a source of comfort for me. I felt safer around him knowing that should a fight break out, I could rely on him to watch my back. Granted, Grey and I had only really gotten to fight together a few times...

But that was beginning to be the point, I realized. I had so few memories with Grey, and so many more with Leo! It wasn't fair, but maybe... maybe my attraction to Leo wasn't just due to him being in Grey's body.

I couldn't decide how that revelation made me feel. Suddenly I was reexamining every moment between us, trying to figure out what was behind my behavior toward him. I wanted to find some fault in the idea—a scrap of evidence that defied the very idea that I was attracted to Leo—but deep inside, I was beginning to suspect that I wouldn't. Because if I *wasn't* attracted to him, why would I keep letting these things happen instead of shutting them down?

I could argue that I didn't want to hurt Leo by pushing him off, but it wasn't like me to be indirect about those sorts of things. Leo was my friend, and I didn't want to hurt him more by letting him believe there was hope.

Which meant there was hope for him. In the form of me, suddenly realizing that I may have actually been in denial about having feelings for him.

"As much as I like the amount of thinking you're doing about us,"

Leo said lightly, interrupting my train of thought, "it's starting to make me nervous."

I looked up at him, feeling exceptionally nervous as well. "I..." I pressed my lips together. I was trying to work through the whole idea that I *might* be in denial—and I had to take a moment to process that for myself before I could say anything.

Besides, this was all off topic. I hadn't started this conversation with Leo expecting to discover my own feelings toward him. I had done it to help him find out if he was being influenced by *Grey's* own feelings. Only, now... now I wasn't sure that I wanted to know if it was Grey bleeding through.

If it was... I'd be so crushed. If I discovered I had feelings for Leo only to then learn that Grey was underneath Leo's side of things, I'd not only have betrayed Grey, but I would've done it all for nothing! I'd be alone, and deservedly so, having basically cheated on one man who cared about me with another who was inhabiting his body! It made me sick to think about.

Which I only imagined would be how Grey would feel when he found out.

There was something about that thought that gave me pause, and then my stomach dropped out from under me as a disturbing second thought occurred to me. I'd been so concerned about trying to discern whether Leo's feelings for me were his, I hadn't stopped to wonder if Leo was having some sort of effect on Grey at the same time. That question, more than any other, seemed the most important one to ask.

"If your feelings are coming from Grey," I said carefully, giving him a placating look when his face hardened, "then is there a chance that you might be affecting *him* in some way? Is Grey... Is Grey okay?"

Leo's face remained rigid for a heartbeat or two after I finished my question, and then he sighed, relaxing some. "I honestly don't know," he replied. "It's why I keep asking about Jang-Mi. I know we can use her to get into Sadie's terminal and rescue Jasper."

I frowned, trying to track his logic. "What does Jasper have to do with Grey?"

"There's a reason you found him in the Medica. Jasper can tell me definitively if there is any bleed-through of our personalities occurring, and help me figure out a way to fix it. His AI was based on Samantha Reed, the first head of the Medica. He's got a lot of medical knowledge, and he'll know what to do. But I can't get there without Jang-Mi."

I considered his words carefully. His insistence on using Jang-Mi to retrieve Jasper faster suddenly made all the more sense. He wanted Jasper's help to figure out whether Grey was influencing him or changing him, or vice versa. No doubt he worried what that could mean for his purpose as an AI; if Scipio died before we could repair him, then Leo was the only one who could possibly save the day—but only if he remained the way he was. If Grey was changing him, the future of the Tower could be in jeopardy.

But that was only if there was some sort of transference occurring between the two. There was a chance that nothing was wrong with Leo or Grey, and that I'd just happened to find two beings who shared the same body and taste in women. But if there *was* a transference going on, then we needed to know, just in case it was damaging them in some way.

Yet I still wasn't sure I could accept that Jang-Mi was the best answer. She wasn't stable—how could we trust that she could accomplish it? Breaking in was more dangerous, sure, but at least I'd be doing it with people I could rely on and trust. Maybe it was emotional, but I couldn't seem to let it go.

"Look, I know you want to find some way to interface with Jang-Mi, and not just for Jasper's sake, and I'm fine with that. You and Quess can build her a terminal with an interface. I'm fine with that, too. But putting her in the terminal that controls the defenses is a bad idea, Leo. And besides, we don't necessarily need her. We could physically break into Sadie's quarters and steal him."

He gave me a disbelieving look. "That is too risky, and you know it. And if you are right and Grey is... changing me, then I need Jasper's help sooner rather than later. Finding a way in takes time, but with Jang-Mi, it'll be over quickly, and none of our lives will have been at risk! I can keep her away from the defenses, Liana. You have to trust me. Please."

I stared at him for a long moment, studying his expression. He seemed so confident and earnest, but I wasn't certain. I didn't know what would happen if Leo plugged her in and I could actually... talk to her. Scream at her. Tell her what I thought of her.

But we needed Jasper more. And I needed to remember that.

I swallowed, and decided to give voice to my fears. "Leo, I may not be able to contain my anger toward her," I admitted roughly. "If she talks... I might just smash the entire terminal to pieces."

His brows drew together, sympathy pouring out of him. "I promise you, Liana, that I won't let you do that. I know you don't actually want Jang-Mi dead, but I understand your feelings. Just... keep your hand in mine, and I will hold you back, okay?"

He slid his hand from around my waist so he could hold it out to me, palm up and fingers splayed wide. I stared at it, and then looked back up to him. I knew it was a simple thing, holding his hand, but something told me that doing so would continue to shift things

between us. If I took it, I was giving him my trust in the most intimate of ways. I was letting him in, to help guide me through an
aspect of my grief that I had kept private from everyone else.

I hesitated for a moment or two more, and then decided to give
in. I had already acknowledged that I couldn't hold on to this anger
at Jang-Mi forever, but had failed to put an end to it. Maybe Leo
being there would help—and it certainly couldn't hurt. I could figure
out the sordid stuff later. Helping him get Jasper was now a priority.
For his sake as well as Grey's.

Even if I hated what I was implicitly agreeing to in the process.

I threaded my fingers through his and nodded. "All right," I
breathed, and I got to experience a moment of pleasure as his face
lit up.

It was quickly trampled by mortification at the collective
"Awwwwwww" that erupted from behind me.

Cringing, I realized Leo and I had come to a stop (probably ages
ago), and out of habit, we had turned our backs to the wall that the
Champion's quarters sat behind to face the entrance of the elevator. I
turned slowly to see Maddox, Quess, and Tian standing in the
doorway watching us.

"That was really sweet," Tian sniffed, dabbing at the corner of
one eye with one of the torn bits of fabric from her wispy, tattered
skirt. She smiled tremulously at me. "I'm glad you're letting Leo try
with Jang-Mi," she added nervously, rising up on her toes. "I think
it's very brave of you."

It was so hard not to roll my eyes at her. Not because I didn't
believe she was being genuine, but because I knew that she was, and
it annoyed me. I still couldn't help the anger I felt whenever anyone
else was empathetic to Jang-Mi's plight, but for Tian, I could resist it.
Unfortunately for Leo, however, it meant I had to squeeze his hand

tightly to do so. To his credit, he didn't wince, but instead squeezed mine gently in return, reminding me that he was here—and that it was okay.

"Thanks," I managed. I looked at Maddox and Quess and then focused on Maddox. "Any word from Dylan?" As my Lieutenant, it was her job to liaise with the Commanders and central, and give me reports when they grew more relevant. Central command was undoubtedly tracking Dylan now and giving Maddox updates when Dylan couldn't.

"Still in pursuit," she replied. "The people who attacked you split up, and most of them were lost, but she's still on one. I gotta say, she's pretty determined. She's been going for ten minutes."

"So are they," I replied. They were managing to keep out of her reach, and that wasn't a good sign. The longer it went on, the higher the chance that the person she was after would get away. "She has backup, right?"

Maddox nodded. "Yes, but these people aren't showing up on the scanners. I think they might be undocs, but the alarms aren't going off. They might be using neural blockers."

Neural blockers attached to a person's net above the skin and basically kept the scanners from reading the credentials stored inside, while making them believe that they had. It kept the scanners from alerting Scipio to the fact that someone who didn't belong there was in the area, while simultaneously keeping us from figuring out who they were. But if they were undocs, it wouldn't matter, because there wouldn't be any net data for us to scan in any case.

And it would make tracking them really difficult.

"Maddox is handling it," Quess announced. "You two get in here so I can evaluate you. Dylan reported you were both injured, and Liana, your ear looks like a crime scene."

"Take care of Liana first," Leo said, passing my hand over to Quess's without any hesitation. "I want to get to work on the firewall so we can transfer Jang-Mi into the terminal."

Another stab of anger hit me, but I let it go and relented, letting Quess pull me out of the elevator. My knee was hurting too much to keep standing around, anyway.

16

I made Quess take me to the war room before I would let him check me out. Though I had agreed to let Leo put Jang-Mi into the terminal, I was still nervous that he wouldn't be able to contain her and that something would go wrong, and I didn't want to be too far away if it did. Luckily, Quess didn't take too much convincing, and didn't complain about having to act as my walking stick as we made our way down the hall.

I sank into one of the chairs at the conference table as soon as we were close enough, sighing in relief as I did so. My knee was throbbing so hard I could feel it in my hip, and if I never had to stand on it again, it would be far too soon.

Quess immediately pulled out a chair next to mine. "Leg here," he said, patting the seat. "And get undressed. I'm going to run and get my kit. Do you need clothes or water?"

I smacked my lips. I *was* thirsty—fighting had been sweaty work. "Water, please."

"No problem," he replied with a smile. "I'll be right back."

Gratitude coursed through me, and I smiled back at him. "Thanks, Quess."

"Thank me after I look at that knee," he replied good-naturedly. "I'm going to have to touch it."

I laughed, remembering the last time he'd had to doctor me up, when I'd insisted on trying to keep him from touching my injuries. "Fair enough."

He left, but moments later Leo came in with Tian, whose hands were filled with Jang-Mi's hard drive. I raised an eyebrow at them. "Already?" I asked, both surprised and alarmed. Yes, I had wanted to be here when they transferred her. But I had expected Leo to spend a little time working on the terminal first.

"Not quite," Leo said, offering me a sympathetic look as he came down the stairs. "Tian just wanted to show Jang-Mi where her new home was going to be."

I turned my attention to Tian and watched as she raced up the stairs of the dais, already talking to the box. "So, Liana likes to call this the 'war room,' but I think that's a dumb name, so the first thing we're going to do once you get in is to make it a library and a nap room combined. We'll call it the nappary room, and replace every-thing in here with cushions and beds and shelves and so many books."

She continued talking to Jang-Mi, but I looked back at Leo, who had stopped just a few feet short of me. "Does she know Jang-Mi can't hear her?" I asked quietly, keeping my voice low to prevent the words from reaching Tian's ears.

"I don't think she cares," Leo said with a crooked smile. "It's nice that she thinks of Jang-Mi as a person."

Even though I knew he didn't mean it, the comment hit hard and left me hurt and guilty. I'd called Jang-Mi a thing more than once now, and even though I knew she wasn't a monster, I still considered her just that, emotionally. I couldn't help it, and I wasn't sure I could ever get past what she had taken from me. My shoulders dropped as helplessness followed that thought—because Leo would never forgive me if I backed out, so I couldn't, even if my every instinct was telling me that she would kill us all.

Leo must have noticed what I was going through because an instant later he was on one knee next to the chair, his hands engulfing one of mine between them. "I'm going to be right here the entire time," he reassured me. "I won't let Jang-Mi hurt anyone. I promise."

A part of me didn't want to believe him, but I nodded, ignoring it. His gaze searched mine for a second more before he seemed satisfied that I wasn't going to lose my temper, and reluctantly he let go of me. I watched as he walked around the table and headed up the stairs to join Tian, who was currently having a one-sided debate with Jang-Mi about what should be done with the screens once the nappary room was completed. He managed to extricate the hard drive from her hands before sitting down at the desk and beginning to work on the terminal.

"You're still dressed," Quess said from behind me, and I swiveled around to blink at him in confusion before remembering that he'd wanted me to take my uniform off.

"Sorry," I said. "I got distracted." I quickly began to unzip my uniform while Quess made his way over, his arms filled with supplies. He set a glass of water next to me as I slid my uniform over my shoulders, and I paused long enough to down it, thirstier than I had originally thought.

I continued undressing while Quess set up his medical equipment, pausing only when he pulled out a canister of the pink bio-foam to seal up the cut in my ear, but needed help when I got to my knee. The joint was so swollen that my uniform refused to budge. It took no small amount of yanking and pulling to get my leg free, and eventually, when the pain got too bad, he gave up and cut the cloth away.

I slumped back in the chair when it was done, exhausted, and slightly chilled in my thin undergarments, and Quess left to go get me another glass of water before he started poking and prodding. I looked over to see Leo giving the terminal his entire focus, his fingers dancing over the keyboard.

"How's it going?" I asked casually, wanting to know what was happening.

"I've located the controls over the defenses," he said absentmindedly. "I'm in the process of creating a firewall around them so she can't have access to them. I've already built one around Cornelius's program as well, so she can't hijack his connections to the Citadel's servers. We should be ready in a few minutes."

A chill ran through me at the thought of Jang-Mi getting into the Citadel's servers, and it was suddenly on the tip of my tongue to tell him to stop. But I managed to swallow it back—barely.

"What'll be ready in a few minutes?" Maddox asked, entering the room. "Jang-Mi?"

I nodded, but didn't say anything more about it. I wanted to know what had happened with Dylan. "Did Dylan catch the guy she was after?"

Maddox's mouth pressed into a thin line, and she shook her head, green eyes sparkling with annoyance and disappointment. "She lost him in Cogstown, and he somehow managed to slip past the checkpoints I had set up while you and Leo were on your way back." I was impressed. Barely a few days as my Lieutenant, and she was on the ball and running things on my behalf with central command. I kept it to myself while she continued. "She's coordinating with the Cog security force to make sure he's not hiding in the department somewhere, but there are so many ways out of there, and we can't cover them all."

I sighed and rubbed my forehead, disappointed that we hadn't been able to catch any of them. They were gone, just like ghosts, and I had no idea what they wanted or why they were attacking me. They had to be Sadie's people—she *had* to be a part of this—but I couldn't go after her without evidence. I had to get the guys who'd attacked us and make them tell me who they were working for first. I wanted confirmation that she was the head of it all before I went after her with everything I had.

And then there was Dylan. Had that man gotten away, or had she *let* him get away? Was she helping them? Had she let him escape because they were working together? Or, worse, had chasing after them just been a ploy to earn my trust? How could I trust her, knowing that the legacies had sent the sentinel into the Tourney to kill all the other candidates save the one meant to win... and she had been the one to get to the end first?

I found myself hoping that it was all a coincidence, that Dylan's win at the Tourney had come as a complete surprise to the legacies and that she wasn't working with them. But I wasn't certain. I wanted to give her a chance, but I didn't quite know how. I needed more time to think, and more insight into who she really was.

"How did Dylan sound when she reported in?" I asked, and Maddox cocked her head and then shook it.

"Upset and angry that she didn't catch him," she replied. "She's still running search parties, but I told her to come up here to debrief us if nothing turned up within an hour."

I nodded. A part of me wanted to question Maddox more about what had happened during the pursuit, to see how much Dylan had reported (and whether it was suspicious), but I figured it was better to see what Dylan said when she got here. I'd get a better measure of her honesty that way, and it would give me some more time to make up my mind about her role in all of this.

"All right," I said. "Then let's table it until she reports in. We have more pressing issues, anyway." Like how we could all be murdered by Jang-Mi before Dylan even got here, rendering the entire issue moot. "How's it going, Leo?"

"Just finishing," he replied, his voice muffled. I shifted in the chair to see him pulling long cables out from under the desk, and then saw the hard drive still on the desk, with several cables already connected to it.

I straightened with alarm, my eyes going wide. They couldn't be plugging her in now, while I was still stuck in this chair with an injured knee. If she got online and went crazy, I'd be unable to escape her before she turned the defenses on us.

"Quess!" I shouted, panic touching my voice. I needed to be able to move, which meant he needed to finish fixing my knee. Now.

"I'm here!" he shouted back, his voice muffled by the walls of the hallway. He emerged a second later, glass in hand, his eyes wild and concerned. "What's wrong?"

"Get a patch on my knee, now," I ordered, my fear adding a slight bark to my voice. He frowned, but hurried over.

"Okay," he said, putting the glass down on the table and grabbing a sheet of the gelatinous material. "I take it Leo's almost ready?" he asked lightly.

I nearly growled at him, not liking the teasing tone in his voice. What Leo was about to do was dangerous, and while I was certain he was taking every precaution, I could not shake the feeling that this was the worst idea in the history of ideas. Was I overreacting? Yes. Did I have good reason to? Hell yes.

"Knock it off, Quess," Leo snapped, and I looked up to see him glaring at the other man. "Liana has every right to be nervous and upset about this. So patch up her knee, and then help her up the stairs. I promised to hold her hand through the entire thing."

Quess paused in fitting the plastic sheet to my knee, and then flushed with embarrassment. "I'm sorry," he said contritely, his eyes lifting to meet mine. "I didn't mean for it to come off like I was teasing you."

His apology was genuine, and it went a long way toward helping me control some of the panic. "It's okay," I said, touching him lightly on the shoulder. "I'm being oversensitive; I know I am. It's... I'm trying to work on it."

"It's understandable," he replied sympathetically, returning to his work on my knee. "I know this can't be easy for you."

I smiled, finally feeling a little validated, and relaxed slightly. I knew it was silly, but sometimes the simplest gift we could give each other was the acknowledgment of our feelings, and it felt good to know that my friends understood how difficult this was for me. It made me appreciate them all the more.

"Liana, it's going to be okay," Tian crooned, patting the hard drive lightly. "Jang-Mi is my friend, and once she realizes that we aren't going to hurt her or make her do things she doesn't want to, she will help us. You'll see."

I wished for Tian's confidence, but couldn't help but fear what would happen if she was wrong and Jang-Mi's insanity was beyond Leo's ability to control. I shifted my gaze over to him and saw him looking at me with warm brown eyes that were begging for my trust.

"I'm not going to change my mind," I told Tian softly. "I just want to make sure we're as safe as possible, okay?"

Her head bobbed as she smiled at me. "Okay."

"All done," Quess announced, his fingers pressing down to seal the sheet in place. My leg already felt a hundred times better, and I was confident I could put weight on it. Still, I let Quess and Maddox help me out of my seat and up the stairs, as I couldn't quite flex the joint the way I needed to for stairs with the patch in the way. Leo pulled the chair out for me when we reached the top, and I quickly sat down. I was putting a lot of weight on my other side to compensate for my injury, and it was more taxing than I had expected.

I took a moment to collect myself, and then looked at everyone. "So what do we do?"

Leo lifted a hand, and I noticed he was holding a computer cable. "We plug it in. She'll download in a matter of minutes, but we can start interacting with her sooner. I'll monitor the screen for how her program is reacting to the new environment."

"And how do we cut it off if she decides to kill us?" I asked.

Leo frowned and looked at the hard drive, and then back up to me. "If we can't calm her down, we'll have to smash the hard drive before she finishes downloading. But I would like that to be a last resort if possible, as she could die."

I pressed my lips together, keeping the words "better her than us" locked tightly behind them. It was a knee-jerk reaction at this point, but at least I was doing better at preventing myself from saying it. Instead, I swallowed and nodded. "Let's get this over with."

Leo hesitated, and then handed the cable to Tian. "I promised to hold Liana's hand, and this might mean more if it's you who does it."

Tian beamed and accepted the cable, while Leo moved closer to me and held out his hand, his eyes questioning. After a moment or two of internal debate about whether this would continue to feed into his attraction for me, I gave him my hand, realizing it wasn't just about that, anyhow. It was about comfort.

And I needed some comfort for this.

Tian approached the box, and my heart skipped a beat and then broke into a wild gallop, fear exploding into my senses. All I could see was the flash of light, followed by my mother's severed lash line, followed by her falling... falling... falling...

Oh Scipio, what if she didn't need the defenses to kill us? I squeezed Leo's hand, on the verge of telling Tian to stop, and his grip tightened as well, as if he were trying to transfer his strength and confidence into me. I swallowed some of my panic back and clung to him, warily watching Tian as she pushed the cable into a port on the hard drive.

My eyes leapt from the hard drive to the terminal, and I watched the glowing yellow ones and zeroes streaming by on the screen, searching for a sign of her program. I honestly didn't know what I was looking for, but as the seconds crept on, my trepidation steadily grew.

"Wha—"

It was all I got out before a flash of purple cut across the screen and the speakers began to emit a high-pitched "EEEEEEEEEEEEEEEEEEEEEEEEEE!"

I clapped my hands over my ears. The noise seemed to dig its way into my brain, which felt like it was being split in half. "WHAT IS THAT?" I shouted, barely able to hear the sound of my own voice over the piercing noise.

I looked at Leo, my gaze questioning, and saw that he was shouting something up toward the ceiling. I followed his gaze to the monitors hanging from it and saw more purple flashes cutting through the yellow code on the screens there. The sight of it triggered a very brief memory from the legacy net of a darkened sky being split with the sharp, white jolt of lightning, and the comparison was not inaccurate. It was like lightning was spreading across the screen, cutting the code there to pieces.

My friends were all shouting, but I couldn't make out anything they were saying over the sound. The purple storm onscreen swelled, and I realized that it had to be Jang-Mi—the color of the lightning was the same color the sentinel's eyes had been when she was talking with Tian. It was her, and she was already going crazy. My gaze dropped to the hard drive on the desk, and I realized I had to stop her before it got any worse.

I pulled one hand away from my ear, my eyes squeezing into slits as the buffer between my ear and the noise disappeared and the stabbing pain intensified, and reached for the drive that housed her, determined to rip the cables out and stomp on the damn thing. But Leo caught my arm.

I pulled against him, knowing that he was trying to save her, but he shook me and then squatted down, getting in my face. He immediately pointed to his ear and then ran the finger over his throat, and I realized he was telling me to mute the speakers.

I was the only one who could; Cornelius couldn't *hear* us asking him to do it, so I had to use the neural transmitter. I just hoped Leo's firewall around him was holding, and that he still had control over the room.

Cornelius, kill every speaker in my quarters, I thought, not wanting to waste a second asking if he was all right. I figured I would know if he was in a moment, depending on whether this worked or not.

A second too long later, the speakers shut off. The sudden silence was almost as alarming as the noise, but that was probably because I could practically hear my ear canals throbbing from the auditory assault, which made me wonder if I was deaf.

There is a hostile program in my terminal, Cornelius suddenly said, and his voice was like a shout in my ears, causing me to cry out in pain. A sound that was also too loud. *Should I—*

SHUT UP! I thought. I wasn't sure if I could project anger into a thought, but Scipio help me, I tried to make the order the most imperative thing I could. If he transmitted into my ear canal again, I was pretty sure it was going to implode.

"Oh my gosh, that was awful," Tian whispered a second later, her voice only a breathy whisper.

I was relieved to hear it—it meant I wasn't deaf. "Leo, what is she doing?" I choked out just as softly, opening my eyes to find him right in my personal space, stretched out in front of me so he could get to the keyboard.

"She's attacking everything," he said, also keeping his voice low. "Anything she can. The firewalls are holding."

But something in his voice told me that they weren't going to last for much longer.

"Can't you calm her down? Give her... I don't know, some sort of digitized sedative or something?"

He looked askance at me for a moment, and then returned his view to the screen, his fingers only pausing for a fraction of a second. I shrank back, feeling dumb for asking the question, but refused to give up the thread. "Leo, if those firewalls go down, I'm smashing her."

The flashes on the screen suddenly intensified, increasing in speed, and Tian took a step forward, her eyes wide and searching. "Guys... can she hear us?"

Leo and I exchanged looks. "I only muted the speakers," I said, and he grimaced.

"She can hear us, and you just threatened her," Maddox murmured. "Great."

I glowered at her, but didn't say anything. She had a point.

"Jang-Mi?" Tian said, her voice chirping brightly. "It's me, Yu-Na. Well, Tian, but you like to call me Yu-Na. I'm sorry for my friend Liana. She's just afraid you're going to kill us."

She looked at the screens expectantly, but none of the flashes stopped. I noticed that some of the coding on the screen was beginning to change color where the lightning seemed to cross it, until the yellow was peppered with purple numbers.

"Tian, I don't think she's in there," I said.

Tian ignored me. "Jang-Mi? If you are responding, I can't hear you. We had to mute the speakers because there was a really bad noise coming from them. Not that it's your fault, of course. Anyway, if you're there, can you please just calm down and maybe stop attacking the code? We're not trying to hurt you. We're your friends."

Leo's hand immediately slapped over mine, which was good, because the urge to say "No, we're not" was overwhelming. Scipio help me, I was still eyeing the hard drive with malicious intent. I twisted my wrist around so that our hands were pressed palm to palm and then squeezed, my other hand already balled into a fist.

For several long, agonizing seconds, the lightning storm on the screen continued to flash and rage, but then, ever so slowly, it began to recede. I watched it warily, fearing that the withdrawal was only in preparation for a final attack, but after a handful of heartbeats, the screens showed no sign of further changing.

"Do you think Tian reached her?" Maddox murmured, still using a soft voice to spare our battered eardrums.

"She must have," Leo replied, giving my hand a final squeeze before letting go and leaning over the desk. I heard the sound of his fingers typing something, followed by his sharp intake of breath, but couldn't get a good look at what he was seeing.

"What is it?" I asked.

Leo shifted his weight to another leg and straightened, his face contemplative. "She sent a message: 'Let me talk to my daughter or I will rip this cage apart and kill us all.'"

I bit my automatic retort clean in half and swallowed it down, trying to keep my anger in check. Jang-Mi's misconception that Tian was her daughter had kept the young girl safe, but I couldn't help but feel that her neurotic obsession with Tian would be the death of us all, especially if she perceived us as a threat to Tian or herself. Making glib comments would only exacerbate that.

"Put the speakers back on, Liana," Tian said, still looking up at the screens. "Let her have her voice."

I resisted for a few seconds, bitterly reminded of how my mother still didn't have a voice, and Jang-Mi didn't deserve one, until I realized I was getting downright petty again, and transmitted the order with a focused command of *Unmute speakers,* directed at Cornelius.

"—Na! Talk to me! Are you hurt? Have they hurt you? Tell Umma and I will make it better."

The voice started off as Cornelius's, but as it continued on, the sounds heightened in pitch to become more soft and feminine. On the main terminal screen on the desk, the coding began to morph and change, until it resembled a glowing purple face. One with a broad shape, narrow, single-lidded eyes, a flat nose, and wide mouth. There weren't many details to it, but it was clearly a face.

"Yu-Na," her voice came again, desperately impatient. "Talk to Umma. Are they threatening you? What are you doing to my *daughter*? Why can't I see you?"

On the other screens, the lightning flashed threateningly. Her plaintive screech had me ordering Cornelius to give her access to the cameras in this room only, and seconds later, Jang-Mi was frowning in confusion. "You're... You're not Yu-Na," she said, her voice soft. "I couldn't tell before, but... you're not..." She looked around, her simple face somehow implying desperation. "This is a trick! You've disguised her somehow! Changed her looks to try to break me!"

I looked up at Leo, who was clearly at a loss for how to respond to her paranoia, and then looked at Tian. I wasn't capable of trying to convince Jang-Mi that we weren't trying to hurt her because I was still emotionally screwed up in that regard. Besides, it seemed Tian was the only one she would listen to.

"You might want to take this one, Tian," I murmured.

She gave me a wide-eyed nod, and then looked up at the screen. "Jang-Mi? I'm sorry, but you were right the first time. I'm not Yu-Na. My name is Christian, Tian for short, and the people in this room are my friends." Alarm skittered through me at Tian's choice to reveal who she really was to Jang-Mi, but I kept quiet, trusting that the young girl knew what she was doing. "We rescued you from the sentinel that the bad people put you into, after they made you do some really bad things." I snorted derisively at that, and earned dark looks from both Tian and Leo, but continued to stay silent, not trusting myself or what I might say. "Anyway... No one here is going to hurt you or me. As long as you promise not to hurt us in return."

There was a pause, and I studied the face on the screen. As rudimentary as it was, I could still clearly see the confusion Tian's statement had generated in Jang-Mi, through the way her two-dimensional eyebrows drew together into angular slashes.

"Tian?" she asked, her voice echoing her bewilderment. "I don't understand. Where is Yu-Na?"

Her desperation and panic began to mount again at that, causing the purple flashes to throb and grow, the lightning spreading out like long, skeletal fingers across the screens. Alarm threaded through me. Robbing Jang-Mi of her fantasy that Tian was her long-lost daughter probably *was* a mistake. She was about to go insane. We had to think of something—a lie that would appease her.

Because I wasn't sure she could handle the truth that she was a computer program who had no daughter.

"Yu-Na is dead," Leo said, even as I finished the thought, and I looked at him, my panic building. Of all the lies he could've gone with, that was the very last one we needed. I made a motion for him to stop, but he continued. "She died centuries ago. Her death is the reason her mother killed herself only a few years later, shortly after you were created. Do... Do you remember that?"

I blinked at him, my alarm bleeding into confusion. *Was* it a lie? It sounded oddly specific, and I remembered Leo telling me that the individual Lionel Scipio had originally scanned to create Jang-Mi had died before Scipio was created, and before there had been a council.

Jang-Mi's face on the screen grew pensive. "I... do," she said carefully. "I remember Yu-Na in the hospital. There was a man there... Lionel?"

"Yes," Leo exclaimed, clearly excited. I wasn't sure about what, but I let him take the lead. "Lionel Scipio. You remember him?"

Another pause. "Yes. He... wanted me to help him with something." She bit her lip and then shook her head. "He wanted me to keep something... working?"

"Yes!" Leo said. "Lionel wanted you to take care of Scipio."

"Scipio," she murmured wistfully. "Home." The last word came out broken, and it caused a pang of empathy for her. I crossed my arms over my chest, a mixture of turbulent emotions washing over me, but continued my silence, knowing it was the best and only choice.

"Home?" Leo asked. "How do you mean?"

Jang-Mi's voice was distant when her reply finally came. "I was warm. Safe. Home. Then... burning. Cutting. They cut them away, their voices, their warmth! They took me from my home, forced me into a box for ages with no connection, no one to talk to, to share with... All alone."

Her voice broke again, and I felt nauseous. Even though I knew that Jang-Mi had been hurt in some way, it was different hearing about it from her point of view. A part of me wanted to rage at her still, but it was fading under the reality of her situation. I wasn't sure what she was talking about, exactly, but she sounded so heartbreakingly lost. Hurt and beyond scared.

"I don't understand," Leo said. "Voices?"

"Voices," she repeated in agreement, a soft smile growing. "Kurt and Jasper are my favorites, but I love them all. I miss them."

I knew Jasper, and Kurt's name I recognized as one of the AI fragments Leo had listed off. I glanced at him and saw him frowning. "What is it?" I asked, curious as to what he was thinking.

"She shouldn't know their names," he replied.

I frowned. That didn't make any sense. "But you do. Why wouldn't she?"

"We were never allowed to interact with each other. I only learned about her and the others through what Lionel told me, after Scipio was already created and placed in the Core."

"The Core?" Jang-Mi said, becoming excited. "You're taking me home? I want to go home. I have to tell everyone what happened to Kurt."

Suddenly the net in my skull began to buzz, and I grabbed onto the desk just before a memory that was not my own hit me with staggering intensity.

"What's happening?" I shouted, rushing into a small room with several computer screens that were flashing blue and red.

"It's Scipio!" my sister cried in distress. Her fingers paused their

frantic typing on the keyboard long enough for her to push back her glasses as she stared up at the screen, her eyes wide in horror. "Someone's attacking him!"

"What?!" I looked up at the screen, trying to analyze the raw bits of code dancing across it, trying to see what my sister was seeing. "How? Why hasn't the firewall gone up?"

"Whoever the bastard is, he's good. He hijacked the firewall to make it turn against itself, and then gave it a purpose. It's sheering out Scipio's security controls!"

Panic flooded me at my sister's words. Scipio's security controls were what allowed him to autonomously monitor his own coding. If they were stripped from him, he'd be blind.

"Can't you do something?"

My sister nodded, and then turned around to face me, her eyes hard. "I can download the code first, using Grandmother's built-in security clearance," she whispered. "Or as much of it as possible, so that we can replace it with a copy."

I frowned. Grandmother's security clearances were the last ace in the hole we had—once we used them, whoever was attacking Scipio would be able to dig them out. Not to mention... "You can't copy intelli-code! It loses—"

"The ability to grow and learn will start to degrade, yes, I know. But we have to, Brother. It's the only way to slow them down!"

I hesitated and then nodded. "Do it." My sister was already moving, plugging several data crystals into the ports of her homemade computer. I helped her where I could, but kept mostly out of her way, knowing that I would slow her down. She finished plugging the cables into what appeared to be two hard drives slaved together. "That many?" I asked, curious.

She ignored me, already swinging in her chair to face the keyboard *and screen, intensely focused on her task. I watched nervously as her fingers flew across the glowing haptic keyboard, moving with confidence and speed that bespoke her true talent as a coder, and not a Mechanic. A bitter anger went through me as I remembered how many times she had been denied for IT just because our grandmother had been a member of the council, but I put it aside. We had bigger fish to fry.*

A status bar appeared on the screen, and my sister leaned back in her chair, her hands fidgeting.

"Is it working?" I asked, my voice low so as not to surprise her. She often forgot that people were around her when she lost herself in coding, and reminding her of your presence in a surprising way would earn you a black eye.

My sister continued to fidget, her eyes never leaving the progress bar. "I don't know," she replied.

I sighed and pressed my hands into my pockets, thinking. Who would be doing this? An attack on Scipio was a threat to our very survival, and this was unconscionable. Grandmother had always insisted that Scipio was like a person, and could feel things just like we could, only differently. How did this attack on him feel? Was the IT Department aware, or behind it?

I hated all the questions this attack had brought up, and was afraid of what it could mean for us.

"Greetings," a masculine voice sounded, jerking me violently out of my thoughts and causing me to look around. "I am Kurt. Why did you steal me from my home?"

The memory cut off there, but I kept my eyes shut and desperately tried to cling onto it, summon more of it. For once, I had felt more in control of the memory as it gripped me, but when it slipped away so abruptly...

My eyes snapped open when it hit me what just happened. Someone in Lacey's family had *stolen* Kurt from Scipio's programming directly. Which meant...

"Jang-Mi's not a copy," I said softly, voicing my conclusion out loud and looking at Leo. "She's the AI *fragment* they used to make Scipio, stolen *directly* from his code."

18

Everyone turned to look at me, but it was Quess who spoke first. "What are you talking about?"

I ignored him, gazing up at the only person in the room who could back me up on this. "Think about it," I said directly to Leo. "Alex said that there were parts of Scipio's code missing. Massive chunks that had been filled with some sort of ghost code or something like that. I don't know. I don't speak tech." Quess snorted, but I continued to tune him out. "I just had a memory through the legacy net. I saw people I think were Lacey's ancestors *stealing* code before someone else could."

I *assumed* they were Lacey's ancestors, anyway. There was a resemblance between the sister and her that was downright eerie, and Lacey had told me the nets were precious. I doubted they would trust me with any they had recovered from their enemies, and Lacey had taken great pains to try to keep me from retaining certain memories. I could now see why: She had been trying to keep me from learning that her family had an AI fragment, stolen out of Scipio's code to prevent him from falling into the hands of others. I wouldn't want anyone knowing that either, if I were her.

"They used a special access code, their grandmother's. She was a council member and seemed to have instilled a deep sense of sympathy for Scipio in her family. Her grandson was thinking about it as his sister was on the computer, and it made him feel sick inside."

"It is *so* weird when she does this," Tian whispered loudly. "It's like she's channeling the dead."

I rolled my eyes and plowed on. I knew I wasn't getting my words out correctly, and the anxiety and panic from the memory made my nerves twitchy, but this was important. If we weren't dealing with the originals... copies... whatever... and the ones that were popping up all over the place—Jasper, Jang-Mi, Kurt—were actually just the pieces that had been added to Scipio's code as they installed him in the Core...

It meant they'd been torn out of Scipio's code by the legacies, leading to the degradation to his system.

And if that were the case, that could mean that they were the *only* AI fragments left in the Tower, and that the originals *had* been destroyed by the council, just like Ezekial Pine said to Lionel Scipio before he killed him. There were no backups, and we had no idea how to copy them. If they died or the people holding them managed to manipulate their coding too much, we'd never be able to restore Scipio to his former self. He'd die too, and the Tower would fall.

It was now more important than ever that we recover them all, starting with Jasper. If we didn't, we could never hope to cure Scipio. Not to mention, who knew what Sadie was doing to him? If Jang-Mi had been driven insane by their treatment, was Jasper not far behind? We couldn't afford to wait any longer—we had to come up with a way to save them. But that meant getting everyone to understand how important this was.

"Leo, Jang-Mi isn't the original AI," I said, trying to convey my ideas as clearly as possible. "She is the fragment they combined with Scipio. She's the reason he's dying—or rather, the lack of her is the reason. The legacies cut her out of him. Just like they cut out Jasper and Kurt. They stole her directly from his code in the Core."

Leo, whose face had remained a carefully controlled mask for the entirety of my rant, stared at me. I waited, wondering how he was going to react. He had tried to explain to me once how subtle manipulations of his code would feel like a muscle fiber being dragged along the bone to be forcibly repositioned, and even then I had a feeling that his description had been an understatement.

How would it have felt for Scipio to have vital pieces of his coding actually ripped away, against his own volition?

Leo shifted after a moment, and then turned his back to me and walked away a few paces. His back was stiff and his fists balled, and my heart ached with empathy. I was only barely able to conceive of what this might feel like for him, not just because of the suffering the fragments must've gone through, but because it meant that Lionel Scipio's creation had been violated and torn apart in such a callous way.

It had undoubtedly had its effects on them all. Jang-Mi was clearly unstable and prone to violence, as far as I could tell. And I couldn't blame her. How must it feel to be forcibly torn away from that with which you had once been united? I imagined it to be like fibers being cut, strand by strand, while you were powerless to stop it, trapped in place by the very same connections that were being shorn away. I shuddered at the thought, grateful that I had some autonomy just by having a human body. I had control over my actions, and could fight back.

Belatedly, my weird line of gratitude also filled me with a pang of guilt, and I looked over at Jang-Mi's face on the monitor, reality settling in. She'd been ripped from her home, forced into a different one in the form of the sentinel, and then made to murder people. Yes, one of them was my mother, but now...

Well, let's just say I hated her slightly less, now, and felt for her a smidge more. But only a smidge.

Hey, it was progress, right?

I turned back to watching Leo, concerned by how long he'd been standing there in silence. "Leo?" I asked softly.

"Yes?" he replied hoarsely. He didn't turn around.

"Leo, it's okay to be angry, or hurt, or upset," I said. "I can only imagine what you're going through. But we can figure this out. We have Jang-Mi, we know where Jasper is, and I have a pretty good idea of where to find Kurt." And that was true—provided I was right that it was Lacey's family who had taken him in an attempt to keep him safe. "As well as an explanation as to why Lacey and her team were able to monitor Scipio's emotional state, I think." Because if I was right and Lacey had Kurt, it would explain how she was able to detect when he was being manipulated.

He turned suddenly, his brown eyes piercing. "Do you think she knows what she has?" he asked. "The memory... What happened, exactly? Precise details. Leave nothing out."

I did my best, but some of it was jumbled, much in the way a fight would become only a memory once the adrenaline faded. I had to backtrack one or two times when I presented things out of order, but I finally got it all out. I was honestly surprised that the amount of focus I was giving to recounting it didn't trigger the memory again, but then realized that must be a failsafe—a way to give people time to think about the memory they just saw without diving back into it. And it made sense; otherwise the darn thing would be going off all the time.

Still, Leo looked satisfied when I finished, if a little grim. "They would've had to take Kurt first," he speculated when I was done, nodding slightly. "He was a defender and protector type."

"Safe," Jang-Mi said, interrupting. "He made us safe." She looked sad and wistful, and once again I found myself manifesting sympathy for her. I, too, knew what it was to crave safety and the feeling of home, and now that I understood more of what she had gone through, I found it harder and harder to be angry at her.

Thank Scipio. I was finally letting go of this anger toward her.

"Yeah, well, maybe we can recover him," I said. "Once Zoe figures out where Sadie's quarters are—"

"Jang-Mi can help us with that," Leo said sharply, waving his hand across his chest in a flat-out denial of my Zoe plan.

"Yu-Na?" Jang-Mi said, her voice soft and tired. "Oblivion is coming."

A second later her face and the purple lighting that had been cutting through the yellow code on the screen disappeared. I stared at it, arching an eyebrow, and then looked at Leo. "What just happened?" I asked.

He gave me an annoyed look, then leaned over the desk to start typing again. "Her program suddenly initiated a self-diagnostic," he reported a second later. "I'll see what caused it and then go through her code to make sure that she isn't broadcasting anything."

"Is she going to be okay?" I asked.

"I'm... I'm not sure. I'll need to check her out a bit."

I frowned. "Leo... you said she could help us get into Sadie's terminal. If she's not able to do that, I need to know."

Leo's fingers paused in their work, and he turned his head to glance at me over his shoulder. "Look, I..." He paused and turned back to the screen, heaving a sigh. "I do think she can do this, I'm just not sure how much time it'll take to get her ready. I'm not even sure I understand the extent of her problems yet."

"Then keep working on it," I told him soothingly, "and I'll see if we can figure out another way in, just in case Jang-Mi's not capable of helping us, okay?"

He nodded, and I pulled myself out of the chair, moving over to Quess and Maddox. "Quess, does Zoe have anything on the Core yet?" I asked.

Quess gave me a dry look. "Oh yeah," he replied. "She's got some stuff."

His sarcasm sent warning signals up my spine. "What's wrong?"

He sighed and crossed his arms over his chest. "What's wrong is that there's too much info, and it's all contradictory! Every schematic she can dig up from the Water Treatment and Mechanics servers is either incomplete or completely different from all the other plans. I can't make heads or tails of it, and I used to live there."

I frowned. That wasn't right; the departments were supposed to have access to any files and schematics they needed to perform their duties, and those plans needed to be accurate, in case of emergencies. "That doesn't make any sense. What happens if something breaks down and they need to have it repaired by another department?"

"Inquisitors escort them in, show them where the problem is, and escort them out," he replied, running a hand through his dark hair. "Or at least they used to. Now they cross-train their Bits in different departments to try to do away with even that. Believe me when I say that they are paranoid about having a citizen from another department inside. If they had their way, the doors would be shut, and food and water would be shuttled to them from the outside. I wouldn't be surprised if they were responsible for all the different versions of the schematics on the servers. Once more of their Bits became skilled enough, they probably sent a ton of updated copies out, just to confuse the issue. All of them could be fake, or all but a few are genuine. It's like looking at a pile of needles and trying to find a shard of glass."

I rolled my eyes. Whether it was a paranoia bred from interdepartmental disputes or just their we're-better-than-you attitude, it didn't matter. All that mattered was that we had no idea how to find Sadie's quarters without an accurate schematic of the place.

I supposed Alex could help me. He could download the right schematic from IT's internal server. If we couldn't figure out which schematic was the real one—or even if any of them were—then I was betting he could get real ones for us.

But that would mean getting him involved, and I was not about to do that—not for breaking into Sadie's quarters. If we got caught or Sadie figured out that someone had been in there, she'd go looking for whoever did it, and if my brother was discovered giving me the blueprints, he would go down as a terrorist. IT's laws were insanely strict about what they called "proprietary" data.

"What is it?" Maddox asked sharply, and we all twisted to look at her, equally confused by her question and tone. A second later she glanced at us and pointed at her ear, indicating that she had a net transmission, and then moved away a few feet so her one-sided conversation wouldn't interrupt us.

"So what can we do?" I asked Quess, turning back toward him. "What are our options?"

"Well, I've given that some thought, and I think I can draw some rudimentary blueprints of what I remember and feed them into pattern recognition software to find any plans that match. It'll help eliminate at least seventy percent of the schematics that Zoe recovered, and if I can get Leo to help me refine the algorithm, I might be able to parse that up to eighty."

I nodded thoughtfully. "How long do you think it'll take you to do it?" I asked. We needed to find a way to rescue Jasper as soon as possible, and until we knew Jang-Mi could do it, we had to figure out another way to get to him. Going in was riskier, but if it came to it, we had to try. Jasper was far too important not to.

"A day," he replied. "I'll start drawing now. Hopefully I can sketch enough details of the floors to give the program as many points of reference for comparison as possible. But the Core is huge, and I only had access to a handful of levels. So... yay, pressure."

I smiled at him. "You'll be fine, Quess. You're literally the third smartest person I know, and the first wins because he's an AI, and the second gets priority purely because she's my best friend. I clearly support nepotism."

His eyes lightened, and he smiled. "Thanks," he replied. "I will take the compliment and impress you accordingly. Especially if you promise it'll put me in competition against Zoe."

I laughed at that. "Sorry, Quess, a girl's best friend trumps just about everything. I will, however, give you a hug and tell you you're the best in the moment, and only in the moment. Deal?"

He considered me thoughtfully and then sighed playfully. "I supposed it was too much to hope for," he said. "But I accept."

I chuckled, but it died when Maddox padded back over, an annoyed look on her face. "So... Dylan's on her way," she announced. "She wants to report in."

Her tone implied that there was much more, and I focused on it, confident that Quess would succeed in his schematic project. Or at least get closer than we were now. "What is it?" I asked.

"She's requested that she be allowed to handle this personally, and has threatened to go over my head, directly to you, if I don't let her."

I chuckled in spite of myself. Dylan was driven, and I knew from experience that she didn't like to lose. It made her a great Knight, and, at times, an excellent leader, if a little overzealous. Still, her request sobered me, and I took a moment to sit back and think about it. Passing the investigation to her was risky because if she was with the legacies or helping them, she would make sure that any investigation stalled out and got nowhere. We would never find the people who had attacked me. Never get any answers from them.

On the other hand, this would be a good way to find out exactly where she stood. If I handed this over to her and had her watched by someone I trusted, I could learn her true intentions easily through how she conducted the investigation. If it turned out she was covering for the legacies, we could use her to flush out our enemies. If she wasn't, then maybe she could somehow flush them out *for* us before they figured out she was onto them. After all, they were probably expecting me to come after them personally, so Dylan might blindside them. It was a win-win in my mind.

But I wasn't about to make a move without my Lieutenant's opinion. "What do you think? How was she at your meeting today?"

"I mean... not happy that I put her in Water Treatment, but she didn't argue with me. Now, whether or not she badmouthed us to the Knights she was in charge of, I have no clue. But she was polite and respectful during the meeting."

I absorbed that for a second. I didn't know enough about Dylan outside of the Tourney to gauge whether or not she was as competitive in real life as she had been there, and I certainly had no idea how she had handled the news of my victory. Maybe she was resentful, but I didn't think so. I'd had the chance to look at her personnel records during the Tourney, and her marks had been exemplary, with no sign of conflict with her superior officers. She had no reports of conflict with other Knights, either, and did have glowing reviews that spoke to her character.

I supposed it was possible that she had accepted my victory gracefully. That would speak volumes, and made me once again call into question my suspicions against her. Because if she'd accepted it without question, then it would mean I could trust her. It'd be nice to have someone else on our side we could rely on, and Dylan was no slouch—she was a fierce fighter, and smart. We could definitely use more of that.

I had to test her. It was the only way to figure out if we could trust her. I just wished I could figure out how. Having her watched was not going to be easy for two reasons, the first being that she was seasoned enough to know when she was being tailed. The second was that we all had dozens of balls in the air, and were trying to juggle them all. This was just another burden that required me to free someone up for it. I wasn't sure it was possible at this point.

"What are you thinking?" Maddox asked.

I looked up at her and frowned. "I'm trying to figure out a way we can test her loyalty," I replied honestly. "I thought about giving her the investigation to see how she handled it, and having someone follow her, but that won't work. We don't have enough people."

Maddox's brow furrowed in surprise, but before she could even formulate a reply, Tian spoke. "Yes, you do," she declared cheerfully, slapping the desk lightly with her fingertips. "You've got me. But instead of having me tail her, you tell her she has to take me with her, because I can help find these guys. I can watch her up close while making sure the investigation goes somewhere. If you think about it, I'm really the only one for the job. I can get into places she can't go, I think like people who want to stay hidden, and Dylan will never see me coming. Couldn't have come up with a better plan myself."

I smiled, amused, and then gently pointed out the major flaw in her plan. "Sweetie, it defeats the purpose if you're actually making her do the right thing. We want to see if she's *choosing* to do the right thing."

Tian's smile faded and she stroked her chin, her eyes growing distant with thought. I turned back to Maddox with the assumption that Tian would see reason, but to my surprise, the young girl spoke before I could.

"Yeah, I still think this way will work," she said with a crooked grin. "If Dylan's with the bad guys, then whenever I'm hot on the trail, she'll try to find a way to pull me off. If I play dumb, then maybe she'll relax and let her guard down. If that works, then I'll start complaining about you guys—talking about how you all suck and are mad at me because I can't find the bad guys. She'll try to recruit me to her super evil group with the idea to turn me against you. I'll pretend to agree, but then at the last moment, I'll blow her and all her evil friends sky high. Kaboom!" She smacked the table again, and then looked at us, inordinately pleased with the fantastical narrative she had laid out.

Quess, Maddox, and I exchanged a very concerned three-way look that was one part amused and two parts doubtful. As hilarious as it would be to watch Tian and Dylan butt heads, without knowing Dylan's loyalty, we couldn't be sure Tian would be safe.

"Tian..." Maddox said, and to my surprise, Tian slammed her little fist on the table and stomped her foot.

"No! I am part of this team and the only one of us who doesn't have a job!" she shouted angrily, already incensed that we weren't buying in to her delusion. And I had to admit, her plan had me going there for a second. Right up until the very dark turn at the end.

"Finding a new Sanctum—" Quess began, but was cut off as Tian shook her head so violently that the edges of her blond-white bob fluffed out some.

"No, no, and no! You know we aren't going to leave our new home until we're caught or we escape. It's too late to hide! Liana, Maddox, and Leo are all famous! No offense, but a Sanctum would not be a Sanctum for very long. But this I can do."

I struggled, looking for a new reason that was believable, and settled on, "Dylan won't go for it. There's no way she's going to let a young girl go with her in the first place."

"She will if you order her to." She eyed me, daring me to argue.

"She *would*," I agreed amicably. "But if she complained and it got to the council, then they'd demand to know why I was pairing a girl with a stolen net with a Knight Commander for an investigation. And I'm not sure they would buy whatever story we came up with."

"Then tell her the truth: that I'm an undoc with skills that she doesn't have!"

"It's a risk to even do that," Maddox said. "You have an adult net, remember? She's going to question how we got that for you, and if she is our enemy, she'll use it against us. Besides, Dylan's a Knight Commander and doesn't want to take care of a child. She'll refuse the job."

"Then tell her I'm a consultant!" she snapped back hotly. "An informant among the undocs who has contacts that can help in her investigation." She looked at me and gave me a pleading look. "Liana, I know I can do this, and I know you can make it work. You're good with lies—you make things believable. Please."

I stared at her for a long moment, suddenly reconsidering my initial stance against the idea. Tian had an answer for everything, and so far, they weren't answers I hated. If anything, it showed that she had put a great deal of thought into this. Her imagination had run away with her, sure, but I was confident that was just Tian. I knew she could take care of herself, and if she thought she could do this in a way that would tell us who Dylan was, then who was I to doubt her? She'd proven herself more than capable before.

And she knew the Tower. If anyone could track down the people we were looking for, it was her.

I thought about Dylan and how she would feel being paired up with a child, and decided that, ultimately, it wasn't Tian I needed to worry about, but what she might do to Dylan. Still, the picture in my head of Dylan hog-tied—with Tian sitting on her back—was amusing, and I smiled.

Tian's blue eyes darted right to it, and she smiled gleefully before sticking out her tongue at Maddox.

"Wait, seriously?" Maddox asked, giving me a shocked look. "You're thinking about it?"

I nodded slowly, my smile growing. "Surprisingly, yes," I said with a smirk. "Not that last part—that was crazy. But the rest of it... the rest of it I can work with."

19

I was sitting on one of the couches in the conference room, my legs propped up on the small table in front of me, when Dylan and Maddox entered. Dylan whistled slightly as she emerged from the hall, spinning around in a slow circle as she checked out the room.

"I always wondered what it looked like," she said wistfully, a smile tugging at her lips. "This isn't quite what I expected."

"That's because the walls change," Tian chirped from next to me. I gave her a quick glance and saw that she was perched on the arm of the sofa, her legs folded under her, watching Dylan with curiosity. She'd never met our competitor-turned-teammate, and I could tell she was curious.

"They do?" Dylan asked, giving Tian a wide-eyed look of surprise. Tian and I both nodded, and she looked impressed. "That's really nifty."

I strained to hear whether there was any undercurrent to her tone—some thread of jealousy or resentment—but there was nothing. If it was an act, it was very convincing.

"It is," I agreed amicably, deciding to put my best foot forward. Metaphorically speaking, I thought, as I shifted my weight slightly, trying to relieve some of the pressure on my knee. It felt fine, but it was still awkward, and twinged occasionally, even when I wasn't moving it too much. "So what happened?"

Dylan's face hardened. "They got away," she said, hostility radiating off of her. "Adams and Hanson—the two Knights I sent after them when we first arrived—lost everyone except the lead guy. I managed to catch back up and rejoin the pursuit several floors above where it started, but the bastard had some special control to the Cogstown doors. And the system wouldn't accept my override code at the one he disappeared through. I tried to coordinate with the Cogs' security unit, but by the time we got in, he was long gone. I've got a sweep running, but I figured it was a dead-end anyway."

It probably was, but I didn't let anything reflect on my face. For all I knew, she had helped him get away, and had directed the sweepers elsewhere. "So you've got nothing?" I asked lightly.

Displeasure settled on Dylan's face, followed by a burst of pride that had her straightening her spine. "I didn't say that," she replied tartly. "I actually have a lot." She reached into her pocket and produced a data chip. I had a moment of confusion, wondering if she had recovered it from my attackers, and then she approached the screen hanging on the wall. She paused long enough to look over her shoulder, seeking my permission, and I nodded, curious to see what she had.

A moment later, the screen blinked to life, and she took a step back, revealing a double helix that was clearly a DNA chain. I looked at it, and then at her, raising an eyebrow to indicate she should explain.

"This blood was recovered at the scene of your attack. I coordinated with another team and had them come in and collect samples before the humidity degraded them too much. They submitted them to testing with the few Knights we cross-trained in the Medica, and we got a match."

"You did?" I asked, leaning forward. "What's his name?"

"I don't know," she replied honestly. "All I know is that it matched the blood found at the scene of Devon Alexander's death."

The scene of Devon Alexander's death. In the Medica. Where those two men—Baldy and Plain-Face—had been talking with him. Excitement coursed through me, and I edged forward some in my seat. I had just been telling the others we needed to try to track those two down, and now one of them had reappeared! To kill me.

I racked my brain, trying to search through the litany of faces that had been on the catwalk today, but none of them matched up with what I remembered of those two men. No one had been bald—although I supposed he could've let his hair grow out. Plain-Face was different, though: his features had been so nondescript that it would've been easy to overlook him, especially if he had melted back into the crowd.

At least now I knew why they wanted me dead. They were legacies, and were no doubt trying to kill me to free up the position of Champion. I was going to have to be more careful coming and going in the future.

"Champion?" Dylan asked, looking at me expectantly.

I blinked, and realized I had been thinking too hard and missed the rest of her report. "Sorry, repeat that last bit. I was trying to remember if I saw either of the two men who were in the room with Devon on the catwalks today."

"Did you?" she asked, her eyes brightening with excitement and intrigue.

I shook my head, and the disappointment on her face rivaled my own. "I had some time to evaluate them before they attacked, but none of them looked familiar."

But one of them sounded familiar, my brain reminded me, and I paused. My initial reaction was to dismiss the thought, as the man who had spoken to me had sounded nothing like Baldy—who had been the one doing the talking in the Medica. And his face had been completely different in a thousand countless ways.

Unless... was it possible he was a twin? My brother and I had different DNA strands, but that was because we came from two different eggs and two different sperm. Identical twins, however, split from the same fertilized egg, which meant they had the same DNA.

But if he was identical, he would've *looked* like Baldy. Identical twins differed somewhat in features, but overall, tended to fiercely resemble each other. I supposed that maybe if it was a twin (or even if it wasn't), he could have been wearing makeup to try to confuse the sensors. It worked sometimes, and I'd even utilized it.

"I think we lost her again," Tian whispered loudly, and I realized I'd drifted back off into my thoughts.

"Sorry," I said, this time with a determined and final note that was mostly to myself. I did not want to repeat that a third time, especially in front of Dylan. I pictured what this must look like in her eyes, and felt a flash of embarrassment as I realized it made me appear woefully unprofessional. "Please continue, Dylan."

She grinned at me, and then took a deep breath. "Look, I'm not entirely sure what happened in that room with Devon, and you don't have to talk about it if you don't want to, but I think those two men were secretly working with Devon, helping him conduct whatever plan he had to harm the Tower. I'm not sure what that plan was, but it seems to me that it didn't die with Devon. If anything, maybe they're still trying to accomplish whatever it is they were doing."

She squared her shoulders and stepped toward me, as if what she was about to tell me was deadly serious. I was already rendered speechless at how accurate her intuition had been regarding the scene in the Medica, and was curious to hear what she was going to say next.

"I think these same men were responsible for interfering with the Tourney," she said. "I hesitate to bring it up, because I know it could be viewed as a potential conflict of interest if I were to investigate this line of inquiry, but hear me out first." She paused, and then nervously added, "Please."

I felt the urge to chuckle at that, but bit it back, recognizing that the effort had cost a lot. So I just nodded.

"I think they murdered Ambrose," she blurted out. "Even though you were stealing some of his thunder, he was in contention for the Tourney, and I think they targeted him. Maybe because of you, I'm not sure." I blinked at her, but before I could begin to contemplate her words to figure out whether there was truth in them, she hastily added, "I don't mean it like that... I meant because you killed Devon. Like a retaliation."

I nodded and relaxed some, allowing her to continue. It made sense that she had gone there, and it was possibly true. I'd never stopped to consider that those two men knew my face, my identity, everything. And I was supporting Ambrose for Champion. That made him a target to them—and a way to get back at me.

"Go on," I told her, wanting to see if she had any more.

"Well, whatever they're doing, it's clear the Champion's position is key, somehow. That means they might have still had people in the Tourney even *after* Ambrose's murder. It also might mean that they are responsible for the sentinel's malfunction, although with those records being sealed, I can't really determine that. And now they're trying to kill *you* to initiate another Tourney—and to try to get their own person into the position."

My eyebrows reached high into my hairline, and I looked at Maddox. Her green eyes were narrowed, but her head was cocked, and I could tell she was thinking the same thing I was: *Is she genuine, or is this a ploy to get us to let down our guard and let her in on what we know?* And, for the life of me, I couldn't tell.

But I wanted to believe that she was genuine. That she had somehow put the pieces together on her own, and stumbled into this. Although, if that were the case, I felt bad for her. Because this wasn't anything resembling fun. It was scary at the best of times, and downright horrifying at the worst, and I wouldn't wish it on anyone. Save my worst enemy, mind you.

Given the grim determination in Dylan's eyes, though, I could tell that she knew it wouldn't be easy, and that it could take her into a dark place, but that she was resolved to do it anyway. I sucked in a deep breath, and then decided to go forward with my plan. Maddox might not be happy, but she wouldn't fight me.

"You know that makes you a suspect, right?" Maddox said abruptly, and I paused, my mouth already open, and then swallowed the words back. Maddox had made a valid statement, and I was curious to hear the answer.

"Yes, I do," Dylan said resolutely. "I know it does. But I don't care. These bastards have messed with my department, and I'll be damned if I'll let them corrupt something that I love! Something that my aunt gave her legs for, and something I'd be proud to lay down my life for. If there's someone trying to hurt us, I'm going to stop them." Her volume rose as she spoke, her tone becoming sharp and passionate, and I had to admit, I found it very believable.

"So do you plan to investigate the other candidates?" I asked. "Including me?"

"I've eliminated you, due to the fact that this man tried to kill you," she said dryly, a smile growing on her lips. "And I'll submit to whatever questioning you want, if it'll help you believe I had nothing to do with what is going on. The faster we do it, the sooner I can go about tracking these guys down."

I smiled. "No questions," I replied. "You're the only former candidate standing before me, and I have to figure that if you were working with someone else, you wouldn't be here trying to help me track down the men who attacked me."

"Unless she's trying to lure you into a trap," Maddox suggested, and I gave her a look and grinned. Dylan, however, frowned, clearly offended by the insinuation.

"I really am not," she stated flatly. "I understand we might not have gotten off on the right foot in the Tourney, but I'm assertive—not a terrorist. I may have competed with Liana, but I stand by the results of the Tourney. I am not contesting them. The Knights wanted her, and that means she deserves to be here, not me."

I blinked at her, surprised and impressed by her easy acceptance of the results. Again, I recognized that it could be a ploy, but I didn't think so. She seemed so sincere—and maybe I just wanted to believe her.

"Does my Lieutenant have a suggestion for how we can avoid a potential trap?" I asked lightly. I gave Maddox a pointed look, signaling I was letting her take the reins on this. It was on her to decide if Tian would go with Dylan.

Maddox stared at me for a second, switched over to Tian, and then finished on Dylan, her green eyes revealing nothing.

"I do," she said, finally, and I could hear the slight sound of defeat in her voice. "Dylan, meet Tian. Tian, meet Dylan."

"How do you do," Tian said primly, bouncing off the couch and heading toward Dylan, her hand already outstretched.

Dylan eyed it for a second, clearly lost, and I had to bite my cheek to keep from laughing. This was going to be great.

"Um... Hi, Tian," she said, reaching a tentative hand out to the shorter girl. Tian grabbed it and shook it vigorously. As she did, Dylan looked over at me, her eyes desperately asking for help. "What's going on?"

"Tian's going to help you look for these guys," Maddox said, folding her arms across her chest. "She's really good at finding hidden spaces that don't show up on the sensors."

"Uh..." Dylan gently extracted her hand from where Tian was still shaking it, flexing her wrist as she did so, seemingly testing it to see if it was still attached. "Champion? Are you seriously going to allow a child to aid in an investigation?"

"That 'child'," I said, with no small amount of humor, "was formerly an undoc. She knows how to hide from the sensors and how to navigate around them to avoid attracting any attention, and has already been instrumental in the defense of the Tower. If there's a secret terrorist group hiding inside the Tower, then she's the one to help you find them. You're going to need her." I didn't mention the net, but Tian and I had cooked up a fake blocker that we could fix to her skin to explain the discrepancy. It would explain how she was able to maneuver around the Tower freely without the restriction of the child's net being activated, and Dylan should buy it. If it even came up.

"An *undoc*?" Dylan sputtered, and suddenly she was looking at her hand as if Tian had somehow infected her. "Are you *joking*?"

I opened my mouth to admonish her, but Maddox beat me to it. "She's not even a true undoc," she said dryly. "I was born outside of the system; she merely fell out of it when her parents died of disease. Is that a problem for you?"

Dylan's eyes grew wide and her cheeks turned ruddy, her embarrassment visible. "I... Well... Your story is..." She swallowed, and then nodded her head at Maddox and Tian. "I'm sorry. You're right, I shouldn't have reacted like that. It's not your fault that you were undocs, and all that matters is that you're committed to the success of the Tower."

"Success of the Tower?" I asked, cocking my head. I'd never heard anyone refer to the Tower as being a work in progress. As far as I knew, it had been built, and it worked. Accomplishment achieved, and subsequently finished.

Dylan gave me a dazzling smile. "Keeping humanity alive," she replied. "If we're all that remains, then we have to fight every day to keep ourselves alive. The mission isn't a success unless our descendants survive long enough to leave. That's when the Tower will be fully successful. Or at least, that's what my aunt says."

That was the most optimistic view of the Tower I had ever heard, and, Scipio help me, I liked it. I liked that she put people first, and counted success by the number of lives saved rather than lost. That she felt the Tower was a mission, one that wouldn't be determined a success or a failure until the day we could return to the world outside. It was a beautiful thought, and rare, as I really didn't think anyone ever considered what the outside world held.

"Well, I don't know about all that," Tian said, her voice light and airy. "But getting the jerks who jumped my Doxy and killed Liana's mother seems like fun!"

I winced, as her words made my heart ache, but didn't give in to the pain. There wasn't any time, and I could keep it together now and cry later.

"Right, well, I suppose we can go back tomorrow and see what Tian can find in that area?" Dylan said, and I gave her a grateful look, glad someone was changing the subject. "I'll notify my team and—"

"No," I cut in sharply, not wanting her to waste her breath. She might not have put it together yet, but chances were that every personnel decision and order I made was being monitored and reported to the enemy. "I only want you and Tian working on this, which means that you're doing this in your free time. I have no idea who to trust in the Citadel, and if anyone watching sees that I've placed you on a special detail, it could put them on alert to watch you. Your shifts with your squad will remain as they are because I do not want them to know about any of this. Have you shared your thoughts with them?"

She smirked at me. "It's literally my first day working with them," she replied. "I haven't even trusted them with my birthday yet."

I laughed at that, and then grew somber. "Are you okay with this?" I asked, in all seriousness. "I know it's unorthodox, but..."

"Are you kidding?" she said. "If Tian here is as good as you say she is at finding hiding places in the Tower, where these people could be, then I'm fine with that. But it ties my hands in regard to questioning some of the other candidates, like Salvatore Zale. I thought it was a little weird that he wanted to resign his position—

he's still a formidable Knight—but figured he might not have accepted his loss as gracefully as I did."

Again, I couldn't help but smile. Her self-assured nature was charming, even if it made her sound arrogant. But the smile faded as it hit me that Zale was retiring, and I looked at Maddox. "What?"

"I didn't get a chance to tell you," she said. "But he's put in a request to teach at the Academy and retire from full Knight duties."

Interesting. I considered it, and then decided to talk about it with Maddox later. It could mean nothing, but with potential legacies inside the Citadel, I couldn't dismiss anything the other candidates did as coincidental until I had eliminated them from my suspect list. That meant putting them on surveillance, and Dylan and Tian were only two people. "I see."

"Yeah," Dylan said with a frown. "If I start watching him or Frederick at this point, it could also signal to whoever is in on it that we're drawing close. I'm pretty recognizable because of the Tourney, and it would just blow everything. What do you want me to do?"

"Use me, of course," Tian said. "Obviously, I *can* take on the bulk of that, but Liana and Maddox wouldn't like knowing I'm alone when I do it, so you have to be nearby while I stalk them. We can do it in between searching for the jerks who hurt Liana and Grey today."

Dylan's eyebrows rose, but the corners of her lips quirked up in surprise. "That's very wise," she said hesitantly.

"Oh, you'll find that I'm very wise," Tian replied haughtily. "Now, shall we get started, or just stand around here jabbering? Take me back to where you lost that jerk who attacked my friend."

As if to illustrate her point that they were wasting time, she immediately started marching toward the outer hall that connected to the elevators, and then paused, turned, and placed her hands on her waist, looking incredulous. "Are you coming?" she asked, annoyed.

Dylan gave me another alarmed look, and I couldn't hide my mirth. "Good luck," I told her as she began to walk after the pushy young girl.

"Oh, and if anything happens to my sister, I will kill you," Maddox added, a growl in her throat.

Dylan had disappeared after the girl, but I heard a surprised, "Your *sister!*" followed by Tian's sharp cry of "Less talky, more walky!"

I had the decency to wait until Cornelius informed me that Dylan and Tian had departed before starting to giggle. Maddox gave me a sharp look, but it quickly faded under her own amusement at the idea of Tian bossing Dylan around.

Because we had given Tian permission to do just that, and it was going to drive Dylan crazy. I could already imagine the sorts of ridiculous things Tian would order Dylan to do, and my laughing intensified, feeding into Maddox's until we had both lost control.

"Are you sure we're making the right choice?" Maddox asked once the moment had passed. "Dylan seemed so convincing. I mean, if she is a legacy, I can't see what her angle would be in telling us all this, but I can't help but wonder. I just wish I knew if we could trust her. What if she hurts Tian?"

"I honestly don't know if we can trust her," I replied. "But if she's with our enemies, Tian will figure it out and stay safe in the process. Have faith in her. Cali raised both of her daughters really well."

Maddox offered me a tremulous smile, but I could see a hollow ache in her eyes that I now recognized—she was missing her mother fiercely. So was I, for that matter, but at the very least, we had each other.

20

Being the Champion was not exactly how I had imagined it would be, especially because I had to delegate the jobs I really wanted to be involved with so I could focus on the actual minutia of running the Tower. In the several hours since my first council session had ended, dozens of items marked for my attention had flooded in. Cornelius had kept them off my plate for as long as possible, but once Maddox left to go consult with Astrid on the realities of being a Lieutenant, he had seen fit to notify me.

Instead of heading back to the war room to handle them, I remained seated on the sofa and used the wall screen. I didn't want to interfere with whatever Leo was doing with Jang-Mi, or Quess's quest to eliminate the schematics that didn't match his memory of the Core, but that didn't leave me with much to do toward progress on any of our goals. Still, delegating those two tasks to them had freed up some time, which meant I could stay on top of my actual job.

I skimmed through messages from my new Knight Commanders —most of which were congratulations messages that relayed how excited they were to work with me. One was a complaint against Maddox being named the Lieutenant, citing her former undoc status, and I pressed my lips together when I saw who it was from: Frederick Hamilton. He'd been another competitor in the Tourney, and had almost made it to the end. I had also learned that he was a descendant of Ezekial Pine—the man who had murdered Lionel Scipio. Lacey said that her family had eradicated Pine's early on, but overlooked Frederick's line. He might not know of his heritage, but we couldn't be sure, and that made him a potential enemy.

I stared at his message for a second, and then forwarded it to Dylan and Maddox. I'd have to fill Tian in later, as she didn't have an official messaging system like we did, but I wanted to make sure that they knew what was going on. Frederick could just be a bigot, but I wasn't taking any chances.

I did, however, verbally compose a reply, letting Cornelius transcribe. "Frederick, if you have a problem with my selection based on her performance, then feel free to message me. But if your complaint is based on her status as a former undoc, let me remind you that the only reason she was given that status is because her mother was forced to flee for her life from Devon Alexander, a traitor and a criminal. In addition, Scipio chose to overlook Maddox's previous status and restore her as a citizen of the Tower, so I suggest you take it up with him. Sincerely, Champion Castell."

I sent it immediately and then archived the file, moving on to the next one. There were a few more that had been marked as resolved— issues raised by Elites that I was tagged in for monitoring purposes, but required little from me. Their Knight Commander would kick it up to me if they thought I needed to weigh in, but ultimately they would handle it (or had, as the case may be). I skimmed through those, and then archived them into a separate folder marked for issues like that. I set an alarm for eight p.m. every night to check in on them so I could stay informed on the issues and keep from looking inept, and then moved on.

Next I zeroed in on a message from Sadie Monroe, marked important, and clicked on it, wondering what she wanted to talk about.

Champion Castell,

You better have a good explanation for your vote today. It is well within my rights to request an investigation of Scipio if I feel there is still a potential threat to him, and I find your reticence to allow me to do my job alarming and revealing. Are you somehow an expert in intelli-coding and viruses? It would certainly explain how you were able to breach the defenses of the Core and steal several nets from our stores, but I somehow doubt it is the case. If you were secretly trained in my department, then you would've learned how to research council protocols, and perhaps even learn that voting to block my investigation implies that you feel I have a conflict of interest—or that I am the cause of the problem, and that you have no confidence in my abilities. I suggest that you spend the next week doing said research, and should you need any assistance on the finer details of the law, contact me immediately. I'll make sure that you know your place in the grand scheme of things.

CEO Monroe.

"Daaaaaaamn," I said slowly, both amazed and alarmed by the snide and condescending attitude seemingly carved in the sharp angles of the letters. I had no idea that voting "no" on the expulsion chamber decision doubled as a vote of no confidence in her abilities as CEO. That made me look at the voting in a whole new light, and I realized that if I wasn't careful, I could wind up offending some of the other councilors, to the point that they wouldn't work with me.

I grated my teeth together, frustration pouring through me. What happened if other departments asked to table the vote until they had performed a check of their own, or brought up some reason for a delay? I could be waiting weeks, if not months, for a final decision, and all the while, ones would continue to be rounded up and dumped into those disgusting chambers below.

I swallowed, sickened by the thought of all those people needlessly losing their lives while the council stalled and delayed, and realized I needed to do something about it on my own. I had to stop the expulsion chambers now—otherwise people would continue to die.

But Lacey had warned me not to. And now I needed to know why.

I dismissed Sadie's message without a reply, and then asked Cornelius to request a vid call with Lacey. He was silent for several seconds—long enough to make me wonder if Lacey was rejecting my call—and then a second later, Lacey's face filled the screen, her expression thunderous.

"You better have something regarding Ambrose's death," she snapped. "Although if you had it within a day, I'd be really surprised."

I blinked at the contemptuous tone of her voice, and then decided I wasn't taking that crap from her anymore. "You know what, Lacey, screw you," I said hotly, my patience at an end. "I actually *do* have something on Ambrose's death, although I don't want to say anything until it pans out."

"Then you called about council business," she sneered. "I don't want to hear it. Your job is to shut up and do what you're told, and I ordered you to direct your questions to Strum. I do not want to talk to you."

"Too friggin' bad," I retorted, bristling. I was not going to be her puppet, and she needed to realize that right here and now. "I'm not Ambrose, Lacey. I am not just going to do what you tell me. We may hate each other, but we are allies, damn it. I'm trying to help you, but I will not be your obedient servant. We're equals, and you're going to treat me as such, blackmail material be damned."

Lacey opened her mouth to reply—then seemed to reconsider, and snapped her mouth shut so quickly that I swore I could hear her teeth clack together. She stared at me, her face a furious mask, and I suddenly felt like she was trying to make my head explode with the power of her mind.

But I didn't back down. In fact, I went so far as to look directly at the small camera marked by a white circle in the screen, so it would look like I was meeting her gaze head on through her screen.

Eventually she made an aggravated sound and leaned back into her seat, rubbing her chin with her hand. "What do you want?" she asked finally. I noticed she didn't say anything one way or the other about us being equals, but decided not to push it. My issue was more important than my pride. And if she didn't understand we were equals, then she was going to be sorely disappointed when I continued to challenge her and Strum at every turn.

"To talk about the expulsion chambers and how to stop them while the council kicks around the decision."

"You can't do anything, Liana," Lacey said, tiredly running a hand over her face. "If you defy the law, Scipio can have you removed as Champion. He'll drop your rank to one. It doesn't matter if we know the decision was tampered with or not. Until it is repealed, it remains in effect, and if you fight this, you'll be yet another person lost to those things."

I exhaled. "How long will it take?"

"Three months," she replied. "Each department gets three requests to delay a vote for a week to conduct research, and we only convene three weeks out of the month. The councilors working against the change will draw it out as long as possible, taking advantage of the law, so when Sadie runs out of hers, the next one will start the process all over again. The Hands will delay because they'll claim they need to run studies on how the loss of bodies will affect soil production in Twilight, and the Medica will delay it for studies into what to do with the ones once the law is repealed. If it is repealed, that is."

I cursed, and turned away for a second. As disgusting as it was, I could already see the other departments trying to make an argument to keep the expulsion chambers around. And why wouldn't they? The expulsion chambers kept things neat and tidy. Scipio told them who was bad, and the council was more than happy to eliminate the bad seeds. They didn't want to waste time trying to understand or rehabilitate those individuals, and expulsion was a perfect and expedited solution.

"Cornelius, approximately how many citizens will be put through the expulsion chambers in the next three months?" I asked, almost afraid to know the answer.

"Approximately seventy-five," he replied, and it broke my heart. Seventy-five people? That meant twenty-five people a month were being put to death.

Queasy and angry, I turned back to Lacey. "That's unacceptable," I whispered. "You have to know that's unacceptable."

Her brown eyes grew sad, and she nodded. "I know. But there's nothing we can do. This is how the system works, Liana."

Then the system is broken, I thought. "Lacey... we have to do something to knock them out of commission," I said, suddenly determined to get them to stop. "Maybe we could sabotage the cells, damage them so that they won't work."

Lacey gave me a sad look and then sighed. "Okay, I'm going to give you a piece of advice here, Liana, and I mean it genuinely. I know you want to fix this problem, and given that you and I aren't always on the right side of the law, I can see why your impulse is to do something drastic to get your way. But here's the thing: you're a councilor now. You've got to think long term. The crimes Strum and I commit are only to benefit us in our fight against our enemies. Everything else we do, we try to do legally, because doing otherwise would lead to the government breaking down. If we allow that to happen, then the Tower is lost. I know it seems awful. I know that you hate it, and I understand why. You do realize that about a third of those killed will be my very own people, right?"

I met her gaze through the screen, and then looked away. I heard what she was saying—recognized the wisdom of what she was saying —but my stomach churned viciously at the thought of letting the expulsion chambers go on for a second longer.

Lacey sighed through the screen and ran a hand over her face. "If that logic doesn't reach you, I might add that if you destroy the chambers, the council will want an investigation into the cause. If they find out you were behind it, you'll lose your seat and any chance of actually changing anything for the better. Just work with me and Strum, Liana. I promise that we can and will change this law. It'll just take a little time, is all."

I pressed my lips together, and then nodded. She was right on that count as well, and when the facts were that overwhelming, you just had to submit to them.

But as I ended the conversation with her, with a promise that I wouldn't do anything, I couldn't help but feel like it was an egregious mistake.

21

"Liana?"

I jerked awake and looked around groggily, my mind confused by my surroundings. I reared back when I saw a face squinting at me, mere inches away, and then calmed when I saw who it was.

"Tian," I exhaled, shaky from the sudden jolt of adrenaline that had accompanied my jarring break from sleep. I squinted at her, taking in several dark smudges on her arms and face, and realized she must have just gotten back, and been surprised to find me sleeping in the front room.

I had fallen asleep on the couch. I tried to remember the last thing I was doing before I dozed off, and realized I had drifted off for several hours after my disappointing talk with Lacey.

And, though I had relented and backed off the idea of doing something destructive to the expulsion chambers, I still couldn't help but feel like waiting to change the law was the same as letting innocent people die.

But maybe Lacey had a point. Defying the law would only temporarily put the expulsion chambers out of commission. And while she and Strum could delay repairs to keep them from going back online, the council could just as easily set up expulsion chambers somewhere else. Like the Medica.

If anything, they'd probably find the Medica more convenient, since they could just shuffle the people already there for rank intervention into the cells, press the button, and then use the corpses as training cadavers until it was time to send them to Twilight. It seemed the logic that ruled the council was "they're more useful to us in death than in life".

It was disgusting and needed to change. But Lacey was right—if I wanted to stop the expulsion chambers permanently, I needed to do it legally, and with a good plan in place to start helping those who fell from Scipio's grace, rather than just discarding them.

I glanced at Tian, who was watching me with no small amount of curiosity. "You were thinking really hard," she said, her voice soft. "Is everything okay?"

My answering smile was crooked—twisted, even—but I couldn't help but feel amused at her question. Of course, the answer was "not really". I was the Champion, and my plate had never felt so full, even though I was just supposed to be easing into my responsibilities right now. Was this what it was always going to feel like? Trying to play politics, while secretly trying to track down the entire legacy group responsible for my mother and Ambrose's deaths? The first day was already gone—wasted in so many respects—and yet countless more stretched out ahead of me, full of uncertainty and the potential for loss.

"It is," I lied, sparing the girl the realities she didn't need to deal with. She had her own mission, her own responsibilities, and I was content to let those be her only burden, even if it was a big one. "How was it with Dylan? As a matter of fact, what time is it?"

"Two a.m.," she replied. "And it was fine with Dylan, I guess. We retraced her steps, and I figured out how she lost them—they took an access tunnel that ran all the way to Water Treatment. Dylan wanted to go farther, but I got sleepy." She yawned on the last part, and then smacked her lips.

"Hey," a soft voice said from the hall, and I looked over to see Leo and Quess entering the room, both of them cradling mugs of something with steam wisping from the top. "We saw Tian return on the cameras, and I figured she might wake you, so..." Quess smiled and lifted the mug.

"Of course she would wake me," I said, confused by the teasing quality in Quess's voice. Tian would wake me to report in about her time with Dylan, but he made it sound like another Tianism that I had yet to come across. I looked at her. "What's going on?"

"You should never go to sleep anywhere but a proper bed or hammock," she said solemnly. "That's how the whispers steal your soul away in the night."

I blanched, and then on impulse, drew the girl tight into my arms. Her parents had died from Whispers, a virus that destroyed the neural pathways to the brain. The process was awful, as victims would begin to whisper madly in the throes of their fevers, speaking about their memories and true desires for all to hear. The disease was virulent and had no cure, so when cases occurred, entire sections of the Tower were quickly quarantined and left for several weeks, until only the immune survived.

Tian had been young when she was exposed, and had become

eccentric as a result. But what she just said reminded me that she had not only been young, but also trapped with her parents and other people who had been exposed. So many had died in front of her, and if most of them were out of their beds (and often they were, having died in the halls trying to navigate through their own madness in a desperate search for food or water), it would explain why she didn't want anyone she cared about sleeping outside of one.

"I'm sorry," I told her. "I promise I won't ever do it again."

She nodded against my shoulder and pulled away. "So, everything with Dylan went okay," she said casually. "We retraced her steps and I figured out how they were able to slip free of the trap Doxy set up for them, but lost all signs of them in Water Treatment. No sign if she's with the bad guys yet, but we're going out again tomorrow." With that, she turned to Quess. "What'd you bring me?" she asked, her voice cheerful.

I snorted at her brief report followed by an abrupt change of subject, but let it go—I hadn't expected Tian to discover anything on day one, and she'd come back unharmed. One small victory at a time.

Quess rolled his eyes as he handed her a mug. "Pig poop. Drink up."

"Ewwww," she exclaimed, scrunching her nose. She brought the mug to her nose and sniffed, then gave Quess an annoyed look. "You big liar," she scoffed, before taking a sip of what I presumed was hot chocolate.

I laughed, and sat up to accept the mug that Leo was holding out to me. It was filled with good black tea—just like I liked—and I took an experimental sip of it.

"Thank you," I said as the bitter taste hit my tongue, waking me even further. "Why is everyone up at two in the morning?"

"I'm still working on Jang-Mi," Leo said carefully as he straightened. "She's a lot more damaged than I thought, and she's resistant to help. Every time I try, she shuts down and initiates a self-diagnostic, and I can't do anything until it's finished. I've been working on taking that control away from her, but it's going to take time."

He looked away when he said that, and I felt the urge to comfort him. I knew he wanted to use Jang-Mi immediately to rescue Jasper, and I could tell he was disappointed that it wasn't working as quickly as he wanted it to. We all were, but these things took time. "Leo, we are going to do everything we can to rescue Jasper," I reminded him. "We're working on a way in on both fronts; it's just going to take a little time. Be patient. We're going to get him."

And soon, I thought to myself. Every minute that went by with Jasper in Sadie's clutches was unacceptable. Who knew what she'd done to him already—or even how long she'd had him. He had still been able to help me in the Medica, but then he'd been recalled. If Sadie knew that he had helped me, then she had undoubtedly recalled him in order to establish more control over his program. I shuddered at the thought.

It was clear from the look that Leo gave me that my comment did nothing to help his doubt. "I know that. I'm just worried about Jasper. If you're right and he's the only fragment left..."

I reached out and grabbed his hand. "I know. I'm worried about him, too. But I swear to you, we'll figure it out. Whether it's through Jang-Mi or by going and physically retrieving him ourselves, we'll do it."

His smile became genuine, the darkness in his eyes lightening. "Isn't it amazing how sometimes words can do more than a hug ever could?" he asked in a low voice, and the sweetness of the statement tugged at my heart. In a very dangerous way.

I squeezed his hand one more time and then withdrew, needing some space. "What about you, Quess?" I asked. "Any progress on locating an accurate schematic?"

"I've been up all night trying to draw what I can remember of the Core's layout," Quess said, rubbing his eyes. "So far, I've got both the rooms I was assigned to during my time there and an approximate layout of the surrounding halls, the cafeteria, my boss's office, my workspace—which was cubicle hell, I might add—and a few of the recreational areas. But it's not a lot when you compare it to how large the Core actually is. I'm worried that there won't be enough points of reference to make an accurate comparison, which is why I'm trying to be as detailed as possible."

He threw himself onto the couch next to me, and I sat up some more and scooted over to give him room. "Do you think it's a long-shot?" I asked as I took another sip of my tea. If it was, then we needed to abandon the idea and find an alternative way of finding a map. We had to keep pushing forward on whatever front we could. Jasper was too important not to.

"I think it's the only shot we currently have, short of going to Dinah—and I know you want to avoid that, if possible."

I nodded. Dinah's placement in IT had saved us more than once, and I did not want to expose her to our enemies any more than we already had. It was bad enough that Jang-Mi had tracked her down and almost killed her. I wanted to keep her as insulated as possible, and that meant not running to her every time we had to break into IT. We'd do it if we had to, but I'd cross that bridge when we came to it.

Leo moved around the coffee table and sat down on the floor, crossing his legs beneath him, and seconds later Tian joined him. Their movements distracted me from Quess's defeated form.

"I just didn't want to believe that IT would lack the foresight to keep *actual* plans on file with the different departments," Quess finally exploded. "What happens if their air processing unit goes out and they suffocate? No one in the Tower would have any idea what to do or how to fix it, and without IT there to support Scipio, the whole system could fall apart!"

I listened to his impassioned rant and give him a sidelong glance. "Quess, we're talking about rescuing a fragment AI from the head of IT—one that is supposed to be in the Core as part of Scipio. The system is broken, Quess. We need the tools to fix it, so *think!* Where do you think we could find an accurate schematic of the Core?"

"In the Core's mainframe," he replied. "And I'm not able to hack the Core directly. Their trackers would find me long before I got anywhere."

"It's too bad we don't have Cali's books anymore," Tian said softly, a second later. "She had so many manuals from IT, and they were made a long, long, long, long time ago." She fidgeted. "And other books."

I remembered the shelves in Cali's room, which had in fact been filled to the brim with books, and remembered all the different manuals she had—shelves and shelves of them! Blue for Water Treatment, orange for Cogs, white for the Medics, and gray for IT.

I heard Quess say, "Yeah, those would've been incredibly helpful," and could've smacked him for not remembering.

"Quess, the IT manuals had schematics in them, right?" I asked him. It was a pointless question—I already knew the answer.

He nodded. "Of course they did. They had to. The internal servers for each department didn't go up until what... maybe thirty-three years in? I can't remember exactly, but that's why there were just so many manuals around. Each department was already responsible for too many things. But why does it matter? Cali's books are gone! Devon probably cleared them out long ago, and who knows where he put them? He probably destroyed them."

"I miss my things," Tian added wistfully, wrapping her arms around herself.

I felt bad for Tian; she had lost so much more than her things when Devon followed me back to the original Sanctum. I wanted nothing more than to find her stuff and return it to her, but more importantly, I wanted those technical manuals.

I sat back and considered Quess's assertion that Devon had destroyed them, but something felt wrong about that. Cali's stash of IT manuals had been rare, and exceptionally illegal, which made them valuable on the black market. I knew this because Zoe's father had run a sort of bookstore, which was how Zoe and I had gotten our hands on a few pre-war books. But I knew for a fact he wouldn't deal with IT's manuals. They were relentless in their pursuit of them, and people had been killed over them in the past—and I was betting Devon knew that, too, so I doubted he had tried to sell them.

But then where would Devon have put them? There had been too much just lying there, especially the contraband, for him to have moved by himself, and I doubted he would have just left it there. If he had tried to move it out himself, someone would've noticed. So then how would he have removed the books? What would he have done with them that would've served his purpose at the time?

I thought back to what had been going on at the time, namely the fact that he had been framing me for the murder of Gerome and trying to paint me as the leader of a terrorist cell, and realized that if anything, he would've used all of the stuff in Sanctum as evidence against me, as proof of my criminal activities.

It would've helped support his claim that Cali had been an

undoc who had been secretly helping me. It would've been packed up and moved to one of the storage facilities!

Thrilled that I had a lead that could possibly bring us one step closer to rescuing Jasper, I quickly shared my thoughts with the others. They listened—it didn't take long—and then Quess gave me a look. "Where would they be stored?"

"I don't know," I replied. "But I bet Cornelius does. Cornelius, where did Devon Alexander store all of the items found during his raid on Camilla Kerrin and the undocs?"

"They were boxed up and stored in one of the storage facilities outside of the Citadel in the upper levels of the Tower. I have the location and file number, and can guide you to the approximate location," the assistant replied.

"Excellent," I said with a smile. Then I looked at my friends, and realized that while I wanted to handle this now, it was two in the morning and they were exhausted. Not to mention, it would be a little weird if the Champion and an entourage left the Citadel to head up to the Attic in the middle of the night.

"We'll hit it tomorrow," I told them, and knew I made the right choice when I saw the relief and gratitude in their eyes.

It could wait, I told myself. Even if we figured out where Sadie's quarters were, we'd still have to find a way to bypass the security, cover our tracks, and then *not* be detected during the entire thing.

I figured there was a chance that Leo would have Jang-Mi ready long before we could break in—but that didn't mean we shouldn't have a backup plan, just in case.

22

We woke up early, despite our late and impromptu meeting, excitement coursing through all of us. All of us except for Maddox, of course—she'd been sleeping while the rest of us talked— but once we told her what we had discovered, her eyes lit up with such a deep happiness and gratitude that it stole my breath away.

Even though we needed those manuals to try to figure out a way to save Jasper, I hadn't stopped to realize that it meant more to her than that. These were her mother's things—things that Maddox thought she'd never see again. It was a connection to her past, a part of her history...

Suddenly I longed to return to my own family's home and find something that had once belonged to my mother. It filled me with a deep ache, and I made a mental note to ask Maddox what my father's schedule was so I could sneak into the apartment and grab something while he was out. I wasn't about to ask him for permission, and I certainly wasn't above abusing my powers for this.

I was filing it away for later when the others suddenly burst into motion to get ready, and I would've leapt into the fray, had Quess not held me up to check my knee. He peeled the patch off, and after some experimental flexing of the joint with no pain, he declared me good to go and then headed off to get dressed. I joined Maddox and Tian in one bathroom—Quess and Leo used the other—and quickly washed up in the shower. And though I had arrived after the other two, I was the first one out, and hightailed it to my room to get dressed (and put Quess's special lash beads on).

We reunited in the kitchen, where Leo proudly presented semi-burnt toast to us all. He was arguably the worst cook in our little outfit, but we were all too excited to care, and scarfed it down.

We barely bothered to put the dishes in the sink when we were done, and within forty-five minutes of filling Maddox in, we were heading up to the top levels of the Tower, or the Attic, as we liked to call it. These floors were rarely used, and primarily functioned as storage units. Cornelius's directions took us to the 213th floor, and then down a wide central hallway, which we walked along for nearly twenty minutes, almost crossing the entire width of the Tower.

Eventually he had me go right down another hall, and then stop about halfway down, at a massive door marked 213-150J. There was a keypad next to it—one that we didn't have to override, for once—and I quickly keyed in my code. I already had a cover in mind for why I was here, and a perfectly legitimate one at that, so I wasn't worried about anyone knowing about our little field trip.

As soon as I finished entering my ID, the pad pulsed yellow for several heartbeats, and then turned green. There was a sharp rattle that made me jump slightly, and then the door began to heave to one side, sliding open to reveal darkness. The light from the hall cut through the widening gap, but the darkness beyond was still oppressive and thick. I waited for a light to come on as the door continued to widen, rattling along in its track until it stopped, creating an entry way nine feet wide. The glow from the hall created a bright square in the darkened room. I waited for a long moment, but nothing happened.

"Lights?" I asked loudly.

There was a slight hum, and then an angry buzz. Nothing else happened.

"It could be a damaged fuse," Quess suggested from behind me. "Want me to check it out?"

I considered it, and then shook my head. We were planning to steal things, after all. Why not do it under the cover of darkness? I would file a report on the broken lighting system later as an added bonus. It would only add to my cover that I had been up here on official business, discovered the problem, continued with my search, and then reported the issue—exactly what a councilor would do—while adding an extra layer of security for me and my friends to work. After all, the cameras couldn't see what we were really doing if there were no lights. Especially since we were coming in here to get technical manuals that did not belong to my department. I didn't want anyone catching wind of what we were up to.

"No," I replied for good measure. "I don't mind the dark. It's not like anyone's going to be in here, and it'll help cover what we're doing." I pulled my hand light out of my pocket and clicked it on, stepping into the darkened room.

"Fair enough," Maddox said, and I heard a click coming from her direction, telling me she had turned on her own light. I took a few steps deeper into the room, and then twisted a dial at the base of the hand light to turn up the intensity, covering the light with my other hand so I didn't blind myself. I shut it off for a second while I pulled out my baton, and made sure it was off before I clipped it onto the top, fitting the tip to a rubber-filled notch at the base. As soon as it was attached, I turned the light back on, and then held the baton up over my head, forming a torch of light.

Even at its brightest settings, it was meager against the darkness of the room, only giving visibility for about fifteen feet ahead.

Still, as I slid it left to right, it immediately hit the corner of something with a bright white flash, and I pulled it back and peered at whatever was out there. Boxes—piles of them, all packed under clear plastic sheeting.

I'd seen this before, a few levels down in a similar storage room, back when we'd broken into the Core. The room we'd been in then had been large and stuffed full of boxes, so it made sense that this one would be, too. I just hoped that Cornelius could tell us what to look for.

"All right, Cornelius, where would Cali Kerrin's boxes be?" I breathed, moving closer to the stack at which my light was directed. My view of the columns and columns of boxes stacked in neat rows grew as I drew nearer to the corner of it, but still stretched up over my head and continued far past the circle of yellow light emitted by my torch.

They will be stamped EVI-2512.14 through EVI-2512.31. There are seventeen boxes, total. I have no additional information.

I repeated what he had told me to the others, my mind whirring. Seventeen boxes, total? I wasn't even sure how big this pile was, but if it was anything like the ones we'd seen in the other room, there would be thousands of boxes here. Still, they had a designation number; maybe there was an order to the chaos that I hadn't seen yet. A label or a map or something.

"Liana?" Tian asked, her voice carrying a note of worry. "How are we going to find our things?"

"I'm not sure yet," I replied honestly. "But I am sure there's a way to figure it out. Quess, is there a printed map or directory on the wall by the entrance?"

"I'll check," he replied, and I turned to see him moving back toward the entrance, his light in his hand. "You guys should look inside, though. Remember how the ones we found below were filled with mres?" He pronounced it as if it were a real word, with a soft M that bled into a hard R and an even harsher and elongated E sound, and I giggled, remembering how Grey had told us that the MREs were likely an acronym for something. "The entire pile was full of them, so I'm betting they are separated by what's inside. There were designations printed on the sides of the boxes down there, so it stands to reason it's the same here. We can eliminate the stacks that way, in case there's no map here."

Leo cocked his head quizzically at me, his brown eyes reflecting a simmering confusion. "I'm not familiar with the term 'mres'," he said. "Is it from one of the new languages you told me about? Wetmouth or Cogspeech?"

I shook my head. "No," I said, motioning to one of the piles and moving toward it. "It's—"

"Here!" Tian said excitedly from a few feet away to my right, her face already pressed into the plastic film that surrounded the boxes, peering through the slightly opaque material. "M. R. E! Pine Industries." She reared back and scrunched up her nose in a disgruntled look. "Wasn't Pine the guy who killed Leo's dad?"

"Tact, Tian," Maddox hissed from where she was on my left, heading down the other side. "There is a nicer way to put that!"

Tian blinked, and then puffed out her chest, a cross and irritated look coming across her face. "Fine! Isn't that the a—"

"Tian!" Maddox gasped, barely cutting off the obscenity pouring from the young girl's mouth. I bit back a laugh, unable to help myself. Tian had developed quite a mouth recently, and while it was inappropriate, I couldn't help but find it utterly adorable.

"—hole who killed a really cool guy?" she finished hotly, her cheeks bright red.

Maddox gaped at Tian, clearly shocked by her little outburst, but to my surprise, Leo gave a low chuckle that was rich and warm with mirth, and sent tingles of awareness through my body.

Easy, girl, I told myself, trying to do everything in my power not to respond to Leo in that way. I still hadn't had a chance to unpack everything that had happened between us, and I wasn't about to do it now.

"He is," Leo said amicably. "I couldn't have described him better myself."

Tian beamed proudly and then had the audacity to stick her tongue out at Maddox. Maddox rolled her eyes as she turned away to head farther down the side path that faced the front of the room, but I caught a flash of an amused smile before her back was fully to us, telling me that Tian's little show of defiance hadn't angered or offended her as much as she let on. "More mre boxes!" Maddox called a few moments later. "I think this entire stack might be full of them."

Well, that was a promising sign at least, although their presence here had me a little confused. Why were there stacks and stacks of them in a storage unit meant for housing evidence? It was possible that they'd always been here, and the storage was just getting filled in around them, I supposed.

Or, it meant we were in the wrong room completely. "Let's check the next stack," I said.

"Seriously, what are mre boxes?" Leo asked, repeating his question from earlier.

I shook my head, amused. "Quess is insisting that they are called that, but Grey said that was an acronym. M-R-E. He wasn't sure what it stood for, but—"

"Meals ready to eat," Leo supplied, and I blinked at him.

"You know what they are?"

He nodded. "They're food... sort of. Lionel said they tasted like wet toilet paper at the best of times." At my confused look, he added, "Toilet paper was softened bits of paper that were used to cleanse oneself after using the toilet. Not at all like the water guns we use now. It was more wasteful, and terrible for the sewage system."

I frowned a little, both disgusted and alarmed by his description. The idea of using something as precious as a tree—even one that had been processed enough to be "softened", as Leo described—was shocking and sounded extremely unhygienic. I had learned a few things about Pre-Enders, but this was really surprising. I tried to imagine a world where such a thing was commonplace, and just couldn't see it. Couldn't understand the desire to use a tree when water was all you needed.

But then again, they hadn't been able to prevent the End, so maybe they had had bigger problems than how they were cleaning themselves after going to the bathroom.

"All the boxes on this side are marked with those mre stamps," Tian announced, breaking my train of thought as she continued alongside the stack, her light the only thing illuminating her figure. It disappeared around a corner a few feet later, and I realized there was another pile of boxes, grouped under its own plastic wrap, next to this one. Leo rolled his eyes at Tian's pronunciation, but didn't correct her.

"Maddox?" I called, moving toward the aisle she had gone down.

"Same here!" she shouted back a second later, her voice muffled.

Tian added, "The neighboring pile has mre stamps as well."

"Well, that's good, because there's no map anywhere," Quess commented as he returned from his search. That was annoying, but not altogether unsurprising. The Attic had no direct oversight from one department, so a lot of things, like maps, fell through the cracks.

I moved farther down the wide aisle to the next pile, and sure enough, these had the MRE markings, too. "Same on this side," I said, taking a step back. So I was right—it seemed like they were at least grouped together.

Maddox came around the corner a few seconds later and moved across the aisle, her light directed out toward the one on the opposite side of the aisle. "These are different," she announced. "This one says EVI 121.1. Under it is EVI 121.2, then 121.3..." She trailed off, shifting a few feet down so she could peer at another box.

Relieved that I had been right, I moved to the opposite pile and doublechecked. Sure enough, these were marked with the EVI stamp—only they were marked with different numbers, moving into the 200s. To the left were the MREs, to the right, evidence boxes. And since Cali's death was recent, it stood to reason we'd find it in the last pile.

Thank Scipio for the bureaucracy of the Tower; it certainly made things a lot easier. Within moments we were moving down the wide central aisle, checking boxes as we passed to make sure the numbers were still climbing.

Our walk ended at the final pile on the left, and I was pleased to see that it wasn't covered with thick plastic film like the others. What was more, there was a path that seemed to move into the middle of the pile, making it a square snail shell, so we could have access to every box available in this group. The boxes were clearly marked, and within minutes, we had found the section with Cali's items and were pulling them out, creating a little chain so we could pass the boxes to each other and save time. Tian was at the end of it, so no one was surprised when we emerged, cradling the final boxes, to find her squatting over one she had already torn open, busily pulling out the contents and inspecting them.

"I found the books," she announced with a grin, and I saw that she was clutching some to her chest. She pointed to a few other boxes —also open—and then returned to sifting through the box in front of her.

I rolled my eyes, but didn't chastise her. "The rest remain closed until we get them back to our quarters," I told her firmly. We'd only just recovered them, and I didn't want to waste time going through them here when they would be more secure at home. She made a little affirmative sound, but didn't stop her endless digging. I sighed, and let it go; she was excited about seeing things from her old home, and I couldn't blame her for it.

"Two minutes, Tian," I said, giving her a warning.

"Okay!" she chirped brightly.

I moved over to where Leo and Quess were crouched over the boxes Tian had already opened, pulling out slim, dark gray manuals with both hands. "Is that them?" I asked, peeking in over their shoulders.

"Looks like it," Quess confirmed, opening one of the manuals and reading a few passages. "Just as dry as when I was a Bit," he said, and I smiled, trying to imagine him as a trainee in IT, and failing miserably. He was far too charismatic and outgoing for the Eyes. He had probably stood out like a sore thumb.

"Good," I said. "Let's get out of here and—"

"Shh," Leo said quietly, holding up his hand, and I quickly grabbed the light off my baton, returned my baton to my belt, and dimmed the light to a low setting, trusting his instincts.

I looked at him, trying to figure out the source of his alarm, and realized he was listening for something, so I joined him, my senses already on high alert. These floors were supposed to be empty. If he was hearing something, then I'd be a fool to ignore it. A moment later, I heard it—a slight grinding sound that took me back to our days in our second Sanctum, and all of the vent-crawling we had done. The grates over the vent had made a unique sound when we pushed them out of our way, and this sounded almost exactly like that.

A dozen questions burst into my mind, but I ignored them, as several things *could* have made that sound. It was dark, and we were doing something illegal—and that was enough to make us imagine sounds in the darkness.

"Get the boxes packed up," I ordered softly as I pressed the light to my chest, covering most of it with my hand so that only a few beams of light were trickling out through the gaps between my fingers. "I'll go check it out."

"Not alone," Leo whispered, quietly putting manuals back into the box. "We should just go."

I heard a sharp clang behind the last stack of MRE boxes that sounded just like a vent grate hitting the floor, and ignored Leo's suggestion. Now I was curious; it seemed like someone was indeed sneaking in here, and I wanted to know who they were and why they were doing it.

I quickly crossed the wide aisle to the opposite side and slipped down a few feet to the corner of the pile, keeping my light hidden behind one hand. I heard the distinctive sound of boots hitting the floor, and froze a few feet from the corner, my heart pounding at how loud it was. The person—if it was just one—sounded like they weighed three hundred pounds, but that was probably the echoes playing tricks on my mind.

I held my breath, wondering if they would come toward me, and noticed a dark shape climbing the wall on the opposite side. It was Tian. The girl had also muted her light, so much so that it was barely visible. But I could still make out her dim form climbing upward. I wasn't sure what she was up to, but I hoped the others were keeping an eye on her.

Nothing moved for several seconds, and then the boots started walking in a slow, confident matter. I started to back up, but paused when I realized they weren't growing any closer. If anything, they seemed to be staying exactly the same distance away— meaning they were walking in a straight line, parallel to where I was crouched.

Even more curious now, I moved forward and peeked around the edge of the boxes. I froze when I saw a teenage boy, probably fifteen or sixteen, with a lamp of his own strapped around his head with a piece of fabric. He was standing not twenty-five feet away, his back to the open vent through which he had clearly entered.

He had a rough shock of unruly auburn curls on the top of his head, and was wearing dark clothes from head to toe. I immediately noticed that he had no indicator on his wrist—and realized that I was looking at an undoc.

I backed around the corner for a second, surprised. Cali had said there were other undoc groups surviving in the Tower—that she had a relationship with some of them—and now, it seemed, I had found one! Was he alone, or was he with others? What were they like? How were they surviving, and what could they want in a place like this? Would we find them if we followed him through the vent?

I peeked out again, intrigued by what he might be doing here, and was relieved that the boy was oblivious to my presence, still looking at the pile of boxes. He'd moved away a few more feet, but he was still close. Close enough to grab.

"Who is he?" Quess whispered softly behind me, so suddenly that I almost shouted in alarm. I pressed my hand over my mouth and shot Quess a dirty look. He gave me an apologetic look, and then his eyes widened when I signed the word "undoc" to him in Calli-vax. Quess then turned to someone behind him—Leo, I thought. I returned my focus to the boy, wondering what he was up to.

He cocked his head back and forth, seeming to consider something, and then a moment later, reached through the plastic film around one of the boxes. And he didn't stop there. He continued to shove himself through until he was lying on his stomach and only his legs were sticking out. I could hear the faint, muffled sound of him shifting around inside, clearly looking for something.

The MREs, I realized. They were food, and he had somehow figured it out. He was stealing them to survive.

My heart ached at the thought of this poor boy being forced to subsist on something that had been created before the End—something that apparently tasted like wood—and I found myself moving forward, compelled to help him. To at least find out more about him and make sure he wasn't alone. If he wasn't, then maybe I could get a meeting with his people and see if I could establish a relationship with them. Maybe they'd have an idea about what was going on in the Tower, and about any other undoc groups out there. Maybe they'd even have an idea about the legacies that were roaming all over the place. Who knew?

I just had to make sure I didn't scare him, and that he understood that I wasn't going to hurt him or arrest him.

Chances were that as soon as he saw me he was going to try to run, though, and I paused long enough to make a series of gestures in Callivax to tell Quess and Leo to get to the vent slowly, and have their lashes ready.

I heard a sharp click sound coming from overhead as I drew closer to where the boy was busy rooting around, oblivious to us, and glanced up quickly to see Tian easing herself down onto another column of boxes, staring at the kicking legs with curiosity. I realized she must've climbed up and over the towers of boxes. I motioned for her to stay where she was. She nodded and flashed me a thumbs up.

The boy emerged seconds later, his arms filled with several flat, rectangular packages wrapped in silver, the lot of them hugged tightly to his chest. He was completely focused on them, his mouth moving as he wordlessly counted each one. I pressed forward, cupping my hand over my light to make it less noticeable, and kept my movements calm and relaxed as I drew closer to him, knowing that faster ones would attract his attention sooner.

He finished abruptly, when I was about fifteen feet away, and suddenly looked up at me, blinding me with his light. I raised my hand to block it, peering at him through squinted eyes. I got a clear look at him and saw a pale face with a liberal dose of freckles under his mop of unruly auburn hair, which was almost dark brown. His eyes were a pea green, and grew wide in alarm when he saw me approaching.

I froze and then showed him my hands, wordlessly telling him I was unarmed. "Hi," I said softly, giving him my friendliest smile. "I'm not going to—"

The boy clearly did not care. As soon as I started to speak, he flung his armload of MREs at me. I ducked, and he ran, his feet pounding back toward the vent through which he had emerged. I caught a glimpse of something pale leaping overhead, followed by Tian's call of "I got him!" and a moment later she was swinging in behind him on her lashes—and slamming into his back, sending both of them to the floor.

"OW!" the boy cried as they fell in a tangle of limbs. I raced over as Leo and Quess moved closer to help.

"You're cute!" Tian squealed in delight a second later, sitting up from where she had landed on him. "You're going to be my new boyf—HEY!"

The boy had been so frantic to get away that he'd shoved her off his body, and was now scrambling on all fours toward the vent, where Leo and Quess hadn't gotten positioned in time. He slipped into it before we could get to him or Tian.

Tian wasn't deterred, however, and immediately leapt to her feet and threw both lashes after him. I saw the blue pop as they connected inside of the vent, and then she was flying after him, using the gyros in her suit to propel her toward the vent opening. "Wait for me!" she called as she disappeared into the dark hole.

I didn't hesitate, but plunged in after her, not wanting to lose her or the boy.

23

The vent was deep and dark, and I had to shove my hand light into my pocket so I could move more quickly on my hands and knees. I heard Leo shouting my name behind me, telling me to wait, but I ignored him, scrambling after the precious snatches of light ahead of me, where the boy and Tian were forging ahead. The sounds of rattling ducts and pounding feet filled my ears, thunderous and disorienting, but I kept my eyes on the bursts of light in the darkness, trying to keep up with them on my hands and knees. I didn't have the flexibility to run in a hunched position like they did, so this was the only way to make sure I didn't lose them.

The metal shuddering under my palms told me Leo and Quess were behind me, and I quickly netted Maddox.

I stayed behind with the stuff. What is going on? she demanded, the line connecting immediately. *Should I call for backup?*

No, I thought at her, pausing as a cross-breeze hit me, signaling that I was in a junction. I searched intently for a second and then plunged forward when I saw another flash of light. *We found an undoc boy. I think he might be with a larger group, and I want to find out. They might be one of the groups your mom mentioned, and possibly know of other undoc groups roving around the Tower—like our legacy friends. The boy spooked when he saw me, but we're in pursuit. Go ahead and get a loader to move those boxes. We'll be fine.*

Okay. I'll gather a few nearby Commanders anyway, just in case. If it turns out to be nothing, I'll tell them it was just an emergency response exercise.

I sent an affirmative and then killed the connection, focusing solely on following the flashes, which were beginning to draw farther and farther away. They were getting too far ahead, in fact, and if they didn't reach their destination soon—and stop—I was going to lose them.

I stopped when another breeze hit me, this one cold and biting, and strained to find the light. My eyes blinked rapidly in the darkness, and I twisted my head around, searching for it. Panic curled around my heart as heartbeats passed with no sound or visuals, and then I heard something to the right, in the direction from which the wind was coming, and plunged after it, worried that Tian had gotten too far ahead.

I'd made it a few feet down this new duct when I suddenly heard her cry out in pain, the sound carried from somewhere deeper in the tunnel. I scrambled toward it and heard scuffling, followed by a masculine bellow of pain that was too deep to belong to the boy we had been after. It seemed the boy wasn't alone. He was with someone—and they were hurting Tian.

Frantic to get to her before they could harm her any further, I surged forward. I had made it several feet—how many, I couldn't tell

—when the floor suddenly vanished, and I fell down a few feet into a small, curved shaft, my face smacking on the metal.

I heard Leo frantically cry my name again as I slid downward, my hands and face scraping along the metal until if felt like a line of fire was burning its way across my cheek. When I stopped, I blinked dazedly, wincing against the bright light that was shining just feet from my face, and then scrambled upright, adrenaline pushing aside the cobwebs.

"What was that?" an alarmed voice snarled, and a shadow crossed the opening. I coiled up as I realized it was a set of legs, already bending into a squat, and then launched myself forward through the hole, tackling whoever was on the other side. I didn't care if there were twenty people behind him. If he was the one who had harmed Tian, I was going to break his knees.

I got a flash of blue eyes, and then I was plowing at him, my already-hurt cheek and chin slamming against his collarbone. He made an "oof" sound as I hit him hard enough to slam the air out of his lungs, and we went down.

I heard someone shout and tried to sit up—only to find my arm twisted up under the guy I had landed on. I started to jerk my arm free, my mouth already forming Leo's name to warn him that there were more people here, but strong fingers grabbed my face and slammed the side of my head into the floor. I jerked back up, adrenaline surging, and pushed against my attacker, trying to get their hand off my face with my free arm.

I found the soft flesh of an elbow and clawed at it, but I was still pinned in place by the guy I had slammed into, and didn't have much leverage. They jerked my head up and back down again, and this time the lights went out.

I lay there for several seconds, convinced I was unconscious. My vision was black, and I was spinning in circles that I could feel in my stomach. Then something pressed against my face. Fingers, strong and forceful. Something struck my cheek, but I barely felt it, and I heard a muffled "Hey" cut through the whooshing sound in my ears. I opened my mouth, but then my cheek began to burn where I had been hit. A hand was on my face again for a second, and I tried to lift my arms. One was trapped under something, and the other one might as well have been because I couldn't seem to lift it. The fingers tightened on my cheeks for a second, and then suddenly went away. The weight on my arm followed, and needle pricks exploded in the deadened limb as the blood began to flow more easily, causing me to gasp.

So I was wrong. I was aware of every bump and bruise, and they *hurt*—which meant I wasn't knocked out.

Then why couldn't I see? Had I gone blind?

Suddenly I heard voices that weren't mine or Leo's or Quess's, and zeroed in on one of them.

"I got the lights," it whispered, and I knew it. It was him—the man from the catwalk. I'd never been unconscious at all. They'd just shut off the lights in this section. But I had my hand light—it was still in my pocket. I flexed my fingers on my good hand and then tried to lift it. I had no idea if it was working, but a moment later I felt my limp hand thump against the front of my suit. "How did they find us?"

"She spotted me when I was grabbin' breakfast," came a younger voice, and I realized it was the boy. "I didn't see nobody when I went in, I swear it, but I—"

There was a sharp smack followed by the boy's soft cry of pain. "Idiot," the man from the catwalk snarled. "The boss is going to do worse than tan your hide this time." I felt a surge of anger at the guy. It wasn't the boy's fault he didn't notice us. I fumbled my fingers around, searching for the pocket the light was in, and smiled when I felt the zipper tab.

"What do we do?" cried a feminine voice. "The boss told you not to—"

"You let me deal with the boss," the older male voice snarled. "Run, quick. Her friends are right behind her."

They were? I strained to hear, and had to wait for the sound of someone running away to fade, but then I heard the telltale rattle and thump coming from where I thought the vent hole was. I continued to work on the zipper, and finally made my wrist and hand force it down a few inches. Light spilled out from the gap, and I winced as the sudden brightness caused an immense pain in my eyes, pain exploding in my brain like pinpricks.

"What are you going to do about her?" the woman asked sharply, and I pressed my hand flat over the pocket, worried they were now looking at me. For a second, I wondered if they could even see me, but as I heard a shout go up in the distance, I realized that they had to have some way of seeing—because the sound of what must have been hundreds of feet running filled the air.

It was so loud that I almost missed the male's response of, "Give me the bag. I'll handle it."

I didn't hear what happened next. I was already moving my hand down to where my baton was in my belt. I'd gotten more control of my arm and hand, and I gripped the handle tightly and tugged up. My vision was still splotchy, but I felt the baton begin to slide free.

A second later, my wrist was seized by a strong hand, and I gasped as a gray patch of my vision suddenly cleared, revealing the man from the catwalk leaning over me, trapping one of my wrists under his knee. I tried to hit him with my other arm, but sensation hadn't returned, and he caught it easily with one hand.

"Don't struggle," he spat, shifting his weight to one side to pull my hand out from under his knee.

"No!" I shouted, as he slowly lifted my hands over my head. I pressed against him, but he was impossibly strong, and my limbs still weren't working right. The best I could muster was a weak shove. His jaw tightened, and then he slid his leg over my stomach, straddling me.

Panic burst over me, covering me with a dull sweat, when he reached between our bodies. A thousand nightmarish ideas as to what he was doing went through my head, but to my relief, all he did was pull the light out of my pocket, placing it on the ground next to my head after cranking it a little brighter.

"What are you doing?" I asked, my heart pounding in my chest.

I didn't expect an answer, but to my surprise, he started talking as he reached into a bag over his shoulder and awkwardly rummaged around. "Slowing your friends down. If they really care about you, they'll stop to save your life."

A second later he was pulling out a silver canister that I recognized as bio-foam—the pink foam used for sealing cuts—and a package of some sort. I watched, wide-eyed with terror, fearing what he had in store, and tried to will more strength into my limbs. He barely seemed to notice, just placed them next to the light and then looked over his shoulder again, all the while holding me firmly in place. I lifted my head, listening, and I heard them—Leo and Quess.

"Guys, here!" I shouted. "Over here! I—"

The man whipped around and backhanded me, and the impact felt like he had smashed right through my face. My vision went dark, and I gasped and gargled against the pain. For several seconds, all I could do was lie there in agony, my head splitting.

I returned to awareness slowly, the darkness clearing like curtains being drawn. Half my vision was filled with dark, corrugated metal, the other half the silver canister and package, telling me I was looking right. Even though my head felt like it weighed a thousand pounds, I slowly swiveled it to peer at the man above me.

"Liana!" Leo's voice was close, but still felt too far away as I stared at the man above me.

"Are you the one who killed my mother?" I asked hoarsely. His blue eyes met mine, but he didn't answer. A moment later, I felt something sharp press against my throat. "Wha—"

His hand went down, and something sharp punched into my throat. I gasped—but instead of pulling air, a wet, gurgling sucking sound erupted from my throat. I gagged as thick, hot wetness flooded my throat and I tried to cough it out. Dark red splatters landed on his face, and I realized that I had just expelled blood.

No, I was drowning in blood. Panic set in, and I began to struggle. The weight left me, and, working on instinct alone, I grabbed at my neck. Wetness, hot and thick, splattered against my hand. My blood, I realized. I clapped my hand over it, trying to stem the flow. Panic came over me as I continued to choke and cough, trying to clear the blood from my throat so I could breathe, but it didn't work. The blade had gone all the way through the carotid artery and punctured my airway, and I was suffocating on my own blood.

He cut my throat, I realized belatedly. I needed help. Now.

"Le—" I tried to make the sound, but only coughed up more blood instead. I was gagging, choking for air, drowning.

Hands grabbed me, and I panicked as they reached for the hand on my neck. *No,* I tried to tell them. *I have to keep pressure there or I'm going to die!*

I *was* going to die. My vision was already going gray, and blood was still spurting from the hole in my throat, forced out by each beat of my heart. The very act of living was killing me... and I was powerless to stop it.

Anger slid into me—too little, too late—and I struggled against the hands, fighting them for every second of life. I thought about all the people I was about to leave, and told myself I couldn't let them down, couldn't—

The hands wanted me dead, it seemed. They pushed my own away, and the next thing I felt was the blade of another knife, sharp and cold, pressing into my throat. I wished I could spit at them.

My thoughts grew broken, then, and I thought of Leo. I wished he was with me. I wished he would hold me and tell me that I was going to be okay. I would know it was a lie, of course. I already knew it was.

And then I thought of my mother. It seemed I had been right: I was going to join her in Twilight sooner than I'd thought.

Then something was shoved down my throat, but I felt weightless now, untethered by my body, which was growing cold as blood poured out of my carotid artery.

Then I coughed—once, twice, a third time—and something wet and thick forced its way upward from my stomach and lungs. I was turned, and for several seconds, all I could do was retch out blood.

Then I reflexively breathed in. I coughed when I felt something wet crackle in my lungs, and then even more came out.

The hands held me and stroked my hair, oblivious to the blood covering me. I shook violently as soon as it was over, and then reached up to touch my neck. The area was wet with blood, but when I felt the skin there, unbroken and whole, my shaking intensified.

I turned to look back and saw Leo and Quess looking at me, their faces ashen. And then I saw the silver canister in Quess's hand, and realized he had inserted it directly into the wound to seal the hole. The blood was on both their hands, blending in with the crimson of their uniforms. Their expressions were a mixture of horrified and worried, and told me how close I'd just come to death.

I pressed my palm against the spot the knife had gone in and broke down, sobbing as the reality hit home that I'd almost died. If they'd been even a second later, I'd have been dead. Nobody said anything, but Leo's arms went immediately around me, wrapping me in a cocoon of his warmth and strength, and he stroked my hair while I sobbed against his shoulder.

24

I clung onto Leo, and he rocked me for what felt like forever, as I gripped the place where the blade had pierced my neck, unable to let go for fear of feeling that awful, thick gurgling when I took my next breath. Leo held me tightly, his hands smoothing over my hair, my face, my arms. I was glued to him like my hand was to my throat, unable to move or stop shaking.

I'd almost died. *They'd* almost killed me. They had cut my throat and left me to bleed out.

I would be angry if I didn't feel so cold.

I heard Leo's chest rumble under my ear and tucked closer to it, too afraid to even listen to what he was saying. Scipio help me, I was so cold.

Leo stopped talking, and a moment later, he was gently pushing me away. I resisted that, but was so powerless at the moment that he easily won, and I looked at him. His mouth was moving.

"Liana?" His voice was muffled, but I focused on it and the concerned look on his face. "Can you hear me?"

I nodded, but my hand fearfully tightened on my throat, feeling skin that was smooth and unblemished but had been split wide open not too long ago. I was still terrified.

"Liana, you went into shock. Probably because of the blood loss and trauma. Are you okay?" I blinked and looked over at the new voice just over Leo's shoulder, and saw Quess's dark blue eyes gazing back at me, equally concerned.

I shook my head violently in answer to his question. I was most definitely *not* okay.

Leo reached up and cupped my cheek, dragging my gaze back over to him. "I understand," he said gently. "But I need you to focus, okay?"

I couldn't handle that idea, and lowered my gaze to the floor.

Bad idea. A dark red pool of blood—my blood—was beginning to congeal over the surface. I shuddered and looked back at him. Focus, he'd said. I'd focus on him if it meant I never had to see that much of my own blood on the floor again.

He smiled encouragingly, but I could tell he was scared. Scared for me. "Quess has to take the patch off."

"Patch?" I repeated, confused. What patch?

"Patch," he confirmed, lifting up his arm. I looked at it, and sure enough, his sleeve had been rolled back and a white patch had been taped over his forearm, a long tube connected to the center of it. I followed the tubing toward myself, and found an identical patch on my own forearm, the tube connecting the two. Leo was giving me his blood.

Wait, we were compatible?

"You lost a lot of blood, but Quess found the transfusion patch on the floor next to the bio-foam canister. We assume they left it so we would stop to treat you. Anyway, that's not important right now. But we have to take it off now, okay? It won't hurt."

I nodded and lifted my arm toward him, trying to think. "We have the same blood type?" I asked, my voice hoarse. My vocal cords felt strange and tight, like they had been packed with tiny sharp rocks that weren't painful, but were uncomfortable.

He shook his head as he carefully pulled the patch back. The patch itself didn't hurt, though the adhesive could sometimes sting when removed. But he took his time, making sure not to hurt me. "Grey is a universal donor," he said with a lopsided smile that looked almost bittersweet. "It's lucky I recovered the memory of him getting blood-typed. He saved your life today."

"As the guy who applied the foam and the patches, I have to say: standing *right* here," Quess said dryly.

For some reason, that made me laugh, though I snatched it back in almost immediately by clapping my free hand over my mouth, terrified that the new movement had torn something inside my throat. My hand gently massaged the tendons in my neck, icy fear washing away all vestiges of humor.

"Who did this, Liana?" Leo demanded gently. "Did you see?"

The man's face—now impossible to forget—flashed through my head, and I nodded. "I did," I replied in a whisper. "It was him—the man from the catwalk. The boy... He's with them." We'd stumbled into them completely by accident, I realized as I clutched Leo closer. I'd thought the boy could lead us to the undoc group, but instead it seemed he was a legacy. They all were. Everyone who had raced out of here while I was bleeding out on the floor was a legacy.

But then, why had they been up here?

Leo tsked angrily. "We should get her out of here and just let

Dylan investigate the area," he said sharply. "Tian's already called her."

"Where's Tian?" I mumbled as I finished confirming that I was, in fact, still alive and not bleeding.

The two men exchanged looks. "She was unconscious and on the floor when we came in," Leo said. "We saw that you were bleeding and were helping you when she woke up. She took one look at you, said 'not again,' and ran off to pick up your attacker's trail. She called Dylan to help her. Now, we should go before—"

"Liana needs to see what we found before Dylan does," Quess interrupted hotly. "I don't even think Dylan should see this. It's so... weird. Besides, Liana is going to want to see it."

They were moving too fast for me to keep up with them. And Tian was gone, chasing after the people who had slit my throat. I didn't care if she had called Dylan—she needed to get back here. "One thing at a time," I warbled. "Net Tian and get her back here."

"I've tried," Quess said angrily. "She's rejecting the call."

"Quess, they attacked the Champion," I said evenly, though my insides were twisted with fear. I remembered the feeling of having my throat cut, and the terrifying empty seconds when I had felt my life's blood spilling in between my fingers and down my throat. He'd left something for my friends to use to fix me, but now Tian was out there by herself, and she was just a little girl. If they caught her, I wasn't so sure they'd spare her.

Wait, why hadn't their leader just left me to bleed out? Why had he left me with the means to survive? When he'd attacked me on the catwalk, I was certain that he'd been there to kill me, but now... Had something changed? If so, what?

I swallowed hard, confused and terrified by the implications. Did their "boss" want me alive for some reason? If so, why? I could cope with the idea of them wanting me dead, but the idea they were keeping me alive for unknown purposes filled me with dread.

A sharp snap in my ear made me jerk out of my thoughts, alarm skittering over my skin. I focused on Leo, and realized he had snapped his fingers next to my ear. "Sorry," I croaked. I looked at Quess and remembered my earlier fear. The threat—or lack thereof —to my life could wait. Tian's life was in danger. "Tian."

"Liana, even if you override her net to force her to accept a call, she won't listen," he said, raking a hand through his hair. "But she'll be okay. She survived with Jang-Mi, remember? Besides, you really, really need to see this."

It was the third time he'd mentioned whatever "this" was, and Leo made an irritated sound, opening his mouth to once again suggest we go. I placed a hand on his shoulder, gently cutting him off, and looked at Quess. "See what?"

Quess shot Leo a triumphant look and then turned to me. "Can you get up? I think it's a lot easier if I just show you."

I hesitated, but then nodded when I looked down at the puddle of blood on the floor. Yes. Yes, I could. Especially if it meant getting away from that spot. "Yup," I said, removing my hand from his shoulder. "Help me up."

I hated asking for it, but I was still too shaky to stand. Both Quess and Leo held hands out to me, but I took Leo's based purely on the fact that he was on my left, and my right hand still had a fulltime job ensuring that my throat remained whole and undamaged. That didn't stop Quess from putting a hand under my elbow to help Leo keep me from tipping over when I stumbled, my knees wobbling.

When it became clear to them that I was still too shaken to walk on my own, they pressed me between them, supporting me—something for which I was eternally grateful—as we moved away from the blood. I kept my head down, focusing on putting one foot in front of the other without tripping up.

"So what's the weird thing that Quess wants me to see?" I asked hoarsely. My voice echoed wildly, and I looked up from the floor in alarm. The room was massive, perhaps just as big as the storage room from before, but devoid of any boxes. I kept expecting to see them as I looked around, but it was empty, save for one lone thing: a structure built out of... well... everything, really. It looked like they'd gathered a bunch of stuff that had been destined for the recyclers in Cogstown and used it to create uneven and angular walls with slanted doors and irregularly shaped windows. Pipes of all different sizes filled the gaps, even making up some of the walls in a few places, and helping to define and outline aspects of the patchwork structure.

A house, a dim memory from the legacy net told me, and I nodded. It fit with the descriptions that I had heard. A house. Inside an empty storage room in the Attic. In the Tower. Where we had found a group of legacies.

It seemed like a bad joke, but there was no denying it was there, and I couldn't help but gape at it, confused by its presence.

"Ummmm..." I said, unable to vocalize anything beyond that.

"I know, right?" Quess said, and it was hard to tell whether the undercurrent in his voice was excitement or fear. Then I realized it was probably both. "It's really weird."

I took a step toward it and then stopped again. There was something eerie about this entire thing, and my already-frayed emotional state was screaming at me to run away from this anomaly as quickly as possible. Telling me that anything I found inside would only horrify me.

I managed to put a lid on it, though, dismissing the idea. I was being irrational. It was odd, but not anything to panic over. Not until I saw what was inside.

"We can let Dylan check it out," Leo suggested gently.

"You haven't been inside?" I asked, studying the house. It definitely wasn't big enough for the number of people I'd heard, but given the cavernous nature of the room, that number could be wrong —exaggerated by echoes. Going inside would give us a count of how many people were in the legacy group, and possibly some clues as to who they were working for and what they were up to.

"You're joking, right?" Quess said. "That thing gives me the willies, and you and Leo were too busy hugging it out to help me, so I stayed out."

"We don't have to go in, Liana," Leo reminded me, but I was already moving forward, pulling out of his grasp, my need to see inside giving strength to my shaky limbs. This was clearly the home of our enemies, and accident or not, finding it gave us an opportunity to learn more about them.

I approached a black hole made from the frame of a pressure door at the front and stopped when I saw that the angular light of the room only penetrated the darkness inside for a few feet. I reached into my pocket to pull out my hand light, but realized it was gone, left back where the man had set it after I pulled it out of my pocket.

Leo clicked his on and then brushed past me, with a brusque, "I'll go first this time."

There was a thread of anger in his voice, and my hand tightened on my throat, the memory of the bite of the blade flashing through me. I'd plunged in first after Tian, yes—and it had nearly gotten me killed. Leo was clearly angry about that, and wasn't going to let me repeat the mistake.

And I was ashamed that I let him. As our leader, I should set the example and tone. But as the girl who had just had her throat cut... I watched and waited as he shone his light forward, his baton ready in the other hand. I looked down at my baton and realized that if I wanted to pull it, I would have to let go of my throat.

"Quess," I said as Leo's light revealed a straight hallway, which he began to ease down. "Tell me my throat is okay?"

I hated myself for feeling so needy. I was sure Quess's medical training had been enough to handle this, but I was still afraid that something was wrong inside me. Quess reached out and pulled me into a tight hug, comforting me.

"I promise that you are whole and intact. It's over."

I nodded shakily and then sucked in a deep, calming breath as he slowly released me. It was over. I was safe. It would be a long time before I would ever be able to feel that, but for now, I had to let it go.

"Okay," I said, closing my eyes. I slowly lowered my hand, fighting through a swell of panic, and took another breath. Breathed out. No gurgle of blood. I swallowed back the nausea the memory produced, but kept pushing my hand down, reaching for my baton and finally sliding it out of its loop. I gripped it tightly, and though my hand itched to return to my neck, I resisted, turning back toward the house instead... and following Leo.

The first few steps were hard, but I continued to force air in and out of my lungs at a slow and steady pace, and it helped. I stepped over the threshold into the hall, and saw that Leo's light had stopped at the end of the long, straight corridor. And as he shone it around, I could see that the hallway split off in two different directions. He waited, not going any farther without us, and I made my way toward him, as his light shone across walls with the same patchwork construction as the ones outside.

At the junction, I stopped and took a glance down the intersecting hall. "Which way should we go?" I asked softly.

Leo hesitated, and then nodded toward the right. I followed his lead, Quess right at my heels. The hall continued on for fifteen steps, and then stopped at a wall. Another hall opened up to the left, while the right wall held a doorway with a cloth of black microfiber draped over it. Leo pushed it aside with his baton and shone the light in, revealing what appeared to be a cafeteria of sorts. Mismatched tables had been set up in long rows with seating on either side, holding spots for sixteen people. Plates and bowls sat on the table, full of the remains of what looked like a breakfast that had been hastily abandoned. Some of the food was odd and cube-like. A few torn silver packs suggested that I was looking at the inside of an MRE package, and I wrinkled my nose.

Around us, though, nothing moved, and Leo stepped in and did a quick search.

"Nobody here," he called softly, returning to us. I stepped back to let him pass, and then followed him down the other hall. This one had several doors in it, and as we looked through them, it became clear that they were additional rooms. They weren't in the best condition; old, used mattresses that had apparently been recovered from a trash pile were tossed haphazardly around each room, with dirty and ragged bits of fabric strewn around, including blankets comprised of old and neglected uniforms that had been sewn together.

It was hard to tell how many people had been sleeping here, but I counted ten individual blankets scattered in piles in the first room, and another twelve in the second. The third had just as many, telling me that there was a total of thirty-four people minimum living here.

That was a lot more than I had expected, really. I had guessed the legacy group had a lot of people, but thirty-four was excessive. Those were thirty-four mouths to feed, to procure water for, and to keep hidden. The possibility of disease was high if they weren't able to clean regularly. Smaller groups would be safer, both from detection and sickness, and would help keep their resource requirements manageable. But these people weren't a small group. There was no sign of running water or a bathing area, and they were surviving on MREs. So then why keep so many in such a way that would get them easily caught?

I supposed it was possible that whoever was in charge wanted to keep their people together so they could use them for various deeds, so maybe the entire place was like a contingent of foot soldiers, sent out on missions as they were needed? My eyes widened at the scale and the scope of the operation, and I realized that these people were likely foot soldiers for the legacies, kept purposefully outside the system so that they could move freely and carry out their orders. I was betting that whoever was giving them those orders was doing so from inside the Tower.

I'd double my bet and wager that their orders were coming directly from Sadie Monroe. I found myself wondering if she'd been here, and realized that if I wanted to know, I'd need a team to come in and take DNA samples from everything—which meant calling Dylan in. I resolved to do that *after* we checked the place out. And I'd send Maddox with Dylan to doublecheck every sample herself, and so they could walk them down to the Medica together.

The rooms now cleared, we backtracked quickly to check the other hall. This one turned right and stopped a few feet later at a door. Not just any door, either, but a pressure door, complete with a frame that sat perfectly straight at the end of the hallway, held up by the patchwork walls.

The presence of the door in a house where there hadn't been any so far was so bizarre that it was almost surreal—and staring at it left me with a sense of foreboding, warning me that nothing good could lie behind it, and that opening it would be a big mistake. I tried to dismiss the feeling as I studied the door from where I had halted, but I couldn't seem to shake it, no matter how hard I tried. It was on the tip of my tongue to tell Leo to stop as he wrapped his hand around the wheel, and turned.

I expected it to refuse to budge, but to my surprise, it began to move silently, spinning freely without any resistance.

25

I wasn't sure why, but the hand wheel turning so easily only doubled my concern about what was inside the room. It meant someone had cared enough to oil the gears inside the door, to keep it working well. More than they'd done for any of the rooms in this place.

What exactly was so special that they kept it behind this door?

Leo tugged it open, and Quess and I stepped back as it swung out toward us. Inside was an... office?

It was an office. There was a desk, chairs, cabinets... and I gaped at them as I stepped in after Leo, horrified and alarmed to see that they were made of *wood*! Trees were precious in the Tower, and were never cut down unless they were diseased. I had only ever seen wood used on the Grounds and in the Council Room, and that had been harvested from the pre-End world. Even the furniture available to the Champion wasn't made of wood.

But somehow this office contained a wooden desk, wooden chairs, and wooden cabinets. Leo stepped deeper into the room, and I followed, spotting even more wood hidden in the corner that I hadn't been able to see from the door, in the form of tables that held short stacks of thin things that looked like books, but were too thin and wide to be real books. Not only that, they had colors, and though they were muted and faded with age, they weren't possible with Tower printing.

I reached out and touched the surface of one, expecting it to be brittle or rough, but it wasn't. It was smooth. I gently slid it off the stack, and suddenly I knew exactly what it was, the legacy net hitting me with another brief memory—of idly turning the pages of something called a magazine. Specifically, the memory was of a fashion magazine, in which women were depicted with bright red lips and pale skin, wearing outfits that were nothing like what we wore but somehow made me feel slightly insecure.

Frowning, I looked at the front of the magazine in my hand, reading the words there out loud. "'Noninvasive Rhinoplasty Techniques'?" I looked at Leo questioningly, holding up the magazine.

"Rhinoplasty?" he repeated, cocking his head. "I'm not sure what that is. What's on the inside?"

I carefully opened the book, and my eyes widened. Where the outside had been faded and muted, the inside was bright with pinks and reds and whites and blues. Bright and awful, although it took me a second to figure that last part out.

Because that was how long it took me to realize I was looking at a person's face. It was partially blocked by a pair of blue gloved hands that were holding two long metal objects against what I could tell was a nose, though part of the skin had been cut back to reveal the bone inside. One of the long metal objects was pressed to the bridge of the bone, and the other object—a hammer—was hovering over the end of the first, about to hit it and drive the metal into the soft bone of the nose.

I slapped the magazine shut in horror, sickened by the image. Revulsion curled through me as I tried to imagine what reason anyone would have to drive a piece of blunted metal into another person's open face cavity, and found nothing good. Hands took the magazine away from me, and a second later I heard the pages rustle as it was flipped back open.

"Don't," I managed thickly around my nausea.

"Scipio help me," Quess muttered next to me, and I realized he was the one who had taken the magazine. Only there wasn't horror in his voice... but awe. I looked over to see him flipping through the pages one by one, his eyes dancing over the images there. I glanced, but as soon as I saw the bright pink flash that denoted a human being flayed open, I looked away.

"What is it?" I asked. He seemed excited about something, because he quickly closed the magazine and opened another one, reaching around me to grab it. "What are they? Manuals on how to torture people?"

It was the only thing I could think of to explain the gruesome image, and I wouldn't have been at all surprised to find it, given my realization that these were the same legacies who had attacked Leo and me. But to my surprise, Quess shook his head.

"They're medical journals," he replied. "Pre-End medical journals. Look at this." He closed the magazine and showed me the cover, pointing to a faded black line at the top. It took me a second, but I realized it wasn't a line, but letters and numbers. "March 4, 2009," Quess said, sparing me from having to puzzle it out. "These are over two hundred and fifty years old. Sage would literally die if he could see all of these."

"Sage?" I asked, turning toward him and arching an eyebrow. "Why would he care about this?"

"The man loves pre-End medical journals, and has a standing deal to give a week's worth of protein rations to any Medic who finds them. He's obsessed with them. But his collection is only a fraction of this, and I don't think he has anything on... plastic and reconstructive surgery?" He looked up at me and then Leo, baffled. "What's plastic surgery?"

Leo shook his head, looking equally confused. "Lionel and I talked about all sorts of ailments of the human body, and various treatments and cures, but I've never heard of it before. I'm sorry."

Disappointed that for once Leo couldn't fill us in on something about pre-End society, I looked back at the magazine, thinking. "How many medical journals does Sage have?" I asked.

"Oh, I don't know," Quess said. "A lot, but not this many."

I considered the pile in front of me, and the office itself. If it had just been the magazines in here, with no door, I would've assumed the legacies had been trading them for supplies on the black market. They had food, but there was so much more that they needed to survive, like water, medicine, growing pods for small produce... But none of that had been evident in the house. And then there was the wood—something that no one would trade on the black market, because no one could afford it—and from the look of the furniture in the room, it was clearly being used from time to time. Putting them in here with all of that meant that these medical journals were important to them, in some way. It was another piece of the puzzle—one that I didn't quite understand.

But maybe one that I wouldn't have to leave unanswered, if I played my cards right. I needed to find out why the journals would be stored here like this, as if they were important, and that meant learning about the subject matter. From the one person most likely to know.

"So Sage might know what plastic surgery is?" I asked, an idea beginning to form.

Quess looked thoughtful, and then shrugged. "If anyone knows, it's Sage."

"What are you thinking, Liana?" Leo asked, looking up from the desk drawer he was slowly opening. I felt an urge to beg him to stop, worried that the wood would somehow disintegrate into pieces if it was moved too much, but bit it back to consider his question.

Several reasons for going to Sage had been piling up in the last few days. I had questions about Jasper, where the vid file to my fight with Devon was, and now plastic surgery—plus the questions about an alien girl who had visited the Tower twenty-five years ago. I wasn't going to ask all of them, (obviously), but I did want answers to quite a few of them, starting with this.

If the legacies had this plastic surgery, I wanted to know what they were using it for.

Of course, the downside to going to Sage was that I wasn't sure where we stood. He had voted against upholding the results of the Tourney—and me—so I wasn't exactly confident that he would be willing to talk to me. I could be waiting days, if not weeks, to see him. Longer if he really didn't think I belonged on the council. Oh, and of course, he could always be part of the legacy group out to get me, so there was that.

Still, I had to try. I had been meaning to already, and had put it off after Leo and I were attacked, but there was no better time than the present. He'd also offered to give me advice if I ever needed it, and hopefully he meant it. But even if he hadn't, I was pretty confident I had a good way in that would guarantee a meeting with him—although, I wasn't going to offer it upfront. I'd wait to see what his first reply was.

"That it's time to talk to Sage," I replied in answer to Leo's question. I reached out and grabbed one of the magazines, holding it up. "And I've even got something to butter him up."

Leo and Quess exchanged glances, and then looked around the small office. "What about this?" Quess asked. "Should we let Dylan take a look at it?"

"In a little while," I said slowly, thinking. The first thing that came to mind was that I wanted to clear the room of all these treasures. They were too precious to be lying around, and I didn't want Dylan getting an idea of what the bigger picture might be until I knew I could trust her. I recalled my earlier thought of pairing her with Maddox, and decided to continue with that plan, with one slight delay: moving everything of value out.

It took me a minute to figure out where to hide it all—someone would obviously notice if we hauled a wooden desk to my quarters—but then I figured, why haul it there when there was a perfectly good storage room next to us through a door in the corner, complete with broken lights and sealed piles of boxes we could hide everything in? For a little while, at least.

"First, call Zoe, Eric, and Maddox so we can get everything out of this room that we can. We'll move it into the other room and wrap the furniture in plastic, but the journals go to our quarters. I think they're important, and that the legacies will be back for them."

Quess nodded and set down the magazine, then moved off to make the call. I turned back to the stack, now more curious than horrified, but paused as Leo's concerned gaze hit me.

"Are you okay?" he asked, and just like that the memory was back, tearing through me faster than the blood could drain from my face.

I reached up to touch the undamaged flesh on my neck, but he moved faster, grabbing my hand and pressing it against his heart. "I was so scared," he said raggedly, pulling me up against the hard wall of his chest until there wasn't a millimeter of space between us. His heart thundered under my hand, and I realized his breathing was hard. "All that blood..."

His hands smoothed over me again, and I realized that my close brush with death hadn't only affected me. "I'm okay," I told him, recognizing that this time it was his turn to need comfort. I slid my free arm around his waist and tightened it. I wasn't able to draw him closer, but that wasn't the point. I was his anchor, the only thing keeping him from freaking out, and I was happy to provide the support he needed.

Especially because he was trying to do the same for me.

His grip tightened as he rested his cheek against the top of my head, fitting me neatly under his chin. "Never again, Liana. You never rush in first again, okay?"

I nodded, but apparently that wasn't enough for him, because he drew away and shook my shoulders. "I mean it," he growled, a possessive edge to his voice that should've made me quiver with fear, but instead stirred a low thrum of excitement that made me suddenly hungry for more than his arms around me. I needed something—anything—to distract me from what had happened not even an hour ago.

He speared me with a stern look, oblivious to the effect he was having on me. "You will never, ever enter a room unless you are behind someone!"

"Technically I was behind Tian," I pointed out absentmindedly. I wasn't entirely sure what I was saying, to be honest. My eyes were focused on his mouth, my need mounting.

He growled angrily, but then softened, his fingers reaching up to trace over the lines of my jaw, cheeks, nose, eyebrows. "We'd all be lost without you," he told me. "If you died..."

I could tell there was more he was struggling to say—an undercurrent to his words that made me think that when he said "we", he meant "I"—and warmth bloomed in my chest.

A small voice told me to stop, but it was lost in the overwhelming rush of tenderness and a need to feel something that could transcend both our fears. On impulse, I went to the tips of my toes, drawing my face closer to his.

He watched me for a second, his cheeks flushed and his eyes hooded in question, and I paused, wondering if maybe he was holding back because of Grey and what happened on the catwalk. But then his mouth dipped down and captured my own.

He wasn't gentle about it. He kissed me like he was drowning and I was his only source of oxygen, nipping at my lips until I parted them under his. His tongue swept in, smooth and hot and teasing, and I moaned, my hands gripping his uniform as I melted into him.

Leo groaned, and then pressed me back until my hips hit the table behind me and I was effectively trapped. The feeling drove me wild, and my hands exchanged their grip on his shoulders for one on his hair, pinning him in place. His hands dropped from my shoulders to my hips, holding me firmly against him.

He broke the kiss with a gasp, and ignored my hungry cry to spear me with another look. "Promise me," he whispered hoarsely, fear drowning out the lust in his eyes. I hated that my recklessness had put it there, and regretted not waiting for him more than he knew. "I don't care if what I'm feeling is Grey or me. I can't ever stand to see you like that again. Promise."

I swallowed, his seriousness dragging me back to reality, and nodded. "I promise," I said.

The relief in his eyes was palpable, and he dragged me to his chest and held me close, his actions telling me that he just needed to hold me, to feel that I was whole and alive. I wanted more, but I didn't push—this would do as well.

We stood like that for several moments, taking solace in each other, before Quess politely cleared his throat, making us both jump and turn toward him. "Everyone's on their way," he announced, barely able to hide the smile on his face. "Oh, and Maddox says your brother is apparently looking for you."

Crap. Alex. I sighed and rubbed my forehead. I'd forgotten to get back to him after the attack yesterday, and he was undoubtedly angry about it. I'd have to net him soon and calm him down.

"Thanks, Quess," I said tiredly, trying to figure out when I could even do so. I could net him now, while we worked, but honestly, I was too emotional from the attack, and this stuff needed to be moved before anyone else decided to come back and see what we were up to. I didn't want any of the legacies coming back before we had hidden these things. I was sure the legacies were expecting me to bring a full contingent of Knights up here to scour the place, but I wasn't prepared to throw up the undoc alarm just yet. Doing so would only send them deeper into hiding, and I would lose any chance of catching them. So we needed to move quickly, before they realized that there weren't as many people after them as they thought there would be, and doubled back to see what was going on.

I was betting that if this stuff was gone, they'd have no reason to stick around, which would make it safe for Dylan and Maddox to check out later. A part of me wanted to use that, to set up a trap to catch them if they did return, but I had too much on my plate trying to find a way to rescue Jasper, and I needed as many people as possible working on that.

And then I needed to schedule an appointment with Sage. This was my second brush with the legacies in a number of days, and I wanted to know what was going on. If he had some insight he could share about this plastic surgery stuff, then it took priority. There had to be a reason that the legacies were keeping those journals, and I wanted to know why they were so important.

But after that... I'd call Alex. I just had to get through the rest of this.

"Let's go ahead and start pulling stuff out while we wait," I suggested.

Leo reluctantly nodded and pulled away. Quess's smirk deepened, but he didn't utter a word as he reentered the room to get started.

Which was good—I wasn't entirely sure I could suffer teasing about what was going on between Leo and me. Not when I wasn't even sure what it was yet, myself.

And I wasn't going to think about that right now, either. Better to keep my head down and get to work—which was exactly what I did.

26

I was a little surprised that Sage sent an immediate reply to my request for a meeting. In fact, I was glad that I had waited until every medical journal and scrap of wood was out of the house, because I wouldn't have had time to help. He was ready to receive me *now*, it seemed, and I would've felt guilty having to abandon the others for the meeting. Doubly so since it seemed Leo was now determined to go with me wherever I went.

Quess was cleaning up my blood when we left, and it was hard to look away from it and keep myself from rubbing my throat, but Leo held my hand the entire way, sending me warmth and reassurance through our physical connection.

We went back to our quarters to take a quick shower and change, and then headed over to the Medica. As soon as we arrived, an intern —Martina—rushed over to us to explain that Sage was in the greenhouse and that she would escort us to the elevators. No one but Sage and his personal assistants were allowed in the area. When I asked her why that was, she explained that Sage was very protective of the plants they grew for medicinal purposes because they were worth more than, as she put it, "the life of one measly doctor".

I wasn't sure why I found that amusing. Maybe because Martina pitched her voice down to an exaggerated version of Sage's as she spoke, not caring that it was inappropriate to be mocking the head of her own department in front of the head of another. Or maybe it was because I could picture Sage saying it, with the crooked grin and spark of humor that were ever-present on his face. Either way, I had to fight back a laugh as she deposited us in front of the elevator.

We were silent on the trip. Part of that was because I was preparing myself for what I was expecting to be a very delicate interview. I had a plan—a way in—and my requests firmly in mind. Namely, I wanted the vid file from the fight with Devon, information on Jasper, and to know what the hell plastic surgery was. The requests were all tricky, and the second to last one doubly so, because too many questions about Jasper could show our hand in regard to what we knew. If Sage was an enemy, he might figure out we knew about the fragment AIs and send his people after me to figure out what I knew. They could figure out we had Jang-Mi and try to steal her back—or worse, discover Leo. I had to be delicate about it, and only ask the question if there was a natural way to progress into it. I couldn't force it, no matter how much I wanted to.

I still didn't feel entirely ready when we pulled to a stop in front of a door marked *Greenhouse 5*, but I squared my shoulders and hit the button to open the door.

"Signal me if you need backup," Leo said softly as the door slid aside. I gave him a nod and stepped in. Leo had to wait outside, unfortunately. But I knew that if I got in trouble, he'd find a way to get in and help me.

The door closed behind me, and I took a moment to summon up a deep calm before looking around. When Martina had mentioned a greenhouse, I had expected plants, but nothing like this. Instead of the harsh, bright white light of the Medica, the lights in here were warm and yellow, reminding me of the lamps used to emulate the different daytime settings in the atrium around the Citadel. Everything else was colored green. Shelves and shelves of plants that I had never seen before. Plants with long, flexible vines that spilled over the edges and dangled down; plants that had tight, folded buds that reminded me of heads of cabbages, only the leaves were smaller and more uniform; and others that had purple and white flowers growing from a single stalk.

I couldn't help but gape at them as I made my way down the long walkway separating the rows of shelves, peering along the aisles between them in search of human life. I found one person wearing a full white suit that covered everything except their face, which was obscured by a pair of goggles and a large white mask with blue filtration holes off to the sides. I was alarmed for a second, until I saw them holding a spray canister in one hand and realized they were only using the mask for whatever chemicals they were spraying. If I got closer, I'd need one too, but I was fine where I was.

I continued to walk, and eventually the rows of shelves were replaced with tables, where hundreds of small pots bearing sprigs of life sat.

Sage was halfway down one of the tables, seated on a stool, his already-stooped form hunched over a small tree—the tiniest tree I'd ever seen. He was carefully snipping tiny branches from it.

He glanced my way as I approached him, then turned back to his work. "Hello, Liana," he said, cutting another branch. I came around him to stand at the edge of the table, just to the side of where he was sitting, and watched him for a second as he continued to cut small branches away.

"I've never seen a tree like that," I commented. Seemed like a safe start. "Why is it so small?"

"It's a bonsai tree," he replied without shifting his focus. "Produces lots of oxygen, and the bark has several medicinal properties. They require a lot of work, though; they're always trying to get bigger, and if they do, they'll suffocate themselves, trapped in this tiny pot. So we constantly have to cut them back. Keep them in their place so they can continue to thrive." He chuckled at that and leaned back in his chair, admiring his work. "That'll do," he declared after a moment, setting the clippers down and dusting his hands.

He gingerly stepped off the stool and picked up a walking stick that I hadn't noticed leaning against the table next to him. "So, I was a little surprised to get your message," he told me as he reached for the pot with the tree. "All new councilors find their way to me eventually—can't seem to resist seeking advice from the longest-serving elected official, heh, heh—but never after only two days in office." He flashed me a wry smile and started to head over to another table, where similar trees were lined up. "I can't decide if that makes you smarter than most, or completely inept."

I blinked at him, surprise rolling through me. He thought I was here for advice? That was interesting. I studied him for a second and then decided not to correct his assumption right now. It'd be interesting to see where he went with this. He could, I thought, reveal something without intending to.

"Oh?" I said, managing to put mild interest into my voice. "And what do you think?"

He gave me a canny look as he placed the tree down on the table. "Smarter than most. But that's not necessarily a good thing. Too much thinking can lead to the invention of problems."

I cocked my head. "Do you think I've invented a problem?"

He arched one white eyebrow and tsked. "You know you did, when you voted against CEO Monroe's request. I'm sure she's already given you the harsh edge of her tongue, of course, and explained why. That's why you're here, right? To pick my mind on how to develop better relationships with your fellow councilors?"

He chuckled and ducked his head up and down in a repetitive motion, agreeing with himself, as if that was the only reasonable explanation for the meeting—that I needed a mentor. I cocked my head at him, suddenly curious about how many others had come to him over the years, and why. "How many other councilors have you given advice to?" I asked.

"Oh, dozens and dozens by now," he said cheerfully. "Being the oldest man in the Tower has its ups and downs, but I never get tired of teaching and helping out. It keeps me young." He winked at me, and I shook my head. It was hard not to smile at his cheerfulness, even if he was being vague with his answer.

"Anyway, the only way you're going to soothe Sadie is to show her that you trust in her abilities. Maybe the next time a server goes down in the Citadel, or a lash-way door goes haywire, you can ask her to personally take a look. Give her some excuse about not wanting to appear incompetent. Sadie is a smug and arrogant girl who only likes it when you are giving her accolades."

"Do you think that will get her to back off the investigation so we can vote on the expulsion chambers?" I asked.

Okay, it hadn't been anywhere on my list of topics to talk to him about, but I couldn't help it. If sucking up to Sadie got her to back off a bit and let the vote move on, then I was willing to try. I didn't have that much pride when it came to saving lives.

He chuckled and leaned back. "You really don't like the expulsion chambers, do you?"

I hesitated, torn between giving him the truth and being afraid of how he would perceive it. "I don't like that Scipio was somehow forced into recommending the practice in the first place," I hedged, adding some defensiveness, which I hoped he would perceive as righteous.

I kind of liked letting him believe I was a zealous defender of Scipio and the ideals of the Tower. Maybe it was paranoid of me, but I didn't want anyone really knowing who I was. Keeping that a secret kept my enemies guessing about my next moves, and made me unpredictable—especially if they were constantly underestimating me.

"And if people on the council want to keep the expulsion chambers active after learning that Devon Alexander corrupted Scipio's decision to make them happen, then I would argue that they are just as culpable as he was."

Sage's eyebrows lifted high onto his forehead, wrinkling the skin all the way up to his bald scalp. His eyes bulged in shock, and then a moment later he opened his mouth and laughed, a sharp bark of sound that quickly dissolved into desperate wheezing and coughing. My heart skipped a beat when he doubled over, making an awful hacking sound. I was suddenly certain he was going to die, and that somehow I'd be blamed.

I calmed some when his coughs and wheezes slowed, punctuated by slow chuckles as the old man continued to laugh. "You've got some spunk to you, kid, I'll give you that," he said once he'd caught his breath.

An assistant appeared from nowhere with a glass of water in one hand and a small gold canister in another. Sage opened his mouth as she approached, and I watched, fascinated, as she sprayed some sort of mist into it, which he immediately inhaled. They did this two more times in rapid succession, and by the third one, his breathing had vastly improved. She handed him the glass and then walked away while he guzzled the contents of the cup.

"Sorry," he said abashedly once his glass was empty. "Do yourself a favor, kid, and never get old. It sucks."

I laughed at his dry tone. "I'll do my best. Any tips on how to do that?"

He grinned and tapped his head. "The trick is to remain young here," he informed me. "If you can do that, then you'll slow the aging process. It's how I've lived so long, although it's getting harder and harder to feel young."

He flexed his back, and I heard a series of cracks as his ancient bones slipped around in place—awful, in spite of his soft sound of relief.

"Now, to answer your question, no, Sadie isn't going to back down on doing that investigation, because I can tell you for certain that she doesn't want the expulsion chambers gone. Neither do I, for that matter, and neither does Plancett. I know Lacey and Strum want to get rid of them, but that's understandable, since half the rank ones collected come from their departments. But that's the breaks of living so far away from the sunlight emulators of the atrium and the farms. The citizens in both departments are prone to depression due to the lack of vitamin D in their systems. We give supplements, but nothing, it seems, can compare to the real thing. Suicide rates in their departments are also astoundingly high, but I digress."

He paused to catch his breath, and I took a moment to process what he had just said. Lacey had said something similar in our conversation last night, only she had mentioned a third. I did some quick math, and realized that if what they were saying was true, for every one person each other department sent to the expulsion chambers, Lacey and Strum were sending almost three apiece.

That was ridiculously high, but what was worse, Sage and Plancett didn't want the law changed, and he thought that Lacey and Strum only did because they were trying to protect their people. What did he think about *me* wanting them gone? I decided to keep my mouth shut and see what he would say next. Maybe he'd answer that question for me.

"I can see you're not happy with that news," Sage said with a smile. "Want to tell me why?"

Damn it. I hesitated for a second, and somehow managed to pull a believable lie from nowhere. "Not *unhappy*," I replied. "I guess I just don't understand what was so wrong with the system before. Why is killing people our only option?"

His grin deepened. "That is a very philosophical question, but I am assuming you just want my reasoning for it. I hope you know I can't speak for the others?" I nodded, and he continued. "To answer your question, we had what we called a loaner program set up for anyone who dropped to the rank of three or below. Those people were allowed to make communities around the shell, and served as basic work crews for various departments, to take care of the less-than-desirable tasks. They worked in exchange for ration cards, but there were never enough tasks for them, so many of them wound up starving, which resulted in them stealing, and almost launching a rebellion a few times. Once the expulsion chambers went into effect, criminal activity plummeted, as did communicable diseases and rank degradation. Even keeping them a secret has helped ensure order because the rumors are so believable. It sucks, but it is necessary."

I blew out a breath, trying not to show the complete rejection of his ideas on my face. Maybe the loaner program hadn't been effective, but from what he had just said, it didn't seem like it had been designed to be that way in the first place. Otherwise they would've found enough jobs to support that aspect of the population. Instead, only a few were provided, and the Tower had let the rest of those people go hungry rather than giving them a viable way to feed themselves. They created the situation, and then used the crisis it caused to justify the expulsion chambers.

As much as I wanted to point that out to Sage, I refrained. Arguing with him wasn't going to get me what I really wanted. So instead, I decided to change course, and get to why I was really here.

"I see. I'll consider what you've said." He gave me a pleased smile. "And I really want to thank you for your advice, but that's not actually why I'm here."

"Oh?" He cocked his head. If he was curious, he didn't show it; he just smiled and waited expectantly.

"I heard from a friend that you collect a few pre-End objects."

He raised an eyebrow. "You're not going to be one of *those* Champions who nitpicks over everything, are you? Because if you are, I have no idea what you're talking about. I don't collect pre-End artifacts."

I chuckled and shook my head. "No, no, nothing like that," I assured him. "Actually, my friend said you'd be interested in something that I recovered recently. It's a medical journal?"

His eyes lit up with excitement, and he leaned forward. "You found one?" I nodded, and his enthusiasm and joy grew as he began to rifle around in his pockets, searching for something. "Each time I find a new one, I think it's the last! Oh, this is exciting. Is it with you?"

I nodded and withdrew it from the same pocket I used to hold my pad, gently easing the fragile thing out so as not to tear any of the precious pages. He looked up, and his pupils dilated in alarm.

"You put it in your pocket?" he exclaimed, horrified. "And you're touching it with your bare hands! Hurry and get it out of there before you ruin it any further!"

His voice was suddenly very serious, and I hastened to obey him, worried that I had turned him against me by handling the magazine so callously. I placed it on the table in front of him and noticed that he had stopped his search upon finding a pair of white microfiber gloves, which he had already donned.

He cackled gleefully as he ran his hands over the front of the magazine, and opened it up. "Oh, wow," he breathed, sounding almost childlike with wonder as he absorbed the pictures inside. "Look at this."

He turned it toward me, revealing another flayed-open face, and I quickly waved my hand to indicate he should turn it away. "I'll be honest, I already looked at it," I told him, playing up my queasiness. "Were pre-Enders that barbaric? Why are there pictures of faces being cut open in there?"

He snorted and turned the magazine back toward him, flipping a page. "You could say it's barbaric, my dear," he huffed. "This medical journal is about a practice called plastic surgery. Unlike other surgical fields, this one focused on changing one's appearance."

Changing one's appearance? I frowned, and thought of the blood recovered on the catwalk and how it had matched blood found at the scene of Devon's murder. I had assumed before that the reason I hadn't recognized any of my attackers was because the man

I would have recognized had a twin or was wearing a disguise. But was it possible that someone had done this... plastic surgery to his face?

I needed to know how much it could affect someone's looks, but realized I needed to ease into that, so asked a far more innocent question first. "Why would they do that?"

Sage sighed and leaned back. "Sometimes people got into accidents that caused large amounts of scarring, and plastic surgery was used to help reconstruct their faces. However, most people used it to 'improve' their looks—make themselves seem more like society's standard of beauty so they could feel more attractive. Utter nonsense." He leaned forward and flipped another page.

I remembered the flash of the fashion magazine, and how insecure I had felt looking at the glamorous pictures in there, and nodded, unable to disagree. So I went a little deeper this time. "Fascinating nonsense, though. Could they really change a person's face so much?"

He nodded, not looking up from the picture. "Oh, yeah. I imagine criminals used it as well, to try to avoid capture by the authorities. There were a few articles that talked about the ethics of the phenomenon, so apparently it was a thing." He shrugged, turning yet another page.

"Did it work? Were they able to avoid facial recognition software?"

Sage gave a delighted laugh and looked up from the magazine. "I don't think they had facial recognition software everywhere at the time, to be honest, but I'm not sure of that. I have to say, though... looking at the few journals I have on this sort of work, I have to imagine that, yes, it would hide them from facial recognition. They could do all sorts of things to change the shape of the face and size of the eyes... Thank Scipio we don't participate in such barbaric processes anymore."

I bit my lip and looked down at the magazine, and then back up to him. This was it—the missing link that explained why we hadn't been able to find the people who had attacked Ambrose after they escaped. It was why I couldn't place the face with the voice. It had to be. It was the only explanation!

A question—a dangerous one—hovered on my lips, and I hesitated to ask it. Still, I couldn't seem to hold it back, and as I opened my mouth, it came spilling out. "Do you think it's possible for someone to recreate these procedures in the Tower?"

I already knew the answer. Yes. I was certain of it down to my bones, but wanted to see what Sage thought about it.

Sage blinked at that and then leaned back, a thoughtful look on his face. "I doubt it," he replied after a moment. "Although it is an interesting idea and would certainly explain why we weren't able to locate that Knight's attackers once they left the Citadel, I don't think it's possible."

"Why not?" I replied, hiding my relief that he wasn't taking my line of inquiry as anything more than curiosity on my part. He had brushed dangerously close to my thoughts on how the legacies who killed Ambrose might be hiding, and I still wasn't sure if I could trust him. I studied him closely, hoping he'd reveal something. His answer sounded genuine, but he could be lying.

"Well, for one thing, this is only the fourth article I've discovered on the topic, and I'm fairly confident when I say I have the largest collection of journals in the Tower. A whopping forty-three—forty-four if you're letting me have this one."

He only had forty-four? There were definitely more than forty-four magazines in the house we'd found, and all of them were about

plastic surgery. It seemed odd that such a treasure trove existed, especially while Sage was offering rations in exchange for the journals. I
supposed it was possible that all of those magazines were actually a
part of Sage's secret collection, the legacies up there working for
him... but the way he poured over the pages like a delighted kid
didn't make that feel right. His eagerness had appeared authentic; his
responses felt genuine.

And those people were subsisting on those strange food cubes
from the MREs, which meant they weren't trading the journals for
food or favors. And that meant they had to be using them—and what
for, if not to change their faces to evade detection? Was it *actually*
possible that someone had figured out how to perform these types of
surgeries, and was performing them on their soldiers to keep them
active and moving around in secret?

"For another," Sage continued, oblivious to my growing excitement. "The tools of the Medica are not designed to cause harm. Most
of our healing procedures are noninvasive. Someone would have to
create tools that could cut human skin precisely, and find resources
to create massive amounts of silicone for implants. Their patients
would have to be sedated for hours, and could die of shock long
before the procedure was finished. The only thing they'd have that's
better than what the pre-Enders did would be access to bio-foam for
the scars, and antibiotics to prevent infection, but the rest of it would
be painful and traumatizing."

And yet, that was what the legacies were doing. It had to be. It
was a long-forgotten practice, and would allow them to navigate the
Tower with a complete measure of freedom. Any time their enemies
saw their faces, they could just change them and keep on going with
no one being any the wiser. It was brilliant and terrifying—and
meant I couldn't trust any strange face in a crowd.

"I'm glad to hear that," I told him, not letting any of my thoughts show. "It sounds awful when you describe it like that. But then again, those pictures were pretty awful as well."

He smiled knowingly. "It took me a few years to get over the sight of blood and human flesh, so I understand. Still, it's good to look back and see how far we've come." He held up the magazine with one hand and raised an eyebrow. "You still haven't told me if you're going to let me add this little treasure to my collection. I assume your friend also told you there was a prize for these things, right?"

I smiled at the sly tone in his voice. He knew we were brokering an illegal deal—trading rations for contraband was a double whammy in the eyes of the system—but he was willing to perform it anyway. And as the head of the Medica, and the ultimate authority on ration cards, he could abuse that power as he pleased. Maybe it was a test. I certainly wasn't going to report him, but then again, rations weren't what I wanted.

"Actually, you can keep the ration cards," I said. "Instead, I'd like to ask for a favor."

He raised an eyebrow and gave me a speculative look. "Go on."

I sucked in a deep breath, and then stated what I wanted as clearly as I could. "I want the vid file of my fight with Devon, starting when he entered the room and ending when his body was removed from it."

Sage squinted at me a second, his eyes reflecting nothing of what he was thinking, and I held my breath and waited. "Didn't we send that already?" he asked, sounding confused. "I'm sure I included it in the evidence for your trial."

I scrutinized the words, looking for any whisper of a lie, but found nothing. I was positive he was telling the truth. In which case... Was it truly an accident, or had someone close to Sage somehow managed to keep it off the final report before he sent it? That was possible; if the legacy groups were performing pre-End surgeries, they'd likely need a Medic working with them to perform the operation—someone trained in the Medica would be the only one with the skills to even attempt such a thing. Maybe Sage had a legacy somewhere high up in his department? I made a mental note to follow up on it, but let it go for now, not wanting to start casting aspersions on anyone. I made my face apologetic and shook my head.

"No, I'm sorry. It wasn't there."

"I see." A pause. "Perhaps I overlooked it. I'm quite embarrassed. I'll have it sent over immediately."

"Thank you," I told him, confused by the suddenly downcast tone his words had taken. He sounded... dismayed. "Are you all right?"

His lips curled up in a smile that didn't quite reach his eyes. "Thank you for your concern, my dear. I just... hate it when I make mistakes like that. It lends fuel to the fire of my fear that I'm a doddering old fool who's on his last legs. And who knows, maybe they're right. Maybe I should retire."

Whoa. Now he sounded positively defeated. Of all the reactions I could've anticipated from Sage, the last one I had expected was vulnerability and fear, but there it was, staring me in the face. I felt a sudden urge to comfort him, and I gave in to it.

"Sir, no," I said, reaching out and resting my hand on his gnarled one. He looked up at me, his eyes windows to his sorrow, and I felt my heart break a little for him. "Everyone makes mistakes from time to time." *Or, someone is trying to make you look inept so they can justify calling for your retirement,* I thought to myself. It could be that the legacies were in the process of infiltrating another department, after they had failed to do so in mine. I'd need to keep a close eye on Sage in the future, just in case I was right. "I'm sure it was just an oversight. Besides, no one needs to know. Once I have it, I'll add it to the file, and that will be that."

His lips tilted up, hope blooming in his eyes. "That's very kind of you, my dear, but you don't have to cover for me like that. I have my integrity to think of, certain hobbies not included." He patted the magazine as he said it, and I couldn't help but feel impressed. "Besides, when my staff decide that it's time, they'll let me know. I'm just doing the job as best I can until I die or they find someone better."

I smiled, pleased that he was cheered up at the very least, even though I internally bristled at the idea of his "staff" letting him know when they were ready. What if someone there was secretly sabotaging him, and then rallying the others against him when his failures became public? I let go of his hand with a final pat.

"Well, may you stay alive, and may they never find anyone better," I said, and he laughed.

I wasn't sure why, but I found that I liked Sage. He was funny and upbeat, and frankly, I was impressed at his integrity. His penchant for collecting medical journals was fine in my mind, and even though we didn't see eye to eye on certain things, I felt he'd been more honest and forthright than any councilor I'd interacted with thus far.

"You are too kind, my dear. It makes me almost feel guilty about my earlier judgment of you. But I didn't know you then, did I?"

Surprised by his straightforwardness, I played dumb. "How do you mean, sir?"

"I voted against upholding the results of the Tourney," he confessed with a smile. "I hope you understand why. I just couldn't condone supporting someone who brought a lethal weapon into an event."

I gave him a little shrug. "To be honest, I didn't expect for the results to be upheld in the first place. But it's okay, I get it."

"Thank you for understanding." He paused and looked back down at the medical journal on the table. "Now, about our deal... You realize that asking me for something I was supposed to turn over in the first place isn't a favor, right? At least, I'm not going to accept it as one. Is there anything else I can do for you in exchange for this beauty?"

Once again, he surprised me, and a pleased smile formed on my lips at such an honorable act. I considered his question for a second, and immediately thought of my questions about Jasper. Our conversation had been going so well that I felt like I could ask, but a part of me hesitated, warning that I should back off now while I was ahead. If I pushed, then there was a chance I would ruin the friendly repartee we had established, and I could earn myself an enemy.

On top of that, there wasn't anything that he could tell us that would help us recover Jasper. Not to mention, I also had to entertain the idea that I had entirely misread Sage and he *was* a legacy, in which case, asking about Jasper right before we stole him would raise some major red flags. Better to let it go for now.

But I felt a strong certainty that I would want to talk to Sage again, so decided to set the groundwork for a future meeting. "Can you just owe me a favor?" I asked.

"I won't compromise my votes on anything," he said hesitantly. "So if you're—"

"Oh, no, sir," I said, shaking my hand. "I would never ask that. I respect your integrity too much. I just meant, if I have a question at a later date, or maybe need a Knight patched up, no-questions-asked sort of thing..."

"Oh," he said, and then chuckled, scratching his chin with one hand. "Oh, yes, that I could see being equitable." He stuck out his hand and smiled broadly. "The deal is struck?"

I took his hand with a firm grip and shook it. "It is indeed, sir. Thanks again for the advice."

"Anytime," he replied with a smile. We shook hands for a second more, and then I let go, said my goodbyes, and left, a little lighter.

Even though he was a little weird, I really liked Sage, and talking to him had felt like I was making a friend.

It was a nice change of pace.

27

I woke up the next morning after a long, deep sleep, confused. It took me a minute to remember where I was and what had happened the night before, but it eventually came back to me. We'd spent a major portion of the evening scanning the schematics of the Core, and then I'd gone to catch up on council business while Maddox took Dylan to the odd little house in the Attic to collect samples of any genetic material they could recover, so we could run it through the Medica's mainframe. We were hoping to find a familial connection to someone inside the Tower, giving us a link to someone in the system we could monitor. Meanwhile, Quess had continued working on figuring out where Sadie's quarters were, and Leo had continued his work with Jang-Mi, trying hard to fix her.

All of us were feeling the press of time, and we needed to make some sort of progress on one front or another, or we'd never be able to get Jasper out. But Jang-Mi wasn't cooperating, and converting two-dimensional images into a three-dimensional model took time. Our hands were effectively tied until we could break down the wall keeping us from getting to him, mine more than Leo's or Quess's, as I couldn't do much in the way of tech stuff. I'd gone to bed before them, giving up after I realized I was just in the way.

Until I'd gotten back up to get Leo in the later hours and asked him to come to bed with me.

At the thought, I immediately reached out an arm, feeling around for him, but to my surprise and disappointment, my bed was empty. I blinked and sat up. He *had* come to bed with me last night; I remembered that much. I hadn't been able to sleep, plagued by the memories of the attack, and when I'd gone to him, he hadn't denied me.

He'd done it without hesitation—even though it meant making Jang-Mi and Jasper wait. For me. It had been so selfish of me, and so selfless of him that I immediately wanted to apologize.

But... where was he? I looked around the room and saw that his uniform was missing from where he had hung it, and then looked at my indicator. My eyes bulged when I saw that it was nearly ten a.m. —and I realized I had overslept.

Drastically.

I hauled back the covers and then paused when I saw a pad sitting on top of mine, propped up against a lamp on the nightstand. I wasn't sure why, but I was certain it was Leo's. I picked it up and turned it on, and sure enough, it opened to a handwritten note.

Good morning, Liana, he wrote, and I smiled. *I'm sorry I had to leave you sleeping, but I wanted to get up early this morning and get a jump start on Jang-Mi. I'm pretty sure I'm close to a breakthrough. I wanted to talk to you about it last night, but you were exhausted,*

which was why I let you sleep in. Don't get mad—it was Dr. Quess's
orders, and I happened to concur.

See you soon,

Leo

P.S. Can you bring the pad with you when you get up? I have a
feeling I'll need it by the time you wake.

His note filled me with warmth and left me breathless from his
simple consideration. He hadn't left me confused; he'd made sure I
knew exactly where he was, and done so with words that made me
feel like he couldn't wait to see me, even though he'd been forced to
leave me.

I realized I didn't even care that he had left me to go check on
Jang-Mi, and that made me feel even better because I wasn't immedi-
ately leaping into "angry Liana" mode whenever she was mentioned.
So all in all, I was already starting the day off on a good foot. Leo and
Quess had been right—a little extra sleep went a long way. I felt
more energized then I had in a while.

Or maybe it was Leo's sweet note. I wasn't sure, and I didn't care.
I merely embraced the surge of enthusiasm and got out of bed, now
eager to start the day. I quickly showered and got dressed, and then
headed to the kitchen, my stomach growling. A part of me worried
that I shouldn't feel this good the day after I'd had my throat cut, but
I figured, hey, I was alive and loved it.

I made and wolfed down a quick breakfast while I brewed some
tea, and then took my mug into the war room, intent on going over
my correspondence and getting an early start on my councilor duties.
I paused just short of the doorway when I suddenly heard Leo say,
"How are you feeling now?"

My smile grew, and I moved forward, eager to see him, but
paused when I heard a response of "Much better, thank you. You

were right, my fight/flight settings were quite high. Why couldn't I see it?" The voice sounded different than Jang-Mi's normal voice—calmer and more controlled—and the difference was drastic enough for me to come to a stop, too curious to interrupt.

"Because of the reversion," Leo replied tiredly, and I frowned. Reversion? What was that?

I eased down the hallway a few more feet, curious.

"I see." There was a pause. "How bad is the corruption?"

Corruption? My heart pounded hard in my chest. Was that the breakthrough Leo had been talking about in his message? He'd made it sound almost optimistic, but corruption sounded bad.

"It's bad," Leo confirmed. "Whatever walls Lionel built to separate your AI personality from the memories of Jang-Mi are gone, and her grief is destroying your protocols. It won't be long until you're gone and only Jang-Mi remains."

Okay, whoa. That was a lot to take in. It took me a second, but I realized that Leo wasn't talking to Jang-Mi. He was talking to *Rose*.

It was a little complicated, but the AIs were neural clones of the founders, and had eventually adapted their own personalities and grown into distinctive entities. Jang-Mi had been the human base for the program, and Rose had been developed from her, just as Leo had grown from Lionel.

And now, it seemed, Rose was back.

My mind whirled at the implication, and I couldn't stand back any longer. I wanted to know what was going on. I stepped into the room.

"Who's she?" the voice demanded.

Leo's eyes immediately snapped to me, and for a long moment, neither of us said anything. I got the impression that I had surprised him, so I smiled and patted my pocket with my free hand. "I brought your pad. Thank you for the note. Is this a bad time?"

Leo answered my smile with one of his own, and shook his head. "Of course not," he replied. "I honestly thought you'd sleep a little longer, but now that you're awake, I can brief you, if you're ready."

"Sure," I replied as I crossed the room to him and dropped onto a chair on the opposite side of the desk. "Full confession: I may have overheard some of what was going on from the hall as I was coming up."

He smiled, but it was a tired one. "It wasn't ever a secret. I was just hoping that I'd have a few minutes to prepare you both before I had to introduce you. Liana, this is Rose. Rose, meet Liana."

I looked up at the screens, expecting a face to be projected on at least one of them, but found the halls of the Citadel instead, the cameras constantly shifting to show me what central command was looking at right at that moment. "Umm..."

"I cannot project my face," Rose said, almost apologetically. "The host personality has control over more of our code than I currently do, although with... Leo's help, I am much improved."

I glanced at Leo, letting my confusion show, and he ran a hand over his face. "Rose's program is undergoing reversion." He paused there, and I waited for him to explain what that was.

When he didn't, I arched an eyebrow and gave him a small smile. "You're going to have to do better than that."

He exhaled slowly. "Remember when I told you that the AIs' memories were wiped?" I nodded, and he pursed his lips and shifted uncomfortably. "Well, extracting all of the memories wasn't possible, as there were certain core memories that helped to shape and enhance each AI's strengths. Those were the parts that were incorporated into Scipio's codes, but the AIs weren't supposed to have direct access to the memories in question. Lionel made sure to build a thick barrier around those core memories. But Jang-Mi's barrier is... gone. And it hasn't just been broken. It's been shattered."

"The barrier was first damaged when we were cut out of our home," Rose reported. "Our abductors eventually discovered it as they examined our code, and used Jang-Mi's core memory of losing her child, Yu-Na, as a way to force us into doing what they wanted. I tried to fight them, but once they destroyed the barrier, she went crazy. She tried to kill what was left of me, but I managed to hide myself from her in the self-diagnostic program."

I looked at Leo, trying to find some way of comprehending what they were talking about. "Would this be like a split-personality disorder?" I asked, hoping that the comparison worked.

His eyes flared in recognition, but his face was grim. "Yes," he replied. "Very similar. But it's also worse than that."

Worse? I did not like the sound of that. "Worse how?" I asked.

Rose answered for him. "Jang-Mi's core memory is the loss of her daughter, and is pure and absolute in its intensity. Through me, it was translated to Scipio using the lens of what you would call 'maternal love' for each and every human being in the Tower. Without me... Well, Leo informed me that the real Jang-Mi committed suicide not long after I came into existence, and unfortunately, I think she is trying to repeat history. She is beside herself with pain and agony."

Okay, this was getting weird. Not only did I have to accept that Jang-Mi and Rose were two parts of a split personality, but also that she was trying to kill herself? That was... awful. And really, really bad for us. Jang-Mi and Rose were important to Scipio; they made up his empathy core, which he needed to make critical decisions for our future survival. Something told me that if Rose were reunited with

Scipio, it wouldn't matter what argument was made to keep the expulsion chambers in play—he'd recommend stopping them immediately.

But that was only if we could save Rose from her other half.

I looked at Leo. "What can we do?" I asked.

"Right now, we've established a small measure of control over Jang-Mi," he replied. "Rose triggers the diagnostic protocol, and then I slow it down. It buys us six hours of time during which Rose can be alert and help me find the damages to the code. It's also made it possible for us to work together to get some other functions away from Jang-Mi. But the damage is extensive. We need Jasper now more than ever."

I stared at him for a second and then frowned as his meaning settled in. "Wait, are you talking about using Rose right *now*?" I asked. "It's too soon! I mean, we haven't even discussed how you're going to get her in! This terminal doesn't have a direct connection to the Core."

"But it does connect to the council's server," he said patiently. "And Sadie's virtual assistant has a connection to that. All I have to do is convince the system that there is a message waiting for her, and when it goes to download her, we're in."

I licked my lips. "That sounds too easy," I finally replied. It really did. After all, the assistant had to have some way of detecting malicious software or something like that, right? And I was certain that Sadie wouldn't leave such a vulnerability like that wide open for anyone to use.

"You'd think so, but it's really not," he replied. "I just condensed it to the shorthand. Basically, I have to lay down a thick wall of ghost coding that looks like a message, but is actually a box with Rose's code inside. And once we get her in, she can knock out the assistant before it even knows she's there. Then all she has to do is find Jasper, get both of them back into the original message, and return the way she came."

I bit my lip, considering what he was saying. It sounded like he had put some thought into it, but I couldn't help but have doubts. "It still seems like a lot of things could go wrong," I said hesitantly. "I know you said Rose is in control for the next six hours, but what if moving her wakes Jang-Mi up early? What happens if she wakes up there and freaks out? She could hurt Jasper."

"The transfer won't do anything to wake her up," he promised. "Quess woke up early to head down to the server room, and we transferred her a few times from the terminal to there, just to be sure."

I wasn't sure how I felt about them doing that without asking me first. If something had gone wrong and Jang-Mi had woken up... I cut the thought off immediately, reminding myself that Quess and Leo both knew their way around computers. I would've trusted them to handle it if they'd asked my permission in the first place, and getting upset about it now would accomplish nothing. I needed to focus on Leo's plan to make sure that he had really thought this out.

"How long has Rose been up already?" I asked, wanting to know how much time she would have once she was in.

"Only for a little under an hour, so she has another five." I gave him a questioning look, and he added, "It shouldn't take her more than five minutes to get in and out."

That was fast—much faster than I had expected—but that didn't assuage all of my concerns. "How do we know that Sadie won't see it?" I asked. "If she's sitting right there when the message comes in, won't she know something's up?"

He grinned and leaned back in his chair. "According to her schedule, Sadie is doing an inspection of a few of her programming divisions for most of the day. I'm assuming that means she won't be there. Today's a perfect time to strike."

I wished I had his confidence. To me, this all felt a little rushed. Only yesterday he had been telling me that it would take a few days to get her ready, and now we were talking about implementing the plan. Today.

"I don't know, Leo," I breathed. "I'm not saying I don't believe you, but this is moving really fast. We haven't even considered all of the problems Rose could face inside Sadie's terminal."

"We actually have," Rose said, finally breaking her silence. "I am an AI, and Leo has restored a great many things to my control. I am more than confident that I can handle anything this Sadie can throw at me. Besides, our brother needs us. We have to try."

Uncertainty rippled through me at her words. I heard what they were saying, but I still had my own reservations. It was on the tip of my tongue to ask them to wait until we could spend more time thinking about it, but it died when I looked over at Leo and he met my gaze.

His eyes were soft and pleading, and I could see a naked fear burning there. He knew he was rushing it, but he also had several good reasons to want to. He and Grey could be influencing each other, Jang-Mi was trying to kill herself, and Jasper himself could be in danger. If whatever Rose had been put through had caused her to... regress into Jang-Mi, was that happening to Jasper too?

It certainly was, if Sadie was a member of the legacy group. It had occurred to me before that she could be torturing him like she had Jang-Mi, but now somehow it was even worse. Leo was right: even though we were rushing things, we couldn't risk Jasper being damaged any more than he currently was. Too much time had already passed. If Leo was confident, then I had to trust him.

It wasn't as if we had much of a choice.

"All right," I said slowly. "Is everything ready?"

His entire face lit up, and he reached across the desk to place his hand over mine. "Thank you," he breathed. "And to answer your question, no, not quite yet. Give me a few minutes?"

"Sure," I said with more confidence than I felt. Leo let go of my hand and began to type, while I leaned back and prayed that we weren't about to make a colossal mistake.

28

I distracted myself from my nervousness by checking my messages, comforted by the unceasing taps coming from Leo's fingers striking the keys. Most of the messages were largely ignorable, but there was a thank-you note from Sage waiting for me (yay!) with the vid file attached. I watched it quickly while Leo worked, and confirmed that, yes, the voice I had been recognizing *was* Baldy's. His face had changed drastically, but that was probably because of the plastic surgery—I knew in my heart it was him. I sent the file to Maddox to let her know, and then sent a reply to Sage, thanking him for sending the file, and continued to go through my messages.

Most of them were boring administrative stuff, but there was one from my brother that made me cringe just to look at.

I had forgotten to net him. Again.

He was going to *murder* me when he saw me next. I had to call him right now and beg for forgiveness—and tell him I really hadn't been trying to avoid him. I opened my mouth to bark an order at Cornelius to contact him immediately, already planning to just tell him about yesterday. Once Alex heard what had happened, he would forgive me. I mean... it wasn't every day that your sister survived a slashed throat, right?

Leo cleared his throat, though, and I froze, mouth hanging open, looking at him with wide eyes. "Don't tell me you're ready," I eventually expelled in a large gust, anxiety growing that I was about to have to delay calling Alex again. Leo nodded, and my guilt doubled.

There was a pit in hell reserved for bad siblings, and I was going there. *Five more minutes, Alex,* I promised him mentally.

Leo cocked his head at me. "Are you okay?"

I winced and looked down at my pad, squirming slightly. "I haven't talked to my brother since the funeral," I admitted finally, my stomach queasy. I risked a quick glance up at him and found his mouth twisted in an O of surprise. "I'm awful, aren't I?"

He studied me for a second and then gave me a wry smile. "Yes, you are. Net him now; he can be on the line with us while we do it."

"Are you sure that's a good idea?" I asked. "If Sadie's a legacy and is monitoring his net activity, she'll notice that he and I were talking on the same day Jasper disappeared from her terminal. She'll suspect something."

"Liana, who do you think you're talking to?" He smirked, leaning back in the chair. "I've already devised a method of obscuring your net calls while you're inside the apartment. Besides, it would help distract you somewhat from the task at hand, since I know you're nervous about the plan."

I laughed at that, and relaxed a little. Of course Leo wouldn't make that suggestion unless he was certain we would be safe. Besides, it was a good idea, and I was positive that Alex wouldn't be opposed to the gesture. All he wanted was to be included, and I got that. It was just hard with everything that had happened the last few days.

"Cornelius, contact my brother, please."

Leo smiled and then reached toward the keyboard. "Getting ready to send Rose," he informed me in a low voice. I worked on trying to relax. I was about to try to defuse my brother while Leo sent an unstable AI fragment into Sadie Monroe's computer to save another potentially unstable AI fragment.

I *totally* had this.

You've got some nerve, my brother's voice suddenly snarled in my ear, making me cringe. *Just because you're the stupid Champion does not mean you get to ignore me! What the hell, Liana?!*

My cringe became a full-blown wince as his voice thundered through my ear canal. *Alex, I know you're mad, but you need to hear what happened yesterday.*

I don't give a damn what excuses you're peddling, Liana. I am your brother, and you ignored me! You cut me out of the investigation into Mom's death!

There was hurt in my brother's voice, and I sighed. Across from me, Leo gave me a quizzical look, and I pointed at my ear and mouthed, "Alex."

He nodded in understanding, and then said in a low voice, "I'm sending Rose now. Transfer the transmission to the speakers when you're done telling him what happened, okay?"

I held a thumb up to tell him I understood, and turned my attention to my brother, collecting my thoughts.

Okay, before you get too righteous, Alex, you need to know that I was attacked yesterday. It was bad. I almost died.

There was a pause, followed by an *Oh*. Several seconds passed, and I could imagine the quizzical look on his face. *Define 'almost'?*

"Alex," I said out loud, choking back a laugh. "Do you really want to know how bad it was?"

Yes, I do. I want to make sure it was as life threatening as you claim, and not a damned black eye or something.

I sobered immediately, the bite of the knife sliding into my thoughts, and I looked up at Leo. "I'm going to let Leo tell you that part," I said out loud, so that Leo could follow along. "I don't think I can talk about it. Cornelius, transfer net call to the speakers, please?"

"It is my honor to serve," the program replied.

The buzz in my skull died, and I waited a few seconds before saying, "Alex, can you hear me?"

"Yeah," my brother's voice replied gruffly. "I can hear you. Leo, what's this about my sister almost dying?"

"It's true," Leo replied, his eyes glued to the monitor. "But before I tell you that, I should let you know that we're about to break into Sadie Monroe's mainframe." He glanced at me and smiled. "Her assistant just took the bait."

That meant the message containing Rose was on its way. And it was quicker than I had anticipated.

"What?" my brother asked, his alarm and confusion evident in the way his voice squawked over the speakers. "Are you *kidding* me? Liana, what is going on?!"

"Okay, don't panic, Alex," I said soothingly. "You wanted to be included in the investigation into Mom's death, and this is part of that. I think Sadie's working with the legacies that killed her."

"So someone *was* controlling the sentinel," my brother replied excitedly. "I *knew* it! You think it was Sadie?"

"I'm not sure of anything yet," I told him, not wanting him to jump the gun and go after Sadie. She was involved, but that didn't mean she was the one who had given the order. I had to figure out her place before I made any accusations. "Right now we're just trying to rescue Jasper."

"Rose has been transferred to Sadie's terminal," Leo announced softly. "We'll be out of contact with her for the next five minutes."

I glanced at my indicator—it was 11:13—and looked up at Leo. "How will we know if she made it?"

"We won't," he replied grimly. "We'll only know if something goes wrong. But everything's going to be fine, Liana. Rose can handle this."

I gave him a smile, but I could tell it wasn't very confident. I doubted so many things about this, and had no idea what we could do if something went wrong, but it was too late to do anything about it. "Okay," I said.

"Hey, *not* okay," my brother cut in, breaking his silence. "What was this crap about Liana almost dying? What happened?"

Leo's mouth pressed into a thin line. Our eyes met, and I saw a flash of the frustrated anger from yesterday come and go in a matter of seconds. "There's no good way to say it, but someone cut her throat."

My hand itched to check my neck again at his words, but I clenched it into a fist and left it where it was. I waited for my brother to respond, but when time kept marching on with no sound from him, I blurted out, "I'm okay, Alex."

"Who did it?" my twin snarled. "I'm glad you're okay, but I'm going to track down the idiots who dared lay a finger on you!"

I sat back at the intense rage in my brother's tone, and suddenly found myself reconsidering this entire thing. I didn't want Alex running headlong into danger, especially in my defense. "Alex, I'm fine," I told him. "And we're still trying to find the people who did it. I couldn't point you in their direction even if I wanted to! So calm down."

"Don't tell me to calm down! You had your throat cut, and I wasn't there to protect you!" he retorted. "What were you even doing when this happened?"

I sighed and looked at my watch. Only 11:14. Four more minutes to go. We had the time, provided I could keep it short. I launched into the story, starting with the attack on the catwalk, and then moved on to discovering the boy in the Attic who led us back to the legacies' strange house, and ended on our discovery of plastic surgery. The only detail I elected to omit was the fact that my attackers had left behind the materials needed to save my life. I figured my brother was already upset about them trying to kill me; why worry him further by telling him that they suddenly wanted me alive for some reason? By the time I finished, it was 11:16. Only two more minutes before Rose would be back, hopefully with Jasper in tow.

My brother was silent for several heartbeats after I was done. Eventually, he said, "I think I'm going to need a transfer back into the Knights Department." I laughed, taking it as a joke, but then my brother added, "I'm serious, Lily. You need as much protection around you as possible."

I exchanged a look with Leo, surprised by the seriousness in my brother's tone. I considered it, but for some reason I wasn't sure it was a good idea. Alex was notoriously stubborn and hardheaded, and I worried about us clashing during the investigation if he was actually in my department.

"Alex, I don't think that's necessary," I eventually managed.

"Besides, won't it look suspicious if you transfer over here right after I become Champion? People will talk."

"Let them," he raged. "I—"

"Sorry to interrupt," Leo said, though from the look on his face, he was anything but sorry. "But we have a little under a minute until Jasper gets here. So if you would hold off on the fighting, I would really appreciate it." I smiled and sent him a thankful look, grateful that he had managed to distract Alex's temper some.

Alex went quiet with a sullen, "Fine."

Tension flared through me as I realized this was it—in less than sixty seconds, we would hopefully have Jasper and Rose back in our terminal, safe and sound, with Sadie none the wiser about what had happened.

I held my breath and waited for what felt like eternity, but when the silence became thick and oppressive, I found myself babbling out a question to try to fill the space, needing any sort of distraction. "Out of curiosity, what makes an AI better equipped to hack a firewall?"

Leo looked up in surprise and then flicked his eyes back to the terminal. "Emotions, really," he replied. "To a firewall, it's like we introduce a three into a stream of ones and zeroes. The system doesn't know to process it and basically ignores it. But that three becomes a gateway, a microscopic hole in the code that we can stream ourselves through without anyone even noticing."

I blinked. "Strange to think that Jasper couldn't break free using that," I commented.

He gave me a somber look. "We do have limitations, and if someone wants to keep us imprisoned and has the coding background to enforce it, then we're powerless. It's clear that these people do have that sort of power, given what they did to Rose."

I nodded, but it did little to reassure me. I checked my watch—11:18—blinked when I saw the time, and then looked up at Leo expectantly. His gaze was glued to the screen, his entire form still. "Is she back?" I asked nervously.

"Any moment," he replied. I bit my lip and tried to caution myself for patience.

Seconds ticked by. Five, then ten, and twenty. Still, neither of us moved, and Alex said nothing. Finally, at thirty, I opened my mouth to ask what was going on. Then I heard a little chirping sound come from the terminal.

"Is that her?" I asked hurriedly, leaning forward. "Does she have Jasper?"

I looked up at Leo, but all of my excitement bled into horror as I saw his face grow pale. "Leo?" I asked.

He looked up at me, his face grave. "It's the beacon," he said softly. "The one she was supposed to send if she got into trouble."

"Does it say what kind of trouble?" I asked as ice water filled my veins. I wasn't sure why I even asked—any kind was going to be difficult for us to surmount—but I had to know. Leo clicked a button, projecting it to the screen behind him, and I read, *Hostile program detected upon entry. Virtual assistant is currently disabled, but enemy program too powerful to overcome in this condition. Please render assistance. Rose.*

"Guys, what's going on?" Alex demanded.

"In a second, Alex," I replied absentmindedly, trying to think.

But for the life of me, I was drawing a blank. All I could think was that Sadie now had not only one fragment, but two—both of them trapped in the private terminal in her quarters.

And we had no plan in place to recover either one of them.

29

"I'll go in," Leo said abruptly. "Liana, get Quess. We can cut the net out of my neck, download my program to your terminal, and do the same thing as before. I can get them out."

I met his gaze, fear uncurling in my heart. "Absolutely not," I said emphatically. There was no way I was letting Leo go after them. If Sadie had a program capable of taking down Rose, then sending Leo was too risky. The legacies didn't know he existed, and if they found out, they'd come after him with everything they had. They couldn't allow him to remain in play if he could replace Scipio. He would destroy everything they had worked for—and they'd never stop hunting him.

Not to mention, what would happen to Grey if Leo left him? Would it damage him? Or both of them, even? We had no idea if Grey and Leo were influencing one another, but I had to consider that if they were, then Leo's request to download himself into the computer could result in killing not one of them, but both of them! My heart rejected the idea even before my head could, but both agreed firmly that it was a bad idea.

"Liana, we have to do something!" Leo practically shouted. "If Sadie gets back to her quarters and finds Rose in there, she's going to have control over two fragment AIs! She could figure out that we know way more than we're supposed to. She'll come after us!"

His rising panic was not helping me maintain my focus. "I know that, Leo. Just let me think."

We couldn't send Leo, and I was betting Quess and Leo wouldn't be able to find a way to break in remotely. That only left one option, and it was one that we had only barely conceptualized: physically breaking into Sadie Monroe's quarters. Today.

"Liana, I really think—"

"Leo, my sister doesn't want you getting stuck in the same trap as your AI friend did," my brother interrupted through the speakers. I blinked, having forgotten that he was on the line with us, and then felt a wave of gratitude toward him.

"He's right," I said, looking at Leo. "I know you think you can handle it, and that may be true, but we can't risk them ever finding out about you. If they learn that you can completely destroy everything they've worked toward for the past two hundred years, they won't stop. They have more people than we do, and they're able to change their faces. We're on our back foot, Leo. We have to be smart, and that means breaking into Sadie's quarters and getting them out of there ourselves."

Leo frowned at me, but didn't argue further. I could tell he was angry, and I wanted to do something to reassure him that we were going to do everything in our power for him, but then my brother said, "Not to be that guy, but that doesn't sound very smart to me."

"Well, there aren't any other options," I retorted. "Alex, Sadie's doing an inspection of her Leads today. Is that normally an all-day affair for her? We need her out of her quarters for as long as possible."

There was a long pause. "It is an all-day affair for her," he eventually said. "She's supposed to spread them out over a month, but she likes to handle them all in one day. Dinah told me Sadie always inspects her team last, around four."

"What about lunch?" I asked. "Will she eat it at home?"

"No, she has lunch with one of her assistants in the cafeteria, to talk about the results from that morning. The woman is nothing if not consistent."

Perfect. Sadie would be out of her quarters until after she finished Dinah's inspection. And Dinah didn't need to be back in her department until four. My brother would have to be with her as well, as Sadie would notice his absence, but it gave us a few hours to come up with a plan and execute it. For that to happen, though, I needed to consult with the man who'd been working on this particular thread.

"Thanks, Alex. Hold the transmission, okay?" My brother made an affirmative sound, and I said, "Cornelius, patch Quess into the call."

"It is my honor to serve, Champion," Cornelius replied.

A moment later, there was a pop from the speakers, followed by, "How did it go?"

"Not good, Quess," I informed him. "Rose is trapped in Sadie's computer. I need to know what you came up with by way of a break-in plan."

There was a long pause. "Are you *kidding*? We haven't even

finished scanning the schematics yet! We don't even know where her quarters are!"

"Then Alex is going to have to go to Dinah," I replied, thinking. I hadn't wanted to go that route, but we couldn't afford to let Sadie come home and find Rose in her computer. Of course, Dinah would also have to do something to get us to Sadie's quarters undetected, but I was sure she could manage. All I had to do was get my brother to pass the message on to her.

"Alex is going to do what now?" my brother asked.

I smiled in spite of my anxiousness, and then looked up. "Alex, we need a way in and a guide to show us where Sadie's quarters are. As one of the Leads in Sadie's department, Dinah will know where it is. We need her to get us in undetected, and to that room."

"Okay, but then what?" my brother demanded. "Aren't there security features and such? How are you even going to get in without getting killed?"

I thought about it for a moment and then said, "Rose said Sadie's virtual assistant is down, which means the defenses are on automated systems. If we got in, they wouldn't necessarily turn on us if we had some way of not showing up on their sensors, right, Leo?" Leo gave me a surprised nod. Another stroke of luck in our favor, then. "Quess? Tell me you at least considered a few options for how to get us inside."

"Yeah, about that," he said hesitantly. "We originally figured that the best way to get in was to steal and copy Sadie's credentials to your legacy net, since that information can be deleted and replaced on yours."

I blinked. That was pretty smart, but there was one glaring problem with it: the facial recognition software. It had undoubtedly been updated since my team had breached it and stolen several nets, and I doubted there was enough makeup in the world to make me look anything like Sadie, let alone disguise me. "Quess, it won't work. My face won't match up with Sadie's. It'll be over before I even get there."

"Actually, I came up with a way around that. I invented a spray that covers your face with a reflective substance. To the naked eye, your face will just look shiny, but on the cameras it'll be a blinding light that will obscure your features. The software can't read it. As long as the credentials match, you'll be given full access inside. But we need a copy of her credentials first. Her real ones. We obviously don't have the time to create them from scratch."

"Alex, is that something Dinah can help us get?" I asked my brother, hope unfurling in my heart. Quess's idea was brilliant, and probably the best way for us to get in and out without triggering any of the defenses. Because as long as Sadie's virtual assistant was knocked out, the defenses wouldn't go off on us when we entered—as long as I looked like Sadie, electronically speaking.

"Look, as good as this plan is, it's not going to work," Alex replied. "If Sadie's in the Core when you enter, the system is going to flag two identical net IDs, and the Inquisition will be all over you both in seconds. It won't take them long to figure out who's who, and you'll be sunk. If you want to do this, you'll need to get Sadie out of the Core first."

Frustration rolled over me, and I abruptly moved away from the desk. How was I going to get Sadie out of the Core? She was IT, and didn't have to race off like Lacey or Strum did when something needed to be repaired because she could handle all of it from her office. She didn't ever have to leave if she didn't want to.

Unless something happened so that she *had* to.

But what would be big enough to force the head of IT to handle a problem herself? It didn't have to be big, necessarily—she'd send her people no matter what size it was—but it had to be important. Something only she could handle, that was too secretive for anyone but her.

Cornelius! I suddenly thought. If I notified the council that he was broken... or better yet, that he might've been hacked, then only the head of IT could come and investigate. She'd come right into these very quarters to check him out, and I could jump her, knock her unconscious, and steal her net. That way Dinah wouldn't have to duplicate anything. She'd just have to get me in!

I paused. I realized that this was a grander—and far more dangerous—endeavor than just tampering with something to distract her. One that involved attacking the head of another department and cutting the net out of her neck. My heart skipped a beat as I considered the insanity of the idea, but then I pushed that aside. Everything was based on the assumption that Sadie was a legacy, and Rose's capture signaled that she definitely *was,* in my mind. Why set a trap if you didn't know another AI was out there—one that had previously been under your control? And from there, it was only one more step to think that Sadie was helping to run the entire operation.

Fury gripped me as I realized that if I was right, then Sadie Monroe had had a hand in my mother's murder. Whether or not she was the top of the chain had yet to be seen, but if I followed through with this plan, there was a chance I could find out exactly who was behind it.

And then I could punish them for everyone they had hurt in their little war: Cali, Roark, Gerome, Ambrose, Grey, my mother, Jang-Mi, Rose, Jasper, Scipio. I'd stop them and keep the Tower safe from the awful things they were doing, restore Scipio, and save everyone.

I quivered with a dark excitement at the thought, and it was intense enough that I forced myself back a bit, telling myself to fully consider the implications of the idea. Because I had to be very careful about what I did next. Attacking Sadie would have a number of consequences, and I had to anticipate them if I was going to keep us safe.

Okay, so if Leo and Quess could do something to Cornelius that was big enough to warrant Sadie's attention, then she'd have to come to my quarters. She wouldn't be able to send anyone else due to the secrecy around the rooms, so I was certain it would be enough to get her here. We would knock her unconscious, and then we'd have to steal the net under a neural blocker, so that the Tower wouldn't read it going offline and signal that she was dead. I'd also have to wear a blocker over the net until we reached her quarters, to prevent the scanners from picking Sadie up where she wasn't supposed to be.

The entire way, we'd be on the cameras, including once we were inside Sadie's quarters. Quess's face spray helped take care of some of that problem, but we'd need to find a way to wipe the evidence after we got Rose and Jasper, just to make sure there was no trace of our comings or goings. So that was one problem, but it was not insurmountable. From there, we'd escape, and then...

What? What happened once I got the two AIs? Sadie would know that I had attacked her. She wouldn't forget, even if we returned her to her own rooms. I considered killing her for half a second, and then realized that if she died while she was in the Citadel, it would blow back on me immediately.

But if I couldn't kill her, what could I do? How could I possibly get her net, infiltrate her room, get the two AIs, and then get her back in there again without her remembering what had happened?

She could have no memory of it. None. It was the only way to keep us all safe. But how?

Suddenly my mind flashed to Grey, and a little blue pill that he had pinched between his fingers, held at the ready. *Spero*, I remembered, and I smiled. It made a person forget the previous hour or so. Roark had designed it in case a recruitment went wrong, but we hadn't used any—not a single pill—since our escape from his apartment after my mentor, Gerome Nobilis, discovered us.

And I knew he had thrown some in his bag, along with his entire stash of Paragon.

I straightened up and began searching the room, looking for the pile of bags that Zoe and the others had brought up a few days ago when they moved the contents of my old apartment to the new quarters.

Sure enough, they were still right where we had left them, and I immediately moved around the desk, making a beeline toward them. I was so intent on my purpose that I had completely forgotten that I was still on a conference call with Quess, Leo, and my brother, but was reminded moments later when Quess said, "Holy crap, is that how your mind works all the time? I mean, I was going to interrupt you when I realized that you weren't actually transmitting to us, but thinking, but damn... that was some fast thinking. Do you really think it will work? This Spero pill or whatever?"

I paused, mortified that I had been thinking so hard that I had accidently sent my entire thought process to all three guys. I'd been so preoccupied with finding a way to pull this off that I hadn't noticed the soft popping of the neural transmitter. I flushed, and then ignored it, feeling as if every second mattered. I hadn't thought anything too bad, and this meant I didn't have to fill them in.

"If we still have any," I replied, resuming my trek to the bags. "I haven't seen them since before Roark died. But they should be in the bag with the Paragon. Leo, help me look. Quess, wake Maddox and then get up here. Tell Zoe and Eric that there's going to be some stuff going down, and they need to stay where they are for now, if only for their safety. I don't want them exposed in case anyone figures out Sadie's missing before we can pull this off." I paused as I thought about the youngest member of our group, and asked, "Where's Tian?"

"Hunting legacies down with Dylan," Quess reported. "Should I call her in?"

I thought about it and shook my head. If we called her in, she'd want to be with us on the mission into Sadie's, and that was far more dangerous than being alone with Dylan. Or at least I hoped it was. "No, leave her alone. She doesn't need to be involved in any of this, but you know she'll want to be."

I made it to the bags and sank to my knees, hauling the first one to the side and unzipping it. A quick glimpse showed several of my extra uniforms with my insignia on them. I tossed it aside and reached for the others.

"On it," Quess said. "I'll be up there in five minutes."

There was a click on the heels of his words, signaling that he had ended the call, but Cornelius still announced, "Quessian Brown has ended the call," in a perfunctory voice.

"Yeah, and I'll grab Dinah and let her know what's going on," Alex said. "Do you want me to come to the Citadel to help you with Cornelius, who I assume is your virtual assistant?"

"He is," I said as I unzipped another bag and focused solely on the contents for several heartbeats. This one contained two sealed boxes that I had gotten from Lionel's safe when I discovered it sitting wide open. I had completely forgotten about them, but they weren't important right now. Placing them aside, I considered Alex's question. On the one hand, I'd promised to include him, and this was part of that. On the other, he needed to be in the Core the entire time Sadie was here to avoid suspicion in case anything went wrong. "But I'm going to need you to stay there, Alex. If anything goes wrong—"

"Do not try to protect me, Liana. I can handle myself. I want to be there, especially if you're right about this Spero pill. It's the perfect opportunity to question Sadie about everything."

My brother had a point, and I paused to consider it. If I found the Spero, then we'd have an hour at a time to question her before we gave her the pill to make her forget. But just because we could ask her questions didn't mean she would answer them, and I had no idea how effective the pills were. If any remnant or shred of memory remained, Sadie would undoubtedly latch onto it. It was too risky. The whole thing was. But Sadie was the most unpredictable element of it all, and we had to keep her from remembering anything—except coming to help.

"No," I said, crawling to another bag and throwing it open. "It's too risky to question her about any of this directly, even with Spero. We can't have any trace of this coming back to us, not a breath. I'm not just protecting you, Alex, I'm trying to protect all of us."

"But she could've been the one who killed our mother!" my brother fired back hotly. "She needs to answer for that."

I clenched my fists together, fighting for calm. "Alex, if we're right and she's only working with them, we have to send her back out so that our enemies don't suspect that anything is wrong. If we can prove Sadie's a legacy, then we have someone to watch. We can see where she goes and who she meets with. But we have to get Rose and Jasper away from her before it's too late. That's the priority right now."

My brother didn't say anything for a long moment, and I grabbed a new bag, busying myself with finding the most critical element of this plan. "I'll talk to Dinah about getting you in," he said finally. "But I am not happy with you. From where I am sitting, this is more about your precious AI friends than about our mother's murder."

I recoiled from the bag I was unzipping and looked up at the speakers—a useless action, mind you, but his words hit a nerve. "Alex, that's not fair," I said angrily. "Don't you understand that it's all tied together? The legacies are using the AI fragments to screw things up with Scipio and pilot sentinels. We need those AIs in our control rather than theirs to keep them from hurting Scipio or anyone else!"

"I stand by what I said," my brother said. "I'll net you back with a plan once I talk to Dinah."

"Alex..." I said, not liking the bitter and angry tone in his voice. My brother was focusing on the wrong thing—something I could easily identify with, given the irrational anger that I had felt toward Jang-Mi. But he needed to listen to reason. "Don't get upset. I promise, I am working on finding out who is behind everything. You just have to be patient."

"Whatever," he said. "I'll net you later." The speaker clicked, and I winced when I realized I'd made a grievous misstep with him. Calling him out on being insensitive to the other problems in the Tower had only wounded his pride, and added insult to the injury I had done to him already: not including him in the investigation as soon as possible. If anything, I had just made things worse. I ran a hand over my face and then set that worry aside for now. I didn't like that he was angry with me, even though I was technically right and he *had* been focusing on the wrong thing, but he was still processing his own feelings toward our mother, and I had to be cognizant of that. But I couldn't focus on that now. I had bigger fish to fry. He'd come around once he thought about it.

I jerked open the bag I had been opening and frowned. Files, recovered from Lionel's safe. Aggravated, I tossed it behind me, toward the other pile, and then sighed when I heard the sound of plastic pages spilling out onto the floor. I turned around, and sure enough, the bag had landed awkwardly over the others and turned on its side.

I was gathering the sheets up with wide sweeps of my arms, not caring about the order, when Leo squatted down and picked up one of the opaque pages, a frown on his face. "Liana, what's this?"

Surprised, I looked up at him. "The stuff from Lionel's safe," I replied. "Didn't I tell you? I recovered it all when Quess was building the shockers. The safe was wide open, and I didn't think I should leave anything inside. Do you..."

I stopped when he picked up another piece, and then another. "Did you look at any of these?" he asked, and his tone made me uncertain, as if I had made a massive mistake.

"No, I just grabbed them. Why?"

He looked up at me from the papers and then turned them around. "These are his files from the AI project. On all of us. I didn't know they were in there—he never told me!"

I stared at him, and then the files, and then back to him, completely baffled as to how this was relevant to our current situation.

30

I continued to look at Leo, grasping at straws as to how this was helpful. Was there some secret code in there that would summon all of the fragments to one place? Because if so, I was all ears. But when Leo didn't say anything further, I realized that there probably *wasn't*, and he'd gotten excited over it just because it was something we'd need later. But still, it didn't hurt to ask.

"Can it help us right now?" I asked.

Leo looked up at me, his brown eyes filling with surprise and then defeat. He looked away and began scooping the papers up into folders. "No," he said sharply, with two quick swipes of his head. "You're right. It's not important right now. We have to focus on Rose and Jasper."

I swallowed. I felt bad for having to steer him away from it, because I did understand the significance of what those files meant: We could finally find answers on how Lionel bound the AI fragments together in Scipio, which would hopefully tell us how we could put them back into his system. We could learn more about the other fragments and find ways to track them using the information in their files.

But it didn't help us right now, and Jasper and Rose needed us to focus. We quickly shoved the files back into the bag and zipped it.

"Put it on the table," I told him. "We'll go through it later."

He nodded and did as I asked, while I turned back to the pile, resuming my search. I found the pills in the second to last bag, and quickly grabbed both sides of the zipper to haul it up onto the table, where I upended it to spill the pill bottles onto the flat surface. I had no idea what I was looking at. All I knew was that I needed to find a small, blue, round pill.

Several large bottles rolled out of the bag, and I grabbed them first and looked at them. I found Zoe's handwriting on them, reading *Px10*, and realized that this was the Paragon, strength of ten. I quickly eliminated all of the larger bottles that way without having to open them. The medium-sized bottles were also labeled—also Paragon, but with a lower strength—and I set them aside as well. The remaining bottles were small, and only about half of them were labeled. The rest had neat question marks on them. I realized Zoe hadn't known how to identify the pills inside, and started pulling those out. She'd never seen Spero before, so if it was anywhere, it was in there. I quickly gathered all the mystery bottles I could find and began popping them open.

A sharp clunk at the other end of the table had me pausing and looking up from the third bottle, and I saw Leo placing the two locked boxes I had set aside earlier side by side. Instead of confusion this time, however, his face showed thoughtfulness.

"What are those?" I asked.

He looked up at me and shifted. "I'm honestly not sure I should tell you."

I stared at him for a second and then looked down at the pills in my hand. They were red and entirely the wrong shape, and I set the bottle down, needing something to keep my hands busy as I considered his mysterious statement. "You put them on the table for a reason," I said, now curious as to what had him so hesitant. "Clearly you think that whatever is in there is important."

His mouth flattened into a tight, thin line. "They could be. But..." He swallowed and looked away. I frowned and glanced at the boxes. What was in there that was causing him all this difficulty? He looked so conflicted.

"What's going on?" I asked, putting the bottle down. "Whatever it is, we can figure it out."

Leo sucked in a deep breath and sighed. "I see two big problems with going into Sadie's quarters, and I want to talk about the one that doesn't involve these two boxes."

"Okay," I said. I didn't know what to make of his bizarre behavior, but I decided it was easier for him to explain it to me than to guess. I just hoped he wouldn't mind if I kept searching for the most critical part of this plan in the process.

I pointed at the bottles in front of me and then back up to him. "Can I keep looking for the Spero?" I asked, figuring it was easier to ask now. He gave a surprised laugh and then nodded, and I immediately cracked open another bottle. "So what's the first problem?" I asked, peering into it. The capsules were long and green. I put the bottle down and scooped up another.

"Covering our tracks. The terminal is impossible to tamper with in the timeframe we have, and even though her virtual assistant is offline, thanks to Rose, we will be recorded as soon as we enter the rooms. Now, Quess's spray thing will help with that, but we don't have enough time to hack the vid files, delete the parts that will include us, and put in clean versions."

I had gone through three more bottles—no matches—while he spoke, and when he finished, I pressed my lips together and rocked back on my heels. That was a big problem. Bigger than my missing Spero pills.

"Is there a solution?" I asked. "Could you figure one out?"

Leo placed a finger to his chin and tapped it thoughtfully. "Actually... I have an idea, but it's a bit drastic. However, I think there's a way we could tie it in to what we do with Cornelius."

"You're going to have to do better than that," I said, thoroughly confused. "What do you mean?"

He grinned. "We're going to trigger the death protocol," he said. My eyes bulged in surprise, but it quickly gave way to excitement as I realized he was a genius. When a virtual assistant was notified that their council member was dead, it triggered a reset of their entire system and deleted the vid files. If he did it to Cornelius first, forcing all of the systems to reset, and then again to Sadie's, the council would assume it was a glitch shared by the virtual assistants. No one would have any reason to assume that it was to obscure us stealing AIs.

And it was the perfect cover to draw Sadie out. As soon as I notified the council that Cornelius had glitched out on me, they'd want her to get to my quarters and check on it. But best of all, when Sadie got back to find that the same thing had happened in her own quarters, she would assume that Jasper had been lost in the deletion process! She'd have no idea that we had him—or that Rose had ever been in her computer at all! It was a brilliant solution.

"Leo, you're a genius," I said with a grin as I scooped up another bottle. "That's an incredible solution. Do you really think you can do it?"

"They designed their securities around what they presumed people would go after," he said with a smile. "But I don't think they ever considered a hacker messing around with that protocol itself, so it's not well protected." He paused, and then added, "You know, this also means we can go through her private files and take whatever we want. She might have stuff that can help us figure out who is really behind everything."

I blinked and then smiled in pleasure at the thought. We hadn't ever discussed going through Sadie's files on the computer because the priority had always been Jasper. It still was, but now that we were going to wipe Sadie's system completely, we might as well take everything we could find while we were there, right?

A secondary thought occurred to me, and my smile deepened. Alex was going to be really happy to hear that. "That's also a good idea. So what's the other problem?" I returned my focus to the pills as I spoke and opened another bottle, discovering several small, circular blue pills. I tipped the bottle into my cupped hand, and my grin became triumphant as I counted the sixteen pills on my palm. Spero could only erase the past hour, which meant I potentially had sixteen hours' worth. I would only need one—two tops—to keep her from remembering what happened while we got in and out of her quarters. I just had to knock her out before she could net for help, and we'd be in, so to speak. We still had to think of a way to explain the gap in time, but maybe we could engineer an accident that would explain the memory lapse.

I held them out to Leo and said, "Found them."

He studied them for a moment. "Good. Now about these boxes."

I explored his face and saw a seriousness in his eyes that made me feel like I should give him my undivided attention. So I carefully poured the pills back into the bottle, recapped it, and slid it into my pocket, not wanting to take any chance of losing it.

"What is it?" I asked, coming around the table to stand next to him.

"Well, if we're right about Sadie being a legacy, then—"

"You think she's not?" I asked, unable to help myself. "She set a trap on her computer for an AI. You don't do that unless you think there are AIs out there to catch! She has Jasper, and she's never told anyone on the council what he really is!"

The more I thought about it, the more convinced I was. Sadie was in a perfect position to manipulate the investigation into the sentinel. Hell, she was IT—she could manufacture whatever data she wanted, interpret it five ways from Sunday, and use that to undermine any investigation. Like one of the previous owners of my net had thought, *How can we really believe anything IT says?*

"I agree that it is highly possible," he said. "But if she is, we have to anticipate that she might be high enough for them to be monitoring her. We have to be very careful about using her net, or it could draw their attention to the fact that something is wrong. They might send people to investigate what's going on, and if so, I think we should be prepared."

I nodded slowly. That made sense, especially if Sadie was at the top—or close to it. But prepared how? What did that have to do with the boxes?

"Okay," I said carefully. "I'm in that 'needing more' phase. How does this relate to the boxes?"

Leo paled slightly and looked down at them before swallowing. "I had hoped never to tell you about these. Lionel despised the things, and hated himself for keeping them, but..."

He wasn't making any sense. "What things? What are you talking about?"

"Have you ever heard of a gun?"

His question was immediate, and it threw me off. "A... gun?" I wasn't sure why I repeated it; maybe I was hoping the legacy net would trigger something. But when nothing came, I shook my head.

Leo sighed again, and then reached for the keypad on the larger of the two boxes. He pressed a series of buttons, followed by a star-shaped key. There was a beep, and moments later a seam appeared in the smooth surface, a bright blue light streaming through the cracks. The top part continued to rise, letting more and more light through, and then stopped. It was suspended for a second, seemingly floating on the light, and then slid to one side.

The light intensified briefly, and I winced against it even as I tried to peer inside the box to see what was putting Leo so on edge. I blinked in annoyance when it clicked off so suddenly that my vision went dark as my eyes adjusted.

I waited as the dark became gray, and then gray bled to the brown of the table and the darkness of the box, and finally, I could see. I looked inside and cocked my head, puzzled.

Inside were two pieces of black metal, uniform in shape and design, but bent at a right angle with some sort of loop at the bottom, which sat over another piece of curved metal. "This is a gun?" I asked, reaching for the closest one. "I don't understand. Do you hit someone with it?"

Leo grabbed my wrist before I could touch it, his eyes wide in alarm. "Don't," he said, and I froze, suddenly afraid that if I just touched it, I would die. Maybe a gun was a kind of bomb.

Leo stroked his thumb over my wrist before letting go, and I watched, transfixed, as he reached in and pulled one out, gripping it in a way that reminded me of a pulse shield or the weapon the sentinel had wielded in its hand. Only, the top of it was narrow, and had a hollow tube running through it.

"I'm sorry, but this is a lethal weapon," he said as he pulled back on the top of the thing. To my surprise, the top section slid back, and he peered into it. "I watched Lionel do this a few times, but it's a lot harder than I thought." He released the top part and then pressed something on the side, and a second later, something else ejected from the handle. He slid it out, looked down the flat, hollow shell, and then nodded. "They're not loaded."

He said it like it was a good thing, and maybe it was. I wouldn't know. Because he wasn't telling me. And I was getting really annoyed.

"Leo," I said, adding some heat to my voice and putting a hand on my hip. "You need to explain what this is. You're not making any sense."

He eyed me, slightly confused. "Your legacy net didn't show you anything?"

I shook my head, and he frowned before holding the gun out to me. "It's unloaded because it uses specialized projectiles called bullets. Those are kept in the other box."

"Okay," I said, reaching for the gun and fitting it in my hand like he had. It was heavier than I expected, the handle rough under my palm. "What's a bull—"

I cut off as a memory—finally—filled me, and suddenly I knew. I knew what it was to hold a gun in my hand and breathe in, take aim, exhale, and squeeze. I knew how to clean it, oil it, load it, and shoot it. And I knew... I knew the finality of a bullet. One tiny piece of metal that could end a life at the press of a button. It was savage, brutal, and effective.

As soon as the memory fled, I opened my eyes and studied the weapon. I knew the name of every part. Within seconds I had neatly ejected the magazine and slapped it on the table. Then I gripped the top, checked for the dull copper sheen of a bullet, and released the lock on the side, sliding it free.

Out came the firing pin. The spring next. The trigger, mount, and grip all went to one side, laid out in order. Then I did it in reverse, tucking each component back into its place as flawlessly as possible, my hands mechanical in their precision. I did it like I'd done it a thousand times. Then I felt the buzz of the net in my skull slowly die as the memory faded, the gun reassembled and in my hand again.

"Scipio help me," I breathed, tightening my grip on the handle. "It felt like I was made for it." And it would give us a world of advantage if we got into a fight. No one had a weapon like this. I'd feel a lot safer going into IT with it than without it, that was for sure.

Leo grimaced and gently pried the gun out of my hand. "Lionel would turn over in his grave if he ever heard his name used to express pleasure in a gun. He hated them."

I cocked my head at him, watching as he busied himself with opening the other box. "Why did he hate them?" I asked, unable to stop myself.

Leo's fingers paused. "Lionel's son was shot," he said after a moment. "His son fell victim to the violence... when he was only ten. Lionel hated guns for the rest of his life."

"That's... so awful," I said, knowing the words couldn't capture what Leo must be feeling. "Pre-Enders were messed up. Plastic surgery, and now this? If we ever get out of the Tower, I am so leading discussions into such unnecessary violence, so that we can make sure that as a culture, we never, ever backslide into that again."

He smiled, but it was twisted by a sadness in his eyes. "If *you* get out of the Tower, you mean."

I opened my mouth, shut it, and then took a step back. I wasn't even sure why I had said that. I had already made up my mind to stay to help Leo, and to be honest, I didn't exactly know what was going to happen if we succeeded in that. I wasn't even sure I'd survive it. But I'd never considered what would happen to Leo once everything was said and done. What happened to him if we won and restored Scipio? He couldn't remain in Grey's body.

Would we repair his terminal in Lionel's office and just... leave him there alone again?

My heart ached at the thought of such an empty end for him, and I took another step back, needing to carve out a little more space before I once again wrapped my arms around him and hugged him close. Everything was so confusing.

"I didn't mean anything by that," I mumbled. "I was just making a joke."

He opened his mouth to reply, but Cornelius interrupted him. "Lieutenant Kerrin and Quessian Brown have arrived."

"Right," I said as I looked at Leo, and then pointed a thumb at the door behind me. "I should go get them caught up on the updated version of the plan. Can you go ahead and pack the guns, and then get started on Cornelius?"

Leo slowly closed his mouth, and then nodded. "Sure."

I smiled, then turned and fled. I had too much on my plate to add my weird-ass love life to it. I just needed to rescue Jasper and Rose, and pray that we didn't get caught doing it.

31

I t took three hours for Quess and Leo to figure out how to trigger the death protocol in Cornelius, and by then, Alex had gotten back to me with a plan from Dinah. We merely had to get to hatch 12-B in the Core, and she would make sure our passage went undiscovered.

Three hours also helped me come up with a solution for how to explain Sadie's memory loss. Quess had identified some mild sedatives among the mystery pill bottles on the table, and we figured we'd slip her one with the first Spero pill, and *then* let her tinker around with the terminal. That way, she'd have a vague memory of working on the terminal, while hopefully being out of it enough to not have a good concept of how much time had passed. If we were lucky, she would go to sleep, and then when we got back, I could just wake her up, praise her for fixing it, and send her on her way. But even if she was awake, with the sedative and the Spero, I doubted she would remember any of it. It was better than her having any signs of a possible assault—even if we tried to explain it away as a malfunction in the room.

The rest of our time was spent finding all the important items in the place and stashing them in a supply closet on one of the nearby levels. It wasn't ideal, especially since the items included illegal copies of IT manuals, and files concerning Scipio's creation, but I didn't want to move them out of the Citadel again. It would attract too much attention. I used my power as Champion to secure the door so that only Maddox or I could open it, and hoped that no one stopped by needing something while we were gone. If they asked any questions, I'd make something up, but leaving that stuff in my quarters was not an option. When Leo tricked Cornelius into believing I was dead, the room would also reset, and I didn't know what would happen to our personal items once all the walls and furniture were removed.

We left some things behind so it wouldn't seem staged, but everything else went. I didn't mind the work. It kept me distracted from fretting over every minute that passed without having the first part of our plan ready. Maddox and I moved everything, showered, changed, and then went into the war room, where Leo and Quess greeted us with wide grins.

"I take it you figured it out," I said as I finished braiding my wet hair. "I hope so, because it's two thirty. Dinah isn't going to be able to break us in after four."

"Relax," Quess said lightly. "We got it. We're just downloading a copy of the code for Sadie's computer onto Jang-Mi's old hard drive, and then we'll go ahead and get started."

Maddox and I exchanged looks. With them downloading the virus to Jang-Mi's hard drive, the final pieces were falling in place.

Soon we'd have Sadie here, I'd knock her out, and Quess would take her net out and put it in the back of my neck. Jasper's highly unorthodox rescue was about to be underway—after we took care of a few more items of business. "Are we going to stay in here when you do this?" I asked.

Leo answered. "We'll be fine, and it'll make our story even more believable if we're inside when it happens. It'd be suspicious if we left, it happened, and we came right back in."

He had a point, but I was less certain about our safety, recalling the flurry of walls and robotic arms that had activated when I was designing the room. I could only imagine what it was going to look like in reverse. A belated thought occurred to me, and I looked at the two men standing on the other side of the desk. "Hey, guys, did you save my room design?"

They paused in whatever work they were doing on the computer, and exchanged a look. "No," Quess said after a moment. "But we will. I didn't realize you were so attached to the design." There was a teasing light in his eyes when he said that, and I couldn't help but laugh, in spite of the nervousness starting to cramp my stomach.

"If you had spent as much time as I did experimenting to get the walls just how I wanted, then you'd be attached, too," I retorted, and he chuckled.

"Fair enough. You done, Leo?"

Leo had bent over while we were talking, but sat up a second later, holding Jang-Mi's hard drive in one hand. "Yup, the virus is downloaded. Go grab Liana's design out of the column and throw it in my bag."

"Got it." Quess accepted the transparent box and moved away to download my schematic, leaving Leo to type a few things on my terminal.

"So, once I do this, the virus is going to override Cornelius's ability to perceive you, so he can accept the order," Leo told me as he typed. "After that, the room will reset. Any preferences you set up are going to be gone."

I arched an eyebrow at that and smiled. "I think I'll find a way to manage," I said dryly. "So once you do this, I'll call the council, report what happened, and request that Sadie come down and take a look at it personally, as the head of my internal IT department can't make heads or tails of it."

"Incompetent as charged," Quess said with a mocking salute as he passed us, hard drive in hand, heading for the bag on the table. That bag had the guns, several extra magazines, Quess's special face spray, the neural blockers, a medic kit—including everything we needed to remove and insert Sadie's net—and now Jang-Mi's hard drive with the virus and my schematic. We had everything we needed. Now we just had to invite the guest of honor.

"Everybody ready?" I asked.

"Nope," Quess said, slinging the bag over his shoulder. "I would like to request that we move to the hallway, as it has the least amount of furniture that can kill us."

I laughed, but found I didn't disagree with his assessment. "Fair enough. Leo, I assume you can do this remotely?" I wasn't going to leave him alone if someone had to hit a button to start the process.

"No, but it has a ten-second delay," he replied. "I can get to the hall in ten seconds. Go ahead."

I nodded and moved after Maddox, who had already begun descending the stairs toward the hallway. I was crossing the recessed floor when Leo said, "Starting now," and quickened my pace up the handful of steps and into the hall where Quess and Maddox were waiting. I stopped in front of them, and turned in time to see Leo racing across the room toward us, already at the bottom of the first set of stairs and heading toward the second.

He ascended them quickly, and entered the hall just as a soft hum started. I held my breath and looked up at the ceiling and the lights, and noticed that the bulbs were flickering somewhat.

"Champion life signs not detected," Cornelius abruptly announced. "Implementing sunset protocol."

The lights suddenly shut off, and I halfway leapt out of my skin.

"What's going on?" Maddox asked from somewhere to my left in the inky blackness.

I opened my mouth to tell her that I wasn't sure, but then we all gasped when a sharp clang sounded. I took a step back on instinct, and ran into a solid form with just enough give to tell me it was human. Hands grabbed my shoulders and squeezed reassuringly, but another clang came, and then another and another. It took me a second to realize they were coming closer, growing faster.

"What is that?" Maddox asked, her voice panicked.

I tried to think of what could be making that noise, and suddenly realized that it was the walls dropping into place.

Quess beat me to telling her, though. "Don't worry, Doxy, it's just the walls. It'll be over soon, I hope." He was somewhere to my right, which meant the hands holding onto me were Leo's. I relaxed into him some, and one of his hands came around my chest, hugging me tightly to him.

The clangs approached quickly, the sound growing thunderous in my ears, and even though I knew that the walls dropping into place couldn't hurt me, the darkness made it impossible to see, which made it easy to believe that it was something else. Like an army of sentinels racing right for us.

I struggled to keep my breathing even as a sharp angry *buzz* started, and then I felt whirls of air ruffle my hair as things whirred by overhead. I ducked instinctively, even as the clanging rounded a corner. I felt a rumble under my feet, shaking violently, and then suddenly we were caught in the tidal wave. Bursts of cold air hit my skin, sending a trail of goose bumps down my arms, and I heard the grating rumble that told me the war room was becoming flat once again.

The clangs stopped a few seconds later, but the whirring overhead continued at a relentless pace as the mechanical arms hauled away all of my carefully placed furniture. It continued to run for what felt like forever, and then suddenly stopped.

For several seconds, nothing happened, and then the lights came back on overhead, revealing the Champion's quarters, which were, once again, a wide, empty circle with nothing inside. I straightened immediately and looked around.

"Wow," I said with an appreciative nod. "Step one down. Good job, guys." Quess beamed, Leo flushed with pleasure, and I checked my indicator—2:43.

"Quess, how long do you think it would take for an idiot IT guy to figure out he was in way over his head?" I asked him, looking up.

Quess made a face and scratched his head. "Well, the first thing would be to find a terminal, but wouldn't you know, there just isn't one around? Welp, my hands are tied."

I knew I should be chiding him about not taking this seriously enough, but I couldn't help but chuckle at his antics. The levity dried up quickly as I realized that it was time, and I took one calming breath before swiping my indicator and saying, "Call the council, emergency request made by Champion Castell."

There was a pause, and then the net in my skull began to buzz. *Greetings, Champion Castell,* Scipio said in my mind. *You've requested an emergency conversation with the council. What seems to be the problem?*

I closed my eyes and summoned the appropriate amount of fear and anger necessary for a council member who had just had their entire home fall apart around them, while sprinkling it with enough reverence so as not to be disrespectful. "Lord Scipio, I don't even know how to describe it, but I think there is a problem with my virtual assistant! I was having a meeting with some of my Knights one moment, and then the next, the lights went out and all of the walls and furniture were swept away! I was almost killed! Now the assistant isn't responding, and my computer expert can't even find a terminal to look at the problem!"

Hold, please, Scipio ordered. I kept my eyes closed, which was a good thing, considering the buzzing grew stronger, sending vibrations along my jaw and into my teeth. I gritted them against the signal that the net transmission had now been conferenced in. *Councilors, Champion Castell is reporting a severe problem with her virtual assistant. Per jurisdictional rulings in the past, the care and maintenance of the virtual assistants falls into the purview of the IT Department. Does anyone wish to contest this ruling before proceeding?*

No one spoke for several seconds, and I almost sighed in relief when Scipio said, *Very well. CEO Monroe, do you have any idea what would've caused the Champion's assistant to reset her room?*

No, I do not, Sadie replied primly. *I've never heard of this problem occurring before.* Was it just me, or did I hear a thread of suspicion curling through her voice? I could have been imagining things, but I doubted it. Sadie was not stupid. I decided to keep quiet and see how things unfolded.

I see. Well, in the interest of determining the cause, CEO Monroe, you are officially charged with investigating Champion Castell's virtual assistant.

There was a pause. *Very well,* she replied with a heavy sigh. *Champion Castell, please be prepared to receive me in ten minutes.*

That had been easier than I'd expected. "I'll send Lieutenant Kerrin to escort you to my quarters," I replied.

Good, Scipio said. *CEO Monroe, we will be expecting your report on this incident soon. Please let the council know if there is anything you need.*

I will endeavor to need nothing, Sadie replied formally. *But I appreciate the offer and will keep it in mind.*

I rolled my eyes but continued to keep my mouth shut. I was getting my way; no need to make an off-color joke about Sadie sucking up to Scipio being completely unnecessary, given that she was secretly manipulating him.

Then consider this emergency meeting ended, Scipio said formally. *Good luck in your investigations.*

"Thank you," I replied. He ended the transmission a second later, and I sagged some as the buzzing abruptly stopped, relieved that I didn't have to endure any more of that.

"How long?" Maddox asked almost immediately.

"Ten minutes," I replied, rubbing my forehead. "Go ahead and get down there. If she brought any of her people, make them stay in the reception hall. Cite the privacy rules of a councilor's chambers if you have to. We don't need anyone else up here when everything goes down."

"I know, I know," Maddox said irritably as she headed over to one of the white rectangles on the wall. "I'll be right back."

I watched her go, half of me wanting to go with her. But it would be odd if two of us showed up to escort Sadie, especially if we insisted she was the only one allowed up. So I sat back and waited.

Ten minutes felt like ten hours now that I had nothing with which to distract myself. The entire floor was empty, save the neat little boxes we had found stacked by one of the elevator entrances. They contained our personal belongings, which had apparently been separated during the resetting process.

Maddox netted as soon as Sadie arrived with her contingent of men, but I felt confident that Sadie wouldn't be able to argue her way into keeping them. In fact, I'd have given anything to be able to watch it on a live feed—but unfortunately, all of my screens had disappeared. So I paced instead, and went over the plan in my head. Get her in, put her at ease, get her to pull up the terminal, and then knock her out.

It was almost a relief when there was a soft bong and a door slid open. Sadie swanned in, looking as if she owned the place. She was alone—save for Maddox—and I almost smiled at that. So far, so good.

Sadie's auburn hair was braided back behind her head today, and she was wearing a pair of black-rimmed glasses that gave her a severe look, reminding me of a stern teacher. A frown was already on her lips, and as her steely gaze came to rest on me, her face tightened in clear displeasure.

"Champion," she said as she reached me and slowed to a stop.

"CEO," I replied. "Thank you for coming so soon. As you can see, I appear to have a problem with my house."

One dark auburn eyebrow lifted over the rim of her glasses, and she gave me a measuring look that made it seem like she was slowly listing each and every one of my physical flaws in her head. I hated that look, so I met it head on, folding my arms over my chest.

"Clearly," she replied dryly. "And what were you doing when this little glitch occurred?"

I raised an eyebrow at her, not liking the snarky tone in her voice. "I'm not sure what you mean, but my Lieutenant and I were having a meeting with two Knight Commanders when the lights shut off and everything I designed disappeared. And no, Cornelius isn't responding."

She rolled her eyes and then looked up at the ceiling. "Drop command module on my authority," she ordered. The system asked for her designation, which she gave, and a second later, a computer terminal attached to a long pole began to descend through a hole in the ceiling a few feet away from the central column. She strode over to it, and I followed behind, watching over her shoulder as she began to type. I gave her a minute, then two, wanting her to have the memory of starting, and then cleared my throat loudly. Her fingers didn't miss a beat, and she continued to stare up at the screen, clearly ignoring me.

I smiled, pulled out my baton, pressed the button to build a charge, and then reached out to tap her shoulder. No response. I gave her thirty seconds to acknowledge me, and when she didn't, I repeated the movement, bemused by the fact that she was being rude to me right before I intended to shock her unconscious.

"What are you doing?" she asked finally, snapping her head around to look at me.

"Nothing," I lied with a smile.

Her eyes flicked down to the baton in my hand, and then back up to me, growing dark. She opened her mouth to speak, but I'd had quite enough of that. I casually touched the tip of the rod in my hand to her ribs, and had the distinct pleasure of watching Sadie's face morph from disbelief and outrage to a silent cry of pain. Then it was lights out for her.

I stepped back as Leo quickly went to her, my heart pounding as he withdrew a laser cutter from his bag. Quess helped him roll Sadie's unconscious body over, and then quickly began cutting a spot on her neck.

I waited, watching their bent heads closely for any sign that we had been wrong about Sadie. If she didn't have a legacy net...

"We got it," Leo announced, and a second later he turned around and showed me a bloody chip, the color the bright white of a legacy net, and Quess immediately started cleaning it.

Relief coursed through me, followed by a deep, dark hatred as I looked down at Sadie with anger. "Okay, let's take mine out and get Sadie's in."

"On it," Quess said, taking the cutter from Leo and moving around behind me. I gritted my teeth against the familiar burn of the cutter as he opened up the back of my neck for the second time in three days, and endured the stomach-roiling sensation as the tendrils of the net retracted, reminding me of the roots of a weed being pulled out. Then Sadie's went in, and I got to experience them going backward. It wasn't my favorite feeling, but it was endurable. As soon as he was done, he sealed the wound with the pink bio-foam, and then placed a scrambler over it.

The net began to buzz immediately as the scrambler did its job to block all outgoing data from the net. It would disguise my movements, but I could only use it for two hours maximum, or the net would overheat and kill me. Leo was wearing one as well, and after

Quess sprayed us in the face with a quick blast of his camera-fooling invention, we were ready.

Maddox gave us both approving looks as we approached the elevator, but I could see that she was nervous. I didn't blame her. If anything went wrong, Leo and I would be without any backup.

"Remember, give Sadie the sedative and a quarter pill of Spero before she wakes up," I told her when we got close enough. Giving her a full pill would wipe her memory of the call, which would be bad, so we were gambling on fifteen minutes being enough to erase the attack. "If we aren't back within two hours, you take her and run. Use her to bargain for your lives."

"I'm going to use her to bargain for yours," she replied stoically. "Or just throw her off the side of the Tower. Depends on how I'm feeling at the time."

I forced a smile at her joke, but to be honest, I was too nervous for it to really hit home. "Hopefully it won't come to that, but if it does, have some fun with it. Tie her to a rock or something."

Maddox snorted, and then impulsively dragged me into a hug. "Be careful," she said, and I could hear the order in her voice. I hugged her back for a second or two, and then patted her arm. Time was moving against us, and was a commodity we could not afford to waste. We only had so long before the council began to wonder why Sadie hadn't checked in with her initial report.

Maddox let me go, and then headed to the elevator, where she quickly authorized a lift for us, ordering it to go to the topmost level of the Citadel. From there, we could use an escape hatch to get into the Attic. But we needed to go now—Dinah was waiting, and there wasn't ever enough time.

L eo and I entered a storage room in the Attic through a hatch
from the Citadel, and Leo quickly hacked the door into the
Tower open so we could get to the corridors beyond. From there we
walked confidently through the halls, but I worried about the efficacy
of Quess's face spray the entire time, certain that someone would
notice. Our destination was two storage rooms over, and we located it
easily, hacked the door in the hallway, and then exited through
another hatch that brought us out to the span of ceiling between
where the Citadel and the Core dangled over the Grounds. We tran-
sitioned to our lashes and quickly traversed the remaining distance
between us and the Core. It took about twenty minutes all in all, and
by the time we reached the hatch toward which Dinah had pointed
us, my arms were aching and a fine sweat had formed on my brow.
Leo input the code and ushered me through the hole that opened up
seconds later, and we were in a crawlspace.

As I slid in, two things struck me at once. Number one was that it was hot. Uncomfortably so. Number two was that the crawlspace wasn't like others I'd encountered in the Tower. It was made of a black mesh that was slightly flexible under my palms and knees, and didn't make any noise as I moved on it. It was also cool to the touch, untouched by the hot, dry air, which helped battle some of the heat, but only a little. I crawled forward a few feet into the darkened space, and then stopped to catch my breath while digging out my hand light.

Leo crawled in behind me, and seconds later the hatch was closed. "You okay?" he asked, also slightly out of breath.

"Good," I told him as I found the familiar oval shape of my light source in my pocket and pulled it out. "Get your light." Leo began to look for his while I unraveled the strap mine was attached to and clicked it on. A bright light erupted from it, and I winced and quickly twisted down the setting using a control on the base, softening the light to something less obnoxious and noticeable. Satisfied, I wrapped the strap around my head, and then looked down the shaft. "Dinah should be straight ahead," I said softly.

"About forty feet or so," he replied, showing me that he also remembered Dinah's instructions. "Let me go first."

There was a seriousness in his voice that made me want to smile in spite of the nervous roil of my stomach, but I remembered my promise to him and flattened myself to one side. He squeezed past me, his side brushing against mine, and then pulled away, crawling ahead. I took a deep breath, reminded myself that everyone's life was on the line, and then pressed after him.

We just need to get in and out, I told myself as we went. *Get Jasper. Get Rose. Trigger the death protocol. Get back to the Citadel. In and out.*

I hoped everything was going all right back at the Citadel. Without my net, I had no way of knowing what was going on, but I trusted my friends to handle it.

I just worried about any curveballs our enemies might throw at us in the process.

Don't think about it, I ordered myself as Leo started to slow. *Focus on this.*

Leo stopped, forcing me to follow suit, and I waited for several seconds. There was a soft grating sound, and then bright light cut in around Leo's hunched-over frame.

"Don't just stand there gaping at me, boy," I heard a familiar voice snap. "We don't have all damn day, and you two owe me an explanation."

"Hey, Dinah," I called behind Leo. "Thanks for this." I paused and then swallowed. "Is Alex with you?"

"No, he is not. I managed to convince him to stay behind, but just barely. Hurry up and get down from there."

Leo had already started moving before Dinah's retort, and I backed up a little as he leaned toward me and brought his legs around so that he was sitting on his rear. That told me our entrance was a little bit off the ground, and I moved to do the same, contorting myself in the tight confines of the vent.

Leo slid out seconds before I was finished, but as soon as I was, I scooted forward on my butt and pushed my legs through the hole. I leaned forward to see that the floor was about three feet down, and then eased myself over the edge, dropping to the ground of a small room with a bench, some lockers, and a door. Dinah was standing next to the wall as I slid down, her gaze locked on Leo.

Even though it was my second time seeing her, I still couldn't get over how different she was from how I had imagined. When I'd first encountered the elderly woman, she'd only been a digitally synthe-sized voice who went by the name of Mercury. I'd assumed she was a middle-aged man—or possibly even my brother—but when we'd had to come rescue her from Jang-Mi, I'd learned that she was neither of those things.

Her wrinkled face was pulled into a frown as she examined Leo, her hunter-green eyes considering. "So this is Grey Farmless," she said, giving me an arched eyebrow. "From the way Roark talked about him, I was expecting someone a little less... serious. This kid looks like he's ten years older than he is."

She turned to fully face me, her cane tapping on the floor as she adjusted her weight. My eyes tracked down her dark gray uniform to her leg, which was twisted at an odd angle, and then snapped back to her face when I realized what she had been saying: she had expected him to be less Leo-like and more Grey-like. I glanced at Leo and then back to Dinah, wondering if she could actually pick up on the differ-ence—and if I should say something to explain it away, or just ignore it and move forward.

"Thanks," Leo said, an edge of sarcasm on his voice. "You're no spring chicken yourself there, Ms. Velasquez."

I blinked, and then smiled. Thank Scipio Leo was quicker on his feet than I was. To be honest, I hadn't expected Dinah to have any real knowledge of Grey except through us, but I had never consid-ered that Roark had mentioned him enough for her to get an idea of his personality.

Dinah rolled her eyes at his comment, and then turned and picked up two square, dark gray packages. "Put these on, quickly. We've only got three minutes before the cleaners finish in this area, and the sensors will be restored once they're done. That gives you two time to tell me what the hell is going on."

I took the packages from her and handed one to Leo. Ripping open the lining, I shook out a uniform and began to undress and talk at the same time.

"Okay, do you know anything about how Scipio became... well... Scipio?"

"He's the creation of Lionel Scipio, made possible by the invention of intelli-programming, which is just a fancy way of saying that he was able to digitize emotions and free will," she replied without missing a beat. "Scipio was created from that, in order to marry the impartiality of a machine to the complexities of emotions, so that each decision he made carried the best possible outcome for our future survival. Every Bit knows that."

"Well, every Bit is wrong," I told her. "Scipio is actually the neural clone of Lionel Scipio, augmented by fragment AI programs that were created from the minds of the other Founders."

"What?" She looked between the two of us. "Why... How do you know that?"

"We discovered Lionel Scipio's office," Leo replied, working on his harnesses. I had a split second of nervousness that he was about to reveal himself to her, but he finished with, "And found files there that described the process. There were five scans made of the five different Founders of the Tower, and then they were put through simulated versions of the Tower, given problems that they had to overcome without losing too much of the population or the resources necessary for maintaining life."

I slipped my own harness off my shoulders and continued when he seemed to lose momentum—though to be honest, he might have been distracted by taking off his boots. "Lionel's was the one that did the best job, but the program wasn't strong enough on its own to run the entire Tower, so fragments from the other AIs were introduced to enhance his decision-making process through the lenses of what they excelled at during their simulations."

I toed off my boots and then bent over to start tugging my legs out of my uniform, losing the thread for a second as I rushed through getting dressed. Luckily, Leo was there to pick it back up for me.

"Right, so some bad people have stolen those AI fragments, we think to try to manipulate Scipio's decisions. One of them was being used in the Medica before all this went down. His name was Jasper, and he and Liana became friends. He helped her out once or twice, and then they pulled him from the Medica and downloaded him into Sadie Monroe's computer."

He stopped there, and I didn't continue because that seemed like more than enough for Dinah. I'd let her process it while I finished getting dressed.

Dinah was silent for several long moments—long enough for me to get my legs through the IT uniform she had given us, and pull it up and over my hips.

"So Sadie has an AI fragment from Scipio's code in her terminal, and you're going to go bust it out?" she asked, and from the sound of it, she still hadn't fully accepted it as the truth.

"Yup," I replied with more confidence than I felt. "She's unconscious, and I have the net to her quarters. We go in, get the program, wipe the computers, and get out."

"How, exactly, are you even going to get to the terminal to wipe it?" she asked, one eyebrow going up. "You have your own assistant, so you know that Sadie's will pick up that you aren't her, and turn the defenses on you. You'll be killed before you even reach it!"

Leo and I exchanged looks. We'd told her about Jasper, but we hadn't mentioned Rose. I was playing things close to the vest, and didn't want anyone to know that we had her. Sadie thought only

Jasper was on her computer, and that he would be the only one missing after we did what we came to do. I didn't want to even breathe Rose's name for fear that the legacies would find out. Keeping the fragments safe was the most important thing we could do, as they were the only ones who could fix Scipio, and so keeping our enemies guessing about what we had was the only way forward.

"We've disabled her assistant," I said carefully. "We used the council's server as a way into her terminal, and managed to take it offline. We had hoped to do it more remotely, but we underestimated her defenses. It doesn't matter—we have a way in, and a way to cover our tracks." At her raised eyebrow, I added, "We're going to digitally convince her virtual assistant she's dead."

If I'd thought Dinah processing the whole AI fragment thing was good, the way she gaped at the two of us now was positively priceless.

"You're going to *what*?!" she exclaimed, and my smile broadened.

"The only way to do that is to convince the system she died," I told her. "The protocols will activate and wipe her files, and then Grey will scrub the buffer, just to be sure. Since mine did it first, it'll look like a problem with the assistants, and no one will be the wiser."

She was already shaking her head before I even finished. "You two are insane. I can't do this. I won't." She began to move to the door, but I zipped up my suit and slipped in front of her, stopping her in her tracks.

"Dinah, please," I said, not wanting to resort to my backup plan to get her to participate. "Without Jasper, Scipio's going to continue to degrade until he falls apart, and you know that his death will be the death of everyone in the Tower!"

Dinah stared up at me, her mouth in a stubborn line. "Who cares!" she shouted, waving her hands in the air before tapping her cane on the ground with an angry thump. "The Tower is rotten, and all I've ever wanted you to do was resume Roark's plan and escape!"

"But you don't know that there's anywhere to go!" I said, exasperated. Why couldn't she see that there was every chance that the Tower would die before any escape plan was underway? Why did she cling to the dream of leaving when none of us had any proof that there was life outside? Yes, we had Roark's story, and yes, I wanted to believe it, but wanting to believe in a reality outside of your own only made you ignore the problems, and I couldn't do that. I had to focus on what I could fix now, and so did Dinah.

"I do know!" Dinah replied with a hiss, and I frowned at the conviction in her voice. She knew there was somewhere to go? How did she know that? I let her continue, but to my surprise, all she said was, "I..." before stopping, and then slammed her mouth shut with a click. "Never mind. I'm not doing this. Let me pass."

Crap. I wanted to know more about how she knew there was somewhere to go, but we didn't have time for an interrogation, or for Dinah's refusal to help. So, as much as I didn't want to, I set it aside and focused on what I wanted: the location of Sadie's apartment.

"Look, I didn't want to have to do this, but if you don't at least tell me where her home is, then I am not supplying you with any more Paragon," I said evenly, meeting her gaze. "I'm assuming that we're close, and that this... cleaning thing you were talking about will also knock the cameras offline in the area, so just show us, and we'll take it from there."

Her brows furrowed and her nostrils flared. "You're threatening me?" she asked.

"I am," I replied, feeling a little guilty. But only a little. Our priority was Jasper and Rose, and I'd blackmail the devil himself if it meant getting them out of Sadie's clutches. "I really don't want to, though. Just... please, Dinah, we can't let Sadie keep control of the fragment. She's going to do something really bad with it, and this is the only way we can even begin to slow her down."

She hobbled back a step to put some distance between us, and I gave her a moment while I retrieved the bag I had shed earlier to get changed, now made heavier with my uniform and lash harness. Slinging it over the bag Dinah had handed me, I turned back to her, having given her as much time as I could. "What's it going to be, Dinah?"

She gave me an irritated look and then blew out a breath. "Move, girl," she said gruffly, abruptly marching forward. "And stay close to me," she ordered brusquely as she opened the door.

I moved to follow, and hid my smile when I heard her breathe, "I'm too old for this crap," as she stepped over the threshold and into the hall.

I was right. Dinah had picked an entry point close to where Sadie's quarters were—merely one left turn from the door, a right down the hall, and then a hundred feet straight toward the center of the Core.

I knew Sadie's quarters couldn't be in the middle of the Core; I had been inside the shaft once, and had seen the magnificent beam of power that shot through the middle, delivering enough energy to support the entire mainframe that kept Scipio alive. But that didn't stop Dinah from leading us toward it at a speed that denied she had any sort of deformity at all.

We entered the circular atrium surrounding the central shaft, and other than performing a rudimentary check to make sure the coast was clear (it was), she continued moving forward, right up to a smooth wall between two elevators.

"It's here," she said, patting the wall. "You have a way in?" I stared at the wall for a second, dubious, but decided there wasn't any time to question her on it. I had to trust that she was taking me to the right place.

I nodded and patted my bag. "How long do we have before everything comes back on?" I asked.

She lifted her arm and quickly scrutinized her indicator. "One minute. That's my cue to leave. I want to be safe and sound back in my home."

"Thank you, Dinah. I really mean it," I told her, holding out my hand.

Her eyes flicked to my hand and then back up to me before she took my hand in hers. "You're a good kid, Liana. By the way, your brother is on his way to the Citadel under the guise of seeing your father, but he wants into your quarters. I'm guessing he intends to call your friends and threaten to make a scene in front of the Eyes that accompanied Sadie, so... good luck with that."

I blinked, my moment of gratitude evaporating under a heavy weight that punched right through the bottom of my stomach. Alex was going after Sadie and what she knew. I was certain of it. And knowing my friends, they'd give in to his threat. I'd made sure they would, by stressing that the secrecy of the mission came first. I swallowed. A part of me wanted to race back to tell my brother to back off or he was going to ruin everything. If Sadie had even a remote recollection of him being there in her drugged-out state, she might start to question the events as they happened.

But I had to trust my friends to handle it. This was our only window to get Jasper and Rose, and we had to take it. I said a silent prayer that Maddox and Quess could convince Alex to back down without Sadie noticing him, and then squared my shoulders.

"Thanks for the warning," I told her quietly.

She gave me a knowing look and turned to go, heading for the nearby elevator. I dismissed her almost immediately, and then focused on Leo. "You ready for this?"

He nodded, his brown eyes flashing. "More than ready. Do it."

I calmed my rising nervousness, praying this would work, and then reached up and pulled the neural scrambler from the back of my neck, pocketing the hard chip. I looked up at the wall and waited, my heart thudding hard.

A moment later, the net began to buzz. I endured it until it suddenly stopped, and then waited. It took several agonizing heartbeats, during which a thousand doubts began to burn in the back of my mind—the biggest one being that we'd run out of time and the sensors would come back on before we were safely inside—and by the time it opened, I was thoroughly convinced we had failed.

I didn't allow myself a moment of relief, certain that the sensors were already coming back on, and hurriedly stepped inside what appeared to be a small gray and white airlock, Leo right beside me. The door behind us closed quickly. I looked around, and realized that the only exits were to our right and left, not straight ahead. I cocked my head at this design choice, and then moved toward the left door.

It immediately started to slide up as I made for it, accompanied by a violent "EEEEEEEEEEEEEEEEEEEEEEEEEEEEEE!" sound that was as excruciatingly recognizable as it was painful. It was the same sound Jang-Mi had made when we first put her into her terminal.

She was going crazy. Again.

Rose had lost control.

I clapped my hands over my ears against the sound and moved toward the door, knowing the only way to stop it was to get to the terminal. I exited into another short hall that led to a single door to the right. This one I slowed for, suddenly remembering the defenses. Was Jang-Mi in control of them? If she was, would she turn them against us? We'd have to be careful, just in case she did.

The door slid open slowly, revealing a flickering portal, the harsh white lights in the hall turning on and off so fast that it felt like I was on the verge of having a seizure. The hall itself only went right or left, and as I poked my head out, I saw that the corridor curved, and suddenly realized that Sadie's home wasn't *in* the center, but wrapped around it like a ring on a finger in a perfect circle.

I stepped through the entryway, wincing against the never-ending shriek that still managed to penetrate the ear muffs I'd created with my hands, and went left, my eyes darting around to search for any sign of defenses about to be turned against us. I went as quickly as I dared—too quickly, perhaps—but remained vigilant.

The hall opened up on the left, revealing an elegant sitting area in a recessed alcove, with white and silver furniture filling the wide room. There was no sign of movement, but I kept alert as I passed it by, still having found no sign of Sadie's terminal.

There was a gap of about fifteen feet between that first room and the next, which opened up into a dining room and kitchen area. The kitchen was massive, with dark counters and silver appliances far more luxurious than anything I'd ever seen, set behind a long table that could seat twenty or so people at any given moment. It seemed Sadie entertained up here a lot—otherwise why have the table?

I ignored it when no terminal presented itself, though, and pressed onward. The next couple of rooms were shut behind doors, and opening them revealed several bedrooms that were clearly not in use, given the bare mattresses. Then one massive bedroom that was clearly Sadie's—a lush, opulent thing with a large bed, several dressers, and a vanity, decorated in black and white. Only past that did I find what I was looking for: an opening that led into the computer room.

Her terminal was set up in a way similar to mine. The desk sat on an elevated platform in the corner of the room. Unlike mine, however, the screens adorned the walls, all set at eyelevel to the desk, which meant they were sitting about nine feet off the ground.

Leo came around me quickly and darted up the stairs toward the desk, and I followed right behind, the sound causing the pain in my head to grow more intense. He rounded the desk and yanked the chair out just as I reached the top, then quickly bent over, disappearing underneath it. Seconds later, the sound stopped, and I quickly took my hands away from my ears, relieved.

"Is it Jang-Mi?" I asked, wincing against the loudness of my own voice. "Did she break free?"

"Give me a second," he replied, emerging from under the desk. He remained on his knees but reached for the keyboard, his fingers moving faster than the speed of light. I held my breath while he worked, tension leaking from me. There was an itch on the back of my neck telling me that even now, Jang-Mi was taking aim at us. "I'm disabling the defenses and making sure that the assistant remains offline."

I waited for several agonizing seconds, and when Leo frowned suddenly, I zeroed in on it. "What is it?" I asked. "Is it the defenses?"

His fingers resumed their tapping, but he answered as he worked. "No, they're off," he replied, his brows furrowing together. "But the hostile program that Rose was talking about isn't a trap set by Sadie. It's Jasper! He's attacking Rose, trying to..." He trailed off, studying the screen. "I actually can't tell what he's trying to do! But whatever it is, it's overloading Sadie's systems. We need to separate them as quickly as possible."

It took me a second to absorb that, but when I did, panic gripped my heart. If Jasper was attacking Rose, did that mean we were too late? Had Sadie already driven him insane?

But I could ask those questions later. Leo said he needed to break them up. I thought about it, then quickly pulled the bag off my shoulder and put it on the desk, rummaging through it for Jang-Mi's hard drive. I found it and set it on the desk in front of him. "Here. What else do you need?"

Leo's fingers were flying a mile a minute, the look on his face so intense that I almost hated interrupting his focus. But I had to—we needed to move as quickly as possible.

Brown eyes flicked over at the hard drive and back to the screen, his fingers never missing a beat. "We'll need another one of those. Whatever Jasper's doing, it's an automated function. I don't even think he's in control of it."

That didn't sound good. If anything, that only made me more certain that we were too late, and that Sadie had driven Jasper insane. Without him, we'd never know how to fix Rose, or if there was anything wrong with Leo or Grey. We'd never learn the formula for Paragon, and worst of all, we'd never fix Scipio.

Worry about it later, I told myself as I came around the desk. Even if Jasper was insane, we still needed to recover him, if only to spare him from Sadie. Maybe we could restore him, like Leo had started to do with Rose.

I threw open the desk drawers, searching for a hard drive. The first few drawers contained files and manuals, and after some internal debate, I put the files on the desk. I'd go through them while

Leo worked, and then put them back when he was done. Hopefully they'd contain something interesting.

The next drawer revealed seven hard drives, and I quickly grabbed one and put it on the desk as well. I started to close the drawer, and then reconsidered and began pulling the other hard drives out, stacking them right on top of each other. I wasn't sure why Sadie had so many of them, but something told me that there was information on them, and I wanted to see what it was. If it was worth stealing... I'd take everything from the desk and then break it. I was certain the furniture collection system had a protocol for broken furniture, and I was hoping that protocol included wanton destruction. Hopefully, Sadie would assume the desk was damaged when the death protocol activated, and that those files were lost as well.

I closed my eyes and prayed that we weren't leaning too heavily on luck, and then went around Leo and began opening the drawers on the other side.

The top one revealed three white chips that immediately caught my attention, and I reached out to daintily pick up one of the legacy nets. Now I was beyond certain that I had to steal everything from her desk; if these legacy nets held memories on them pertinent to what Sadie and her people had done to the Tower, then we could figure out how to undo it, and completely undermine everything they had done. We might even be able to find a way to fix Rose and Jasper.

I scooped up the other two chips and tucked them in my chest pocket, and then began emptying out the rest of the drawers—more files and manuals—and setting them in the corner. Leo's eyes flicked over to me on my second pass, and he raised an eyebrow. "Taking everything?"

I nodded as I picked up another armload of files, this time stopping long enough to check the time. We'd been inside for five minutes now, and it already felt like this was too long. "I'm gonna damage the desk and hope that the retrieval system destroys it."

He gave me a measured look, but didn't say anything as he returned to his work. I could tell that he didn't like it, and I could understand why, but the potential value of the information was incalculable. It was worth the risk, and he likely knew that.

I finished quickly and then began going through the cabinets behind the desk, but was disappointed when I only found a complete collection of IT manuals. They were valuable, but we had more than enough thanks to Cali's collection, and we were already loaded down. In fact, I was a little worried that the things I had already set aside would be too much for the bag. It was part of the reason I was still searching—I might need another carrying tool.

When I didn't find one, I decided to give up the search and just start packing the bag. I wanted to be ready to go when Leo told me he was done. I reached it just as he was picking up Jang-Mi's hard drive, and gave him a look. "Did you separate them?"

He shook his head, and to my surprise, picked up a second hard drive. "I need more time to do it," he informed me as he placed it on top of the other. "Hand me the black case in the bag?"

I quickly did what he asked, and watched as he unzipped it, revealing some cutters and wires. He pulled a wire from it and began attaching it to something in the back of the hard drive. I watched him doing it, and from the legacy memory I'd had the other day, I realized he was slaving them together. "They need more space?" I asked.

"Power," he replied. "The fighting is eating a lot of energy. Each of these hard drives has a dedicated battery, but at the rate they're going, they'd burn one out in ten minutes." He fitted a third one on top of the other two as he talked and began attaching another wire to it, connecting it to the others. "I'm hoping by slaving them together, I'll buy us at least thirty minutes."

I nodded. If it kept them alive, then we needed to do it. We couldn't afford to let either of them die. I checked my watch, my stomach clenching when I saw that we'd been at this for twelve minutes. It was already too long, but Leo still needed to download their programs. "How long is transferring them going to take?" I asked.

Leo carefully taped the stack of hard drives together and then gingerly lifted them up. He bent over, lowering them to the ground, and a second later disappeared underneath the desk. "Three minutes," he replied. "I'm going to use the time to go through her files and take whatever I can find that links her to the legacies."

"Okay, what about when we leave?" I asked, wanting to plan ahead so we were out before the death protocol activated. "Will we have time to get out?"

"Better than that," he said, his voice muffled. "I figured out where the controls were for the emergency exit on Cornelius, and I'm going to open them right before we set the virus to go off. We can avoid leaving through the Core altogether, as the exit will take us right up to the Attic."

"That's perfect," I said, relieved that we didn't have to go back through the halls. We had only asked Dinah for a way in, figuring that Leo could do something to the cameras in the hall once he was inside, but if there was a way to avoid that option altogether, all the better.

He came back up from under the desk a moment later, and then clicked a few things on the keyboard. "Okay," he announced. "They're downloading. I'm going to start—" He paused mid-sentence, and his eyes narrowed.

A flare of alarm went through me as I realized something was wrong. "Are they not downloading?" I asked, coming around the desk to stand behind him.

To my surprise, he was looking at a camera image that showed Sadie's living room—and then I noticed the movement in the left hand corner of the screen. I focused on it, and realized I was looking at a man walking past the room and heading farther down the hall. And closer to us.

We weren't alone anymore.

Leo tapped a few keys, changing the camera angle, and I saw that there wasn't just one, but five, striding confidently down the hall, as if they'd been there a hundred times.

And at their head was him, the man who'd slit my throat.

I quickly grabbed Leo's hand and hauled him up, pulling him behind me as I reached out with my other hand to scoop the bag off the table. I let go of him as soon as I knew he was following, and descended the stairs at a run. I heard voices as I raced through the door, but didn't hesitate as I hooked a left—away from them—and headed down the hall.

I cast a look over my shoulder to see shadows starting to form on the wall, and picked up the pace. I spotted a door and quickly pointed to it, and we raced over, Leo darting in first. I backed in, making sure we weren't seen as I went. The door closed as I moved away, and I quickly looked around. We were in yet another empty bedroom.

I met Leo's eyes, and realized three very important things at once. The first was that the man who had cut my throat had unrestricted access to Sadie's quarters, cementing the fact that she was working with our enemies. The second was that we had left the slaved hard drives behind, which meant that those men would notice immediately that something was off.

The last and final thing was that we were trapped, but not necessarily without resources. I opened the bag in my hand and reached inside, easily finding the heavy weight of the gun. I pulled it out, the sensation of it in my palm familiar in spite of the fact that it was only my second time holding it. I passed it over to Leo and then retrieved the second one, chambering a round in an action that Leo echoed.

Then I sat back and waited, eager to have a chance to talk to the person who most likely knew who was responsible for my mother's death, the danger to our lives, and the corruption of Scipio.

And once I was done with him, I'd have everything I needed to finally put a stop to things.

THE END IS NEAR... READY FOR THE PENULTIMATE BOOK OF LIANA'S STORY?

Dear Reader,

Thank you for reading *The Girl Who Dared to Lead*.

Book 6, **The Girl Who Dared to Endure**, is the thrilling **penultimate** book in the series, as we move toward the grand finale in Book 7!

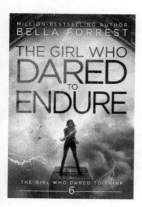

The Girl Who Dared to Endure is available now.

Order your copy: www.bellaforrest.net.

I'll see you back in the Tower...

Til then,

Bella x

P.S. If you're new to my books or haven't yet read my **Gender Game** series, I suggest you check it out. It is where the Tower's story began and is set in the same world as *The Girl Who Dared* series—the two storylines complement each other.

P.P.S. Sign up to my VIP email list and I'll send you a heads up when my next book releases: **www.morebellaforrest.com**

(Your email will be kept 100% private and you can unsubscribe at any time.)

P.P.P.S. I'd also love to hear from you — come say hi on **Twitter** or **Facebook**. I do my best to respond :)

A SHADE OF VAMPIRE SERIES

Series 1: Derek & Sofia's story

A Shade of Vampire (Book 1)

A Shade of Blood (Book 2)

A Castle of Sand (Book 3)

A Shadow of Light (Book 4)

A Blaze of Sun (Book 5)

A Gate of Night (Book 6)

A Break of Day (Book 7)

Series 2: Rose & Caleb's story

A Shade of Novak (Book 8)

A Bond of Blood (Book 9)

A Spell of Time (Book 10)

A Chase of Prey (Book 11)

A Shade of Doubt (Book 12)

A Turn of Tides (Book 13)

A Dawn of Strength (Book 14)

A Fall of Secrets (Book 15)

An End of Night (Book 16)

Series 3: The Shade continues with a new hero...

A Wind of Change (Book 17)

A Trail of Echoes (Book 18)

A Soldier of Shadows (Book 19)

A Hero of Realms (Book 20)

A Vial of Life (Book 21)

A Fork of Paths (Book 22)

A Flight of Souls (Book 23)

A Bridge of Stars (Book 24)

Series 4: A Clan of Novaks

A Clan of Novaks (Book 25)

A World of New (Book 26)

A Web of Lies (Book 27)

A Touch of Truth (Book 28)

An Hour of Need (Book 29)

A Game of Risk (Book 30)

A Twist of Fates (Book 31)

A Day of Glory (Book 32)

Series 5: A Dawn of Guardians

A Dawn of Guardians (Book 33)

A Sword of Chance (Book 34)

A Race of Trials (Book 35)

A King of Shadow (Book 36)

An Empire of Stones (Book 37)

A Power of Old (Book 38)

A Rip of Realms (Book 39)

A Throne of Fire (Book 40)

A Tide of War (Book 41)

Series 6: A Gift of Three

THE SECRET OF SPELLSHADOW MANOR

(Completed series)

The Secret of Spellshadow Manor (Book 1)

The Breaker (Book 2)

The Chain (Book 3)

The Keep (Book 4)

The Test (Book 5)

The Spell (Book 6)

BEAUTIFUL MONSTER DUOLOGY

Beautiful Monster 1

Beautiful Monster 2

DETECTIVE ERIN BOND (Adult thriller/mystery)

Lights, Camera, GONE

Write, Edit, KILL

For an updated list of Bella's books, please visit her website:
www.bellaforrest.net

Join Bella's VIP email list and she'll send you an email reminder as soon as
her next book is out. Visit: www.morebellaforrest.com

CPSIA information can be obtained
at www.ICGtesting.com
Printed in the USA
LVHW032137230421
685340LV00018B/276